CW01370901

2

THE CAPTIVE PRINCESS

ELEANOR FAIR MAID OF BRITTANY

BY J.P. REEDMAN

Copyright May 2018 J.P. Reedman/Herne's Cave

Cover Art by FRINA ART/ selfpubbookcovers.com

PROLOGUE

"Parchment! Bring me parchment!" I call to my solitary tiring woman, Agace. "And a quill pen, with ink. Be swift!"

"But…my Lady Eleanor," Agace cries, "You know they won't permit…"

"Get de Williton! Tell him it is important!"

Agace scuttles away, a timid mouse beneath her heavy wimple. Moments later, she returns with my keeper, de Williton. Keeper. A kinder word than gaoler.

"My lady," he says, all frowns. "What ails you? Is anything amiss?"

"I have the need to write. Have you brought the parchment?

I saw that he had; it hung limply from his hand. "Give that to me, Williton!"

He licked his lips, nervous, shifting from foot to foot. "Begging your pardon, my Lady, but I will need to know to whom you write…and I will need to read the content ere any courier takes it."

"I am not sending it to anyone, Williton," I tell him, extricating parchment, pen and ink from his grip. "I…I wish to tell the tale of a saint!"

"A saint, my Lady?" He blinks, confused.

"Yes! Last night in the dark before dawn, I dreamt. I dreamt of a saint, the young Saint Melor from my homeland of Brittany. It was so real…maybe it was not a dream but a vision and Melor has designs for me. A desire has overcome me to tell the tale of his martyrdom. Perhaps he wishes the knowledge of his sanctity spread throughout England."

De Williton crosses himself. Saints were an important business and not to be denied. "So be it, Lady. I wish you well in your holy endeavour." He scurried out of my chamber, no doubt to tell tales in the local alehouse of saintly goings-on in Bristol Castle.

Bristol, my prison, one of many over the years. How many? I have lost track. At least I can smell the sea here.

Retiring to my small desk, I place the parchment down, pinning its edges to keep them from curling. Using the stylus, I began to write, squinting in the dim light; my eyes are not good these days. Not good at all. Nor are my fingers, and many years have passed since I last wrote a letter, let alone hagiography. Biting my lip in concentration, I write awkwardly in my crabbed hand…

Many years before the present, when King Arthur was not long slain at Badon, a young and holy boy lived in Brittany. Fair of face, pious and learned for one so tender of years, he delighted all he knew with his wisdom and humility. He was the son of the local king Milio—Brittany had many petty kings in that troubled, time—and the name he bore was Melor, which some say comes from the word 'honey', that is to say sweet. Melor had all the attributes of a saint, and as all saints who vowed their lives to God Almighty, Prince Melor was doomed to die...

As I write the word 'die,' great melancholy consumes me. The quill droops in my hand. Could I bear to go on?

In that moment, I thought not of the martyred boy-saint, but my own brother, Arthur—lost to me, lost to the world.

Arthur and Eleanor of Brittany we were, long ago, children of royal lineage. Our grandmother, whose name I bear, was Eleanor of Aquitaine, that most celebrated of Queens. Clearly, I remember her from my youth, strong, powerful, wearing the wreckage of her great beauty like a mantle. She is long dead and lies in Fontevraud Abbey, a House of nuns she ever loved. Men say her effigy, brightly painted in blue and umber, shows her clasping a book rather than lying in the usual prayerful pose. That was grandmother—different from other women and not afraid to be so. I have little doubt that a thousand years hence men will still remember her and marvel.

Not so, her unfortunate granddaughter and namesake. Within the King's castle at Bristol, I grow old and rheumy-handed, with cracks upon my visage like those lining summer-parched ground. Beneath my wimple, my hair has grown springy, coarse beneath my touch; it has turned iron grey, replacing locks of vivid, Plantagenet red-gold.

I am over fifty now.

But once I was young and as fair of face as my fabled grandmother of Aquitaine. Men called me the Pearl of Brittany and The Fair Maid. I was one of the most marriageable girls in all Europe, the eldest child of Constance Penthievre, Duchess of Brittany, and Geoffrey Plantagenet, brother of the King known as Lionheart and his successor, King John—John Softsword, whom I curse to Hell for the harm he brought to my family. Like Eleanor, John is dead now, many years dead, and a good riddance. Hell is too good for him; it is no wonder men state, 'Foul as it is, Hell itself is made fouler by the presence of John'.

For most of my adult life, I have been a prisoner, torn from the rocky coasts of Brittany to reside behind stern, grey, English castle

5

walls. I survived one bad King and went on in my imprisonment to watch his son Henry grow from unsure boy-ruler to a cultured man with a doting Queen and promising heir. Once I entertained the idea Henry might help me, release me from my prison; I was wrong.

I was a threat, a threat to all he held dear….

So I remained a prisoner, charged with no crime, convicted of no offence. My only crime was bearing royal blood in my veins.

My freedom was lost because many believed my claim to the English throne was superior to that of John. Or Henry.

Despite my loss, I am lucky.

My brother, Arthur, Duke of Brittany, was not. Arthur is dead and tale is one of bitterness and woe. To remember, pains me still, even after all these years.

Thrusting my sorrows aside, I return to my parchment, the spidery scribbles in drying ink. Irritably, I beckon Agace to light another candle to ease my bad eyes. The saint, the saint who sent a visitation to me…Jesu, I almost wrote his name as Arthur instead of Melor. Melor, sweet as honey…

Young Prince Melor, the treasured son of Milio, lived a life of great happiness and respect until his father was taken by apoplexy whilst at table. Men whispered behind their hands of poison and many pointed fingers at Melor's uncle, the ambitious Riwal, who ever despised the lot of a second son. But men were afraid to rise against Riwal, known for his cruelty and his love of war. Now, in ancient Brittany, as in its sister isle Britain, the laws of the land stated that a king could only rule if he was unblemished in body. So Riwal, eager to remove Melor from the succession, secretly ordered his henchmen to lead Melor to the woods, there to suffer mutilation, his hand and foot struck from his body. Despite the Prince's pleas for mercy, this awful act was duly done and the gravely injured boy sent to the monks in the abbey at Quimper. The monks thought he would die of his wounds but God had other plans—under the ministration of the holy brothers, Melor recovered and they fitted him with a hand of silver and a foot of bronze. By the workings of the Almighty, those lifeless metal appendages soon began to work as if wrought of flesh and bone. The monks in their abbey gave praise, but Melor's good fortune meant he was once more a threat to the unrightful reign of Riwal…

I let the pen fall. Sweat breaks on my brow and I slump on my stool, wiping my forehead with my sleeve. I have not been well, not for some time. The words I write agitate me, make my heavy head spin…for it is not Saint Melor I see in my mind's eyes, not that sad little saint with his false hand and foot.

"Lady Eleanor, can I get you anything?" squeaks Agace, wringing her hands to see my distress. "You look so pale!"

"Hush, Agace," I say, calming her. "It will pass. It always does I just need time to think…"

Eyes closed, I lean back against faded, moth-bitten tapestries of David and Goliath, the Wise Men with their gifts, a grinning Woodwose in a gown of green leaves, and through my troubled mind leaps a panoply of memories—memories of a land beyond the sea, where a golden boy once lived, the hope of my people, the lad who should one day have been crowned King Arthur.

Chapter One

My father, Geoffrey Plantagenet, had the misfortune to die young whilst competing at a tourney in Paris—showing off to the French, my mother Constance would say with disdain. Eager to exhibit his prowess, he launched himself recklessly into the heart of the melee, smiting helms and driving back lesser men. However, in the press of men and horses, his steed stumbled and went down and so did Geoffrey…he was trampled to death beneath the dancing feet of his opponent's horses, his red, royal blood mingling with the churned soil.

His funeral beneath the soaring arches of Notre Dame had been both a grand and startling affair. King Philip of France, his dearest friend, had fallen into a fit of grief at the sight of Geoffrey's battered corpse lying upon its pall. Weeping, he cried out that death should take him too and attempted to leap into my father's coffin until his equerries restrained him.

Not all men were as sorrowful as King Philip on hearing of my sire's unfortunate demise. My mother Constance remained remarkably indifferent—for it must be said, my parents' union was no love match. When they were both children, the powerful and land-hungry King Henry, Geoffrey's sire and my grandfather, had ordered Count Conan of Brittany to hand the duchy over to five-year-old Constance…so that Henry could marry her to his middle son and have Geoffrey claim Brittany as Duke through the right of his wife.

However, whilst mother had tolerated my father's Plantagenet excesses, the church did not. They praised God on bended knee when they heard of his fatal accident for father was renowned for razing churches and monasteries when he needed funds to support his extravagant lifestyle. Gerald of Wales, full of acerbic malice but not without some truth in his words, wrote of Geoffrey's behaviour years later: '*He has more aloes in him than honey…he is of tireless endeavour, a hypocrite in all matters, a deceiver and a dissembler…*'

When father was killed, I was but a little maid up to my nurse's knee, while my sister Maude was a babe in swaddling and my brother Arthur still within my mother's belly—Geoffrey died before his longed-for male heir took his first breath. Being so young, I did not mourn a father who spent so little time in Brittany he was but a shadow in my child's mind, but I did remember my mother's lying-in upon a hot, hazy

8

summer's day when the sea salt and dead fish stench from the beach, reached into the castle bailey.

She struggled for hours, days, seeking to push the babe into the waking world; her screams shook the castle walls, and the servants, whey-faced, crossed themselves for many women did not survive giving birth. The best midwives were summoned, running hither and thither with basins of bloody water, amulets to ease the childbirth pangs, holy relics borrowed from nearby monasteries and convents.

Finally, the child was born, screaming and sound, his copious hair a red-gold crown—a true Plantagenet, mother said—but despite his ancestry, she refused to give him a Plantagenet name. The old King, Geoffrey's father Henry II, wrote and said he expected the child to be named Henry in his honour, but mother would not even for a moment consider calling him after his paternal Angevin and Norman ancestors. He would be called Arthur, after the Great King whose legends were attached to hills, caves, and stones across Brittany and in Britain too.

When mother was well enough to rise, and after her churching had taken place, she took Arthur from his puzzled nurses and carried him up on the battlements of our castle. There, she held his wriggling body up to the sun, almost like some pagan priestess of old, and in a loud voice cried, "My son, my precious son! All I have suffered is worth it now that you are born! One day you will be a great ruler, of Brittany and beyond!"

Oh, mother, how you did tempt Fate with such pridefulness!

Chapter Two

The suddenness of my father's demise and the fears for my mother at Arthur's hard birthing soon faded from my child's mind. While mama tended the business of the Duchy in our castle at Nantes, I sought out the local urchins for amusement, despite my high rank. A lazy but doting woman called Aaliz was my nurse, and when she was not looking, which was often, for she liked to gossip with the cooks and washerwomen, I would creep away to find the peasant children who wandered in and out of the bailey, helping their parents carry in food destined for the castle table. I liked to peer at their chickens in wicker baskets and nibble on fresh fruits and vegetables gathered in the fields that morn.

My favourite of the children was a girl named Tephaine who had leaf-green eyes and curly hair the colour of copper, a much deeper red than my own locks. She came to Nantes Castle with her parents and her aged grandmother, who was blind; the old woman was called Mother Nonne.

Nonne was a storyteller and in her trembling croak she told me of the birth of the Morbihan, the Little Sea, and its hundreds of sea-swept islets—how Fae expelled from the haunted Forest of Broceliande wept sorrowful tears that formed the waters and how the garlands they hurled into the flood created islands such as Hoedic and Houat. She also told me of the Korrigans, a type of Fae who were ancient princesses doomed to eternity for refusing to worship Christ. They had poisonous breath and lurked around the edges of wells, and they could tell the future. They hated the Virgin Mary so much that any poor soul who witnessed them combing their long hair upon Her day would die.

I doubted very much if I would die if I spied a Korrigan, though, for my father Geoffrey was said to descend from such a water-spirit. That is why men called him and his brothers 'the Devil's Brood'. Due to this odd ancestry, I was certain no such creature would have power over me, for I was kindred by blood. Aaliz waggled her finger at me and said I should pray to Mother Mary to be cleansed of such a stain, but I was obstinate and would not apologise for the bloodline I was born with, even then.

Tiphaine's grandmama Nonne liked to tell fortunes too, just like the Korrigans, even though the village priest had forbidden it and would have made her pay harsh penance if he knew. She had a highly polished

10

green stone that she had found; she would ask a question, then spin it and get Tephaine to tell her whether it pointed east, west, north or south. Tephaine said it was a Thunderstone, and that Nonne had found it years ago, back in the days before her blindness, in a field full of stones standing tall like petrified warriors. She kept it because it was lucky and protected the family cottage from lightning.

I remember that stone well; it played its part on a fateful day I will never forget. I was playing with Tephaine in the bailey, making houses out of sticks and stones, while old Nonne was sitting on a stool near the gates, resting her aching limbs against the chill castle stonework.

Growing bored with my game, I skipped over to the elderly woman. "Nonne, tell me who I'll marry!" I tugged on her ragged brown sleeve. Tiphaine had been bragging of her grandmother's prophetic powers yet again, telling me that Nonne predicted she would marry a handsome prince. Even at my young age, I knew that she merely flattered her granddaughter, for peasants did not consort with princes...but a prince or a mighty duke was my eventual destiny and I wanted to know his name and stature.

Nonne sighed in mock exaggeration but she drew the Thunderstone from the pocket stitched to her long, dirty apron. She rolled it in her withered hands, spat upon the surface, then had me do the same, even though it was a most unladylike gesture. When the back of the stone dripped with our spittle, she set it on the sandy ground and spun it around with a flick of her spider-like fingers.

"Tell me which direction it points, Tephaine!" She called her granddaughter over. "East, west, north or south?"

Tephaine flung her thin body down beside the rotating Thunderstone, watching as I peered nervously over her shoulder. "Grandmama, it is spinning and spinning. It will not stop!" she frowned. "What does it mean?"

Nonne's withered-apple face crinkled even more. "There will be no marriage, no marriage ever. But that cannot be, surely…"

A shadow descended over the day. I shivered. I did not want to play this divination game any longer. My squeaky child's voice assumed an imperious tone. "Stop it, stop it right now. My mother would be so displeased!"

Even as I spoke, a trumpet blew outside the castle walls, its call brazen and clear. Guards sprang to attention; villagers flurried around the bailey, excited but also slightly apprehensive. Several riders burst through the open gates, resplendent in bright colours. They rode so fast and furiously they knocked Nonne off her stool, sending her flying into a muddy puddle; Tephaine screamed in alarm and ran to her side, narrowly avoiding the flashing hooves of the horses.

The Thunderstone, still spinning, was crushed beneath a hoof, its ancient shell shattering into many fragments. Nonne, her ears grown keen in the absence of sight, heard the noise and cried out in fear. Tephaine clung to her, terrified.

The horsemen milled about the bailey, raising dust. Their faces were proud and arrogant; on their shields roared a lion guardant, gold on red. I stood staring, afraid and yet angered by their intrusion. I was Duchess Constance's daughter; this was my castle, not theirs. How dare they act as if they had the right to ride about and terrorise us!

The trumpeters blew their horns again. More horsemen flooded into the bailey; a lion passant glared fiercely from surcoats and shields. Dangerously near to the stamping hooves of the newcomers' horses, I teetered forward, wanting to see who broke my friend's magic seeing-stone and destroyed the peace of my mother's castle.

Snoring and pawing, a pitch-dark destrier thundered into the bailey. The man on its back was stout and red-faced, his cropped, bristling hair holding a tint of fire. Age and care had ravaged his face but it still bore vestiges of one-time strength and majesty. His piercing eyes were wolfish yellow-green in colour and his brow encircled by a band of gold.

A man of importance, that was clear. Drawn by curiosity and perhaps by a subtle knowledge, I wandered in his direction, but before I could take a good look at this foreign lord my nurse Aaliz came flying out of the castle kitchens, her aprons blooming like ship's sails, and hoisted me off my feet.

Wrapped in her hefty arms, I was borne inside the castle, kicking and protesting. "Lady Eleanor, I told you not to wander off!" Aaliz admonished loudly, which was nonsense for the benefit of my mother, for the nurse always allowed me free rein while she was about other business.

Inside the Great Hall, mother looked pale and disturbed at the announcement of newcomers. "I did not ask him to come here…," she murmured. And then, eyes flashing fire, she rounded on Aaliz and the other castle nurses. "The child's dress! Disgraceful! What have you been doing, Aaliz? Get her ready! The rest of you—get Arthur and Maude ready. He will want to see the boy in particular."

"My Lady." Aaliz plumped down into a deep curtsey, red with embarrassment after her scolding. "Your will shall be done!"

She dragged me down a corridor and up a flight of winding stairs into the nursery, then started rubbing at the dust whitening my face. "Oh, no time to bathe you now, but at least I can dress you and untangle your hair. You look like...like a street urchin! What on earth were you doing, Lady Eleanor?"

"I was just playing a...a game with Tephaine and her grandmother!" I cried. "Why is everyone so upset? Why is mama making such a fuss?"

Aaliz did not answer; her mouth was a thin white line.

"What is happening, Aaliz?" I continued to plead as the nurse scrubbed at my face with a cloth and tore a comb painfully through the red-gold tangles of my hair. With help from another nurse, Jenefred, they swiftly divested me of my stained, workaday kirtle and brought out my very best garments—a miniature imitation of a highborn ladies' bliaut with threads of gold stitched on hem and collar. "Why is mama upset? Who is the red-faced man on the black horse?"

Lips pursed, Aaliz looked at me, still striving to control my wild hair. "Child, have you not guessed? Do you truly not know? Our visitor is your grandfather, King Henry II of England!"

13

Chapter Three

The King of England looked me over in much the same way as he might look over a new hound or a prize horse. Boldly, I stared back. It was very strange, gazing into that broad, sunburnt face, the face of a great ruler…but also the face of kin.

"God's Teeth!" Henry bent over to examine me more closely. "Save for the hue of hair, she is the image of her grandmother Eleanor, God rot her!"

"Your Grace!" cried mother, outraged at his language. "My daughter cannot help the looks God bestowed upon her."

Henry sighed, rolling his eyes. "Not 'God rot' the child, Constance! God rot my bloody wife, Eleanor of Aquitaine. I thank heaven my dear Queen is far from here, freezing in my castle of Sarum behind doors shut and barred. Finally, I can have some peace."

I continued to scrutinise my grandsire. I had heard the tales of how my grandmother had fomented rebellion, turning Henry's sons against him one by one. Such treachery had resulted in her being imprisoned in England, with only one maid to keep her company. They were in such straitened circumstances they even had to share a bed. "Will you ever set her free?" the words tumbled from my mouth, even as Aaliz and mama both gasped in horror.

Henry glanced at me, one bushy red-brown eyebrow lifted. "Hmmm…Outspoken like the other Eleanor too. I will have to find this child a husband with a firm hand. And the answer to your question is no, little one, not after what she has done. And there are other evils she may have done…by subterfuge."

He turned and walked away, suddenly engrossed with his own thoughts. "There is talk of poison, but I have no proof…I'd have Eleanor's head if I found out…"

"Ah, the fair Rosamund Clifford, who died so mysteriously at Godstow." Mother moved closer to the King. "Do you still mourn her, your Grace? She has been long in her grave, and it said the nuns have made a shrine of her tomb. "

"You are impertinent, woman!" A vein suddenly bulged on the King's brow.

"Am I so? I beg forgiveness, your Grace. It is just that you have put me at a disadvantage. You have come to Nantes unbidden and unannounced; I can only surmise there is some business afoot that you would rather I did not know in advance."

Henry said nothing; he stalked around the fire pit, glancing at everyone gathered in the hall with those wolf-eyes. "Where is the boy? My Geoffrey's son?"

The crowds parted. Arthur entered the room with his nurses; they were late coming because the nursemaids had to deal with an angry two-year-old boy woken from an afternoon sleep.

Blandishments and then threats finally brought him to the hall. He stood like a small and defiant angel, the light from slits high in the walls creating a nimbus around his golden curls. He wore a starched blue linen robe threaded through with gold and bronze stripes in a pattern that mimicked the standard of the Dukes of Brittany.

Henry gazed at him and a sigh broke from his lips. He looked sad for a moment, perhaps remembering his son, my father, trampled in the melee in Paris. "So, this is the child that should have been called 'Henry.'

"Arthur," said mother defiantly.

"He looks a fine lad." Henry's tone softened.

"As is fitting for the heir to Brittany."

"Heir to Brittany?" Henry folded his arms. "You think too low, Constance. I am an old man; my son Richard shall supplant me…but Richard seems disinclined…" a tight grin froze his features, "to produce a royal heir. He is still unmarried and spends more time fighting than ruling his lands. If anything should befall him…" Thoughtfully, he gazed down at Arthur. "This is our hope."

Mother paled. "I knew Arthur had a claim, of course. But you have another son other than Richard."

"I do, and sometimes I think he is the only one loyal to me out of all my brood. But the law of primogeniture places Arthur above John, as many would account it."

Mother said nothing but stared at Arthur and an unnameable fear darkened her face.

"Why do you look so grim, Duchess? What kind of mother would not wish her child to be King?"

"With the Devil's Brood all fighting for supremacy? A wise mother!" she retorted.

"Ah, that insolent tongue strikes like an adder again. You speak through womanish fears. Besides, the boy is one of the 'Devil's Brood' himself! He will enjoy the fight."

15

"Even if it is to the death?"

Henry shrugged. "We Plantagenets live for the fight. To die with glory—what better? Far more honourable than lying in a bed, crippled and incontinent, so old your brains quiver like a jelly!"

Mother turned away, biting her lip.

Henry reached after her, his huge hand coming to rest on her shoulder. "I have offended. No more talk of Devils and warfare!"

"What is the reason you are in Nantes, your Grace?" asked mother. "I cannot believe you have just come to visit your grandchildren."

"And you would be right, Constance. I came to see about you."

Next to me, Aaliz stiffened; reaching down, she clutched my hand. "He would not dare!" she muttered indignantly.

"Dare what?" I asked.

She stared at me as if she had forgotten I was in earshot. "N…nothing a child should bother about, Eleanor. Let us just say your grandfather has a reputation with women…"

I had no understanding of what Aaliz meant, and in any case, Henry had released mother's shoulder and walked away a few paces. When he spoke again, his voice was hard. "At present you rule Brittany while your young son is in his minority. It will not do. As a widow of some charm, you will soon have suitors, if you haven't already…and some of them might be persistent. To the point of abduction. I cannot risk one of them taking you by force and waging war upon my adjacent territories."

"What do you propose?" Mother's face was white as wave-foam, white as her rich silk robes that fell shimmering to the floor.

"You must marry again of course…and soon….to a suitable husband. Do not look so grief-stricken, women; it is for your own safety and your children's…" The King of England, my grandfather, nodded in my direction. "A necessary sacrifice for their futures and for the security of your realm."

"I suppose you speak true, Henry—it is indeed a lawless time." Mother's voice was tight and bitter. "I take it you have some minion of yours in mind? Dare I ask who?"

"One of my closest supporters, Ranulph de Blondeville. I can place my trust in him; his loyalty is unquestionable."

"I have never heard of him. Tell me, what kind of a man he is? A greybeard? A heathen? Or is he one of your mercenaries, seeking special payment for his services? "

Henry snorted. "Do not speak foolishly, Lady Constance. Ranulph is of good stock, a fine fighter whom I value. Far from being aged, he is but eighteen years old. He will give you many more children and protect the borders of your country with the strength of his arm."

"I have protected it well enough since Geoffrey died. What if I say no to this marriage?"

Henry looked at her, expression blank, but eyes flinty. "You will not say no, Duchess. Will you?"

Mother trembled, suddenly realising that the King was firm in his intent. "I must think upon this; give me time at least! You ask much of me, Highness. Much indeed. I…I still mourn…"

Henry ignored her. "In one week the wedding shall take place. Ranulph de Blondeville is already on his way to Brittany. He is eager to sanctify the marriage and receive all it brings. Especially the Earldom of Richmond."

I squirmed, wanting to shout out. Mother marry a stranger? It seemed too horrible for words! I wanted her to scream at grandfather, to fly in his face in a fury and stand her ground. She did not, and her face was livid, like that of a dead woman.

I began to cry and Maude followed, terrified and not understanding. Arthur grew alarmed by our tears but did not cry himself. Blue robe swirling, he ran for comfort to his nurse instead.

Henry, King of England said nothing but a harsh smile played on his lips. My grandfather was like a mountain, stern, stony, immovable.

Ranulph de Blondeville arrived at Nantes with great fanfare—most of it contrived by his own followers, who blew brazen horses, dashed about on fast horses and proclaimed their lord's supposed greatness. A short young man, his lean, dark face bore an expression of hauteur and arrogance. He wore his hair cropped into a gleaming bowl in the old Norman fashion, and upon his tabard, shield and horse's trappings blazed his Arms, a sheaf of golden wheat on an azure background.

Striding into our castle with a swagger, he entered the Great Hall without any niceties, pushing by our servants and guards as if they were invisible. "Madam!" His voice boomed out over the customary buzz of the chamber. He gazed towards mother who, looking frail and defeated, sat stiffly on the dais beneath a canopy. Despite her misgivings about this alliance, she was dressed beautifully in a bliaut girone of fine, imported blue silk and a headdress with a barbette that emphasised her attractive features.

"My lord Ranulph." Raising her hand graciously although without enthusiasm, she gestured to a cupbearer. "You must be weary—and thirsty—after your long ride hither. Drink, I beg you and assuage your thirst."

Ranulph, who had been followed in by three of his henchmen, all brash-faced youths like himself, glanced at his fellows with a grin. "Drink? I will not turn down drink, that is true." He rudely snatched the proffered cup from the page timidly approaching him, drained it and dropped it onto the rush-strewn floor. Wiping his mouth, he glared balefully at mother. "I should have had Fulk or Eudo here taste it for poison first." His fellows sniggered and grinned. "I had word you are not very keen about our match."

Mother's fingers tightened on the arms of her carven seat. "Whatever I may feel, I would not stoop to the poisoner's art. I have been commanded by the King; I will obey."

"So…a woman of morals and of obedience. Good! Let me look at you, my bride!"

Overbold, he strode towards mother, while his companions leered at each other. He looked her up and down, while she stared at the floor.

After a short while, he shrugged. "At least you are not a crone, and Richmond will be mine when we are wed. Smile, a little, will you? You might almost seem winsome if you smiled"

"My lord Ranulph, there is no need for ill manners or mocking speech." Mother lifted her head.

"Exactly! And so you should smile at me, and be warm and welcoming to your new lord. Christ's teeth, I pray you are not frosty and sulking in the bedchamber!"

A horrified gasp went through the hall at his rudeness; Blondeville had clearly overstepped the mark. I did not understand what he meant but knew it was unacceptable for Aaliz's hand clamped over mine in a death-grip. "We must leave at once for the nursery, child. You must not witness…this…this disgrace any longer."

Aaliz tucked me into my bed in the nursery. Unable to sleep, I stared open-eyed at the night-cloaked ceiling, filled by an unnamed fear. Below me in the hall, I could hear the revellers yelling and shouting, and drunken singing—it was Ranulph's party, seldom was mother's household ever so rowdy. Something shattered, and a woman screamed.

I began to sweat beneath the covers, terrified the scream was from my poor mother, who was to be the unwilling bride of Ranulf of Chester.

However, despite my avowals to stay wakeful and listen for more sounds, my lids eventually drooped and I slept, while the raucousness in the Hall below faded away.

The wedding took place outside the doors of the grandest church in Nantes, with Bishops and various dignitaries attending. I waited anxiously in the castle with Arthur, Maude and Aaliz for the wedding party to return for the evening's planned feasting.

When at last the newly married couple appeared with their retinue, clanking over the bridge into the inner ward, the first thing I noticed was my mother's red-streaked eyes. Glum, she hovered on the verge of tears. The servants in the bailey, ever loyal to the family of Conan, the former Duke and my maternal grandsire, muttered darkly and cast furious stares at the swaggering de Blondeville.

"Below her, he is," I heard Aaliz mutter to another nurse, Jenefred. "What was the old King thinking, bestowing such a fine lady on his uncouth follower! Christ's Teeth, my Lady Constance is of royal blood; her mother was sister to two Scottish kings! No good will come of this union, mark my words."

Mother and Ranulph proceeded into the Great Hall with musicians leading the way with skirling pipes and banging drums, and took their place at the head of the high table with its spread rolls of bleached white linen.

As the servers began to emerge from the kitchen and tumblers and mummers filtered in wearing scant costumes, once again I was whisked with my siblings from the frenetic scene to the safety of the nursery. Jenefred was cosseting my fitful brother, who was almost feverish with distress, his golden curls stuck to his head with sweat.

"It is not right" Jenefred rocked Arthur against her breast. "You know what I heard that awful Lord Ranulph say, Aaliz? He said he resented another man's brood in his castle, even though they be royal, and he'd soon see them sent off as wards. What a disgrace, speaking so right in front of Duchess Constance."

"You would think he was the heir to the Duchy, not just some interloper," spat Aaliz. "He knew when he agreed to marry my Lady that she had children. I know it is usual for bairns to be sent to other noble households for their learning…but not yet. They are all too young, all of them."

"He'll have his way, you mark my words," said Jenefred darkly. Arthur was now asleep in her arms, his thumb in his small rosebud mouth. "Everything will change here from this day forward. Poor little mites."

Jenefred was not wrong. Suddenly, within our own castle, we felt like strangers, intruders, as Ranulph's loutish retinue thrust their way in and took over. We stayed hidden and silent in our chambers, which satisfied Lord Ranulph, for he had no liking of his new bride's children.

And then one morn mother came to me in the nursery, clad in a matron's dull garb and a white wimple as severe as that of a nun. She frowned, biting her full lower lip. "You may be too young to understand fully what I am about to tell you, Eleanor, but you must listen intently to what I have to say. My lord husband wishes to depart for his own lands across the narrow sea in England…"

My heart began to thud and I blinked back fearful tears that stung my eyes. I knew what mother would say next. She was leaving, maybe forever, and her children were to be separated and sent to other distant households. We might never see each other again.

"I must go with him, for a time, at least," continued mother, her voice catching in her throat, "but I swear it will not be forever. Arthur shall remain in Brittany with my most trusted advisers, since this land is his rightful place, his inheritance.

"And what of Maudie and me?" Tears began to well in my eyes.

Mother knelt down and wiped the moisture from my cheeks with a thumb. "Do not cry, my little one. After much discussion with my lord husband, he has agreed to allow you to accompany me to England. Maude shall come too."

My heart leapt; I did not want to leave Brittany, but at least such exile would be bearable with mother and Maudie.

Running from Aaliz's hold, I flung my arms around mother's legs. She was stiff, like a statue, staring down at me. "We will be all right, mama. We will be together. And one day we will return to Brittany and Arthur will be Duke, and we will all be happy again."

"Happy again…" Mother gave a little sobbing laugh and took my hand in hers. Her fingers were clammy despite the warmth of the day. "Ah, may your innocence keep, Eleanor. I do not think I shall ever know happiness again. As for you, I can only pray to God and the Virgin that you find contentment one day and not suffer as I have suffered."

Poor mother. The Almighty and the Blessed Mary ignored her prayers all her life.

Chapter Four

We left Brittany the following month, once our baggage was packed and arrangements for Arthur's care had been finalised. Surrounded by newly appointed councillors, mother's handpicked advisers, and his bevvy of doting nurses, young Arthur stood ready to bid us farewell. Mother had ordered him garbed in cloth of gold and wearing his ducal crown for our leave-taking. Mother and I were both very proud that he did not weep or beg us to stay as we bade him farewell then climbed into our litter for the journey to the port.

As we moved off, Ranulph rode up on his charger to trot alongside the litter, a dark presence with his entourage of rough, swaggering young men never far behind. "I shall be glad to reach my own lands," he said. "Too long lingering in a land run by a woman makes a man grow soft. By God, I'll bet my own lands are overrun by wolfsheads and the like in my absence. A few hangings will sort them out, no doubt." He side-eyed mother meanly.

"Simple woman though I be, the folk of Brittany have no complaint about my rule," she said dryly, not deigning to look him in the face. "Besides, ruling was not my choice—it was King Henry who insisted my sire, Conan, abdicate in my favour. Of course, the whole exercise was to find a dukedom for his son Geoffrey, so my father had to go. Better to retire graciously than twist on the tip of Henry's sword, I suppose—though infinitely more dishonourable."

Ranulf flushed, scowling. "You are outspoken for a woman. I do not like that. Bloody hell, I hate this entire wretched land, and all in it…reminds me overmuch of Wales. Both places full of savages and simpletons speaking gibberish. Ugh, I find even the air here oppressive!"

"I am sure you can survive a few more days," said mother. "I will keep those fearsome 'savages' from you. Your men, however, appear to have been infected by the natives' uncouthness. Maybe it was through their frequent 'contact' with the local women…" Voice dripping sarcasm, she nodded towards Ranulph's men, who were drinking while on horseback, belching and farting as they pretended to buffet each other with their fists.

Ranulph cast his new wife a furious glare. "You go too far. My friends are not for you to sneer down upon."

"I am your wife; you will put me before your companions. That is God's law."

"I make my own laws, as does the King," snarled Ranulph.

"Henry is of the Devil's Brood, is he not? So...you say you follow the devil?"

Ranulph's visage purpled. "God's Hooks, I am already regretting this marriage—title of Richmond or no!"

"Good." A devious little smile played on mother's lips. I gazed into her face and saw there a growing strength, a resistance. Inwardly, I swore I would assume her haughty air too. Maybe one day, when I was older, I would be able to face such adversity with as much courage and defiance....

The sea crossing was nightmarish; they say hell is full of flames but I am certain parts of it are also filled with water. Deep, dark water where hidden things creep; fishes with shark-teeth and octopuses the size of castles. I lay in the hold of the ship beside Aaliz, crying as the ship heaved and bucked, timbers groaning under the strain. Vast waves smashed against the side of the ship, and my ears were filled with the roaring of the wind and the whimpers of Maudie as she lay wrapped in a blanket on a straw pallet. The smell of bile reached into my nostrils, making me heave until my throat was red-raw and my belly aching.

And then it was over.

We were alive.

Recovering from their ordeal, the nurses wiped their mouths and attended to Maude and me, brushing our matted hair, flinging off our vomit-soiled gowns and replacing them with fresh linens. We were then escorted to the ship's deck as the vessel sailed into Southampton harbour under a louring sky that spat down a misty drizzle.

Mother was already on deck, headdress sodden and hanging like a shroud, her solemn eyes locked on the green shores of her new country as they opened up before her. Even from this distance, we could hear the bells ringing in Southampton's churches, and after being at sea so long in stormy weather, they seemed somehow magical and welcoming. I clutched Maude's hand. "Do you hear them, Maudie? They ring the bells for our arrival. They ring the bells for the arrival of the King's granddaughters."

It was not true of course and when we finally disembarked upon the cobbled quay, Fulchard, one of Ranulph's henchmen, met mother to inform her that Ranulph, who had travelled in his own ship, had landed the day before and without waiting for his bride, taken horse and headed north with his favourites.

We were to trundle after him, a sad afterthought.

A rather rickety chariot was waiting on the quayside, adorned with Ranulph's coat of arms. "I would rather ride, if I may." Mother looked at the carriage dubiously; it looked dangerous, the wheels bowed out and the axles unstable.

Ranulph's burly henchmen shook his head and gestured impatiently towards the chariot. "Riding astride would not be regarded as seemly in England, my Lady. And it would make you a target."

"A target? For whom?"

"Anyone who would like a wealthy bride, my Lady."

"But I am already married!" She spat the word as if it were poison.

"That would stop but few; wedded wives of good blood have been carried off ere now. Have you not heard of the mistress of the King's grandfather, old Henry I? Beautiful Nest of Wales, raped by Owain in front of her own bairns."

Mother scowled at the oaf, sweating in his tabard decorated with its stupid Blondeville Wheatsheaf. "I bid you not repeat such unpleasant tales before two maid-children. Or me."

The man's eyes—brown and watery, the whites streaked with red veins—raked over us girls. "It's your daughters I also fear for Ladyship. They are a King's granddaughters; they'd be even more valuable for any passing rogue."

Mother looked shocked and distressed. Clasping her hands together, she cast her gaze towards the cloud-strewn heavens. "Jesu, what sin have I committed that I must be sent to this benighted land? Blessed Virgin, please lay your holy hand over my daughters, even if I am too great a sinner to receive your grace. My children are mere innocents."

Impromptu prayer over, she gestured to Aaliz and Jenefred, who were lingering in the background. "Get the children into the chariot. A crowd is forming and it is best if my daughters are kept from view. I will follow you."

"Come, child." Aaliz propelled me along the harbour wall to the waiting chariot with its four champing horses. "You heard her ladyship."

I trotted along, the singing, salty wind lashing my cheeks and the rain making my red-gold hair turn the colour of unpolished copper. I began to notice people creeping from the nearby houses, watching us.

Having overheard the warnings of Ranulph's henchman, my heart began to thud and I clutched Aaliz's hand all the tighter.

Suddenly an aged woman burst from the gathering crowd and scuttled towards me like a crab on the beach. Toothless and sun-ravaged, her face had in old age sunk inwards; it resembled a withered apple, flabby, lined, and rotten. She wore a tight white cap, yellow with unmentionable stains, and her skirts were festering rags. "Oh, it's the princess, the proud, snotty little princess!" she howled in a mocking tone. "True offspring of the great *hoo-ar* of Aquitaine and the Devil King. Eleanor the great *hoo-ar*."

Although I did not understand the meaning of her words, I sensed her overwhelming hostility. I clutched at Aaliz's skirts, nearly tripping her up, as the crone hurled an object she'd hidden within her rank skirts. It clattered on the cobbles before my feet. In Brittany, the locals often hurled posies at their Duchess and her children...but this was no posy. It was a clump of knotted green seaweed tangled around the bleached skull of some unfortunate seagull. "We don't want any more of your kind in England!" the woman shrieked. "A pox on you all...May you have no progeny, may your line die!"

A guard hustled the woman roughly away and two locals beadles took hold of her by either arm and roughly dragged her from the quay, still shrieking. Horrified, I stared at the skull at my feet—the hollow eyes, the long, open beak. Had the woman really cursed me?

"Don't look, Eleanor!" In a panic, Aaliz crushed the skull beneath her heel, grinding it to nothingness. "The woman was mad, that's all. You must pay no heed to her moon-mad words!"

Mother rushed to my side, distressed. "We must not tarry here. Hurry!" She gestured wildly to Aaliz who picked me up like a babe and carried me alongside the still-seasick Maude to the chariot. Mother clambered in beside us and, uncharacteristically for a great Lady, drew us close against her, just as if she were a common nurse or a peasant-woman.

"Try not to be frightened, my dearest daughters," she said as the chariot clattered over the cobbles and out toward the town gates. "We will prevail. In this godforsaken place, we will prevail. You have the blood of kings in you, and I am still the Duchess of Brittany."

Adjusting to the rainy isle of Britain was difficult. Brittany was also damp, buffeted by storms from the Atlantic, but its summers were hotter and balmier. Ranulph's stone keeps at Chester, Chartley and Coventry were bone-chillingly cold, filled with the constant smell of damp wool on unwashed flesh and the unchanged reeds and rushes covering the floor. I grew accustomed in fairly shorter order, but poor Maudie did not fare well in her new environment. She grew pale and thin and was constantly ailing; the nurses rubbed liniments on her chest and gave her possets nearly every day.

Our lives were lonely. Occasionally Ranulph allowed us to ride out on our ponies, with guards around us to keep us from the outlaws that infested the English woodland, but such treats were rare. Mostly the Earl of Chester ignored us, and although we were fed well and duly clothed, he kept mother from visiting our quarters, or so it seemed to two homesick little girls. We were not permitted to mingle with common folk as we had been at Nantes, and we only understood a few words of the peasants' tongue anyway. I often gazed out over the parapet of the castle, wondering about our brother Arthur, if he would remember us, what he looked like now. I wondered if we would ever meet again. The thought that we might be parted forever sent daggers of cold fear needling through my heart. Before long, no doubt, there would be talks of marriage for Maudie and I, and once we were betrothed to stout English lords, our lives would no longer be our own.

As the months rolled by, Maudie's health began to decline further. Her appetite waned and she grew pale and listless. A cough racked her lungs and dark rings circled her eyes. The best doctors were summoned but when they examined her, they shook their heads and had her taken from the nursery to a chamber far from mine, where they applied their near-magical ministrations in secret.

In the castle chapel, I prayed every night that Maudie would grow well, and that mother would come to tend her. Her touch, her kindly voice was what my sister needed...

But Maudie did not return to the nursery and mother did not come—other duties called in London where she resided at court with her hateful husband, Ranulph de Blondeville.

One night in June, an uncharacteristically hot and sticky night punctuated by fierce thunderstorms, I was woken not by the thunder's roar, but by the hooting of an owl outside my window. Blinking in the half-light, I crawled from my bed and went to look. My heart was hammering in fear, for in Brittany, the peasant folk called the owl *Labous An Ankou*—the Bird of Death. As I opened the casement, thunder grumbled and a flash of lightning illuminated the stern walls of

Ranulph's castle. The entire world turned blue-white and the sky was webbed with snarls of lightning, and then, on the retaining wall, lurking in an alcove...I saw him. A tall, dark-hatted, spindly figure holding a scythe. His head bobbed and beyond the edges of his voluminous hood, I spied a naked skull. It was Ankou himself, the collector of souls, the lieutenant of Death. In Brittany he was said to be either Adam and Eve's first son or else an arrogant lord who challenged Death himself hunt down a rare, twelve-tined black stag. The lord lost the bet and his penance was to serve Death for eternity, harvesting the spirits of the recently deceased for his new master...

Terrified, I let out a shriek and staggered backwards, my legs turning to jelly and collapsing under me. Aaliz and Jenefred came running in a panic, but even as they bore my inert form to the bed, other footsteps sounded in the hall amid shrill, frightened shouts. "What is happening?" I moaned. "I want my mother! I want to see my sister Maude!"

But I would never see Maudie again. On that night, amidst the claps of thunder, Ankou had come for her, wielding his scythe, and spirited her away in his death cart.

The nurses did not allow me to see my sister's body but I knew where she was kept: in the chapel, before the altar, wrapped head to foot in a white linen winding sheet and surrounded by tallow candles that burnt throughout the night.

Mother soon arrived, riding up the long road from the south like a whirlwind. De Blondeville had granted permission for her to depart while he remained in London. She looked an old woman, and desperately unhappy, but her eyes stayed dry. Without a solitary word for me, she hurried to the chapel where Maudie lay and stayed there, praying all night and all the next day and accepting no food or any other sustenance. At the dawn of the day following that, my sister's body was carried on a bier to Combermere Abbey, where Ranulph's ancestor Ranulph de Gernon had witnessed the foundation of the monastic house.

She had been dead for over a week; the scent of death, cloying and sickeningly sweet, wafted out of the castle with her.

My heart departed with my poor sister...and only my nurses offered comfort. It was as if my mother Constance, who closeted herself in her apartments and spoke to none, had forgotten her eldest child in her grief.

A month had scarcely passed when on another muggy morn with tepid raindrops slapping the castle walls and a sky the hue of a bruise, I woke to all the bells ringing in the castle and town. Great, mournful bells that tolled on and on and on. Sitting up with a gasp, I glanced towards the window. My nurse—not Aaliz, who had been unwillingly returned to Brittany after Maude's death, but a new one employed by Ranulph ("More appropriate," he'd said)—put her hand on my shoulder, holding me back. Tears trailed down her broad, work-worn face.

"What is it, Muriel? Let me go!" I pulled away from her touch; she was Ranulph's creature, replacement of dear Aaliz; I had no trust in her. "What are those bells? Why do they never stop? I am afraid!"

"There has been a death, my Lady Eleanor. A terrible tragedy for the country, although not altogether unexpected. His Grace King Henry, your noble grandfather, has gone over to God's keeping after illness overtook him at Chinon."

I said nothing, vaguely remembering that craggy red face and flaming hair, the body like a bull with the shoulders broad and deeply muscled. A fearsome man, a fearsome ruler whose decree had brought me to this hated place. Dead. I would not mourn…

"His Highness died after much fighting with hard-headed Richard, who treacherously bowed the knee to the King of France. And then young Prince John threw in his lot with Richard. Henry loved John; the betrayal broke your grandsire's heart—and that was the end for him. Coughing blood, he fell into a fever and after confirming Richard as his heir, he took confession and gave up this life."

Pulling away from Muriel, I sat on the edge of my bed, sullen. If grandfather died broken-hearted, I was glad. I was broken-hearted too, and no one cared On Henry's whim my family had been torn asunder. I almost hoped that in death devils were poking Henry with prongs, but to truly wish hell on a man would be too wicked even for a daughter born of the Devil's Brood.

Muriel must have misread my actions for suddenly she was smothering me in her oversized bosom. "My poor little Lady Eleanor! Losing a sister and a grandfather in such close succession. Let me ready you for chapel where you may pray for both their souls."

I knew I had no choice but make the expected motions. I let Muriel dress me in mourning garb and escort me to the castle chapel upon the third floor of the keep. At last, I saw my mother. She was white with grief and barely looked like the woman who had ruled Brittany so competently after her first husband's death.

"Mama, why did you not come to me?" Tears stood in my eyes. "I miss Maudie too."

"I...I would not have you see me weak as I am now." She bowed her veiled head. "For you must be strong, Eleanor. Strong against the storms that buffet our family."

"I thought you were strong."

"If I was strong, I would put a dagger into Ranulph's heart," she said bitterly.

I was shocked. Wives did not speak so of their husbands, even if they were not good friends. They certainly did not speak so before young children.

Wearily, mother turned to me and wiped a stray hair from my forehead. "With your grandfather dead, more changes will come, Eleanor. Near the end, worn out by warring with his sons, he named Richard his heir....but there is more to the story. Should Richard have no progeny of his own, Henry desired that Arthur would inherit England, even above John, for Geoffrey was older and hence higher in the line of succession. That is how they account the line of descent in Anjou."

"Arthur...Arthur will make a good king, mama...."

"Yes, but remember, my daughter, that if anything happened to him, God forefend, you would have a strong claim on England's throne yourself. French laws are not followed in England; although the barons might object to a woman ruler, there is no impediment to the crowning of a Queen."

A Queen! Me? I bit my lip, nervous, sweat pooling at the nape of my neck. But no, it would never happen; Arthur would reach manhood and have a dozen healthy sons of his own...

"The death of Henry brings me no sorrow but it has brought more worries," mother continued. "Everything will change. Just remember that your rank has risen in the world, along with your value as a marriage partner. Richard the new King will be aware of this...and so too, his mother the Dowager Queen."

"Eleanor of Aquitaine. My grandmother."

"Yes. Soon, the old beldam will be released from her imprisonment in Sarum Castle. I am sure she will begin her usual meddling as soon as she can."

News came to Ranulph's castle of Coventry; I cannot say it was unexpected. King Richard was to take me as his ward and oversee a reputable—and profitable—marriage for his 'dearest niece.' He was

29

faring to England for his Coronation and his mother, freed from her prison, would come to escort me to the celebrations in London.

"You should be glad, Eleanor," said Muriel the nurse. "I can't understand why you wear that sullen frown. A great destiny lies ahead of you. To think, you will see the grandness of London and the majesty of the Coronation. No doubt Richard himself will speak to you; you are most favoured."

"I am scared of the King."

"Why ever so, child?" Her scanty eyebrows lifted into a sea of wrinkles. "He is your uncle and a great warrior."

"They say he is like a Lion, that he shouts and roars when angry," I began but stopped myself speaking further, for that was foolish child's talk. Not like the whispers I'd heard when eavesdropping on two of my mother's ladies-in-waiting, those adult murmurs which I barely understood. "The King is a most lusty man," one woman had laughed, "but he takes no wife yet. It is most…unusual."

The other had smirked knowingly, playing with the trailing sleeves of her dress. "Some claim he has unnatural desires…However, when he used to lead his men against rebellious lords in Aquitaine, he would ravish the women abducted from their captured castles and pass them to his men for sport."

"And they call him chivalrous. That does not sound like chivalry to me, Basilia."

"Chivalry—pah! Made up nonsense encouraged by his mother to fit with her equally foolish 'Courts of Love'. Richard's chivalry is only towards nobles he considers equal…I think he hates women. There are men like that, you know."

"Because of Eve's sin?" asked the other lady-in-waiting.

"Maybe. Or maybe he merely punishes them for not being the one woman he adores…the Dowager Queen."

Eleanor of Aquitaine. I feared her nigh as much as I feared my Uncle Richard. Many rumours circulated about her too—how she left her husband, the French King Louis VII, to marry my grandfather Henry, who was eleven years younger than Eleanor. How she may have bedded Henry's own father, the handsome Geoffrey Le Bel, and her own uncle Raymond of Poitier, Prince of Antioch. And then there were the things that were not rumours—how she pitted her own sons against their father, encouraging faithlessness and bloodshed.

At night, confined in my small chamber, the heat of summer troubling my slumber, I dreamed of Eleanor, by Wrath of God Queen of

England. Her hair flowed free in a great cloud and her eyes gleamed with wildfire, like one of the Fae of Brittany, a portent of doom and death. She rode a bone-white palfrey down from a tall castle on a hill where winds whistled night and day and galloped after me as I ran in terror, scooping me up and laughing in an unpleasant manner as she deposited me, limp as a sack, over her saddle. Pinching my ribs and belly as if she were a witch sizing me up for a pot, she cackled, "You'll do fine, my little namesake. So sweet. We'll find a fine prince for you, little Eleanor! One with coffers bursting with money…"

I would wake up shivering and sweating, but there was no one to whom I could confide my fears. Maudie was dead, Aaliz sent home; mother as distant as the moon. Muriel would only have tutted and called me silly; she could only see good fortune in my closeness to the throne.

Messages reached us, stirring tales of the aftermath of Grandfather Henry's death. Eleanor's gaolers at Sarum had freed her instantly without waiting for the new King's command and she had hurried directly to Winchester to wait for Richard to arrive. Richard had sent his loyal man, William the Marshal, to England with orders for Eleanor's release; Marshal was amazed and taken aback to find Eleanor awaiting him in Winchester's Great Hall, behaving as if she had never suffered imprisonment at all, with a small court already gathered around her. Kneeling at her feet, he told her Richard wished that she rule England as regent in his absence, and that her word would be law.

Such power suited the Dowager Queen just fine. Hastening to Westminster accompanied by the Justiciar Ranulph Glanville, she received oaths of fealty on behalf of Uncle Richard, while the Archbishop of Canterbury hovered behind her seat. Without stopping to rest, she had then set off on a progress, flitting from town to town, castle to castle as she pleased…and now, the latest courier informed us, she was on her way to visit her daughter-in-law and granddaughter.

The castle went mad in preparation. As a prime subject of the Dowager's interest, I was hastily readied for her imminent arrival. Plunged into a wooden tub of tepid water, servants washed my skin and hair with fat soap rolled with rose petals. Then my best gown was brought along with a silver fillet, and Muriel brushed the wild curls of my gilt-rose hair until I felt they would be wrenched from my head. The entire household was in a panic as if this old woman about to visit was as mighty as the King himself.

Perhaps she was, in her own way.

Clean, primped and prettified, I glowered as a beaming Muriel thrust me into the decorated hall, to await my grandmother's grand entrance. I was reminded all too clearly of when King Henry arrived in Brittany to tell mother she must marry Ranulph of Chester. Oh, how his gaze had examined me as if I were a fine cow or broodmare.

Trumpets suddenly blasted out, their shrill fanfare bouncing off wooden beams with carvings of winged angels high above. Everyone rose, their chatter failing as the doors of the hall opened and in strode the Dowager Queen, upright and spry as if still a young woman, her figure showing little thickening despite all the children she had borne. A dour, long-faced lady-in-waiting in a burgundy robe strolled behind her—her faithful maid Amaria, who had endured years of captivity with her mistress. Henry had kept his estranged wife so impoverished she even had to share a bed with her loyal servant.

Mother appeared, dressed in a fitted bliaut with flaring sleeves and a girdle arrayed with golden tassels. She curtseyed deeply to Eleanor. All around her, the household bobbed up and down like ships on a sea, paying their respects to Eleanor of Aquitaine. Their constant movements made me feel slightly nauseous; the rhythm was broken only when Muriel gave me a sharp nudge with her elbow. "Curtsey, Lady Eleanor," she whispered. "You grandmother will expect it."

So intent were my observations, I had completely forgotten my manners. I dropped into the deepest curtsey I could manage without falling.

Eleanor spoke words of greeting to mother, her tone disinterested. Amaria the maid was looking about as if checking out the splendour of the castle and finding it lacking—presumptuous of a servant who'd dwelt in a cold, old-fashioned castle such as Sarum for many years.

Then the Dowager turned, transfixing me with her gaze. Pale eyes of many colours, brown and amber, green and grey, in a face unfashionably brown, even after long imprisonment, probed mine. Black eyebrows hinted at the colour of the tresses hidden beneath the gauzy headdress held in place by a barbette.

It was quite shocking, for to behold Queen Eleanor was to see myself aged, only my colouring was not dark but the red-gold of the Plantagenet line. Eleanor's lips quirked upwards as she examined me, and I gathered our clear resemblance pleased her. "My little namesake, the Maid of Brittany. I see much of myself in her visage. I think Richard will be pleased. She will be most marriageable with a noble lineage and a fair countenance."

She bent over, her face close to mine. Exceptionally tall for a woman, she smelt faintly of musky roses. Damask silk, deep blue and decorated with rayed stars, rustled faintly. "How old are you, Eleanor?" she asked.

"Almost seven, your Grace."

"Not too soon to see about a marriage then. I must take you to Anjou or Aquitaine, though…" She sniffed haughtily. "You will not learn the ladylike arts to your best advantage in the backwater of England."

Anjou! My heart leapt. If Eleanor removed me thence, I would be closer to Arthur, maybe could even visit him in Brittany. But mother sadly would have to remain here, as Ranulph's despised wife.

"It is a pity the other girl died," said the Dowager Queen. "Matilda was it?"

"Maude." the name burst from my lips. "We called her Maude."

"Maude then. She could have made a fine marriage too. But we must not weep; her death was God's will."

"God's will." A strangled little chuckle that was half a sob passed mother's lips.

Queen Eleanor glanced at her former daughter-in-law. "It is a grievous blow to lose a child, Constance; I remember my first son, William, who was taken aged but three, of a seizure at Wallingford Castle. We laid him to rest at his great-grandfather's feet in Reading Abbey. Then there was my poor Henry the Young King, once with such hopes pinned upon him—a man grown, yes, but still the child I bore in pain and blood. One grieves but one must go on, bound by duty as we are. At least, Constance, you are young, you can have more children"

Mother bowed her head. Eleanor looked suddenly knowing. "Ah, so it's like that. Well, you can find a way to unencumber yourself, Constance. It is not impossible, especially now that Henry is dead. Pray to Wilgefortis, whom the English call Saint Uncumber and the French call Liberata—the liberator of women."

"Saint Uncumber had a beard!" Words tore from my lips unbidden, childish and reckless. "Why would mama want a beard, Lady Grandmother?"

"Why, indeed?" said Eleanor. The maid Amaria began to smirk. There were blushes from mama's ladies and mother herself grew even paler, her hands clenched into balls at her side. I realised I had spoken out of turn, had made some dreadful gaff, although I was not sure exactly what it was.

33

Queen Eleanor noticed my red-cheeked discomfort. Laughing, she slapped her hand upon her hip in a most unladylike fashion. "Do not be ashamed of an over-active tongue, little Eleanor. Fewer women should be silent, not more. I was never silent, as I am sure you know, and it is abundantly clear you resemble me in more than mere looks."

I blushed even more deeply and made another curtsey.

Eleanor extended a hand. "No more talk. Have the servants pack your things. A new life awaits you, granddaughter. You will travel with me on my progress and begin an education in the art of Queenship. You may well need to know, one day. I will show you how to deal with court and chancery, and to regulate the measurements of corn and cloth; things necessary in the running of a kingdom."

She rubbed her chin thoughtfully. "I will plan new coinage—new coins for a new King. And I will build a hospital, a safe place for the poor and afflicted. The people of England will be happy with that. Would it please you to learn about such things, Eleanor? The minting of coins and the building of dwellings for the good of the common man?"

"Yes, your Grace," I answered dutifully, although in truth these things sounded deadly dull to my seven-year-old ears.

Eleanor must have noticed my less than enthusiastic expression for she gave a little snort of mirth and shook her head. However, she did not seem angry. Instead, she held out a more interesting proposal. "Have you ever gone hunting in a royal forest, child?"

I shook my head. Ranulph did not even allow my mother to hunt, let alone her young daughter. Needlework was my main pastime, and I was not particularly good at it.

"Well, you shall go with me. I am going to lean heavily on certain Sheriffs who have exceeded their duties and penalised trespassers in unusually harsh ways. I can't restore the hands of any poachers," she said with a grim little smile, "but I can give them their freedom. Such will be my clemency and that of King Richard."

"I shall look forward to it, your Grace." It did sound rather more interesting than coins, weights, and measures.

"And horses…do you like horses?"

"I do, madam."

"And do you have one?"

I shook my head. Ranulph allowed me an old sway-backed pony, supposedly for my own safety, but I doubted he had much care for that. A nag was much cheaper.

"Well, soon you shall. During my late husband's reign, he decreed that the royal horses would be stabled at various monasteries under the monks' care. It was a ridiculous idea and the monks hated it, for it took money from their coffers—and whoever dreamt of monks tending horses full-time as if they were grooms? I plan to relieve the brothers of this burden and present the horses to the abbots, a gift freely given in recompense for their inconvenience. But one mare of good quality and excellent temperament will be chosen for you, Eleanor."

My face brightened. Even though I would have to leave mama, maybe my new life would not be without its joys.

"I can see you like that idea, Eleanor. Your face is bright as a newly lit lantern. I am pleased. Now run along and prepare to depart. Time must not be wasted. I have much to do before Richard reaches England for his Coronation."

Chapter Five

The Dowager Queen did not spend much time in my company but enough to make me realise that my new life as the King's ward was far preferable to being in Ranulph of Chester's household. I got my horse; I got fine clothes worthy of a Plantagenet princess. Halfway through Eleanor's progress, not long after she had founded her hospital in Surrey, a courier reached the Dowager bringing news that Richard's ship had docked in Portsmouth. Her eyes danced, her mood lightened, and suddenly her young granddaughter held no interest for her whatsoever.

"I must fare to Winchester at once!" she announced. "Richard will ride to the castle to claim the treasury, as is his right. He will expect me to meet him there."

"Grandmother, may I come with you?" I asked, not keen on remaining in the company of near-strangers. All her ladies seemed aloof and Amaria, her constant companion, was a sullen, suspicious creature, seemingly wrapped in self-importance due to her closeness to the Queen.

Eleanor looked startled at the idea and then gave a gentle shrug. "Why not? He has made you his ward, after all, and you are his brother's daughter. It would do well for you to meet."

So with a select party of personal guards, we rode for Winchester and its huge castle, one of the favourites of the English Kings. I was quite excited to see the town, for legend told that Winchester was once upon a time Camelot, the capital of King Arthur. Arthur the Bear, the eternal king, for whom my dear younger brother was named.

Thinking of Arthur, a touch of sadness flitted through me; I wished he could visit and we could talk of Merlin and Lancelot and Guinevere…We had loved those tales in Brittany.

My sadness did not last long. Ahead loomed one of the great gates of Winchester, set upon deep-buried Roman foundations. Passing under its low-hanging arch, our party clattered over the cobbles toward a massive fortress standing not far from the gate itself. It dwarfed any castle I had known thus far; its pale, flinty walls over ten foot thick, solid and formidable. It had a single great, whitewashed square tower on a motte, huge protective earthworks, and a long barbican with jutting towers.

The constable of the castle, John de Rebez, walked alone across the narrow bridge to greet us. Overhead, from the peak of the great tower, I could see the royal standard flying, the lion snapping and snarling in the wind. The new King was already in residence.

"Your Grace." De Rebez bowed to Queen Eleanor with all courtesy. "It is with great joy I welcome you to Winchester."

"Oh, enough formalities!" Eleanor waved a hand. She seemed as excited as a girl about to meet her true love. "Just take me to my son, the King."

I wondered if I was to be shunted out of the way once our horses and our baggage was taken but the Dowager beckoned me to follow her. "Come with me, little Eleanor."

Walking briskly, she guided me along the maze of passages burrowing through the enormous keep, past the cabinets and boudoirs, the chapels of Saint Thomas and Saint Judoc with their austere columns and bright wall-paintings, the lavish royal apartments with their fine tapestries and exquisite decoration, down toward the Great Hall.

The hall, as we entered, was high-roofed and very beautiful, lit by hundreds of tallow candles set in gilded candelabras. Tapestries hung down the walls, showing the Nine Worthies, the Magi, and, completely different in tone to the religious hangings, a posse of archers shooting ducks, alongside a woman with a greyhound who bore the Agnus Dei on a chain around her throat. The rushes on the floor were newly plucked and smelt sweet, mixed with copious amounts of lavender and fragrant herbs. The spacious fire pit in the centre burned merrily while minstrels played on flutes, rebec and lyre in the wooden gallery high above.

At the end of the hall, resplendent in deep purple robes, the King sat on a dais. He was my father's brother and I expected them to bear resemblance, but there was little—not that I remembered much of Geoffrey, for I was so young when he died. Richard seemed to embody the very epitome of kingship—tall, well knit and bluff, his shoulder-length hair golden-red and his beard slightly tawnier, his face open and sun-bronzed, with wide, pale blue eyes ringed by laughter lines.

"My Lady Mother!" he roared in a most astonishing fashion and without ceremony or much decorum, rose from his seat and strode to Queen Eleanor's side, clasping her hands in warm welcome.

It was as if the chamber was empty, with no one in it but mother and son. My grandmother pushed me aside in her haste to reach Richard and I stood alone, cheeks burning, not knowing where I should cast my eyes. In the end, I decided the tiled floor was best.

Not for long, however. After their initial greeting, the King and Dowager Queen removed themselves from the hall to talk in private and hawk-faced Amaria swooped upon me, no doubt obeying Eleanor's orders. "Come with me, my Lady. The hour is late and you should be abed."

I went silently, feeling out of place amongst all the great lords and ladies, gorgeously attired and dripping with gold and gems. Our court in Nantes seemed humble and even mean in comparison.

On the way to my quarters, Amaria leaned over, her heavy black brows two crawling slugs across her deep-set eyes. "It is a great miracle you know, my Lady Eleanor. But it was prophesied long ago."

"What was?" I whispered.

"The Queen's return to power. Merlin the sorcerer wrote long ago that 'the Eagle of the Broken Alliance should rejoice in her third nesting.' Her Grace is the eagle, her wings encompassing England and France, while his Grace the King is her third chick, the child who will restore her to her rightful estate."

I was not quick enough to answer with admiration or awe and Amaria snapped, "Do you not feel happy for the restoration of your grandmother?"

"Of course I do. But I know nothing of such prophecies."

"Your education was clearly remiss in the backwater of Brittany! I thought that in Lesser Britain that Merlin…Merlin…was almost seen as a god!" She crossed herself, as if she thought modern-day Bretons were all truly pagans who danced round the old standing stones and venerated Arthur's sorcerer.

Anger knotted inside me. My grandmother's companion and sometime friend she might be, but she had no right to speak of my people with scorn. "Maybe we seem backwards to you but you would do well not to slight Brittany, Amaria. For Arthur of Brittany is my dearest brother and if King Richard has no heir…my brother could one day rule England. I wonder if Merlin has prophesied that?"

My tirade silenced her, although her lips quirked upwards as if she was secretly pleased by my outburst. "So," she said, "the little mouse from Brittany has teeth. That is good, if she is to survive in this hard world."

Dark brows beetling, she took me without further delay to my quarters overlooking the gardens and left me in peace. I was glad. I lay on my bed and stared out the window as the day faded to twilight and stars emerged, twinkling like diamonds around the circlets of the ladies at court. I wondered what Arthur did tonight in Nantes—games of Nine Men's Morris or marbles, maybe. I thought of poor lost Maudie, buried in a strange abbey far from Brittany's shores. I cried a little, then hastily wiped my tears on the counterpane.

Plantagenet princesses did not cry. A descendant of a devil-woman with a serpent's tail did not weep like a hapless babe.

Dowager Eleanor summoned me into the presence of King Richard the next morn. "You sit quietly and do not move or speak unless you are spoken to first," she told me sternly, moments before the King arrived in a great fanfare of horns. "You are to learn today, watching the King and I discuss business. One day you shall be a great chatelaine."

"Yes, Lady Grandmother." I retired to the corner, amongst Eleanor's ladies, with Amaria watching me like a hawk for any improprieties.

Richard entered the room, a lion of a man, his hair a flowing mane that created a sun-bright halo about his head. Moving regally through the awed courtiers, he sat down upon a throne set on a dais. An azure silk canopy embroidered with his lion emblem and a thousand tiny stars stretched over him, a blue and gold sky. Grandmother seated herself at his side, stern-faced and yet serene, her dove-grey gown trimmed with squirrel fur arranged loosely about her.

A nobleman was escorted into the hall by the palace guards—an older man with blunt-cut grey hair who wore a worried expression. Head bowed as if in shame, he fell to his knees before the dais.

"Ranulf de Glanville..." Eleanor's voice rang out like a clear bell. Any remaining buzz of noise in the Great Hall faded to nothingness. "Long were you my gaoler."

"Y...yes, your Grace." De Glanville crouched ever lower, lying almost prostrate before the royal dais "But I beg you remember I only did my duty by the late King Henry. I treated you as best I could with what little I was given to support your comfort."

The corner of Eleanor's mouth flicked upwards. "You were ever courteous, Ranulf, and offered me no affront, that is true. However..." She trailed off.

Ranulf de Glanville curled up like a bug crushed under a boot. I could sense his terror even from my distant seat amidst the women.

"However," continued Richard, taking over from his mother, "you broke your word to my father King Henry when you allowed the Dowager Queen to depart Sarum."

De Glanville glanced up, confused and uneasy. "Y…your Grace?"

"You broke your oath to guard the King's prisoner before you received word from me regarding her release. Even though your actions benefited my dearest mother the Queen, how should I regard such faithlessness? What action should I take?"

"You Grace, I beg you, I meant no…"

Richard lifted his great, sword-calloused hand for silence. De Glanville's mouth shut with an audible snap. "Quiet. I have made a decision. You will pay the Crown a steep fine for your poor judgment. However…I recognise you did your best for your Queen, your intent was good; so you shall have a full pardon."

"Your Grace, you are too merciful…" Sitting between the silent ladies-in- waiting, I watched de Glanville's face turn from white to red. I thought he might weep in relief or even faint.

"Yes, I probably am," said Richard cheerfully. The court clapped in joy to witness their benevolent new ruler's show of clemency. Dazed by his good fortune, Ranulf de Glanville was escorted away by the guards.

"He won't be allowed keep his position as Justiciar." The King glanced sideways at Eleanor. "Some price for his actions must be paid."

"Naturally." Eleanor gave a slight nod.

"As for your other gaolers over the long years—I grant you to right to seek them out and do with them what you will, whether it be imprisonment, or…" He shrugged meaningfully.

Queen Eleanor pursed her lips. "I am in my sixties, Richard; the idea of bloody vengeance no longer ignites a fire in my breast. They only did as Henry ordered. None harmed me; the worst damage to my person came from the cold winds of Sarum and to be truthful, most of my captors suffered more than I did. I have rude good health; the rest all now suffer from rheumatism."

"So, what is your decision then, mother?"

"I grant them all mercy and forgiveness."

Richard reached over and clasped her hand, pressing it to his lips. "You are too good, Lady Mother."

"Just too old!" Eleanor gave a bleak little laugh.

A string of other prisoners, mostly men who had supported Henry against Richard, appeared before the dais; the new King, full of benevolence since attaining his inheritance, pardoned them all with smiles and blessings.

After audience with the King and Dowager Queen ended, a huge banquet was prepared. Wine flowed free and lavish foodstuffs were served—roast swans bearing all their feathers, fine peacocks, roast boar, eels and lampreys swimming in saffron sauce. Eleanor permitted me a place at table, near to her own—an honour for one so young, although I dare say she also wanted to keep an eye on my behaviour. However, sitting in such an obvious place meant I would have to remain in attendance until the King departed for the night, and as hours slid by, my eyelids grew increasingly heavy, aided by the watered-down wine in my goblet.

At last, near midnight, Richard took his leave of the court. Grandmother Eleanor processed to her chamber shortly after, followed by her jewel-like, glowing crowd of ladies…and by her tipsy granddaughter with her circlet hanging askew and wine stains on her gown.

As she reached the door of her apartments, the Dowager halted and gazed at me with appraising eyes. "Well, young Eleanor, it looks like it is long past your bedtime. You will find, as you grow older that sleep is ever less important—there is time enough to lie quiet in the tomb! I look forward to seeing you at Mass early tomorrow morning. While you are at prayer, see that the servants pack your things. We are going on progress."

"Progress, Lady Grandmother? Where?" Disappointment welled in my heart; I had looked forward to relaxing in the castle's herb garden and being escorted through the town to the great cathedral and the Bishop's Palace, and to ancient Nunnaminster and out across the meadows to the Hospital of Saint Cross, where I could do a royal maiden's duty and give alms to the poor.

Eleanor had not seen my downcast face. She beamed as she described the glorious progress of her son. "Richard is not well known in England for he comes here seldom. He needs to meet his people before his Coronation takes place. They must learn to love him as…as I do! Our royal cavalcade shall pass through Salisbury to Marlborough and then on to Windsor, where the King means to meet with his half-brother Geoffrey."

"I did not know his Grace had a half brother! Was the King married be…"

Eleanor's sour expression silenced me. "Ah, you are a dear little innocent, Eleanor. Geoffrey is baseborn, gotten on a woman called Ykenai…" Her lip curled in contempt; it was clear she thought this Ykenai a worthless creature.

Ashamed by my too-swift tongue, I flushed. I hopped nervously from foot to foot, fearing chastisement.

Eleanor ignored my embarrassment and said no more about my lack of discretion. "There will be a wedding at Marlborough, too, my dear child. Weddings are always a joy…of sorts. I should know; I've had two." She let out an unqueenly guffaw and her women tittered behind their hands.

My heart skipped a beat and for a moment, I feared I might spew my dinner at my grandmother's slippered feet. They had found me a husband, surely; without telling me, they had anchored me to some aged, rich old lord with a whiskery chin and hot, probing eyes. Someone even worse than mother's horrible husband, Ranulph of Chester.

The Dowager Queen looked at me, quaking and heartsick, my hands visibly trembling, and she let out another peal of mirth. "It's not your marriage, my overwrought little granddaughter. Soon we will seek an adequate match for you, that is true…but not yet. Richard and I do not believe in haste; your hand is too valuable to throw at someone just because he owns many lands. Marriage must be mulled over—like a game of chess."

"Who is to wed then?" I asked timorously. "Is it the King?"

"No, not the King. Another of your Uncles—John, my youngest son. We call him Johnny; I am certain he would be gladdened if you called him Johnny too. But be cautious around him, I beg you…He can act inappropriately at times."

Unwitting, I gazed at her. What did she mean by inappropriate? That he spoke too loudly, picked his nose, belched at table?

Eleanor sighed and took my face in her long, strong hands. "My little innocent. What can I say? Let me just tell you one of his quirks—when he cannot have his own way he gnaws his own fingers like a beast."

I could not refrain from making a face.

"John also has too keen an eye for beautiful women but I needn't think you need fear him on that front. Yet." Eleanor gestured for her ladies to make her quarters comfortable for the night—bowls of rosewater were brought, pomanders hung, sheets warmed. "Till tomorrow then, little Eleanor."

I curtseyed reverently and grandmother departed into her apartments, the door closing in my face. The sound of a lyre drifted through the wood to reach my ears. My own nurses escorted me to my chamber, where they divested me of my dress, tutting over the stains, and combed out my tangled hair.

John. Johnny.

I thought of my uncle biting his own hands and shuddered primly. He sounded wicked. Despite his youth, John had plotted with Richard against his own father. Men whispered that John's defection had come as a great blow to the ageing monarch, for John had been his favourite son. Three days after learning of John's defection, grandfather had turned his face to the wall and died, filled with a grief born of ultimate betrayal. The betrayal of one's own blood.

John. They called him Lackland because he has no lands of his own.

I shuddered and beckoned to my attendants to close the wooden shutters on my narrow window, keeping out the deepening night beyond.

Marlborough was a small town deep in the county of Wiltshire. Three mills churned alongside the river and the workshops of tanners and fullers clustered along the edges of the broad high street. The bells of the Priory of Saint Margaret of Antioch rang out over all, clashing with those of the nearby churches of Saint Peter and Saint Mary. At the farthest end of the street reared the imposing square tower of the castle, built in the reign of my grandfather and standing on top of an enormous earthen mound.

"That is Merlin's mound." Amaria the handmaid, riding in the litter beside me, peered through the curtains. "They say he is buried there, deep below the earth, waiting to return some day alongside King Arthur."

In silence, I gazed at the huge mound, swollen and immense, a huge boil upon the landscape ready to burst and cast forth the ancient dead into the world of the living. Somehow, its presence felt ominous, its black sides casting long shadows over bailey and frowning stonework. Shivering, I dragged my woollen cloak around my shoulders.

Amaria tittered and let the draperies on the litter fall back into place. "It's only a story, my Lady. I thought it might amuse you."

It didn't, especially after her earlier jibes about Brittany. She had no idea how in Brittany the name of Merlin was whispered as if he still lived, not as a god but as an old one, an ancestor of many powers. We were as Christian as any land and laughed at such foolishness in castle or chapel, of course…but at night beyond the firelight, it was different, not just to children but most adults too. I had no wish to sleep this night over a wizard's grave, even within the King of England's keep…

I had no more time to think of Merlin, lying unbreathing but incorrupt within the hill, for now the entourage was entering the great gate of the castle ward. Saint Martin's church, standing hard by the curtain wall for the use of the castle servants, boomed out a welcome in a noisy peal of bells.

Inside the bailey there was already much activity—the parties of John and his bride-to-be, Hawise of Gloucester, had arrived not long before ours. Grooms ran about leading horses and trumpets blasted strident fanfares as great dignitaries here for Prince John's nuptials ascended the stairs to the first floor of the keep, where they would greet King Richard and his esteemed mother.

Being but a child and not very important in the scheme of things, I was carted away to a small room at the back of the fortress; all of Eleanor's ladies-in-waiting were thrust in with me, since space for the celebrations was severely limited. The stables in the outer ward were bursting with men and beasts and I heard grumbling that all the town inns were full. Lesser men would have to pitch tents in fields beyond or sleep under bushes and pray for no rain.

A small private dinner was held in the royal apartments with only Richard, grandmother, Uncle John and their favourites in attendance; the rest of us had a simple meal in the hall, the highest-born, including myself, seated near the empty dais.

"So that's the lucky bride." Pavia, one of grandmother's ladies, nodded toward the trestle table opposite, packed with strangers in rich garments. "A lamb to the slaughter, I'd say, wouldn't you, Mariot?"

Her fellow laughed and nodded. "The marriage is all about giving Lackland some lands at last. One of the last things old Henry did for his beloved boy. The King made sure John would profit well. Disinherited Hawise's sisters, Mabel and Alice, so that she was made sole heiress of her father's lands."

"Some might call that illegal, Mariot."

Mariot giggled, dabbing her mouth with a cloth. "That's not all that might be illegal, Pavia. The Prince and Lady Hawise are related within the prohibited degree since they both shared Henry One as a grandsire, although Hawise's father, Robert, was born on the wrong side of the blanket. So they are cousins."

"It is not much of an impediment. The Pope will surely grant a dispensation…with a little enticement." Pavia made a motion with her fingers meant to imitate coins rubbing together.

Mariot smirked, then threw her napkin aside. "But I have heard none has been applied for, let alone obtained. John could quite easily get rid of his little bride if she is not pleasing to him."

"Will he do any better than her, though? A King's younger son with no great patrimony? His wealth will come from his wife."

"I'd wager John would find a way to keep Hawise's lands even if the marriage was annulled. He may be a land-poor little fellow but he's clever and. acquisitive…"

I managed to glance past the chicken leg I was nibbling on to observe the Earl of Gloucester's daughter—who was also my distant cousin through Henry I. About sixteen, Hawise was sitting staring miserably into her trencher, a tall, spare girl with a pointed chin, wan complexion and a tiny mouth overcrowded with teeth. She wore a veil with plaits of long, light brown hair flowing under it. Thin hands played nervously with a golden pendant of the Virgin and Child dangling from her neck.

For a moment, Hawise met my gaze with sad, timid grey eyes; blushing, I quickly looked back to my food. So this is how it was with marriage. It was no different to my mother's marriage with Ranulph. The man gloated over lands, the woman endured. It seemed all the stories of great lovers were just that…stories.

The next morning, John and Hawise of Gloucester were wed before the doors of Saint Nicholas's chapel in the castle bailey. Due to my age, I was not invited to the nuptials but left to bide my times with nurses and ladies of the court. As time passed, the day grew hot and thunderous, great clouds rolling in fantastical formations across the darkening sky, and, breathless and bored, I managed to slip away unnoticed into the castle gardens on the far side of the motte.

The gardens were royal purple with criss-crossed hedges of lavender. Pungent fragrance rose from the shrubs to permeate the heavy air. Herbs grew in decorative knots—rosemary, sage, lemon balm and mint, their own pleasant scents mingling with earth and the lavender. In the centre of the garden stood a low deep pond, covered in lilypads; I

45

wondered if carp for the table were contained therein, and on hands and knees tried to search for fish within the watery depths.

Behind me, the castle motte, Merlin's Mound, was a dark presence, its shadow falling over the garden to give it some shade. A hot wind whirred in the grass and the fruit trees that ringed the garden, and I fancied I heard a voice whisper in my ear, "Where lie the bones of wise Merlin? Where lie the bones of noble Arthur?"

On my knees before the pond, crouched like some supplicant at a pagan altar, I froze. And then my heart nearly ceased to beat, for mirrored in the waters, crowned by the cumbrous, yellow-tinged storm clouds was a head, the face of a primaeval god…or was it a demon? It rose up, dark, ominous, white teeth flashing, masses of wild dark hair blotting out the storm light.

I whirled about and the beginning of a thin childish scream tore from my lips. A hand clamped over my mouth, silencing my cry. "Be quiet, girl. It is only your uncle, John."

The hand fell away. I fell too, gracelessly, my legs jelly, and landed unceremoniously on my backside.

John! My kinsman…

Struggling to rise to my feet, I dropped a clumsy curtsey.

The youngest son of the Devil's brood was nothing like his royal brother, King Richard. He was nothing like my time-dimmed memories of my father either. John was short and inclined to stoutness; his body belled out around the middle, even though he was only a young man. On closer inspection, the hair I had thought was black was a very dark shade of red; so dark it appeared black until the sunlight stroked it—then fire bloomed on the curls and snarls. The eyes were brown, as shrewd as grandmother's, and framed by bushy dark brows. His complexion was ruddy, resembling grandfather Henry's, but also, as was common in young men his age, rather spotty.

"So…you are my niece, Eleanor. Geoff's get." John hooked his thumbs into his elaborate belt. "Your mother must be pretty—you look nothing like Geoff. Poor, luckless old Geoff, trampled in the tournament."

I winced at the mention of my unfortunate father's demise. John seemed not to notice…or care. "Mother said she'd brought you along on her progress. You're Richard's ward now, are you not?"

I nodded. John licked his lips; they were rather full for a man and a dark, liverish red. He had no beard yet, but some scruffy bunches of dark hair sprouted on upper lip and chin.

"It's a pity I could not have married you...instead of that whey-faced mare they've shackled me to this very day."

I let out a squeak. "But you...you're my uncle."

He scratched the bristles on his chin. "Aye, I know that...but things can be bought, Eleanor, if one has the money. As you get older, you will understand."

He stalked away, sat on a bench. I felt uncomfortable and even a bit fearful. I did not like his talk of marrying me. I remembered well what the Dowager Queen, John's own mother, had said of her son. "Don't be alone with him..."

"I must go now..."

"Don't be stupid. I only just got here. Surely we should get to...know each other." Suddenly he was back on his feet and capturing my hand, pressing it to those over-ripe lips. "It is my pleasure to meet you, kinswoman."

I tried desperately to rid myself of him. "Yes, it is nice to meet you, sir. But will the Lady Hawise not expect her husband?"

"Oh, yes, yes." He dropped my hand, flapped his own about in frustration. "Hawise, who looks near enough to cry every time I even speak to her. She's brought me a fortune though, so I mustn't complain too much. I am now Earl of Gloucester through right of my wife and will have Hawise's lands to do with as I will. Richard has finally shown me some generosity too and given me both this castle and Ludgershall." He gestured to the keep thrusting like a bleached finger-bone from the summit of Merlin's Mound, the banners on the parapets flapping and coiling in the wind. "This is mine now, all mine! Do you like my gardens, little niece?"

I felt he was mocking me and held my tongue.

"You're afraid of me, aren't you?" he asked. He leaned over, his big, thick head with its wild flame-dark hair close to mine. Shadowed, his eyes appeared almost black. Wine reeked on his breath.

"No..." I lied. I would not admit such a thing. A Plantagenet, even a girl, did not.

John changed the subject. "You have a brother, do you not, Eleanor? Why is he not here for Richard's Coronation?"

"Arthur is Duke of Brittany, so he remains in Brittany," I said. "And...and...he is only five."

"Five! " John's lip curled. "A mere babe, then. And to think, as Geoff's get, he will be considered heir presumptive till Richard begets spawn of his own. Whenever that might be." He began to pace upon the lawn, visage suddenly as thunderous as the sky, muttering to himself like some madman. I remembered grandmother's tales of his enraged finger-biting and wondered if I would witness such horrors this afternoon. "It isn't right, isn't right, I say. I am a man grown. I should be Richard's heir. HIS HEIR!"

His voice lashed out like the crack of a whip, and in the same instant, lightning forked across the dimming sky.

Taking the opportunity to escape, I snatched my skirts in my hands and fled the garden. Rain spewed from above and lightning-needles darned the clouds.

Behind me, mingled with the storm's tumult, I could hear Prince John laughing.

Chapter. Six

Gleaming in the westering September sun, the gates of London gaped open to admit the Dowager Queen's entourage. At last, after many days' travel, we were here for Richard's Coronation. Peering out of the carriage at the streets of the great city, I felt awestruck. It was hard to imagine such a huge place existed; I had never seen so many people gathered together in one place, pushing and shoving to get a better look as the chariot, draped in banners and painted with the Dowager Queen's personal Arms, trundled down the street.

Everything looked so big and tightly packed together—houses of multiple stories and overbearing turreted walls, monastic houses with graceful spires and grand palaces with glass windows and opulent fronts. All manner of humanity gathered in the streets, from monks and nuns, swathed in their dusty robes, to bell-ringing lepers, to wealthy merchants in silks of clashing colours and outrageous hats, to minor nobility wearing jewelled collars and the latest fashions from the continent. The sound of London was overwhelming too—asses braying as they were beaten, horses whinnying as their riders forced them through the mob, townsfolk shouting, singing, swearing, pedlars pitching their wares in booming voices, while overall the bells of the monasteries and churches tolled in endless clangour. Naturally, such a crowded place had its own scent and it was not a pleasant one— unwashed bodies packed close, spoilt meat from the fleshers, the greasy fare of pie-men…and rotting ordure. It startled me to see so much excrement running down gullies in the cobbled street, splashing up in acrid waves as the horses drawing our chariot ambled through it.

Soon, however, the fragrance changed. A wind was blowing off the great river Thames that coiled like a dank green-brown serpent through the heart of London. Scents of waterweed and rancid water struck my nostrils, and in the heavens above white-winged gulls shrieked and dived.

Inquisitive as ever, I poked my head out of the chariot; Amaria, sitting by my side with her sewing in her lap, looked mildly displeased but kept her peace. Squinting in the sunlight, I gazed over at the river, massed with all manner of boats, from little coracles to great barges packed with nobles arriving for the Coronation. Flags fluttered and horns blared, their strident calls bouncing off the nearby buildings. In the far distance, I could see a great bridge, piled high with houses and crawling with onlookers, thick as ants; it bore a huge stone gatehouse and a mill that dashed the river water, and several mighty churches flanked its span.

"What are you staring at, Lady Eleanor?" asked Amaria. "Have you never seen a bridge before?"

Amaria was not kind like Aaliz, whom I still missed, or even bluff Muriel; she seemed to imagine I was some gaping bumpkin and treated me accordingly. "Of course I have seen bridges! Just not as big as that one...London Bridge."

"Yes, that's its name," sniffed Amaria. She was clutching a pomander stuffed with dried rose petals to her rather large nose to cut the worst of London's odours. "I would not stare too hard though, Lady Eleanor. In fact, I think you should withdraw from the window right away. The Dowager Queen would not be pleased if you saw sights unsuitable for a highborn princess. Remember, her Grace is only just riding ahead of us in her own chariot."

"What sights?" I was revelling in the strangeness of the London vistas and feeding off the excitement of the crowds. I wanted to see all that I could.

"The heads." Amaria dangled the pomander before her nose again, inhaling noisily. "Can you not smell them? A scent different and far worse than dung. It clings to your clothes and hair if you come too close."

"Heads? What heads?" Not understanding, I blinked stupidly at my grandmother's maid.

"The heads of traitors, silly!" Amaria disrespectfully rolled her eyes. "The heads of wicked men set on pikes to warn those inclined to evil of their potential fate."

Ignoring Amaria's warning, I stared through the bleary, over-bright afternoon light. Far, far away, black lumps were visible on poles near the gatehouse of London Bridge; gulls and other birds hovered around them, darting in every now and then in a frenzy of beaks and wings.

I sprang back into the depths of the chariot, my mouth gone dry and my throat stinging with bile. I had never seen such a city as London. And I had never seen mutilated remains of dead men before, either.

Amaria seemed pleased that I had finally obeyed her by coming inside. "I told you they weren't fit for a lady's eyes. Disgusting, rotten things that once belonged to disgusting, rotten men."

Screwing my eyes shut, I tried to blot out the memory of what I'd glimpsed. "I...I would like some water, Amaria." The maid heaved a sigh as if she thought me weak and wanting and handed me a flagon.

Fortunately, my discomfiture did not last long. We soon reached the rich London house where the Dowager's party was billeted. Grandmother was heading onward to the Tower of London to join the King for his final night before the Coronation.

"Will we see anything of the King?" I asked Amaria plaintively while servants bustled around us, carrying chests of clothes, crates stuffed with victuals, and barrels of wine. "What a shame if we can see nothing of the ceremonies!"

"We won't be able to go into the Abbey, of course," replied Amaria, "but her Grace has arranged a place for us near the doors on a raised platform so we can see his Highness pass. As for the feast that will be held afterwards, Richard is a man for men—he has invited no females to attend, not even Queen Eleanor."

I made a small unhappy sound.

"However, her Grace has decided to hold her own celebratory feast in honour of King Richard, and she expects her granddaughter will attend."

Happy at the news, my smile returned. Amaria folded her arms, imperious and cross as ever. "But first we will have to do something with that rats-nest of hair, Lady Eleanor!"

The crowd pressed close against the sun-warmed stonework of the great Abbey of Westminster. Under a silken canopy, I sat with other great ladies, including my cousin Richenza of Saxony, who was soon to marry Geoffrey of Perche by the new King's command. Both of us wore gowns threaded with gold to proclaim our status and narrows fillets that swept back our hair. The air buzzed with excitement and my hands dripped with nervous sweat as I clutched the edge of our viewing box.

Away in the busy streets, clarions rang out and the sound of cheering arose in a great wave, growing ever louder and louder. Clergymen appeared carrying a bejewelled ceremonial Cross that shone with a dazzling array of colours. Abbots in heavy cassocks and bishops in soaring mitres trailed in the wake of this Rood, walking in stately cadence along a red woollen carpet that led straight up through the Abbey doors. Another cluster of silk-hooded clergymen waited on the carpet, some swinging censers that emitted clouds of incense, some bearing lighted tapers, while others escorted a crystal vial filled with the Holy Water. Four barons, resplendent in silk and wearing chains of office, marched alongside the religious, holding up four candlesticks of pure gold.

I did not know the men of the King's council, but Amaria did from her long service to Eleanor. She nudged me and exhorted me to listen as she pointed them out and listed their names; one day, she said, it might do me well to know them all.

Godfrey de Lucy, a tall man with a drooping moustache, carried Richard's gilded cap of maintenance on a cushion; with him was John Marshal, whom I had seen at Marlborough, carrying a pair of ornate spurs. Next was William Marshal, one of Richard's stalwarts, bearing the royal sceptre with its ornamental cross, and at his side, William Fitz Patrick, holding a rod of gold surmounted by the figure of a dove. David Earl of Huntingdon was holding a sword of state, likewise the swarthy-faced Earl of Leicester—and between these two dignitaries rollicked Prince John, the newly made Count of Mortaine, like a small, barrel-chested ape. Pulling faces, he jostled against the older, stern-faced lords as if he did not take the occasion of his brother's anointing and crowning seriously.

After John passed into the Abbey's maw, there was a little gap in the procession, and then another cluster of earls and barons appeared, conveying a tableau painted with chequered hues, upon which rested the King's robes and Royal Arms. William de Mandeville, an old warrior greatly respected through grandfather's reign, came next with the domed royal crown clasped firmly in his hands, followed by the King himself, tallest of the gathered lords, his ermine robe trailing in his wake, his hair shining golden-red upon his muscular shoulders. The Bishop of Durham walked on his right, the Bishop of Bath on his left, and a blue and silver canopy held aloft on sharp spear points lifted over them all.

The King paused and glanced around him; the waiting spectators outside Westminster roared and surged forward, eager to touch, to impart the magic of his royalty and nobility in some way to them. In my sheltered stand, I did not move. Something about my Uncle Richard disturbed me—his bored, dismissive glances in my direction and at the ecstatic crowds, even as he smiled. He did not speak the language of the majority here, nor did they speak his. Rumours ran rife that soon he would leave on Crusade. England to my Uncle Richard, I feared, was just a source of money to pay for his foreign wars. And I would be currency for a profitable alliance.

Amaria was nudging me. "Why so solemn, Lady Eleanor? Why do you not wave? Your uncle is King; surely, you are glad! Look at your Cousin Richenza; she is weeping with joy!"

I forced a weak smile, wobbly as ripples on a pond. It would not do to seem reticent. "Huzzah!" I cried unenthusiastically, thrusting my small, curled fist to the sky. "Long live King Richard!"

Chapter Seven

I was ready to attend the Dowager Queen's private banquet in the King's honour. Dressed in my best, with Amaria serving as my lady-in-waiting, I climbed happily into the litter that waited outside the grand mansion where Queen Eleanor's party was lodged.

As we travelled down the street toward Westminster, an uncomfortable feeling gripped me, dousing any vestiges of excitement. Amaria must have felt the same judging by the frozen expression on her face.

Beyond the hangings of the litter, the streets were full of running men and women. The happy mood of the Coronation had died utterly and hostile shouts rang between the houses. A plume of smoke rose over London and spread out across the sky like a winding sheet, darkening the heavens and making the wan sun resemble a malevolent, blood-shot eye.

The scent of burning reached my nostrils and my stomach knotted with fear. "What is happening, Amaria?" I tugged the maid's long sleeve.

Amaria thrust the litter's draperies aside and shouted to our guards, "Hold! You will not proceed further with the Lady Eleanor until we know what is amiss in London. You, man…" She pointed a bony finger at an armoured youth. "You look fleet of foot. Find out why fires burn and men shout. Use her Grace's name, if you must."

More crowds began to pouring into the streets, rushing forward in such numbers that people were crushed against the shops and houses. My little guard drew close, keeping us safe at sword point, but their steeds were frightened and nigh out of control, while the terrified litter-bearers swayed this way and that, striving to keep their footing as the nervous horses bashed into them.

I shrieked as one end of the litter lurched downwards, nearly spilling me out into the dung-filled street. Amaria flung her arms around my waist, holding me back. She was not my favourite person, but she was loyal to grandmother, and in that moment, I was glad of her strong, practical presence.

Our little party struggled onwards, moving from the centre of the street to the shadows of a gateway leading to a small monastic house. We sheltered in the arch as tides of heaving humanity swept through London. At our backs, red, round, monkish faces pressed to the slot in the huge oak door that protected the house from the temptations of the outside world. It took me a few moments to realise these monks were actually shouting imprecations, telling us to leave the premises at once in case we attracted the attention of the mob.

Amaria flushed with rage. Thrusting her head out of the litter, she cried, "How dare you, you cowardly men of God? Would you see us all beaten and robbed or worse?" She grabbed my arm, pushed me forward into view. "This child is the King's own niece, Eleanor Pearl of Brittany. If any harm should come to her, it will not go well for your precious Order! Open up!"

"I will have to ask prior's permission," whined one of the monks, his voice high and nasal. "To have women here is against our…"

"A royal princess, not some doxy from a brothel!" bellowed Amaria. "For love of Christ Himself, let us in."

The monks behind the door shuffled and jostled, whispering to each other. It was with great relief I heard the wooden bar on the far side fall and saw the gate open a few feet. A cowled figure half-leaned out, waving an arm in an agitated manner. "Quickly then! Quickly, before the rabble try to break in here."

My little entourage shoved into a narrow passage that widened into a small quadrangle. Between the ivy-wreathed arches framing the quadrangle, smoke from the burning city whirled and twisted.

Amaria alighted from the litter and I crawled after her. "Do you know what has occurred?" she asked the monk guiding us. "The man I sent never returned. This is terrible…terrible…the King newly crowned and there is rioting, and by the look of it, looting and burning."

The monk took a deep breath. "We have heard it's the Jews."

"Jews?" Amaria's heavy eyebrows lifted. "You are trying to tell me the moneylenders are attacking us? You jest, man."

"No, no, mistress, you misunderstand. The folk of London are attacking the Jews."

"But why ever so? I know rumours linger that Jews murder Christian children, but only backwards places such as Norwich believe such nonsense. Not here in London. Surely you are mistaken."

The monk shook his head miserably. "No, mistress. It all came about from a terrible misunderstanding. The King forbade all women—and Jews—from his Coronation banquet…"

"This is common knowledge," snapped Amaria. "Get on with it!"

The monk chewed on his lip. "Unfortunately, not all Jews were informed of this decision. One wealthy moneylender walked into the

55

banqueting hall, intent upon presenting the King with a gift. He was jumped upon and beaten, then thrown into the street."

"So...this moneylender broke the King's command. He sparked this trouble, unwitting or not. Still, I do not think King Richard ordered there to be burning and depraved acts of destruction in the wake of a fool's error."

The monk wrung his hands. "I want to believe not, Lady. But rumours quickly went abroad that Richard had ordered the deaths of all Jews, both in London and further afield."

Amaria stared at the man, aghast. "This cannot be true! Why...why would he do that? The King owns all the Jews. Their money is very useful to him."

The monk made a small non-committal noise and shook his head. "I would have said the same as you, mistress, but there are those who have sprung upon these rumours as a dog springs upon a meaty bone. The mob has gone to the Old Jewry, fired the Jew's homes and stolen their possessions. There will be deaths...and outrages, you can be sure of it!"

Amaria crossed herself, looking shaken and flustered for the first time. "This is an ill omen, and the King with the crown so recently set upon his head! You will allow us to stay for our own safely...for the princess?" She gestured in my direction; I stood against the ivied wall, shivering miserably in fear.

"The Abbot isn't happy," said the monk wearily," but then again, he's never happy. However, he has granted permission for you to stay until the streets are clear."

Next morning, my little entourage hastily departed the priory. A message had been smuggled out to the Dowager Queen and she'd supplied a contingent of guards to ensure my security. Warily, we passed out into the streets of London—empty now that the King's soldiers had dispersed the rioters. Smoke still hung like a pall over the city and the air smelt ashen, tindery. Items that thieves had attempted to drag away lay scattered everywhere—smashed chests, torn and trampled fabrics, discarded plate. There was even a fine gold candlestick, a Menorah sacred to Jews, flung into the gutter by a thief fleeing the arrival of Richard's men.

We were marched to the mansion and taken immediately to the Dowager Queen, who waited in the solar. As I entered, she rose and looked me up and down as if inspecting for damage. "You are unharmed, little granddaughter?"

I nodded. Unharmed...but I'd learnt a harsh lesson about men that day. They could turn in hateful rage upon their fellows, even if they had once dwelt at peace, if there was something to gain...

"Richard is furious at this atrocity," said Eleanor. "You must believe me on this, child."

"I do, grandmother."

"He has no time to deal with these problems in England. Soon he plans to go on Crusade."

"Crusade!"

"Yes, a noble ambition. He will make preparations and, Christ willing, his flotilla will be ready for departure in the spring. He plans to leave England himself ere Christmas."

"That seems so soon, my lady grandmother! He has just become King!"

"Indeed...but Henry left a goodly sum in the royal treasury and my son always has his way." She laughed throatily. "Do not sound so shocked, Eleanor; you are too young to understand anything. All you need to know is that he will go and fight for the glory of God. We too shall be on the move when the affairs of England are settled."

"We are surely not going on Crusade too?" My eyes widened. The thought of hot burning deserts and swarthy paynims with scimitars was terrifying to a child my age.

"No, no, not to Jerusalem. I have grown too old for such adventure. But we will return to Normandy, and to my lands in Aquitaine. There I can teach you to be a proper lady, and think upon an appropriate future marriage for you. A match must be made for Richard too—he is far too long unwed. He procrastinates with Alais, chosen by his father, and I can hardly blame him, for it is said Henry...laid hands upon her. She is getting old, too, near enough nine and twenty, and he needs a woman who can produce healthy sons. Otherwise, should, God forefend, he fall in battle, it may turn out to be a war between my John and your brother Arthur for England's crown."

As planned, Richard swiftly fared to the continent to attend his business there and prepare for his upcoming Crusade. Grandmother dragged me from castle to castle, Windsor, Canterbury, Salisbury and Winchester, as she dealt with the running of England. All the while, a great flurry of shipbuilding was taking place on the coast as the King's crusaders massed for their expedition to Jerusalem.

Despite being busy provisioning his forces, Richard found time to write to the Holy Father in Rome. A papal bull was circulated stating that no women were permitted to accompany the Crusaders upon their long road to Jerusalem.

The Dowager Queen laughed as she told her ladies-in-waiting, of the papal bull. "Oh, my dear son, Richard; he is terrified of women, really, for all his bluster and the past indiscretions of youth. He wants no women on his journey, he says...yet he still leaves power and his kingdom in my hands."

Christmas court took place at Winchester and the nobles of England feasted and caroused for many days. I was given new, silvered slippers, a marten fur cloak, and a music tutor. The only downside was the arrival of Count John with a downcast Hawise of Gloucester in tow. John had quite taken over the festivities, imagining himself as some kind of a wag and far more amusing than Osbert the court jester. "You should have seen me in Ireland!" he roared, staggering around the hall with goblet in hand, sloshing wine down his brocade tunic. "There I was, dressed like a King's son, as well I might be, and I'm introduced to what? A bunch of hairy savages with beards dangling down to their knees! And they could not speak French, or even English! Not a word of either!"

"Beards to their knees? Surely you exaggerate, John." Eleanor passed his words off as if they were the ramblings of a child and continued sipping from her fluted goblet.

"No, mother, I swear by the Holy Rood—they had beards as twice as long as Hugh here!" He capered over to an elder courtier and gave a tug to the old man's neatly coiled beard. The courtier spluttered in outrage but dared say nothing to his young royal tormentor.

"Count John." John's half-brother, Geoffrey, recently made Archbishop of York, frowned over at his youthful sibling. "It is not fitting to mock one's elders. Or the Irish, for that matter. You know well how your japes went down with their chiefs."

John glowered, clearly annoyed at being rebuked by his bastard half-brother. Geoffrey did not cease his admonishments, however. "They called you an ill-manner child of whom no good could be hoped."

"How dare you bring up the foul words of those savages!" snarled John, stamping his foot on the rush-strewn floor. "I will go back to

Ireland one day and teach them manners. Teach them not to disrespect a prince of the blood!"

I shrank back on my bench. John looked almost demonic; his face suffused with blood and his eyes so dark they were near enough black. The light of the nearby torches flickered on their surfaces, little points of red and gold.

Eleanor half-rose, face stern with displeasure. "We are still enjoying the joys of Christmas; Twelfth Night is not till tomorrow. At least hold your peace till then, the both of you!"

Geoffrey sniffed disdainfully and, taking his leave of the Dowager Queen, glided from the Great Hall with his nose regally held in the air. In the minstrels' gallery, the court musicians began to play on dulcimer, lyre and crumhorn, eager to distract from the tense situation between the half-brothers. John stomped about like a petulant child, kicking at the fire and at a passing dog, who bared its teeth at him before scuttling under a trestle table with its tail tucked between its legs.

Then suddenly John seemed to relax, the tension flowing out of his bull-like shoulders. His grimace became a lopsided smile. He looked past his thin and mouse-like wife Hawise to a newcomer entering the Hall—a tall, broad-faced girl, plump and buxom, the red folds of her dress clinging to the curve of hip and breast. She wore her hair loose, a tumbling mass of waist-length tawny curls. Her lack of a headdress signified she was a maiden but she walked with a womanly sway and looked far too old to be unwed.

Queen Eleanor stiffened with displeasure. "Princess Alais, you've decided to join the festivities. What a surprise."

So this was Alais of France, chosen by Henry to wed Richard but believed by many to have been grandfather's mistress. Still in wardship at nearly thirty, she was another resident of the Dowager's Queen's household, but this appearance at Christmas was the first I'd seen of her. She had been kept comfortably in various properties when Henry was alive, but since his demise had dwelt under a soft house arrest wherever Queen Eleanor dictated.

"Your Grace." Alais dropped a low curtsey. Eleanor watched her with narrowed eyes. John stood hands on hips, openly ogling her overripe figure.

"I did not ask you to come to the banquet, Alais. You were not summoned."

Alais pouted; her lips were painted cherry-red. They were very full, almost overblown. "But madam, I was told to come to Winchester on the King's order. Although I have not been so informed, I assumed that perhaps, now that his Highness is crowned, our long betrothal can finally progress to marriage."

Eleanor stiffened, her fingers clawing the edges of her gilt chair. "You presume too much, Alais. You have been brought to Winchester only because the court is soon to move to Normandy, nothing more."

Alais's pout grew more prominent; it was in danger of making her ugly. "I appeal to you, madam! I must marry Richard…or be returned to my family immediately. Even the Pope said that Richard should not linger and that we should marry at once."

"My son does not want used goods," said Eleanor in a low voice. "Old, used goods."

A hush fell over the assembly. Alais's mouth opened and I thought she might spit at the Queen or at least bombard her with angry retorts.

John stumbled over, still clutching his goblet. "God's teeth, she looks a lusty wench, not like whining Hawise. 'John, please don't do this, don't do that…'" He assumed a high-pitched voice and pretended to wipe his eyes. "I'd marry her, mother. It would keep the French sweet. With no dispensation, I'd easily shed myself of Hawise…although I would fain keep her lands."

"John, be silent!" hissed Eleanor. "You will not touch Alais, do you hear me? Lady Alais, it is my wish that you seek your own chambers. In your past misdeeds, you have brought shame on yourself and on my family too. I want no more commotion in this household, especially at this time of holy celebration."

"I will go, as you desire," said Alais, "but you must decide what to do with me soon, Madam. This matter angers my brother Philip; you must see me wed to Richard as agreed or return me to my family. Your son needs a wife; you, of all people must know that."

A taut, knowing smile crossed the Dowager Queen's features. "I realise he needs a wife, Alais. I am giving that matter much thought even now. Much thought indeed."

The King summoned his mother to come to him in February, after the worst of the winter storms had passed and skies were blue nearly as often as they were dark. The entire household, including Archbishop Geoffrey, Count John, Hawise and the blowzy Princess Alais fared across the channel in a stout royal ship. I prayed for a better crossing than when I first came to England, and God smiled upon me—the Channel was calm, a mirror of glass.

At Bures in Normandy, Richard greeted his mother warmly, John and Geoffrey not so much. I was of no importance but merited a small nod and smile from my kingly uncle. Alais simpered and pursed those red lips into a moue but it did not move Richard; within a few days, the French princess was sent forth under guard to Rouen, a prisoner in all but name. No one now had any doubts that she would never marry England's King.

Watching surreptitiously from my bedroom window, I shivered as saw her pass into the distance surrounded by armed guards. Defeated, she slouched over her horse's neck. How terrible to be cast aside and lose her freedom too!

Much debating went on over the subsequent weeks as Richard laid out plans for the running of England in his absence. At Nonancourt, he summoned Eleanor to meet with him along with John and Geoffrey. I, naturally, took no part in this family meeting but Amaria, in attendance upon the Queen, told me of the shocking events that had occurred.

"The King's face was hard as stone the moment they entered the chamber." Amaria braided my hair, her hot breath tickling the back of my neck. "He did not even smile at his beloved Lady Mother."

"Was he angry at her? Had she done him some wrong?"

Amaria shook her head. "No, he was just showing firmness. He had things to say to his brother John and he knew her Grace would protest."

"I do not like John," I said honestly. "He frightens me."

"He is a capricious man, and full of danger, even though he is young and untried in battle. The King knows that danger...and so he forbade John to return to England for three years."

"Three years! He will be furious!"

"He fell upon the floor and gnawed the rushes as his sire was wont to do." Amaria looked disgusted. "Richard ignored his foolish antics but Eleanor begged that John be allowed to return and live peaceably on his English lands. I deemed her pleas misguided—but it was not for me to judge my dearest liege-lady, and she only did what most mothers would do."

"And the King?"

"In the end, he agreed with her and allowed John's return. John grovelled and kissed his brother's shoes. I hope the King and her Ladyship do not come to regret this reversal in John's favour."

Amaria smirked, giving my hair another twist. "Geoffrey was unlucky, though. Archbishop of York though he may be, he was commanded to stay out of England for several years too—and no one was ready to plead for Geoffrey. He is not much better liked than John; a bastard pumped up with pride just because he bears a smidgen of royal blood."

I had no real knowledge of Geoffrey, other than he was a man who wore a constant air of peevish dissatisfaction, but I was secretly pleased to know that John was returning to England and would not be in close proximity.

Even when I was a child, the youngest of the Devil's Brood made my skin crawl…

Chapter Eight

The King was ready to sally forth on his Crusade, leading a mighty host for the glory of God. I was at Chinon with grandmother when she said farewell and Godspeed to her favourite son. They also discussed marriage. Incredibly, Philip of France still believed Richard would marry Alais when he returned from the Holy Land. In truth, he was now eager to be rid of her. The Dowager Queen had persuaded him to wed Berengaria of Navarre instead. She was the daughter of King Sancho and said to be accomplished and beauteous—which, of course was said of every princess, even if she had fumble-fingers, crossed eyes and missing teeth. Better than being beautiful, Berengaria was known for purity and piety—no chance existed that she had made light of her virtue in the way Alais of France had.

Even at her great age, the Dowager was eager to set off across the Pyrenees. "I am not in my dotage yet!" she said blithely. "I have some life in these old bones, believe me."

Shyly I sidled up to her. "My Lady Grandmother, can it be that you will need companionship on the road?" I was quite eager to see the world beyond the mountains, the Spanish Kingdoms where the sun burned the earth with fury.

Queen Eleanor patted my shoulder affectionately. "Not this time, child. You'd just be another worry to me, travelling so far. Two princesses in tow might be too tempting to kidnappers. I must deliver Berengaria safely to Richard; it is paramount they meet and he begets an heir."

So I was left behind in Chinon, while my ancient grandmother set out on one of her adventures. Meanwhile, the King marched with his forces to Tours and there received the pilgrim's scrip and staff. Almost at once, he broke the staff by bearing down too heavily upon it; the locals whispered of dark omens.

When I heard, I crossed myself and prayed that it meant nothing. In truth, I thought it was only because Richard was stronger than most other men. He had placed too much of his weight upon the staff and hence it had snapped like a twig. He was, apparently, unconcerned. He had laughed at his misadventure.

Soon, in my maiden's closed world, the King's great Crusade was forgotten and I turned my attention to learning the womanly arts and more. I was grilled on Latin and taught music and dancing by stern tutors. My needlework was scrutinised—and heavily criticised. I was shown how to keep the accounts of a great household, and, most importantly, I was given religious instruction and lessons in court etiquette.

In what little time I had free, I wandered the great fortress of Chinon, standing high on a cliff above the River Vienne, with three sides a sheer drop and a mighty defensive ditch on the fourth. It had a series of towers jutting out over the curtain wall—the Tower of the Dogs, the Mill Tower, the Treasure Tower, the Tower of the Grand Portal. The extensive royal apartments were in the Middle Castle; the fortress was divided into three sections for added security. The eastern ward was built by my grandsire Henry, who also died within its walls; the chapel he'd constructed was dedicated to Saint George, the patron saint of England. I spent much time in that chapel, pretending at piety while counting the scales of the dragon in the mural on the wall. Frequently I also visited the older, less grand chapel of Saint Melanie, where I felt at home, for Melanie was a Breton monk from Rennes who outlawed idolatry among the Bretons, one of a host of unusual saints, such as Darerca, Queen of Brittany; Malo, who travelled to the Isles of the Blest; Padarn, whose magical coat was coveted by King Arthur; Corentin, who foresaw the ruin of the drowned city of Ys...and Melor, the boy-saint, with his silver arm and murderous uncle...

God must have sensed my homesickness for Brittany as I prayed before painting of Saint Melanie's image, for it was at this time a messenger came from the land of my birth, riding beneath the black-and-white flag known as the *Kroaz Dhu*, the Black Cross.

My heart beat fast as a sealed scroll was handed over to a secretary to read. So many times such missives betokened death or disaster, and so I feared today...but this time the news that came was joyous.

My mother Constance was home at Nantes with my brother Arthur. She had insisted that Brittany needed her governance, and that Arthur's advisers were inadequate to guide him. Ranulf, tired of her barrenness, of her indifference, had permitted her to go, while reminding her that he could recall her or join her at any time. *I pray we can meet soon again, my dearest daughter Eleanor...* she wrote. *I have worried so for you since the Dowager Queen took you. You are Brittany's Pearl...*

Tears fell from my eyes upon reading her words. Somehow, I doubted Queen Eleanor would permit me to visit mother without good reason. With mother presiding over a court viewed as hostile to the Angevins, Eleanor would never allow me back into her care.

64

She was still abroad anyway, having fared across the winter-bitten Lombardy plains to the coast at Naples where she'd embarked on one of Richard's vessels with poor Princess Berengaria trundling behind her and only Count Philip of Flanders as an escort. Messina had initially been Eleanor's aim, but Tancred, the fractious King of Sicily, had refused her right to land there, sending the Queen's ship further up the coast.

By all reports, had gone nearly mad at this news. "The French King was behind it all, spreading his lies," muttered Amaria, who had remained behind in Normandy to look after me. "He's still insistent that Richard weds his sister, that trollop Alais. God help me, I am glad she has gone from court with her...her haughty French manners!"

"What did Uncle Richard do?" I thought of Richard's sun-bronzed face, serene until he was roused. Then the Lion truly woke, roaring and snarling.

"He threw open the doors of Tancred's keep and smote down the guards that tried to stop him. Sword still in his fist, he stormed into Tancred's presence and demanded a meeting on the spot. Tancred was with his advisors and at first refused...till Richard swung his blade at his head! The court was in uproar, swords clashed and blood was spilt before Tancred's very throne!"

I gasped in alarm, imagining my irate Uncle overwhelmed by his foreign rival's men and hauled away to an ignominious death.

Amaria raised a mocking eyebrow. "Frightened, are you, Eleanor? No need to be. Tancred is a brute and appreciates brutishness—he found the whole event humorous. Soon he was drinking over roast boar with Richard, having realised Philip of France had told him falsehoods to stir up trouble. After dining, the two Kings played chess and draughts—by the end of the night, they were staggering about, deep in their cups, with their arms slung about each other's shoulders. Tancred shouted out that he would give the King nineteen ships as a gift. In return, Richard gave him an even greater prize—the sword of King Arthur, found in a pit at Glastonbury alongside the bones of a mighty man and a woman whose bare skull still retained hair of spun gold..."

"Caliburn, the sword of Arthur!" I cried, quite horrified that Richard had handed away such a priceless weapon—its symbolic value to the Welsh and to the Bretons was beyond any amount of gold...and certainly beyond the value of a foreign King's friendship.

"Indeed." Amaria ignored my distress "Was he not generous, as a great ruler should be? But there's more, Eleanor, in which you might have interest. Your aunt Joanna, Richard's sister, was a prisoner of Tancred after her husband William sadly departed this life. Tancred, that nasty ape of a man, released her into Richard's care readily enough but he had kept her dowry and other possessions. By the time Richard had finished charming Tancred, however, the usurper had changed his mind. He surrendered the dowry without any further aggravation and…and he even agreed to a marriage alliance."

She gazed at me and I went hot then icy cold. I knew not much about Tancred or his family, save that he had usurped his crown from Constance of Hauteville and was rumoured to resemble an ape— a hairy, low-browed man with long arms and a rollicking gait.

Amaria stifled a laugh upon seeing my expression. "Not for you, Lady Eleanor. You escape yet again. The match is for one of his young daughters, either Elvira or Valdrada. The bridegroom, should all go well, is to be your brother Arthur. By these actions, King Richard seems to have unofficially declared Arthur his heir. John will be furious. Poor Hawise."

I stood in shock. So it was true. Arthur was indeed heir presumptive to England and Richard an unmarried King about to embark on a dangerous and lengthy crusade. An image of John's glowering face floated threateningly in my mind. Instantly, I began to cry—so silly and childish, even for a maiden of my tender years.

Amaria seemed to believe my tears were those of joy. "Wipe your eyes, Lady Eleanor; you don't want the court to see you red-eyed and snot-nosed and think you are unhappy about the King's decision. You must not weep! All the crowned heads in Europe will be fighting to have you marry their sons!"

Hastily I wiped my eyes and forced a smile to my lips, although my stomach was churning. What was wrong with me? I had always wanted Arthur to have a high destiny, our father's legacy to a son he never saw.

Why was I so fearful now? What did I fear?

Chapter Nine

Richard and King Philip, even though crusading together, continued to fight bitterly that summer over the future of Princess Alais. Eventually my uncle admitted he would never marry her...and he told Philip of her escapades with his father. Still, Richard did not order her released into her brother's care; he still craved her rich dowry consisting of the Vexin and the castle of Gisors. I knew my uncle would miss the castle far more than the girl.

And now he had another girl to think of—his future wife, the Princess Berengaria of Navarre.

The marriage was, of necessity, delayed—by the time Eleanor got the princess to Richard it was Lent, when no wedding could take place. This at least gave grandmother time to order wedding garb for the King—a rosy tunic of samite girded by a golden belt, and a striped cloak covered in silver suns and white-gold crescent moons. And then, leaving Berengaria in the dutiful care of my Aunt Joanna, Eleanor began her journey back towards Normandy, stopping to view the consecration of Pope Celestine and meet with him about the disturbing news emanating from England, where William Longchamp played the tyrant in absence of the true King. At her request—Celestine had known Eleanor of old—the Pope made Walter of Coutances a super-legate, whose powers would supersede those of the rapacious Longchamp.

It took the Dowager Queen a long time to cross the Alps again, but at last she came into the castle bailey at Rouen riding astride like a young woman—no litter or carriage for Eleanor even in old age.

I ran out to greet her and wondered how I had suddenly come to see her, not as the loud, stern grandmother who wrested me from my mother and lectured me about duty, but as someone I greatly admired...and maybe almost, though not quite, loved. "Grandmother, it has been so long!" I set my lips to her hand. "Are you hale? I heard about wicked Tancred and his fight with the King! Is Berengaria well? And Uncle Richard?"

"I am fine, child, and likewise the King and Berengaria. A pity the wedding and bedding could not have taken place before I left, but the dictates of the Church must take precedence over even my wishes. Once Richard reaches the Holy Land, their union with Berengaria will be completed, no doubt. We will wait for news from couriers."

"I thought the King allowed no women on his Crusade."

Eleanor smiled. "They call my son 'yea and nay' because he often changes his mind! He wants his bride after all, it would seem. He has got around his own rule by sending Berengaria and Joanna in a ship of their own."

And so it happened in the months that followed that Richard wed Berengaria at Limassol in Cyprus, after her ship had foundered on the coast. The island's ruler, another unlawful tyrant called Isaac Comnenus, had threatened to imprison her, but full of rage, Richard vowed to put him in irons if he so much as breathed upon Berengaria. Cowed by the English King whose forces now paraded around his citadel, Isaac had begged not to be placed in irons—to which Richard willingly agreed. Instead, he had Comnenus bound in chains of silver, and the whole isle rejoiced too see the humiliation of its hated ruler.

Then, after taking hostages for Isaac's good behaviour, Richard and his new Queen took ship once more and hastened for Acre and the kingdoms of Outremer. Upon his arrival on those foreign shores, he immediately gave aid to the beleaguered Guy de Lusignan at Acre, and after a vicious attack with his siege engines, destroyed the main gates to the city. While trumpets shouted out a victory song, King Richard headed in triumph to claim the royal palace at Acre for his own.

Eleanor's household was in joyous uproar as tales of the King's valour filtered in from afar. The messengers, eager to collect the riches that came with happy tidings, took pride of place in the middle of the Great Hall, almost taking on the role of storytellers rather than couriers to the appreciative audience.

"Once the King held the palace, he did not become sleepy or overpleased with victory!" The messenger, a young man with his face burnt red from the hot eastern sun, stalked around the chamber. "He could not even be enticed to seek his bed by his new wife, the fair Berengaria!"

A ripple of laughter went through the room. The Dowager Queen's lip curled slightly.

"No!" cried the messenger. "Instead of dalliance, he went straight to treat with that cur Saladin, leader of the Moslem hosts…"

A series of boos and catcalls filled the room.

"The King asked the Saracen leader to surrender and to give up his hold on the True Cross. Saladin was obstinate and with great foolishness refused…"

More boos. The messenger puffed himself up with pride. "And what does a paynim who refuses a great Crusader king expect if he acts with arrogant malice?"

"Death!" someone screamed from near the back of the hall. The shout was taken up and became a chant, even on the lips of the watching women. I remained silent, hiding behind Amaria's back. She, too, was muttering, "Death, death!"

"Yes! Richard showed his might to Saladin that day, and sent him a warning that no infidels would be given mercy. All those he'd taken prisoner in the fall of Acre were put to the sword, be they man, woman or pagan brat!"

The room went wild with clapping and cheering. "Gods will be done!" a woman cried, crossing herself. People began approaching the messenger, pressing coins into his palm. A purse brimming with gold was carried to him by one of the pages circling the Dowager's throne. Minstrels began to play merry tunes while people danced, arm in arm.

I could feel no joy. The King was doing God's work and killing heathens was part of that…but helpless children like myself? What did they have to do with wars? What was glorious about slaying an unarmed child with a sword, even an infidel child? What happened to Richard's fabled chivalry?

Why do you look so forlorn, Eleanor?" Amaria turned to me. "You have grown quite pale. Here…have some wine, it will put colour back in your cheeks." She handed me a crystal goblet; the watered-down wine inside it swirled, the hue of blood.

"The King…at Acre…" I could not quite express the unease I felt.

"A wondrous victory, wasn't it? Splendid. He showed those paynims the true might of the Cross."

My right temple gave a throb. Cramps needled my gut. I clutched my belly with my free hand and was indecorously sick on the expensive rug below my slippers.

Amaria gasped and flung up her hands in horror. "What, by Christ, is wrong with you, girl?"

I heaved again and then ran from the chamber, dropping the wine goblet from numb fingers as I fled. The glass smashed, fragments spiralling up in the air and catching the muted light, while the red wine spattered the tiles, like the spilt blood it resembled.

Thereafter I endeavoured to close my ears to words of Richard's Crusade, even if it made me seem disloyal to my uncle's cause. Many tales of war and death passed me by as I immersed myself in herb-lore, romances (stolen from Eleanor's library; they were too old for me, but I enjoyed the illuminations) and prayer. I could not avoid hearing of the victory at Arsuf, however, where Richard defeated Saladin and placed the important Port of Jaffa back under Christian control—the cheering from the Great Hall was deafening

And then there was the terrible day when I caught grandmother frowning as she pored over a parchment roll that had arrived that morning with a courier. "I do not approve of this! Fie on this dangerous foolery!" she murmured, as she took the parchment and flung it on the brazier.

"Madam!" cried one of her ladies-in-waiting, Amice, as the parchment flared before withering to black ash.

"The contents were an outrage to my eyes!" spluttered Eleanor. "The King suggested that his own widowed sister, my daughter Joanna, marry Al-Adil, the brother of Saladin."

Amaria released a loud gasp and clutched her rosary. "But...but that is shocking! Al-Adil is a heathen! Besides that, as her Grace Joanna is a dowager, she cannot be forced to remarry and I hardly imagine she would agree to such a union. The Pope would also need to give permission for such abomination."

"Joanna has refused in no uncertain terms," said Eleanor sharply. "So, in her place, Richard offered little Eleanor here." She glanced over in my direction.

A rush of blood went to my head; black dots spun before my eyes. I dropped the prayerbook I was reading into my lap. Marriage with a paynim prince! He would have strange foreign ways and probably many wives, sultry women in veils with smoky, judging eyes. Mass would be forbidden, my husband would insist I worship his god Mahommet, and he would hide me away from the world in his harem. I would be hundreds of miles from all I knew in a burning hot land of blood and sand.

"Young Eleanor, of course, would be an ideal choice," continued grandmother. "As Richard's ward, she could marry Al-Adil without interference from the Pope."

"I still think it outrageous, your Grace, if I may dare say so," Amaria huffed furiously. I had never liked her more. "A Christian princess joining the household of an immoral paynim!"

"You may save your outrage," said Queen Eleanor dryly. "And Eleanor, for goodness sake, get hold of yourself! You are always falling and fainting these days. There will be no wedding. Richard's conditions included Al-Adil's conversion to Christianity. He showed no interest, so all deals are off."

"You should not have made me think it could happen!" I cried, standing up abruptly. My prayer book dropped to the tiles, face down, the pages splayed; my hands balled into tight fists at my side. "You should have told me the truth from the start. You are cruel, Grandmother, cruel!"

"Be silent, you silly chit!" the Dowager Queen snapped in irritation. "You had best learn that one day news will come of your marriage arrangements and the last thing I want to deal with is a screaming, hysterical child. You must learn your duty."

"Duty? Like you did? You divorced a king to marry Grandfather when he was scarcely more than a boy. You left your daughters behind in France. So much for 'duty.' I think you did exactly what you wanted!"

The Queen's ladies flushed with embarrassment. Eleanor rose, majestic and terrible, and came to stand before me, a giantess in her flowing robes. And she slapped me with her open hand, sending me reeling against a tapestry of bare-footed peasants crushing wine grapes in a wooden barrel

"What I did of old is not your concern. You are not me. You will never be me, Eleanor. And you will do as I bid you."

I ran weeping from the chamber, my cheek ablaze, my pride hurt after my public chastisement by my grandmother. How I wished I were not a princess, bartered to the highest bidder, be he old, foul, or poxed. How I wished for freedom...

Chapter Ten

"I cannot believe he has behaved in such a manner!" Grandmother stalked around the solar in Bures Castle, where we had moved after Rouen. "Philip, that craven fool, has returned to France and blames my son for his own failures. He has abandoned the Crusade, that coward! He has broken his vows to God."

"Wine, your Grace!" Amaria rushed over to pour a goblet for the Queen. "It will calm your stresses. Shall I call for a brew of chamomile to be brought?"

"Fie on your herbs and the like!" Eleanor grasped the goblet, drained it to the dregs like a man in a tavern and sent it sailing into the fire pit. Flames leapt up and sparks scattered over the floor. Grandmother's ladies, making small fearful noises, trod hastily on them, fearful they would catch the imported carpet or the tapestries. "Would I was a man and could heave a sword at Philip's perfidious skull!"

The Dowager stalked to the window, staring at the sleet that fell outside on the castle walls. "Philip dares to malign Richard in other ways too—he has hinted to his advisers that my son had him poisoned after a dispute!"

"Poisoned?" The word slipped from my lips. "Surely King Philip has a taster...!"

"Of course he does. He is lying. He merely has contracted the fever that often attacks warriors on campaign. This foolishness is all about his sister Alais, the fat little whore. He wants revenge for Richard casting her off."

"What shall you do, my Lady?" asked Amice, perhaps Eleanor's favourite servant after Amaria. She was less acerbic-tongued and very well read and kind.

The Dowager Queen bit her lip thoughtfully. "Philip may well use his false grievances as an excuse to invade us. I must send word to all my castles. The castellans must see that the walls and gates are in good repair, and food hoarded in the event of a siege. The garrisons must be fully manned and batches of weaponry delivered."

Suddenly her shoulders slumped and she sat down heavily on a cushioned couch, holding her head in her hands. For the first time since I'd known her, she truly looked her age and it frightened me. "Grandmother!" I ran to her side followed by Amaria and Amice, unknotting her gown and untying the band beneath her chin that held her headdress in place so she could breathe more freely. Greying dark hair coiled down like storm clouds.

"Don't fuss, you saddle-goose ninnies!" She pushed us away with her hands. "Just get me more wine."

"What is wrong, Grandmother?" I ignored her orders to stop fussing. "Surely it is not just wicked Philip and his lies!"

Queen Eleanor grabbed one of my long, hanging braids and gave it a tug. "You are more observant than you seem, little Eleanor. You have guessed well. It is not just Philip who brings me trouble, it is John."

Why did that news not surprise me? I shuddered at my uncle's name and glanced at the tiles so as not to meet my grandmother's tormented eyes.

She did not look in my direction anyway. Uttering a groan, she pressed her hand to her brow. "How my head aches with it all! John has fallen victim to evil counsel…"

I fear the evil is within him, Grandmother, I thought, but dared not speak. It is naught to do with evil counsel.

"Philip tries to tempt him away from loyalty to the King. With Alais, of all things. The ageing slut. Oh, and John is so susceptible; a comely face, a fat arse, and a few castles thrown into the mix…" Frowning, she halted and glanced at me with perplexity, as if she'd just remembered I was a child and a gentle, well-bred maiden at that. "I have said more than enough. I should not trouble your little head with my woes."

"I do not understand." Amice shook her head. "The Lord John is already married. He would need to put the Lady Hawise aside to wed Alais."

"And you think he wouldn't?" Eleanor's brows rose. "In his mind Hawise is nothing already. With no dispensation ever granted, an annulment should prove straightforward. Add to it, the fact that so far Hawise has proved barren."

The Queen's temper began to rise again; her voice rose in a shout and I feared another cup might be flung. "Not only has Johnny expressed a desire to marry Alais, he has agreed that in the event it should happen, he would give Philip Gisors, which is part of Alais' dowry, in return for properties rightfully belonging to Richard. How dare he? But that is not the worst thing of all…" She took a deep breath, steadying herself. "John is assembling a band of mercenaries and plans to come to France and do homage to Philip. He is going to commit high treason…"

"What are you to do, Madam?" asked Amice uneasily.

"What do you think?" said grandmother with mock cheerfulness. "We must prepare to return to England. I've lost two sons for their sins; I would not have my last two setting against each other like angry curs. I will curb Johnny's tendencies to take that which is not his; like a bad child, I will slap his greedy hands! Henry should have disciplined him more as a boy, but Henry had a soft spot for our youngest. Sparing the rod did no good for my last son. If Henry refused to apply it when John was a child, his mother will apply it now that he is a man."

I did not want to return to England. When Eleanor had left me to escort Berengaria to Richard, I had grown quite content with my lessons and was happy to ignore events in the outside world. Events a child-princess could not control. Now I was being dragged into upheaval once again. Most daunting of all, however, was the prospect of coming into contact with my fractious Uncle John. With every report of his misdeeds, my apprehension grew. The youngest son of Henry II and Queen Eleanor became a lumpen black shadow that haunted my dreams, a spider spinning webs to catch its prey, throwing out sticky tendrils to ensnare me…

We returned to England in February after the worst of the winter storms had passed. How fearless I had become, riding into Portsmouth atop ship with the Dowager Queen standing at my side. The sailors crossed themselves and made signs against evil; women aboard a ship were considered unlucky, even royal ones, and they would much rather we were hidden away in the hold for the entire journey.

Once on shore, we began a trek across the frozen land to the castle of Windsor with its huge shell keep raised high upon a frost-covered motte, pale and shining in the wan winter's light. Inside the Great Hall, grandmother publically swore loyalty to her son, the King, and exhorted the most powerful nobles to likewise renew their oaths of fealty to Richard. Once that was done to her satisfaction, she rode on to Oxford, where in the old, war-battered castle glowering amidst the sunset-reddened spires of the houses of learning, she summoned more barons to swear allegiance to her eldest son. Finally, at Winchester, after she roused another crowd of nobles to hold fast for their sovereign, Prince John arrived to hold audience with her, creeping from whatever fortress he had misappropriated after Richard's leave-taking from England.

With Amaria's connivance, I hid in a gallery in Winchester's Great Hall when my Uncle had his meeting with the Dowager Queen. Peering through a peephole, I saw him enter the chamber and strut like a peacock towards his mother. Swaggering and arrogant, he lounged before his mother's seat, thumbs hooked into the belt that girded his overhanging belly. A thick golden chain hung upon his shoulders and a circlet dotted with blood-red rubies tamed his wild dark-red hair. A long robe of silk hung to his ankles—I noted he wore the royal colours of purple and gold. Ermine trim adorned the hem on his cloak, too; another sign he regarded himself as being of the highest royalty. As high as a King.

Rudely he waved his hands in Eleanor's face; he wore great, gaudy rings on every finger—emeralds, diamonds, sapphires the size of small eggs. "So…you asked for me to come, mother. What is it? You know I am a busy man!"

"Busy, indeed!" Her voice was acid; her fingers curled on the arms of her chair. "Busy causing mayhem in England while Richard is away."

John rolled his eyes. "At least I am in England. Unlike my dear brother."

Eleanor's cheeks flushed with anger. "Richard is doing God's work!"

"God's work," said John, sarcastically, toying with one of his rings and gazing appreciatively at his own reflection in the crudely cut facets of an emerald as green as poison. "Hmm, yes, that's it, God's work…killing Saracens and Jews."

Eleanor looked startled. "They are unbelievers."

He laughed. "But they think the same of us, no doubt! But come; let us not argue over theological matters. You know I am hardly the pious sort, coming as I do from the Devil's Brood. So many of us Devils…and only one God." He grinned impishly at his blasphemous humour.

The Queen cleared her throat, looking sour. "Indeed, your irreligiousness is of little concern to me. It is between you and your Maker when the time comes. I am more concerned about your actions in life. About certain rumours I've heard. About you gathering a band of mercenaries to join Philip of France in harrying Normandy!"

"You mustn't believe all you hear, mother. At your age, it might be more seemly to abscond from politics and do the things…older ladies do. Like sewing."

"You are not the court fool; do not behave like one!" Eleanor banged her fist down on the arm of her chair. All the courtiers gathered around her jumped in alarm. "I have a duty, and unlike you, I will keep to it. To think, I persuaded Richard to let you return to England rather than languish in exile for three years! My motherly affection for you clearly overwhelmed my common sense!" Imperiously she climbed to her feet, towering over her shorter son. "If you continue in your folly, Johnny, it will not go well for you, mark my words. Should you leave these shores with mischief in mind, I will see that all your lands and castles are seized."

John took a step backwards, teeth bared like those of an angry dog. "God's Hooks, why did I ever have a dam so fierce! Fear not, mother, I would not have really gone over to Philip. I hate that French pig as much as any man. I was merely toying with him…"

"Were you?" Eleanor fixed him with a hard stare. "I think you are toying with me now…but I am no fool, far less a fool than Philip, evidently. Go from my court, John, and make yourself quiet and small. Take Hawise with you and get an heir upon her, for you won't be having that trollop Alais, no matter what enticements Philip may offer. Do you understand?"

John scowled, his brows drawing together over his dark eyes. "Yes, mother, I understand perfectly. Richard was always your favourite; I was an afterthought. You could not even stand up and tell him that I should be his heir, not that snotty-nosed brat in Brittany…"

I made a noise of outrage at the insult to my brother. Crouched beside me, Amaria elbowed my ribs and shook her head. "If you wish to listen in on adult talk, then you must learn control," she said sternly. "You must also learn—adults do not always speak…as adults."

Below the gallery, John was striding towards the door of the Great Hall, his cloak blowing backwards in the wind of his speed. "I will be at Wallingford, should you wish to harangue me more!" he shot over his shoulder at the Dowager Queen, and then he thrust the guards at the door aside and departed.

Over the next few months, grandmother processed about England on business, leaving me at Winchester to continue my studies. Her lady-in-waiting Amice was one of my companions and she was in high spirits because the Queen had awarded her the manor of Winterslow. "If her Grace permits it, I shall donate half of my new estate to the sisters of Amesbury Abbey," she told me. "Do you know about Amesbury, Eleanor?"

I shook my head. "Only that it has been made a daughter-house of Fontevraud, of which Grandmother is very fond. The former abbey in the town was closed when Grandfather the Lord King had Becket..." Blushing, I halted. No one at court dared speak of what Henry unwittingly did to his former friend when he shouted, 'Who will rid me of this troublesome priest?' It was long ago: penance was done, with Henry whipped publically in Canterbury Cathedral and the troublesome Thomas lauded as a much-loved Saint...

"I am surprised you did not know more of Amesbury since the older abbey has a connection to your homeland of Brittany. One of your saints' relics was taken there centuries ago."

"Who?" I tried to cast my mind back over the vast array of saints common in Brittany but nowhere else—Cornelly, Brioc, Samson...

"Saint Melor. Many centuries ago, Breton migrants took his bones on tour around Britain. When the remains were placed upon the high altar in Amesbury, they suddenly grew as heavy as lead; the Saint had used his heavenly powers to let the congregation know he wished to be venerated in that spot forevermore. Is that not a charming tale?"

I should have been pleased to hear the little-known legend of the boy-saint from my homeland. Instead, in my mind's eye, I saw the sword of his tormentor, Riwal, slash down to sever Melor's head from his shoulders. I saw the bleached skull upon the altar, wreathed in a haze of incense. I saw a golden-haired boy running on a high cliff against a violet-blue sky. "Eleanor!" he cried. "Save me from my Uncle. Save me!" Then the boy was gone, and there was just the skull, rolling towards me, bouncing from the altar and gliding over the floor to lie, grinning up at me, by my feet...SAVE ME...

"Lady Eleanor, are you unwell?" Amice touched my arm. "Are you having one of your funny turns? Your face is as pale as whey!"

"It must have been the peaches I ate last night!" I cried, and holding my belly, raced for the privy.

But it was not peaches that turned my belly, just my own twisted imaginings.

Amesbury...I shuddered as if a hare had galloped across my future grave.

Amesbury.

Chapter Eleven

John's peace did not hold for long. Having dwelt quietly at Wallingford for a month or two, he began processing around the countryside, taking oaths of loyalty from local knights and nobles as if he were a King.

"I doubt Richard will ever return," he told his followers. "My brother is foolhardy. No doubt, some Saracen's spear or scimitar will find him. Or he will die from a hideous foreign disease, writhing in a pool of his own shite!"

"I thought John would listen to me," said the Dowager Queen, brow creased in a frown. "Alas, he seems to want to play onwards with his dangerous ways. He has taken bribes from certain disloyal barons. They will not nay-say him, no matter what he now asks for. I may have kept him from heading to Philip with his mercenaries, but I that fear soon I will not be able to hold him in check. He will see me as a powerless old woman."

"Never!" cried Amaria, ever Eleanor's stalwart supporter. "The King has trust in you, has given you powers of regent. You are not old or powerless, your Grace!"

"You flatter me," said Eleanor, "but age catches us all. Even me. There is only one thing I can do now…"

"What might that be, grandmother?" I piped up. I was dutifully assisting the maids to prepare the Dowager's bed for the night.

"I must write to Richard," said Eleanor. "He must be told the truth of the situation."

"But he will not come back! He is a Crusader!"

Eleanor sighed. "There is only so much one man can do and Philip has abandoned the cause. Sooner or later, and maybe it is better sooner, Richard must return to his kingdom."

The King had one final victory at Jaffa. Saladin had laid siege to the city, trapping the defenders in the citadel, and my uncle dashed along the coast in his swift-moving ship to assist the besieged. Recklessly he flung himself into the sea to swim to the beleaguered shore. Dripping wet, without even his blade in hand, he waded through the waves, a huge sea-god with streaming mane and beard tangled with seaweed. When his squires brought his steed and weapons, he rode in a passion to the walls of Jaffa with only a small force at his back, heedless of the enemy archers and spearmen on the parapets. "Saladin!" he cried. "You or your champions, hear my words. I will fight each of you, one on one, to free this city."

No one moved. No one answered. Richard roared his challenge again. Within the day, Saladin had retreated and the Crusaders streamed into rejoicing Jaffa.

And then Richard fell ill.

It was the '*mala-aria*' that laid him low, the bad air that rose from stagnant water. Courteous despite their enmity, his opponent Saladin sent him gifts of fresh fruit. Slowly Richard began to recover but he was weak as a newborn lamb, his hands shaking as if with palsy. His heart turned towards his own realm, which he knew from grandmother's messages was in peril from his own faithless brother.

The Third Crusade was over. Once Richard had agreed to a truce with Saladin, he was coming home.

When grandmother heard the news, she was very silent. Then she sought her chapel to pray. Later that evening I saw her light a taper and place it on the windowsill while she gazed out into the swirling darkness. It was almost as if she placed it there as a guiding light to her favourite son. He was still hundreds of miles away, but it was symbolic—a light to bring King Richard safely home.

Grandmother remained there, on her knees before the light, all night.

If Queen Eleanor prayed for a safe journey for her son, then God did not see fit to grant it.

As Christmas approached, the Dowager began to grow fearful, for Richard had sworn to return home before the festivities began. Mariners had spotted his ship, the Franche-Nef hastening toward Marseilles.

But the King never arrived.

"What could have happened?" Eleanor paced the flagstones, her fingers knotting a long string of crystal rosary beads. She turned her gaze towards a tapestry of Saint Christopher bearing aloft the Christ child on his shoulder—he was the patron saint of travellers. "If Richard was delayed for any reason, surely he would have sent me a message."

"I am sure it is just an oversight, your Grace." Amaria tried to soothe her. "He will be here soon. What could stop such a mighty ruler from returning to his land?"

"Treachery," said Eleanor darkly. "Plotting between Philip of France…and John. How I wish I had heeded Richard's wishes to keep John out of England. However, I dare say he might still have made mischief abroad."

"What will we do, grandmother?" I asked. I had never seen the Dowager Queen so disturbed and fretful. Nothing pleased her or eased her troubled soul—not music, books, needlework or hunting. As hard as she tried to hide it, she was distraught.

Christmas flew by at Winchester. Boar, peacock, and a swan fettered in silver links graced the high table, but a heaviness hung over the court, making celebrations feel empty and somehow forced. The high seat where the King should have reclined stood empty. Beside it, Eleanor sat like a watchful dog, her lips unsmiling, eating only tiny morsels, as if the thought of food pained her.

Early in January, a hard winter hit England, freezing the rivers in their beds and leaving long icicles like sword blades hanging from the edges of the palace towers. Wrapped in a marten-furred cloak, I went out with the other children of the court, the maidens in wardship like myself, young, rosy-cheeked pages, and older squires who already mimicked their lords in manners and dress. Watched over by several nurses and chaperones, we cavorted in the knee-deep snow, hurling snowballs at each other and gliding on skates carved from animal bones on the solid surface of the River Itchen.

Wholeheartedly I joined the fun, every bit as rough and tumble as the other children, sliding on my bottom on the ice, thrusting handfuls of snow down the necks of screaming maids and squirming youths.

Suddenly I glanced over my shoulder toward Winchester Castle. To my surprise, I saw Amaria striding toward the river, a loose blue cloak billowing around her. I wondered what she wanted and losing my concentration, my legs went from under me and I ended on my back on the ice, my bones skates slashing at the air.

"My Lady Eleanor." Amaria's voice was sharp. She stood on the riverbank, her dark hair uncovered and straggling, her eyes stark in her face. "Cease this unseemly play. You must come with me at once. At once!"

I scrambled up, fell again, then ripped off my skates and crawled on hands and knees to the riverbank. "Amaria?" I looked up, a damp lock of hair hanging over one eye.

Amaria grabbed my shoulders and hauled me to my feet in a puff of snow. She turned to the other nurses and attendants. "Get your charges," she ordered. "Bring them back to the Castle...immediately."

Taking my arm, she started to march me back uphill towards the gatehouse. "What is it?" I cried. I sensed something was wrong, terribly wrong. Up above, in the bell tower, a great bell began to toll, its rumble booming out across Winchester. Other bells began to sound in churches, priories, and abbeys all over the town. The sound was ominous, almost funereal.

Amaria did not answer me, did not look at me. Her cheeks held no colour; were as grey as the winter sky overhead.

"Tell me!" I cried, dragging on her long, dagged sleeve. "You are frightening me! What has happened? Why do the bells ring out?"

She halted so abruptly I nearly fell over, my shoes finding little purchase on the icy cobbles. "News has arrived, Lady Eleanor. Terrible news. The King...he...he has been taken prisoner by Leopold of Austria."

"I must go to Austria at once!" Grandmother was distraught. She paced the Hall like a wild beast, twisting her rosary beads till the string snapped. The beads fell glittering to the floor; servants dived down to gather them but the Queen kicked them away. "None of you know as well as I do...the Austrians are beasts of men. Savages who are scarcely civilised. I must find my son, the King."

"Your Grace." Walter de Coutances, whose spies on the continent had brought the tidings of Richard's captivity, bowed before Eleanor, "I beg you think upon this matter with a cool head. England needs you. Leopold will not harm the King; he will desire a ransom instead, I am certain. To harm Richard would benefit no one at all. And England needs you to remain here as its protectress, as you must realise."

Eleanor pinched the bridge of her aquiline nose. "Yes, yes, de Coutances, I know you are right but I am his mother, and...and..." Tears suddenly appeared on her cheeks, rivulets that trickled through deepening lines of age and care.

Angrily she wiped the wetness away with the back of her hand as if she despised her own weakness. "Summon a scribe!" she shouted at her chamberlain. "I will send a letter to the Abbots of Robertsbridge and Bexley, commanding them to take sail to Austria. The treasury will cover all expenses. Another letter shall be sent to the Bishop of Bath—

he is the cousin of Emperor Henry of Germany, who is doubtless involved in this outrage along with Leopold and Philip of France."

When the letters were written and sealed, the Dowager retired to her chambers, calling for me to follow in her wake. Together we sat before the brazier in her apartments with their jasmine scents, imported rugs and exquisite tapestries. She sat in silence awhile and I dared not speak to her, just crouched still as a mouse at her feet, giving her whatever small comfort I could.

Her hand reached down to lie upon the crown of my head; I fancied it trembled. Having her son imprisoned was a body blow to the Queen, felling her as a great oak is felled.

At length she spoke, her voice hoarse with emotion. "So…today you see my weakness, young Eleanor."

"It is not weakness, grandmother. We all mourn for the King's misfortune and pray for his release."

"It is weak, for I must keep England safe in his absence, and hence must have the strength of ten men…and now I have been reduced to the weakest of women. All has gone amiss…and Johnny is stirring up trouble again."

These latest ill tidings about John's behaviour did not surprise me. I made no effort to ask what he'd done but grandmother heaved a deep sigh and continued, "Like the little worm he is, he slithered out of England under cover of darkness. He is jubilant over Richard's imprisonment and convinced he will soon wear the crown."

"But what of Arthur!" I burst out, leaping to my feet. "Even if Richard was harmed, Richard declared for Arthur by suggesting Arthur marry Tancred's daughter!"

"Calm yourself, Eleanor. The lords of Normandy were displeased by John's bold announcement that he should be Richard's heir. It is only Philip who supports him in his aim to oust both brother and nephew from the succession."

I sat shivering in my loathing of John as the fire sank to red embers. Glancing up, I saw that the Dowager's head had fallen forward and she slept, worn out from her worries.

Please, Jesu, I prayed, glancing up at the carved crucifix of Nottingham alabaster that hung upon the wall. *Stop John and free the King from his captivity. Let things go back to how they were before….Let me see my brother and my mother in Brittany just one more time…*

Chapter Twelve

The months dragged on. Queen Eleanor began raising a ransom, for she suspected the King's enemies would ask for a great sum. The good Abbots she sent abroad, after hunting high and low, finally found Richard at a place called Ochsenfurt. After much haggling, the churchmen were granted permission to speak briefly with him before his captors bore him away by guarded chariot to the castle of Trifels.

"He is in good humour, your Grace." Fulc, the Abbott of Boxley, assured grandmother when he had returned from Austria. "He is in no doubt that he will soon be freed."

"And what do you believe, Abbot?"

The Abbot, fat and round-faced, stared at his feet. "I believe more careful negotiation will have to take place. Henry Duke of Saxony and many other nobles railed against The Holy Roman Emperor's continued imprisonment of the King, but the Emperor he...he said..." the Abbot's voice trailed away miserably.

"What did he say? Speak, man, I shall not bite the messenger." Eleanor's eyes narrowed.

"The Emperor threatened to execute the King if he does not receive all that he demands."

Eleanor leapt up in a rage; she loomed over the smaller Abbot who cowered before her like a small plump bird. "Execute him! Has the Emperor gone mad? On what grounds would he execute my son?"

Her vehemence clearly shook the Abbot; sweat-beads burst out on his forehead. "They say there are charges for improprieties in the Holy Land, but these charges are doubtless fabrications to keep his Grace's allies from attacking Henry and Leopold in protest. A meeting of the Imperial Council was taking place even as my delegation travelled back to England, and I am sure all will be well...Well, as well as it can be in these unhappy circumstances. Bishop Walter is travelling from Rome to be at the King's side in his time of need."

"Hubert Walter." Eleanor looked slightly mollified. "A fine legal mind and loyal as so few are in these wicked days. To know he is going to the King brings some small comfort to this old woman. You have done well, Abbot. You may return to your abbey at once. I will not require you again."

The Abbot bowed, his cassock straining over almost womanishly rounded buttocks, a sight Eleanor's ladies-in-waiting, huddled by the window embrasures, frowned to behold…before bursting into improper giggles. The Abbot licked his plump red lips and jigged about in a strange, nervous dance. "You…your Grace…" he stammered.

"What is it, man? Do you need the privy? I dismiss you," said the Dowager Queen.

"Ah, your Grace, before I leave, I must ask…Well, it is just that…that my abbey is not rich, and this journey has run up expenses beyond the monies you kindly granted from the royal purse…"

"Oh, so you ask for more money, despite knowing a great ransom will most likely need to be paid for the King?" Eleanor's face registered disgust. "Pah, you men of God…Why are so many of you so damn acquisitive?"

"Your Grace!" The Abbot seemed shocked by her outburst. "I assure you…"

"Oh, be silent, man. You will receive your monetary reward. I suppose you need more puppeteers."

"Puppeteers, Highness?" The old man frowned and shook his head.

"Oh, I'm no fool; I know what goes on at the Abbey of the Holy Cross of Grace….that talking Rood that pilgrims love so."

"The…the Holy Rood, it is a miracle from God."

"If you say so," said grandmother smugly. "The Almighty must favour you very much, for your Abbey also has Saint Rumbold's effigy, does it not? The precious child-saint whose image cannot be lifted unless a pilgrim offers a hefty sum to the Abbey. Once coin is passed on to the monks, Rumbold springs up as spry as a March Hare in all his glory! Between Saint Rumbold and the Rood, you brothers at Holy Cross of Grace are truly blessed—what next will you find, a talking Ass that dwelt in the stable with Christ?"

"I…I assure you, Highness…" the Abbot stammered.

"It matters not what you assure. Now go before I get truly angry, you avaricious charlatan."

The Abbot scuttled from the room like a huge brown beetle, pushing startled onlookers out of the way. The Dowager sighed and beckoned me to her side. You see what one must deal with, child? Perfidy, avarice and greed. Learn your lessons well, here at my side, and never forget what you are told."

"I will not, madam." I curtseyed.

"Now," said the Queen, "I will write to those I deem truly of God—the nuns of Fontevraud, whom I have ever loved. They, I hope, will send words and prayers to comfort me…"

The nuns comforted grandmother as best they could but it was a rather cold comfort. The Pope had not sent a legate to negotiate with Richard's gaolers, although he had promised three times.

Quiet as a mouse in my corner, pretending to sew, I watched and listened as Eleanor stalked about her apartments, dictating to a nervous and sweating scribe: *To the Reverend Holy Father, Lord Celestine, from Eleanor, the most miserable Queen of England...I entreat you, show mercy to a sorrowful mother...*

It was extraordinary; the proud Dowager was begging his Holiness the Pope to listen to her plea!

I am tormented...my flesh wastes...the marrow of my very bones will be washed away with tears...

The Queen dictated her words to the scribe with high drama, almost like a player upon the stage, clutching her heart and wringing her hands.

And still she continued on, while the scribe scribbled in a frenzy, ill at ease to witness his mistress's overbearing passion, not daring to look up at her for even an instant lest she strike him for impertinence.

Oh I am wretched, yet pitied by none! My progeny is ruined and passing from me. The Young King Henry and Count Geoffrey of Brittany..." I jumped in alarm at the unexpected mention of my father. *"They both lie mouldering in the dust. My two surviving sons bring but distress, with one bound in chains and the other destroying his kingdom with fire and sword. Alas, the Lord God has become cruel towards me...*

Almost an hour later, the Queen was finished, her passion spent. The scribe looked about to faint, his hands shaking and sweat curdling on his yellow brow. I brought him a pitcher of wine, placed a .goblet before him and exhorted him to drink. "The wine will steady you, sir. It is her Grace's best."

After her long outburst, Eleanor herself looked pale and unsteady but determined, her jaw outthrust in defiance. "I will see my missive reaches Pope Celestine. Surely, he cannot refuse such a plea...although, who knows? He is aged and with age, some grow timorous..."

"I am sure he will aid you, grandmother," I said, but I was not sure at all. The Emperor of Germany was powerful and noted for cruelty; the Pope, for all his far-reaching powers, was an old man, often sickly. For all the lip-service men paid to Mother Church, they were quick enough to defy it when it suited them...

Lent rolled around. John was back in England recruiting more bands of mercenaries—Welshmen with their man-high longbows this time. He seemed even more determined to put in his claim as King. Without so much as a by your leave, he arrived at court and burst into the Dowager Queen's apartments, eager to plead his case before his mother.

"Get these wenches out!" Clad in red velvet, his beard oiled and his hair hanging in greasy ringlets on his shoulders, he stalked about Eleanor's chamber as if he owned it, his barrel chest puffed out and his walk a swagger. The ladies-in-waiting hesitated, fearful of John but equally fearful of offending their mistress.

Eleanor's lips pursed with annoyance but she nodded at her women. "Go now, my son would see me alone....but he won't take long. Will you, Johnny?"

John's already florid face took on a purplish hue. "I will take as long as it takes, mother!" he said in clipped tones. "Now away with these harridans."

The women began to file from the chamber and I made to follow them but at the very last, I turned aside and hid behind a large silk curtain that shielded Queen Eleanor's bed. What made me do it, I cannot say—perhaps an adventuresome nature inherited from the indomitable woman who sat facing her errant son, perhaps a fear of what the volatile John Plantagenet might do, even to his own mother...

If Eleanor was aware that I still lingered, she made no outward sign.

"Well, Johnny," she said in clipped tones, "out with it. What is your purpose here?"

John pouted like a little boy and folded his arms. "You always believe the worst of me, mother! Always"

"Why shouldn't I? Your behaviour constantly leads me to such conclusions. Such a wayward boy."

"I am not a boy, that is the trouble, mother. You treat me as if I am a child. You always loved my brother Henry and Richard, never me. You did not think much of Geoffrey either, but then, neither did anyone else, not even his Breton wife."

I bridled in fury at the disrespectful way he spoke of my parents, even if he was, in this instance, close to truthful.

John continued to pace the room; nervous, the Queen's favourite hound slunk behind the bed curtain and, wagging its tail, joined me in my spying. "You do realise, don't you, mother, that Richard is unlikely to return, which is the main reason I am here. I want the regency to end and to assume the mantle of power. The country needs a King—not, pardon my honest tongue, an old woman and a gaggle of feuding barons."

"You are mad. He will return." Eleanor's lips became white, compressed lines.

"What makes you so certain? While I was in France I heard all kinds of interesting rumours…" He trailed off, a sly expression on his face.

"What kind of rumours? Tell me!" The Dowager Queen attempted to sound calm but it was clear to see John had touched a nerve with her. She feared for her golden leonine son.

"That the ransom will never be raised. That the Emperor will increase it every time a deal is debated. That poor old brother Dick will meet a nasty accident at one of the German castles, maybe by falling from a tower or having the misfortune to drown in his bath."

"How dare you voice such lies," said Eleanor. "The German Emperor would not dare touch the King of England, God's Anointed, in such a manner."

"I never thought you were naive, mother." John rolled his eyes. "If it served Henry's purpose, Richard would be done away within a trice. Sensible to remove him, since the Germans and Austrians see him as a warmongering troublemaker. And, be true to yourself, madam…you know as well as I that he is! Be that as it may…" He suddenly shrugged. "The latest rumours say he is dead anyway, killed by a fit of apoplexy while in prison."

I could have rushed out and struck John at that moment, had I been bold or foolhardy enough. Eleanor's face became cold as marble. "It is not true."

"It may well be true," said John, shrugging again, "or about to become true. His captors are impatient for the ransom, and he is no easy prisoner to hold."

Eleanor said nothing. Trying a new tactic, John sank down on his knees near her feet. "Mother, Oh mother, I truly have no wish to grieve you…I know he is your favourite, but you must be realistic. The demands are too high. The Emperor hates Richard. You…you should think of me, your lastborn. The regency council set up in Richard's absence should be turned over to me."

Eleanor lifted her chin slightly, the old pride returning. Her voice was resolute. "John, enough. Leave me."

John sprang to his feet, his wheedling mood evaporating in a cloud of rage. "You and the barons will yield to me. None of you has any common sense where Richard is concerned. I would prove a better King of England than my vainglorious brother who thinks of nothing but his foreign wars! Why, he does not even produce an heir for England, despite the pretty girl with the funny name that you procured for him."

"John, say no more lest I deem it treason!" Eleanor snapped. "If you do not leave now, I shall call the guards. Prince or no, you shall cool your temper in a dungeon."

"I will go," John flashed back. "But you are a fool, mother. A comely man's face always charmed you, didn't it, and made a fool of you! It was so with my father, and so it is now with your love for my warmonger brother! Well, you shall come to regret it, I'll wager…you haven't heard the last of me!"

Whirling on his heel, the Count of Mortain stalked from the chamber.

Huddled into a ball, I continued to hide behind the curtain. A few feet away, I could hear a strange, unfamiliar sound—that of my esteemed, strong as tree-roots grandmother weeping.

When it came to creating treasonous mischief, Uncle John was always as good as his word. Fomenting rebellion wherever he could, he promptly took control of several royal castles, including Windsor. Richard's faithful rolled up their siege engines and tried to batter down the gates to no avail. John's hired Welshmen laughed and pelted the besiegers with dung and the contents of piss-pots. From the breastwork of the castle wall, they laughed at their foes; the invaders were prepared for a long siege.

"He will be taught a hard lesson when Richard returns," said grandmother grimly when this latest news of John's perfidy reached her ears. "Why, God help me, did I bear such fractious children? I cannot prise him out of his castles but I can certainly attempt to stop any of his diabolic Flemish mercenaries from following him to England. Land-pirates, that's all they are. If any are captured on these shores, it will mean immediate imprisonment…or death."

A few of these self-same mercenaries did try their luck over the next few weeks, but after one crew was hauled away in chains, beaten by peasants and pricked by sharp spears, the rest leapt back into their ships and fled to their homelands.

One man did arrive on England's shores, however, who was greeted with joy rather than outrage. Richard's loyal man Hubert

Walter, who had visited the King in his imprisonment, had returned. Hastily he sought out Eleanor with news of her son.

"Your Grace," he knelt before her and kissed her ring, "I bring, first of all, greetings from his Highness, that most puissant prince, Richard. He wants you to know he thinks of his mother daily and prays for her, and he hopes she does the same for him."

"I pray daily and have my chaplains say a hundred prayers for my son, the King...so many times do they pray for his good health, their chants much surely reach heaven!" Eleanor leaned over, catching Hubert Walter's hands in her own. "Walter, you are close to Richard, he trusts you. I trust you. I bid you, tell me how he is, and if evil has befallen, do not soften the blow. I am made of sterner stuff than you imagine."

"So is the King, wrought of the same fine stock as her Grace. Richard is well in body, though captivity chaffs and he is almost completely solitary, seeing only his gaolers. He had taken to composing mournful songs."

"Richard?" The Dowager Queen looked amazed. "He never showed much appreciation for music before!"

Hubert Walter nodded. "He is changed, my Lady. He sings, My friends are many but their gifts are few."

"I will make them give 'gifts', friends and foes alike," Grandmother's eyes burned. "You can be sure of it."

"The King will be pleased to hear it, Madam. But he has made another request—he asks that you make terms with John."

Eleanor's sat back, stunned. "Is he aware of the extent of his brother's treachery and wickedness?"

"Yes. Some of it at least. But his Grace the King is a practical man—he said that as he has no heir if evil should befall him, John still has a claim to inherit the Angevin empire, although he is not necessarily the preferred choice. At least the Prince is a man grown."

I shuffled uneasily on my seat near the hearth.

"Maybe Richard is right. We must try to negotiate a truce. John can be vengeful towards those who cross him—how much worse his vengeance if a crown was placed on his head? Peace must be restored in England and all efforts made in raising the ransom for the King's release."

Don't trust John, I wanted to scream, but who was I to query the knowledge of a great statesman such as Hubert Water and my grandmother, the powerful Queen Eleanor?

However, once Walter had departed, I turned to grandmother and drew upon my meagre stores of courage. "Grandmother, why do you pander to John's wish to rule? Arthur is Richard's heir. Richard himself said so by betrothing him to Tancred's daughter. Geoffrey's son should come before John by the laws of Anjou."

Eleanor gazed at me, brows raised. Suddenly her face was a remote, unfriendly mask. It was almost like gazing at a stranger. "Things may change, Eleanor. Things often change. We must change with them."

Fear took hold of me, rose up to choke me. Anger followed it, a surge of red-hot, confused emotion. I had slowly grown to love and admire my grandmother, with her pride and her wilfulness, her ability to reduce barons to quivering wrecks while in her presence. But now, she was letting my family down, denying Arthur's right. For John, for the likes of greedy, avaricious, portly John.

I hated her then. Hated with all my young heart. The Dowager Queen had betrayed me.

Philip of France did all he could to keep my uncle Richard behind strong walls, offering a sumptuous bribe to Emperor Henry to keep him imprisoned. But Henry hated Philip as much as he hated Richard and would not agree. Instead, he set the ransom at 100,000 marks, to be delivered by the barons into the care of the Dowager Queen. Out of solitary confinement now, Richard behaved as a cherished guest at Henry's court, drinking, dining, and hunting with the princes of Europe.

He did not even seem to care about John's behaviour. He shrugged his treachery aside and laughingly heaped scorn on his brother's head. "John, take my kingdom? Fie on him! He could not conquer a country such as England. He would crumble in the face of the feeblest resistance!"

With her thoughts consumed by her captive son, Eleanor left me at Winchester while she went about the country raising the ransom. England groaned under the burden of these payments. The barons were as generous as they could be without harming their tenants overmuch, but John scourged even the poor and infirm to fill the coffers. Not that much of John's fund-raising ever reached Queen Eleanor. Reputedly, once he had gathered a goodly sum, he forged the Great Seal in order to take the money back into his keeping. As for others, the clergy surrendered their tithes, and churches and abbeys offered up chalices of silver and gold and relics stored in musty reliquaries.

And it was not enough.

Amaria, who had been left in charge of the household while the Queen attended a council at Saint Albans, burst breathlessly into my room to tell me the latest news. Of late, as I grew older, she no longer seemed to see me as such an annoying encumbrance and would fill my ears with the latest gossip. "Jesu, Lady Eleanor, it goes not well."

"What do you mean, Amaria?" I put down my Psalter and pulled her deep into a curtained niche in case unwelcome listeners might be hovering.

"The Pope has contacted the Queen...about her letters."

I nodded, remembering the heartfelt pleas, the begging, the recriminations, some subtle, some less so.

"His Holiness is angry, very angry at Eleanor's harsh words and also the slowness of raising the ransom money."

I saw a haunted fear on the lady-in-waiting's dour, black-browed face.

"Eleanor...he is threatening to place England under interdict if the King's subjects do not dole out their last coins! Do you know what would happen then? None of us could take the sacraments. There would be no proper baptisms or burials. It would be like...hell."

I shivered despite the heat of the day. "Surely the Queen will appease him."

"She has begged forgiveness and informed him she would put her finger to her lips and say no more to enrage him. And try harder to get the ransom for the King."

"How much harder can she try? The people of England have little money left as it is."

Amaria's eyes were dark, hollow. "England must be bled dry if that is the case, little Eleanor. Sacrifices must be made." She glanced at me, and I saw her lip quiver, which startled me, for Amaria always seemed unemotional and quick-tongued, hardened by her years of deprivation with the Queen at Sarum.

I also began to feel desperately afraid.

Outside the window, the day suddenly darkened, a black cloud obscuring the midday sun. I poked my head out, saw the sky become a sickly yellow. In the distance, beyond the red and grey rooftops of Winchester town, behind the distant green hump of Saint Catherine's hill, thunder grumbled and lightning began to flare, tangled streaks of deadly silver and gold.

"Come away, child." Amaria weakly drew on my arm. "A storm is coming."

Grandmother returned to Winchester in a better mood than I had expected, given the Pope's threatening missive. Evidently, she had used her powers of persuasion to great effect in various quarters, not just in raising funds but also in gathering hostages. "Henry wants numerous hostages in surety for Richard's behaviour. However, I had problems convincing the barons to let their sons go."

"They believed Emperor Henry would harm them?" I asked, horrified.

"No, not that so much, child. They did not trust William Longchamp to bring them to his court unmolested. He is rumoured to be a sod…Ah, you are too young to hear such talk, Eleanor. Let it suffice to say they would rather see Longchamp escort their daughters than their sons. However, when I said I would provide an escort alongside Walter of Coutances, the barons were satisfied."

I had no idea why the barons feared William Longchamp, who was a man of high standing in the church. Foolish child that I was then, I thought all churchman chaste and honest. I had no time to ponder my grandmother's words, however, for her hands descended on my shoulders and she turned me to face her. The once-lovely face, still strong and handsome, loomed above me, darkly carved against the white of her barbette. Jasmine scent, enticing, reached into my nostrils. "Eleanor, my child…you shall come with me to Germany."

I smiled up at the Dowager Queen, pleased to accompany her once again on her travels. Perhaps we could find the little closeness we had gained…then lost.

She did not smile back at me. "Eleanor," she said, "our negotiations with the Emperor covered many topics. As part of our agreement with Henry, you are to wed Frederick, the eldest son of Leopold of Austria. You are part of Richard's ransom."

I had known the day would come. I had promised myself I would keep my dignity and accept a betrothal as my duty.

Yet the tears came, falling silently down my cheeks. I would never see my kin again….

Floating in the gloom above, grandmother's face showed displeasure. She made no effort to comfort me or call for the ladies in waiting. Picking up her trailing skirts, she walked stiffly away.

The door of the chamber slammed shut behind her with finality.

Chapter Thirteen

The journey to Germany and the Holy Roman Emperor's court had begun. With the silver for Richard's ransom piled on sturdy wains and thousands of soldiers in royal livery guarding the treasure, the royal party proceeded overland towards the German town of Speyer, set upon the banks of the mighty river Rhine.

Along the way, I got to know some of the boys travelling to Germany as hostages. They laughed and misbehaved, seemingly unaffected by the fact they were leaving their families and that their well-being, possibly even their lives, rested on the good behaviour of others. Most of them regarded their travels as a great adventure. They were the younger sons of barons and knights, hence not of great value to their fathers. Many were destined for the church, so were glad of this last chance to see a world that would soon dwindle to the size of a church nave or a cloister. There was quiet Hamelin and mischievous Jack, tall, lanky Robin and fair-haired Gregory, who was always hungry and stealing morsels of food from the trenchers of others.

On the journey, I also made my first true friend—a highborn maiden named Beatrice Maria. She was the daughter of the deposed Isaac Comnenus, the tyrannical governor of Cyprus, whom King Richard had bound in silver instead of iron. Beatrice had descent from the Byzantine royal family of Comnenus, a very old and regal lineage. Taken prisoner at the same time as her sire, Beatrice had journeyed about Europe in the company of Richard's bride Berengaria and my aunt Joanna; evil gossips had whispered that Richard had visited her chambers more often than his wife's. Now the Emperor had decreed her release as part of the terms for my uncle's own release, and, like me, she was set to wed a son of Leopold of Austria. Her groom was my future husband's younger brother, Leopold; once the marriages were solemnised, she would be my close kin. It was nice to think about having a sister again, although sorrowful memories of poor Maudie surfaced to make me melancholy.

Beatrice Maria was about fifteen and, I thought, very beautiful, with fine, flashing dark eyes, coiled raven hair and full, voluptuous lips. She had round breasts and hips, which made me feel ashamed for despite being nearly twelve, I was still a skinny stick indistinguishable from a boy, save for my waist-length hair. Beatrice was well read and educated, and best of all seemed delighted to have another girl as company, despite the difference in our years.

"I wonder what Frederick is like," I said, as we trotted along, side by side, on our caparisoned ponies. On either side, dark primaeval forests rolled into the distance, the treetops capped with layers of dark blue cloud. Fortresses stuck up out of the mist on distant hills, much taller and fiercer than those I had known in Brittany and England.

"Cold, most likely," sniffed Beatrice. A shaft of sun, breaking through the heavy masses of clouds, strayed across her warm-toned skin and made her wide brown eyes glow gold. "These northern men are officious and arrogant, from what I've seen. Leopold's family does have some blood from the Byzantines, though. Maybe that will come through and make our husbands bearable."

"My grandmother described the Austrians as barbarians."

"They are," said Beatrice with the assurance that only a fifteen-year-old could have. "A few generations ago they probably drank from their enemies' skulls... Oh, if only I still lived on Cyprus, where the sun always shines and the seas are the hue of sapphires."

"Tell me about Cyprus." I did not want to talk anymore about my cold, barbaric, possibly blood-drinking future husband. "It is an island, is it not? Like Britain."

"An island but not so large as Britain. It is magnificent, a jewel. The Arabs tried to claim it once, but God be praised, they were driven out. They say in days long before the birth of Christ, the old goddess of the Greeks, Aphrodite, rose out of the waters, naked and magnificent and showering sea-foam—all men quailed and loved her. Adonis was born on Cyprus too—the most handsome man ever to have lived, though born of foul incest. Aphrodite cursed his mother Myrrha with lust and she tricked her own father, King Cinyras, into sharing her bed for nine dark nights. When Cinyras found out, he drew his sword and made to slay her, but Aphrodite intervened and turned Myrrha into a tree."

"A tree!"

"Yes, and when King Cinyras hewed at the tree with his blade, a baby fell out of the gash. Aphrodite gathered it up and bore it to Persephone, goddess of the underworld, who raised it in her bleak kingdom. The goddesses later fell out over Adonis, but that is another story..."

"Can I hear it, Beatrice?"

"Not now, later! Look, we have reached our port on the Rhine!"

Our entourage had reached a small village with tall, timbered houses and the thick block of a fortress guarding the river from atop a rocky eminence. Trumpets sounding and banners flapping in the wind, our company rode through crowds of curious onlookers in the distinctive costumes of the Germans towards the waterside, where a flotilla of barges sent by Emperor Henry tugged at their moorings

The King's ransom was placed on the foremost barge, surrounded by an array of armed guards. Beatrice and I, both accounted part of the treasure, went on with the ransom, followed by all the young hostages. Queen Eleanor sailed separately on a magnificent barge decked with the royal standard, carrying Richard's regalia on her lap, ready to present to him once Henry's grasping hands had taken possession of the ransom.

I stood on the forward deck with Beatrice Maria, the boy hostages milling behind us, squabbling as they pointed out beasts and birds in the unfamiliar landscape—"I saw a fish!" "I saw an eagle!"

Before us, the Rhine swept out like a silver mirror, shining in the feeble light of the winter sun. The wind, chill from the east, blew into our faces and caught at our hair, which, as maidens, we wore uncovered, although we both wore circlets to denote our rank, mine glimmering with sapphires that spelt my name, Beatrice's a thick golden band covered in exotic geometric designs.

The trip started smoothly enough but after a while, we hit fierce waters, tumbling grey and brown over rocks that jabbed through the swell like sword blades. The eastern wind, insistent, seeking, was now threatening snowfall—a few large, wet flakes slapped against the deck of the barge. The hostage boys began to run about trying to catch them on their tongues until their minders settled the lads with threats of a birching.

"I hope this ride does not go on overlong," muttered Beatrice as the barge lurched and a wave crashed against the side. "I may have been born on an island but I am no sailor!"

The winds grew fiercer, shrieking down the vast coiling ribbon of the Rhine. The hills on either side, thronged with fortresses stern as steel, had gone from verdant green to mottled white and black where snow had accumulated on the higher levels. The far distance was naught but blue-tinged dimness, an ominous roiling haze. It felt like we were heading towards the end of the world in a rush of water, wind and snow.

I glanced over at Beatrice. White flakes frosted her dark curls and her hands clenched tightly together, while her lips, blue from the cold, moved in silent prayer.

She saw my look and murmured through chattering teeth, "Jesu, how do men live in such bitter climes? Send me to the pits of hell instead! At least I'd be warm!"

At that moment, I heard a commotion among the young hostages. Hamelin had thrown up over the side of the barge but Robin, his fair hair in a frizzy yellow ball around his red-blotched face, was gesticulating toward the front of the craft. "I can see a city ahead, can't you? Look! Are you all blind?"

I peered into the murk. Yes, sure enough, through the gloomy haze three thin church spires pierced the murk. My heart leapt. "Where is that place?" I cried out to the sailors and servants aboard the barge.

Heads craned; I did not speak German and the sailors were the Emperor's men. At last, one of our retinue, who knew German as well as French, spoke to the captain then came over and bowed. "My Lady, you see ahead the city of Cologne. Your barge will dock there, for it is the will of her Grace the Dowager Queen to spend Advent in the town before moving on to Speyer to meet the Emperor."

"Thank you, Lord Jesu!" Beatrice rubbed her blue fingers vigorously. "We are not properly attired for this weather. I am nigh frozen to death. To death! I cannot feel my toes even in these clumpy northern shoes." She stared mournfully at her feet, encased in sturdy pattens. "And to think, not long ago I wore silk slippers as light as air!"

The barge glided on and the mood lightened, for we could see the city spreading along the riverbanks and smell the aromas of food and fire and see torchlight gleaming through the thin veil of never-ending snow.

Once our barge had docked at the central quay, our party was hustled onto the lantern-lit harbourside, then the hostages were taken one way, and Beatrice and I were guided to a chariot that without preamble carried us to a local convent. I asked if Grandmother would be staying with us too, but the Queen had taken residence in a palace in the town centre and was entertaining various German lords.

It was as if now, with my betrothal soon to take place and her son soon to be released, I was of little interest to her, as long as I was out of harm's way.

I found no time to brood, however. I was cold, weary...and hungry. Although Advent had begun and fasting was encouraged, the kindly nuns brought Beatrice and I fish soup to eat in the privacy of our little chamber, where the fire blazed and chased away the chill of the night.

Later, they even bought little mince pies shaped into the cradle of the Christ-child.

"I wonder where this place might be?" I said, as wrapped in darkness, I snuggled below a warm coverlet next to Beatrice.

"I heard them say it is the Convent of Saint Ursula, who was martyred with 11,000 maidens many years ago. The Huns killed her."

Saint Ursula. She was famed in Brittany too. Legend said her father, a British King, tried to force her to marry a pagan Breton lord but she refused and marched across Europe with her maidens until she reached Cologne where the bloodthirsty Huns fell upon her contingent.

"It is a sad story," I said, thinking of how all those young women died. The elders said it was glorious to die for one's Faith but, being of tender years, I struggled to see why.

"Yes," Beatrice Maria turned over and yawned, "one of many. Female saints…all the same. Vapid virgins slaughtered or tortured needlessly. Katherine on the Wheel, Agatha with her paps cut off, Agnes beheaded."

"Beatrice, you are so irreverent," I cried, half shocked, half laughing at my friend's impious words.

"I know, my father often told me so. Although he was no better! Now, go to sleep! I can scarcely keep my eyes open after all our long travels!"

In the morning, servants sent by the Dowager dressed Beatrice and me, and a nun called Sister Genevieve led us through the abbey cloisters to attend Mass. Afterwards, she took us to the Golden Chamber, an ossuary filled with stacks of bleached human bones arranged into fantastical shapes—spoked wheels formed from leg bones, arches wrought of skullcaps, fringes strung with finger bones. The bones were set in mountings of gold, and crystals glimmered in the eye sockets and open jaws of skulls.

Both fearful and fascinated, I stared at the remains in rapt silence. "These are the bones of the holy virgins martyred with Saint Ursula," said Sister Genevieve reverently. "11,000 of them."

"This one looks more like an ape." Beatrice Maria examined one of the skulls more closely. "If it did belong to a girl, it is no wonder she died a virgin."

Sister Genevieve cast Beatrice a disgusted look, her mouth pursing.

Ignoring my irreligious companion, I turned to the nun. "Would it be fitting for me to pray to Saint Ursula?"

The lined face softened a little. "She is the patron of young girls, especially of those inclined to learn. As you are the granddaughter of Queen Eleanor, I would assume you have been educated well?"

"I can read Latin and speak three tongues, Sister. I would continue my education...but I am told I must marry instead." I made a wry face.

Sister Genevieve's face lit up. "And...and like blessed Ursula, do you feel a calling to the church instead of the marriage bed?"

"I fear not, Sister, and I doubt it would be permitted even if I did," I said, and as she scowled again, "but I would pray to Ursula even so. Pray that even though I marry Duke Leopold's son, he will permit me to continue my studies."

"Pray then, child. If your heart is pure, Ursula may well give you answer and succour."

Kneeling before grotesque bone-wall and the skulls encased in golden boxes, I closed my eyes and prayed fervently to the holy Saint. *Blessed Saint Ursula, you don't know me but my name is Eleanor. Please, if you are a patron of young girls set me free from my bonds to Frederick of Austria. Please Saint Ursula, heed me. I don't want to marry the groom chosen for me,, just as you did not....*

I do not know if it was merely a fancy, a young girl's imaginings born of weariness and the cloying, heady incense in the church, or the fact I had not yet broken my fast, but in my mind's eye I saw the Saint, white-robed but all bloody, holding out her arms in my direction. She seemed to smile with split and stained lips. *You'll never wed, Eleanor. I can promise you...never. Your prayers will be granted...*

Then the vision was gone and I felt a pounding in my skull and saw a shower of sparks in my vision, and I fell swooning and vomiting on the floor while Sister Genevieve shrieked in terror.

The Queen would hear nothing of my vision of Saint Ursula; she wanted to make certain I had not contracted a fatal malady that caused hallucinations. "Richard will not be released unless a royal bride is produced for Leopold's son," she said. "You must be fit and hale for him!"

Worried about her precious son rather than her ill granddaughter, Eleanor sent her best doctors to my bedside; they poked, prodded, and asked impertinent questions; "Have you had such attacks before, my lady?"

"Yes, but none so vivid. Mostly I just feel faint."

"Have your courses begun yet?"

"What...what ...why...Yes, but only twice."

"What other symptoms do you have? Does your head throb?"

"On one side, as if someone strikes me with a hammer! And I see flashes of lightning where there are none…"

"Ah, such symptoms have been known long. Galenus of Pergamon called this malady '*hemi-crania*', the Half-Head. It may afflict you often throughout your days, but it is not lethal."

The doctors conferred, soon declaring that my ailment was merely this fierce type of headache brought on by a young maid's giddiness as she neared womanly ripeness. They gave me tincture of willow-bark for my pounding head and then left, telling me I must lie abed awhile and rest my fevered brain.

Clad in silver, girded with gems, Beatrice happily tripped off to the Epiphany feast while I lay in the convent, stewing in my bed and tremendously bored. At least, when she returned later that night, flushed from dancing, sprigs of holly spiked through her hair, she brought me some tasty sweetmeats wrapped in a kerchief—and my belly had settled enough to devour them.

"It is so unfair I had to miss the feast," I whined.

"Then you shouldn't have started play-acting." Beatrice popped several candied violets into her full red mouth.

"I wasn't play acting. I swear on the Rood I was truly sick...and saw Saint Ursula."

"And I'm the Virgin Mary."

Her impious levity began to irk me slightly. Whilst I appreciated her fearlessness, I was not joking in this matter. "You are as irreligious as my Uncle John, Beatrice."

"Maybe I should meet this Uncle John. He sounds an interesting man from what I've heard." She popped a pilfered sweetmeat in her mouth then licked her fingers with a little cat's tongue.

"John is awful! You have no idea!" I drew my bedclothes tight around myself. "And I still wish I had been allowed to attend the banquet."

"There will be others. Now that Queen Eleanor knows you are not on your deathbed, we are moving on to Speyer. She is eager to see Richard freed...and to hand us to our new masters."

"Masters! You make it sound as if we are servants! Or slaves!"

Her raven brows lifted. "Aren't we, Eleanor?"

The Queen's entourage left Cologne, the great wains holding Richard's ransom rolling slowly through the city gates, their wheels groaning under the immense weight of all the silver. Eleanor sat in an open carriage despite the cold weather so all men could behold her majesty. Beatrice and I were in an enclosed chariot, peering from behind drawn curtains whenever we dared.

After many hours of travel, we reached Speyer, a town of great importance, the burial sites of Salian and Staufer dynasties of Kings. Orderic Vitalis had called it *Metropolis Germaniae* because of its political importance. Twitching aside the gauzy draperies of the carriage, I gazed up at the awe-inspiring Great Gate of the city, the Altportel, a hundred feet high, and attached to a stern wall bristling with dozens of other watchtowers. From there, we journeyed up the crowded street, past the market with its wine, weapons, pottery, spices, cloth and fruit, toward the red sandstone cathedral of Saint Mary and Saint Stephen.

In the shadow of the Romanesque domes with their green copper roofs, our party was met by a delegation from Emperor Henry. Immediately I knew something was wrong. The lords in Henry's contingent looked smug, while the barons and churchmen travelling with Queen Eleanor began to show signs of unease. A foreign bishop in rich ecclesiastical robes was brought before the Queen; he spoke briefly to her, bowing and gesticulating. She turned red, then white, and thrust her hand out as if to push him away. He slunk back amidst his fellows. Flanked by Henry's men, who felt slightly intimidating, almost like gaolers rather than guards, we entered the cathedral and Mass was performed before the gilded tombs of the Emperors and their wives, but I could see the strain on the Queen's face, strain…and rage. Her hands, though clasped piously, shook as if palsied.

Once Mass was over, the Queen's company was escorted to the guesthouse of a nearby abbey. Light was draining from the sky, leaving it a dim, unhealthy blue. Ice crackled on puddles underfoot and a wan moon showed a thin, sly face from behind a rag of cloud. Across the town, bells were booming, their constant clangour putting one's teeth on edge. A group of Jews on their way to the Synagogue in their high knobbed hats scuttled out of an alley and paused, gazing upon us with alarm as if fearful we might bring plague or sword upon them. The guards beckoned impatiently for them to continue on their way.

Once we had reached our accommodation, the Dowager Queen called for her lords to join her in a council. To our surprise, Beatrice and I were summoned to attend.

"Something has gone terribly wrong," hissed Beatrice in my ear as we were ushered down an arcaded cloister to the chamber where the Queen awaited. "Henry should have been here in person to receive the ransom. Richard should have been here. And our prospective husbands, with their father Duke Leopold. No one came but a gaggle of smirking knaves and some sour-faced bishops and priests hovering like black crows."

Stepping down a long flight of torch-lit stairs worn in the middle by a hundred years of feet, we came into the presence of Queen Eleanor sitting in a carven chair. For a moment, I wondered if she was ill, for her eyes looked hollow and her colour was poor. It seemed as if all her years had fallen on her in one bitter moment. At her side stood Walter Coutances and the Bishop of Bath, both grave-faced.

"Today my son, the King, was meant to be released," said the Dowager, her voice flat. "As you can see, all you who assemble here, he is not with me despite the ransom having been raised."

"Your Grace...is it bad news...illness?" a young lord cried out in dismay.

"No, far worse than that, Aimeri. Henry, rot his black heart, has postponed Richard's release."

A gasp of shock rippled through the chamber. "This is outrageous!" cried Hugh de Lusignan, slamming his curled fist into a decorated pillar. Flakes of gold paint came off on his knuckles. "What reason has he to hold the King longer?"

Eleanor's upper lip curled in contempt. "Can you not guess, Hugh? He has had a sumptuous offer of more money—from Philip of France...and from my son John. They wish to hold Richard fast till Michaelmas at least so that they can devastate his lands and break his kingship."

"Henry plays an evil game with us all," said Walter Coutances. "He seeks to better his lot, despite already gaining more than he deserves. What else will he ask for? What more can England give?"

Eleanor's visage was stony. "Whatever he asks for must be given, no matter how bitter the taste it leaves in the mouth. Richard must have freedom, and swiftly. I will send a letter to the Emperor at Mainz, and ask him about providing new terms."

She rose, throwing out her arm in a deliberate, angry motion and knocking over the candelabra to the floor. The candles died with a hiss; tallow pooled on the deep blue tiles with their inlaid images of lions and flowers. "Go now, all of you. The situation, as it stands, has been made clear to you all. Go, but be prepared to move at speed if summoned."

Candlemas was nigh, the feast of the Presentation of Jesus Christ. At the Emperor's request, Eleanor and her company rode to Mainz. As we approached the city, we saw a sea of brightly hued pavilions clustered on the meadows around the city walls. Due to the coming Feast day, candles burned around them and in them, their thin flames dancing in the chill air and shining through open tent flaps. The pavilions spread out from a huge wooden meeting hall with carved spires and gables decorated with saints and dragonheads. A semi-circle of timber houses, built just for this momentous occasion, stood in the shadows of the hall.

The Queen alighted from her chariot, glaring around her at the throng of German knights. "Where is your Emperor? Take me to him. Take me to my son."

"It will be done, Great Lady." Emperor Henry's steward bowed before the Queen, and along with Walter Coutances, the Bishop of Bath, and the Bishop of Cologne who had agreed to treat on Richard's behalf, Eleanor was taken to speak with the Emperor. The rest of us were permitted to follow the party at a respectful distance, surrounded by Germanic knights to ensure our peaceful behaviour.

Within the vast expanse of the wooden hall, the Holy Roman Emperor sat on a dais raised many feet above the floor. The chair he sat on was pure gold, its feet carved into roaring lion's heads. He was clad in gold from head to toe—robe, cloak and gloves. A huge chain dripping tear-shaped diamonds hung about his neck. Clearly seeking to impress his audience, he wore the Imperial Crown, its panels depicting Biblical scenes and its summit surmounted by the fiery opal known as 'The Orphan.'

As we drew near to the Emperor's lofty throne, Beatrice made a small cough and whispered in my ear, "I have heard one panel of his crown says, 'The renowned king delights in doing justice.' Let us hope

Henry takes heed of those words from the Psalms and fears the anger of God if he does not."

The Holy Roman Emperor beckoned the Dowager Queen to come before him; casting suspiciously glances right and left, she stepped in his direction. She did not curtsey, although he seemed to expect it. In her eyes, they were equals, despite that he bore the title 'Holy'.

"My dear Queen Eleanor, I am so glad you have arrived in Mainz in good health…"

"It is a miracle, is it not?" she shot back. Henry's courtiers gasped and fell to whispering amongst themselves. "I made a long journey in winter, expecting to reunite with my son in Speyer, but I was told I must journey here instead. Let us not play with words. Tell me what you want, Emperor, and be done with it. I have your ransom; I will sit and count it with you if you think that England might cheat you."

"Oh, there is no need," said Henry, "now quiet yourself, for here is your son."

A horn rang out, notes high and shrill, and Uncle Richard appeared surrounded by men who gave the appearance of being gaily-dressed courtiers but who bore swords in their hands. Despite his long captivity, the King looked surprisingly fit and well, his face breaking out into a smile. "Madam…mother."

Eleanor rushed forward but stopped just short of embracing him, remembering her position and that a hundred eyes, many hostile, were upon her. Wheeling around to face the Emperor, she said, "I am greatly pleased to see King Richard hale, but I fear you dangle the prospect of his freedom before us both. Is it not true you were considering an offer of money from Count John and Philip of France to keep Richard imprisoned? Did those treacherous lords back off with such an audacious proposal?"

The Emperor's smile was fixed. "Ah…well, yes, that is the problem. The Count of Mortain and Philip of France have outbid you for the King's freedom."

A shocked gasp rippled through the Dowager's entourage. Beatrice clutched my fingers; her own were clammy with sweat. So…we might not ever marry Leopold's sons, after all, but what would happen to Richard if all deals were thrown aside? England had no more to give for his release.

Richard began to utter great oaths, having only just learned of his brother's greatest treachery. He had not expected John to take things so far. The men surrounding him in their gorgeous attire suddenly had their hands on their sword hilts.

The Queen was quick to act. "My lord King," she said to Richard, "be at peace and do not trouble yourself at this time. I will deal with this…problem."

Turning back to Henry, she said in a cold voice, "Emperor, would you have me haggle as one does in an Arab slave market? Let us go into private quarters and discuss how we may reach terms satisfactory to everyone."

Beatrice and I were sent to one of the princes' lodges in the semi-circle outside the hall, while the Dowager and her stalwarts met Henry and his advisers in the Emperor's private closet. Beatrice was pacing the floor. "Maybe Henry will truly never release Richard…Did you note that Leopold of Austria was not here to collect his share of the ransom? To collect us. Maybe we will not have to marry his horrible boys after all."

"But what if Richard is not freed? They would have to kill him to keep him. And what would happen to England if John grabbed hold of Richard's crown? It's not his by right. Should Richard not rule, the crown must go to my brother Arthur. I…I would happily take Leopold's horrid son for Arthur's sake!"

"Really?" Looking startled, Beatrice stopped pacing. "You'd sacrifice yourself to preserve your brother's claim?"

I thought about it for a moment and then nodded. "As much as I am afraid of going to Austria, as much as I prayed to Saint Ursula for my liberty…for Arthur, yes, yes, I would."

"You are a far better person than I, Eleanor." Beatrice shook her head, sending a cascade of midnight curls tumbling about her shoulders. "Let us hope all turns out as you would wish."

We slept well that night, despite the tense situation in the world of the adults beyond, and shortly before dawn, an agent of the Queen came to wake us. "Her Grace wants you to come at once."

Hastily dressing, we followed the servant from the princes' lodge and into the wooden meeting hall. The fire in the centre of the room had died down and it was smoky and dark for the sun had not yet risen. In the centre of the chamber stood Eleanor, red-eyed but somehow radiant, leaning on the arm of…Richard, King of England. Others gathered round, bleary after springing from their beds at the Dowager's summons.

"It is done," said Eleanor. "The King is to be released forthwith. John and Philip's bribe of more money has been rejected. However, his Grace must take the Emperor as his overlord and kneel in homage before him."

The terms were embarrassing, and I was glad the room was dark for felt my cheeks burn.

"Once this is done and the ransom money counted, and the hostages sent to respective lords, we can begin the journey back to England."

"And what of us?" Beatrice whispered under her breath. "What of us?"

Whether Richard overheard her whisper or not, in the next instant the King and his mother were escorting us into an antechamber. The door shut firmly behind us. "Sit, girls," said Eleanor sternly. "We must talk."

We sat on cushioned stools while Richard and Eleanor stood. The King was shaking his great leonine head. "My little niece...I do not want her wed into the family of a blackguard such as Leopold." Fury darkened his eyes. "I pray Pope Innocent heaps wrath upon him for holding a crusader captive. For this outrage alone, he should have to pay back every penny of the ransom. The marriage contract for Eleanor should be nullified!"

"I have heard Pope Celestine is greatly angry," said the Dowager Queen. "I do not think Leopold will remain unscathed. His Holiness will take action, but whether he will rule in the way you desire is debatable. Some of the ransom may be returned but the marriages..." She shrugged. "He may see them as separate, or as a binding force to bring peace between enemy families."

Uneasy, Richard began to pace, his great sword-calloused hands clasped behind his back. "By God's Teeth, if I could, I would burn down Leopold's palace and smash his tower at Durnstein into the dust!"

Eleanor suddenly smiled. "We can delay, surely, if nothing more. See what happens with the Holy Father. Perhaps we can tell Leopold there is an issue of consanguinity that must be investigated. In fact, it is no lie."

"Consanguinity?" Richard's eyes lit up. "What consanguinity do you speak of, mother?"

"Lady Beatrice is the daughter of Isaac Comnenus. Leopold's mother was Theodora Comnena, a kinswoman of Isaac. We can tell the Duke this relatedness has only become clear to us."

"But what of Eleanor? She does not share Leopold's accursed blood. It is Eleanor, daughter of my brother, that I worry most about, not the princess of Cyprus."

"The girls go together," said Eleanor.

"I do not know if Leopold would accept such an answer, lady. He is a hard man...and remember, besides taking his share of the ransom from Henry, he has demanded 20,000 marks for Eleanor's dowry. He would be loath to give up such a sum. While I was imprisoned, he told me all his plans for grand buildings in Vienna—paid for with my money!"

"The 20,000 marks...yes." Eleanor chewed on her lip thoughtfully. "All the more reason to postpone Eleanor's arrival in Austria. At present, the treasury is bare. We have no extra money for such an ample dowry. We can, of course, not let Leopold know such a thing, for it would put the hostages he was sent in danger."

Richard scratched his beard. "Christ, this all grows more entangled! You are the expert in these matters, mother. What reason could we put to Leopold regarding a delay? My mind is dulled by my months of captivity, I fear, and was never sharp when it came to matters matrimonial! The battlefield, not the bedroom, is my delight."

"There is one excuse few would question." Eleanor folded her hands. "Illness."

"Illness?" Richard gestured at me with his mighty hand. "The girl looks the picture of health!"

"True, but children her ages are prone to sudden fevers and poxes. Sometimes they never recover. Eleanor recently had a fainting spell in Saint Ursula's Abbey, witnessed by the nuns...and by Lady Beatrice. My physicians say it is merely headache; the girl just becomes too overwrought. However, she is an intelligent child; she could easily feign real sickness. Would any dare go against the words of her own grandmother, her companion, and the holy nuns?"

"I could crush a cherry and paint spots all over her face," said Beatrice cheerfully, butting in. "No man would look twice at her then. Not even Duke Leopold's spotty sons."

"I hope it shall not come to that." Eleanor laughed dryly. "I don't suppose they would doubt our word so much they would insist on inspecting her. But I am certain Leopold would not want a weak child with an unknown illness to contaminate his precious heirs."

"The subterfuge would only work for a brief while." Richard frowned.

"Giving us time to get the dowry raised and see what Pope Celestine decrees, at least." Eleanor turned to me and placed her hands upon my shoulders. "I know you do not wish to marry this Duke's son. As your lord King also does not wish it, we will work to keep you from such a fate. It may not prove possible to break the arrangement, however. It will depend on a ruling from the Pope…and the grace of God Almighty. Do you understand, little Eleanor?"

"I do, grandmother." Now that Richard was free, any chance to release me from this bond would gratefully be taken.

"Then it will be done. I will write to Leopold at once. In the meantime, the servants must prepare for our departure. Richard…" She gazed lovingly at her son, the golden King, the lion of warriors, "we must return to England in haste. Troubled is your land, and you must put wrongs aright. I fear John's supporters hold Nottingham…"

"A royal castle?" Richard's brows lowered and his upper lip curled in a snarl. He truly looked a lion. "I shall march an army there and teach the defenders, and my brother, the price of treachery!"

"Are we to go back to England too, if we are not sent to Leopold?"

"No," said Eleanor, suddenly hard and business like. "Absolutely not. The land is in upheaval. If your marriage goes through, the journey is longer and more dangerous from England because there is a violent sea to cross. You shall stay in Normandy, maybe in Rouen, maybe Caen, maybe a series of safe nunneries. Gisors is out of the question, alas; Philip went looking for Alais when Richard was still in the Holy Land and captured it for himself."

"It was a fine castle," interjected Richard, folding his arms, "but no matter. Let Philip of France have his little victories, and his harlot of a sister. I will soon build a better, more stalwart castle in Normandy…it shall assume a novel design and will be named Chateau Galliard—the Strong Castle."

"There…all is settled," said the Dowager Queen, motherly words but with a hint of iron. She gave me a little shove with those smooth hands. "Prepare yourself, Eleanor. We must move quickly and get the King away from the lands of his captivity…lest treachery prevails over honour and the Holy Roman Emperor goes back on his word."

Chapter Fourteen

The next few months were quiet. Beatrice and I remained young, unwed girls, doing girlish things on the King's estates—sewing, embroidering, dancing, reading romances supplied by Queen Eleanor. I prayed once again to Saint Ursula to free me from marrying Frederick of Austria, and to Saint Uncumber, patron saint of unwilling brides, who had grown a magical beard to chase off unwelcome suitors. I felt my own smooth chin every morning

After a time, I began to think Duke Leopold might have forgotten about us, although I was wise enough to realise other husbands would soon be found if he had. "I just hope mine is handsome, kindly, and lives somewhere warm!" laughed Beatrice, as we skipped through the gardens of one of Richard's castles. "I grow weak from lack of sun!"

And then news came. A tall man in ragged, sweat-stained leathers arrived at the castle, asking for admittance. After the castellan and steward ascertained his business and verified his identity, he was permitted to come before Beatrice and me, who stood silently with our nurses in the Great Hall.

Although he looked almost ready to drop, he went down courteously on one knee. "Lady Eleanor, Lady Beatrice, you do not know me but my name is Baldwin de Bethune. I have long served the Kings of England and am close friends with William the Marshal. I was with his Grace the King on Crusade and was taken prisoner with him. When the King was released, I remained as one of the hostages."

"If you are a hostage, why are you here?" Beatrice's voice was shaky. "I do not know if I believe you."

"Let me tell my tale, Lady. Pope Celestine has unleashed his fury on Leopold for capturing a crusader and holding him prisoner—both Leopold and Emperor Henry have been excommunicated. The Holy Father demanded they return the ransom to King Richard at once; upon hearing this, Leopold leapt up in rage, swinging his sword about like a madman. He had spent large sums of the money improving Vienna and depended on the dowries of his two future daughters-by-law to continue his works." Baldwin bowed his head. "He has written to King Richard, demanding that you go to Austria at once. I am to take you there. My life will be forfeit if I do not deliver you safe and well to Leopold. Some of the other hostages, mere boys, are slated for death unless I return with you. Leopold has threatened to put out their eyes and hang them from Vienna's walls."

I swallowed, feeling tears rise to my eyes. But I was a Plantagenet princess; I tried to show courage. "What did my uncle the King say to this threatening message from Duke Leopold?"

"He said the man was unreasonable but to save the hostages, he would uphold the bargain. You are to leave for Austria at once, both of you."

So the involvement of the Pope had worsened the situation, not improved it at all. Lives were at stake. Beatrice and I were the sacrifices to save the others. I supposed it was a small price to pay. It could have been worse. Our husbands might have been lecherous old men many times our ages.

"It is late tonight, Sir Baldwin." I tried to adopt the queenly tone of my grandmother. "Chests must be packed before we travel anywhere, but we shall go without protest. It is our duty to my Uncle the King."

The journey to Austria was unpleasant in the extreme. The weather turned icy and sometimes, deep drifts of snow blocked the roads, impeding our progress. Our entourage had to stay in strange little wayside villages, where the sullen peasants gawked at us as if we were monsters. Despite furs and fires, we were continually cold; Beatrice's humour ran out, and for the first time ever, I saw her cry.

"I shall die if I marry young Leopold," she moaned, "and he probably will not care a jot. Look, Eleanor, my very tears have turned to ice on my cheeks!"

The baggage train moved on and a range of towering mountains crowded in on the horizon, jabbing the sky like spears flung by a giant-king's army. Snow mantled their craggy shoulders and on their lower levels grew dark, ominous forests filled with trees—the haunts of bear, boar and witches, I had no doubt.

I glanced over at Sir Baldwin who rode alongside our covered chariot on a bay destrier. "Sir, what is it like at the court of Duke Leopold?"

"Like any other court, my Lady. Business on most days, feasts on the feast days, tourneys when the Duke feels like showing off to his friends. He's holding one in Gratz now. His wife is Helena, a princess of Hungary; plain, quiet, pious. She has no daughters of her own; maybe she will take you and Lady Beatrice under her wing when you are her daughters by marriage."

"It is more likely she will hate us!" said Beatrice. "Many women resent their son's brides."

Sir Baldwin chuckled. "Maybe. I admit I do not know much about the minds of women. I myself am as yet unwed, and doubtless will be until Leopold decides to release all Richard's hostages and I can return home."

"No wife?" Beatrice whispered to me as Sir Baldwin fell silent and fixed his attention on the road ahead. "I think he is very handsome, don't you?"

"I…I do not know…I suppose so." I was still too young to feel any real attraction to men, other than to eschew spots, flabby bellies and ears like jug-handles.

As we rode on, dusk fell over the mountains, staining them pink, then purple, then a glacial blue. A crescent moon emerged and a hard frost crackled under the hooves of the horses. White puffs appeared around men's mouths and the nostrils of their steeds. Beatrice dragged another rug around herself as her teeth started to chatter. I leaned against her like a loyal dog, trying to bring my friend some comfort.

Suddenly Baldwin rose in his stirrups, staring squint-eyed into the descending gloom. He swore under his breath. "Jesu! Soldiers are coming towards us at a goodly march. Men, make ready." His hand fell to his sword hilt; as his thick winter cloak swept back, I saw his mail coat gleam silver beneath.

The guards and attendants in our cavalcade halted in their tracks and drew their weapons. The wains slowly stopped, wheels stuttering on gravel on the road. Beatrice and I clutched each other, sitting in the darkness inside our chariot. The nurses who accompanied us uttered whimpering sounds and crouched down like whipped dogs. Attackers would want the dowries we carried…but they would also want us.

The sound of hooves and marching feet grew louder in the crisp winter air. Gathering my nerve, I peeked from the chariot. Over the backs of the horses, just past Sir Baldwin's red-mantled figure, a sea of torches dipped and swayed. Their wavering light glinted off the tips of conical helmets.

Suddenly my breath, held in fear, whooshed out of me in a noisy rush. The lead soldiers carried a large banner bearing three stripes, the top and bottom blood red, the middle one white. These were the colours of Leopold's House, the House of Babenberg! While we were on the road, Baldwin had told us the tale of how the Duke had obtained such colours. While fighting in a frenzy at the Siege of Acre, Leopold's tunic became soaked with blood, so much so that when he removed his belt, a white line was visible underneath. The Emperor had given him permission to use red and white in a new banner from that day forth.

So these men were not our enemies. While I could not consider them friends, at least they were not brigands or rivals of the Duke, seeking plunder or worse. I noticed Sir Baldwin's tense shoulders relax a little as he too recognised the striped banner.

"Why do you come armed and in haste, men of Leopold?" Baldwin shouted, leaning over the neck of his horse. His hand still rested near his sword hilt. "Does his Grace the Duke not trust my word that I would return? You can clearly see I am making towards the Duke's lands and that I have the Damsels of Brittany and Cyprus in my company."

The leader of Leopold's men removed his helmet; beneath was a stubbled face, grim and hard-eyed. "It is news we bring, grave news, Baldwin of Bethune. News that will affect your journey."

"And what news is that?" Sir Baldwin looked perplexed.

"At the Christmas tourney in Gratz, the Duke was participating in the joust when his horse stumbled and fell upon him, crushing his foot. When taken to the surgeon's tent, the physicians advised him to have the foot cut off...yet none of them dared perform the act. In agony and great fear, Leopold called for his servants to hew the limb from him—taking an axe, they severed it with three mighty blows..." He paused, struggling to speak. "Despite their efforts, the wound became rank with flesh-rot and a few days later his Grace died, God rest his soul. He will be buried at Heiligenkreuz Abbey."

Respectfully all in our cavalcade bowed their heads and crossed themselves.

The Duke's man continued, "The country will be in mourning. Our new lord, Frederick, has said you are not to proceed further into his lands. All may return home. The hostages brought to Mainz are now free to go. You are free to depart, Sir Baldwin."

"But what of Lady Eleanor and Lady Beatrice? I have sworn to accompany them to their new husbands. Their safety is in my hands. Where they go, so shall I." Still suspicious, Baldwin half-drew his blade from its sheath.

"They are to go back with you, Sir. The Lord Frederick has ordered it. The marriages will not take place; the brothers have no inclination to complete the contracts. Now take your company and depart to wherever suits you well."

Surprised but without complaint, Baldwin gave the orders for the cavalcade to turn around. Men steered carts in circles; animals fought their bits. "Well, who would have expected it!" Beatrice, grinning, nudged me with an elbow. "I don't know how to feel about this news! The Austrians have repudiated us!"

"Feel grateful," I laughed. "Feel grateful you don't have to wed Leopold's boy and live in his freezing lands!"

King Richard ordered me to return to England, and it was at Calais, waiting for the ship to bear me across the rough winter sea, that I learnt something that grieved me—Queen Eleanor, worn out from years of imprisonment and striving with her fractious sons, had decided to retire to her beloved convent at Fontevraud, taking Amaria with her. Another blow then came—my dear friend Beatrice would not be crossing the water with me. Richard had decided to grant her wardship and marriage to my Aunt Joanna.

"You will be happy with Joanna," I told her when we parted, standing on the quayside with the wind in our hair and England a dark blur on the distant horizon. "She is kind…and you will not feel the cold so much in Occitania. She will find you a good husband, far better than Leopold's son."

Beatrice hugged me, blinking back tears. "I am sure she will. I beg you visit me sometimes if you are permitted, Eleanor."

"I will, I swear it on the Holy Bible!" I said with all the fieriness and passion a child on the cusp of womanhood could muster.

Alas, I was foresworn. Beatrice rode off into the swirling morning mist and I never saw her again, although I later heard of her wild exploits. When Joanna died in 1199, Beatrice married her bereaved husband, Raymond of Toulouse, but divorced him within two years. She married twice more after that.

Chapter Fifteen

With the Dowager Queen in retirement, my life in England was relatively quiet. Richard departed the country again after a second Coronation in Westminster, an act that represented the cleansing of his past sins and the start of a new, untroubled reign. I was left in the care of various tutors and nurses who sought to mould me into the perfect princess, the ideal wife of a great prince or magnate.

Once King Richard wrote to me, only once—to tell me he wished to patch up his long-standing differences with King Philip and that by marrying Philip's son, Louis, I could unite the warring nations of England and France. I accepted the news with resignation but then heard no more of the match. Later it was said Emperor Henry had forbidden it, along with a prospective match with Duke Odo of Burgundy.

Time passed. I befriended many young damsels. I became an expert dancer; my body blossomed and matured. Beatrice was almost gone from my mind, her friendship passing into time as young friendships often do, and even Queen Eleanor was only a memory, albeit a bright and vivid one. I travelled about the countryside of England, taking residence in various castles; I rode, I hunted, I hawked. Handsome young men danced the pavane and gazed at me with longing eyes, for I was too far above them, a daughter of the House of Plantagenet.

Prince John been sent into exile in France after Richard's return from captivity and hence was no longer about to trouble England—I heard tell he was attempting to be loyal to Richard by besieging Evreux Castle, seizing Gamaches and capturing the Bishop of Beauvais. Throughout all of his adventures, his long-suffering wife, Hawise, barren and neglected, trailed around the courts, as wet as a rainy spring day, her only pleasure found in piety. God might love her; John certainly did not.

Strangely enough, it was one of those strange wet spring days, in April, when rainbows arced across the firmament between sudden storms, that my life was changed forever. I was out hawking and, by chance, the Lady Hawise was with the party, although shuffling about like an aged dowager with downcast looks and constant sighs. The rest of the women were as merry as songbirds; one, Lady Idoune, even carried about her pet canaries in a gilded cage. My hawk was called Gawain, after the legendary hero; high he flew into the sky, striking his

114

prey with accuracy then returning to my wrist where he sat, bloody beaked, upon my ornate glove.

Suddenly the skies darkened, grew ominous, the clouds the hue of bruises. One could smell the wetness in the air. "The rain will come soon," said Hawise, miserably, "and ruin our dresses! God forefend, lightning may strike us."

"Pisht to the rain and the lightning!" I cried, uncaring of the inclement weather. My unbound hair a flash of red-gold flame against the darkening sky, I galloped wildly on my palfrey over the fields around Windsor and loosed Gawain from his jesses once more. Shrieking, he soared into the sky…and vanished into the fastnesses of the Great Park. He did not return.

Burning with the famed Plantagenet temper, I shook my fist at the brooding line of trees. "Curse that poorly trained bird! If he does not return, I will have the falconer cast from his post!"

I was so engrossed in trying to spot Gawain amidst the wind-tossed oaks, that I did not notice riders racing down from the castle towards our little party.

It was only when the other women began to gabble in high-pitched, frightened voices, and Lady Idoine's cage clanged over in the gale, nearly freeing her canaries, that I whirled around to look. Across the green terraces rode Hubert Walter, Archbishop of Canterbury, papal legate and former High Justiciar of England, his silk robes flying behind him, loose and shroud–like in the ascending wind. A band of nobles surrounded him, the rain glistening on helmets and mail.

Staring, I halted what I was doing, pulled on the reins of the palfrey. Why were they here? Why did they come to me, a maiden of little import? Unless…

At that moment, bells began to peal in the castle and in the town beyond, nestled by the river—a dismal noise that rose to assault my ears. Immediately my thoughts flew back to early childhood days when the bells tolled for the death of my grandfather, Henry…

Forgetting my missing hawk, I pressed a nervous hand against my throat. The Dowager Queen, it had to be Eleanor—she was an old woman in her sixties. She had outlived most of her contemporaries, as it was.

Hubert Walter dismounted with the help of a squire and came to stand before me. Although now old and suffering the ailments of age, he remained tall and upright, his face bearing traces of his lost good looks.

But there was no smile upon his lips and his eyes were shadowed as the storm clouds above.

Unable to meet those sorrowful eyes, I stared at the Archbishop's feet—his resplendent shoes were covered in garnets the hue of blood…

"It is her Grace, Queen Eleanor, isn't it?" I asked. I would pray for her, my indomitable grandmother.

"No, my Lady, it is not." Walter's voice grated out, half-strangled with grief.

I dared to glance up from those bejewelled feet. A tear was slipping down the Archbishop's lined cheek, dangling from the end of his chin before falling to the ground.

"My Lady Eleanor, while besieging Chalus in search of fabled treasure, the King was struck by the bolt of a crossbow. The wound festered. The Queen came from Fontevraud to sit at his bedside but no one on this earth could heal his injury. The news I bring is grievous—King Richard is dead."

I stood gaping like a mooncalf, unable to believe that powerful, golden Richard, the Lionheart, the crusader who flung himself into the sea before Jaffa, was dead. Above me, the clouds burst and as thunder rumbled in the distance, rain sluiced over all of us.

A terrible long wailing cry mingled with the crash of the storm, and glancing over I saw John's wife, the meek Hawise, fall down as if possessed, her hands gnarled, her mouth gaping. "No…nooo…" she cried. "John…what if John is made …He will desert me…"

"No!" I shouted back and grabbing her shoulders, I shook her. "Get hold of your wits, Hawise!"

I whirled back to Hubert Walter, now completely rain-soaked, his tears mingling with the water gushing from the skies.

"On his deathbed, did the King speak of the succession?" I cried, terror running through my body like the lightning flashing in the distance. "Tell me, my Lord Bishop."

Hubert Walter took a deep breath. "Before Richard passed to God's waiting arms…he named Count John his heir."

I was rootless and afraid. With Richard dead and John set to inherit, I felt in great danger. When my mother Constance wrote asking that I be returned to her household in Brittany due to the regime change, I joined in by writing to the Justiciar, to various bishops, to the chancellor…to anyone who might hear my plea and feel a frisson of pity for my plight.

No one was overly concerned about the fate of a solitary unmarried maiden, even one of royal birth, in this time of unrest. In the confusion of preparations for John's Coronation on Ascension Day, permission was granted for me to leave England, my wardship over, and fare to my mother's estates in Brittany. Taking ship with a small company of servants, I set out for the land of my birth.

As my company arrived at the castle in Nantes, I stared around the courtyard I had known so well as a small child. After my travels in England, Normandy and Germany, it now seemed rather small and mean, dusty and full of ramshackle outbuildings in need of repair.

Meeting my mother Constance again was disconcerting. I had grown as tall as she, and where I remembered a handsome, strong woman, I now saw a hard-faced matron, her hair beneath her headdress heavily greyed, deep lines streaking from nose to chin. She embraced me perfunctorily while looking me up and down with narrowed, suspicious eyes as if to see whether life in Eleanor's household had ruined me in some visible way.

A little knot of anger tightened in my belly. "Yes, I will seem changed after so many years. And no, I haven't grown horns and a tail, despite living with Eleanor of Aquitaine for many a year."

"You have a sharp tongue, girl," said mother. "That much has changed. If you were not near enough eighteen, I might strike you for insolence."

My wrath suddenly dimmed and my eyes brimmed. "If I have changed, so have you, mama. You never spoke so harshly in the days gone past."

The ice in her melted; her own eyes dampened. Hastily she embraced me. "So much has changed, Eleanor. Life has been hard. Come into the solar and we will talk. There is so much to say."

As I followed her through the halls, noting the moth-eaten tapestries, the smell of damp, the ash from the torches staining the ceilings, I asked her about my brother. "Where is Arthur, mother? I had thought he might come to greet me. How is he taking the news of Richard naming John his successor?"

"He is out hunting…don't look so stricken, Eleanor. He is an active boy and heir to Brittany; even being of tender age, he would not put aside masculine pursuits to see a female relative, no matter how cherished. As for the bad news—he has not taken it well." She laughed harshly. "He is a proud lad. He talks of nothing but meeting John in hand to hand combat and slaying him."

I grimaced. In my memories, Arthur was a golden angel, a well-mannered child studious and courteous. It was clear our entire family had changed.

Entering the cramped solar, with its familiar but badly flaking wall-paintings, I sat down upon a stool and mother seated herself on the cushions in the window embrasure. She summoned a page to bring me an ewer in which to lave my hands and another to press them dry with clean linen. Then her maids brought rock crystal flagons of wine and silver platters with cheese and grapes and sweetmeats. "Grapes!" I cried, fingering one of the fruit before putting it to my mouth. "I have missed grapes…though the King and Queen Eleanor imported much wine."

"I am pleased Coeur de Lion is dead." Mother's voice was harsh. "You may think my words shocking, Eleanor, but he and his father brought nothing but sorrow to me and mine. And now…now he has attempted to steal Arthur's birthright by handing the English crown to that ugly miscreant, John." She took a deep, shuddering breath. "Do you know what happened to me in 1196, Eleanor? Did you hear while you were off cavorting at the English court?"

I flushed. I knew only that her marriage to Ranulph of Chester had been annulled. Some scandal had taken place and Richard had interfered. "I heard but little of that nature, mother. It would not have been considered proper for my youthful ears."

Mother's mouth pursed; when had she started to look like one of the grapes, a withered sack, drained of its juices, unpleasant? "I will tell you. As you know, Ranulph and I began to maintain separate households years ago. It suited us both and Arthur needed my good counsel here in Brittany. All went well until I allowed Arthur to join me in governing the Duchy. Richard, God curse his black soul, went mad with rage. He sent a summons, telling me I must immediately come before him at Bayeux."

"And you went?"

"I was compelled to do so; would I want my castle burnt down and my assets seized? I hurried to Bayeux…but I never reached it. Ranulph lay in waiting for me. Taking me prisoner, he hauled me to Saint James de Beuvron. It was the King's idea, meant to separate me from my son, but he allowed whispers to go abroad that I was imprisoned because I tried to desert my lawful husband."

Embarrassed, I peered into the rich red wine in my goblet. Richard had something else to answer for. He had clearly endeavoured to keep me in the dark about my mother's situation. Shame filled my heart; while mother was held captive I had been hunting, hawking, and dancing….

Mother's eyes blazed and suddenly she looked not angry but triumphant. "The people rose to support me, though. Riots broke out across the land. Arthur was safely hidden away in Brest where neither Ranulph nor Richard's minions would find him."

"Not once did I hear from you, ungrateful girl," mother continued, wrathful once more. "Oh, I had food and finery, but I was separated from my boy, and I was powerless. And to have Ranulph there, still trying to call himself Earl of Richmond jure uxoris and sneering down his long nose at me."

She slammed down her flagon and leapt to her feet, swirling around and around the room in some kind of passion. To my eyes, she looked unwell; her cheeks mottled and her colouring yellowish. As she reached for her wine again, I noticed her right hand seemed odd, wrong, the fingers bent in the way the fingers of the very elderly often were. Only mother's affliction was worse than that borne of age; around her wrist were hardened, scaly patches that had not been there before.

"You must sit," I said. "I am worried for you, mama. Shall I call for a physic?"

"Of course I am unwell! I was a prisoner and my both my children wrest from me. I swore I'd stick a sewing needle through my heart if that pig Ranulph tried to force his marital rights upon me."

I cringed, not wanting to hear any tales of violent intimacies between mother and the hated Earl of Chester. Fortunately, mother changed the subject and returned to listing Richard's injustices towards her. "Richard demanded hostages, the bastard. Many noble lords offered themselves up, but once in captivity, the 'Lionheart' went back on his word. I remained imprisoned and the best of Brittany was locked up too. But my people never wavered in their love of me; they continued to burn the towns on the Normandy border, demanding my release. At last…" her smile became grim, "Richard realised his unlawful actions would gain him naught. He let me go. Once I returned to Brittany, I petitioned for and duly received an annulment of my marriage to Ranulph. I am free of that serpent at last! Free! I only wish I could have seen his face when he received the news."

I was glad mother had rid herself of the odious Ranulph but his absence did not stop my fears for her. Something about her whole demeanour brought unease to my mind.

"I shall have to marry again," she said, "and as soon as possible."

"Wha...what?" In shock, I dropped my glass. It shattered on the floor, sending shards spinning over the tiles. "Blessed Mary, I am sorry, mother."

"Never mind..." She waved one of her crippled-looking hands at me, seemingly unaware that her skirts trailed in wine and broken shards. "The flagons were a gift from Ranulph; I do not care for them. But as for my next marriage—at last, it is a match of my own choice. I am to wed Guy of Thouars before the year's end. He is supportive of my cause, supportive of Arthur. Don't look so shocked, Eleanor; a strong male hand is needed in our country if we are to fight for Arthur's rights."

"Arthur is so young, mother. You would set him up against the likes of John?"

"Arthur, by strict primogeniture, is heir! I will not see him lose the throne he is owed!" Mother stamped her foot like a petulant child. Crystal chips shattered underfoot. I winced again. What had I come home to?

"You do not know the half of it," mother continued to rage. Flecks of spittle whitened her lips; I thought of a mad dog I had seen once, writhing and howling, foam covering its mouth before it died. "Did you know Richard also asked for Arthur to be handed to him? What would he have done—killed him? The very lad he had promised the crown to. A faithless dog was his lordship Yea and Nay—saying one thing when he meant another."

I shook my head. "Richard could be harsh to his enemies but cannot see him harming any of us."

"For Christ's sake, Eleanor, are you another one blinded by the glamour of that dreadful family of Angevins? Richard burnt down a church here in Brittany. A church, and on Good Friday." Mother's pacing grew frantic; the specks on her mouth damper. "I will take no more from the House of Plantagenet. My son may bear half their blood, but he also bears mine and that of my father, Conan, wrongly ousted from his position as Duke!"

She rounded on me, jabbing my arm with a sharp finger as if I bore the blame for her misfortunes. "Arthur and I were away for over a year, even after I was freed, did you know that? With the French king!"

I blinked stupidly. "Philip? But he...he is our foe, surely..." From my days of living with Queen Eleanor, I had always seen the devious Philip as nothing but an enemy.

"No more! He had proved more helpful than any other. He supports Arthur's claim to the crown. His son, Louis, even befriended Arthur while at the court in Paris."

"I would beware, mother," I said dully. "Do not think Philip offers friendship from the kindness of his own heart."

"I do not, but who amongst the ravening kings and lords of these lands does? I will accept help wherever I might receive it." She began to toy with the edge of her long sleeve, knotting it over an over. A muscle jumped in her eyelid. Over and over, it jumped, a twitch, a tic. "If the French can help my son to his rightful inheritance, I will gladly follow them to hell and back and promise my very soul to Lucifer if need be!"

Once again, I attempted to soothe her, to quell these strange, violent words. "You are overwrought. We will talk of this later. It was wicked what Richard did to Arthur, I agree. And although your remarriage has caught me by surprise...I am glad for you. If you are happy to marry Guy of Thouars, let it be so. Yes, you are right; Brittany will always need strong support. Now, where are your ladies-in-waiting? I think they should put you to bed for a while."

"To bed, as if I were an infant or in my dotage!" She was scornful. "I have too much to do."

"Mama," I tried to insist. "Your hand, I have noticed...Surely it is painful."

"Pain is a woman's lot. You would do well to remember that, Eleanor." She gathered her skirts and flounced out of the room, leaving me sorrowing and stunned. What had happened to my bold, brave mother? Her defiance towards her adversaries had turned to bitterness verging on, dare I say it, madness...And what of my brother, new friend to Dauphin Louis, who had not even bothered to forgo the hunt for one day to greet his long-lost sister?

Arthur summoned me to his chamber later that evening. I was irked, for weariness consumed me after my disturbing encounter with mother and I wished to sleep. "Can it not wait till the morrow?" I petulantly asked the squire who knocked upon my door. "Tell him I am indisposed."

The youth flushed, dancing nervously from foot to foot. "My Lady, forgive me, but his lordship was most insistent he sees you before he retires. He would be most upset if you were not to come." I judged that by 'upset' the boy meant that Arthur would have a fit of Plantagenet temper.

Crossing my arms, I sighed. "So be it, then. Take me to my brother."

Arthur was waiting in his own lavishly furnished apartments, where the ceiling gleamed with gold-leaf and shields bearing the Arms of Brittany hung everywhere. A huge Jesse Tree decorated one wall, showing Arthur's descent from Jesse and his son King David. Below in fancy scrollwork was written—A shoot shall come out of the stock of Jesse, and a branch shall grow out of his roots. The Royal Arms of England were graven on his bedstead amidst all sorts of fantastical monsters, including the serpent-woman who had bedazzled the Count of Anjou and from whom the Plantagenets descended.

For a moment, we just stared at each other, then I remembered my manners and curtseyed low—after all, he was Duke of Brittany and rightful heir of England. Seconds later, he laughed and then threw himself at me, flinging his arms about my waist and almost lifting me off the floor. "I did not recognise you at first, Eleanor! You were so small when we parted. Now you are a woman grown!"

"It is the same for me! You too have grown, Arthur." He released my waist and I let my gaze travel over him. Twelve summers old, he bore the air of one older, and if the bright gold of his hair had dimmed a shade since earliest youth, his wide eyes were still the startling blue of the Morbihan, the Little Sea. He was tall for his age, with comely features—no surprise, with Eleanor as his grandmother and the Geoffrey Le Bel, the Fair, the first Plantagenet, as his great grandsire.

"I am glad you have escaped England and come to Brittany," he said, and at first, he genuinely just seemed a lad pleased to meet a long-absent sister. Then a shadow passed over his fair features, and he muttered, "It is best, in case they should try to use you against me in some way. I…mother and I…must work on a marriage for you, to keep you out of harm's way and to gain an advantageous alliance for Brittany. I will speak with my advisors tomorrow after my morning ride."

"Marriage!" Shaken by his words, I laughed nervously. "I have only just arrived home! Surely it is a little early for making such moves."

Sternly he glanced at me, his pretty mouth unsmiling. "No, it is not, Eleanor. There is no time to waste on niceties. John has taken my crown, due to the stupidity of Uncle Richard, who was no doubt already half in hell for all of his unnatural vices when he died! No one of any decency truly wanted John; I heard tell that Hubert Walter desired me as

King but that cur, William the Marshal, insisted upon John. Marshal…an overmighty subject if ever there was one. I'll have him in chains if I ever get my throne back. What I won't have is John Lackland wearing my crown! I won't stay satisfied with a mere Dukedom. I want to be King! I deserve to be King!"

Hands balled, high colour staining his cheeks, he lunged towards me. "You understand, don't you, Eleanor? You must understand! I will be King of England!"

Despite myself, I took a step backwards, disconcerted by his angry ardour. "Yes, yes, Arthur, I understand your need. But not this minute. Let us just renew our kinship in joy."

Arthur must have realised he had frightened me. Expression changing swiftly, he grasped my hands and kissed me on either cheek. "Forgive me, Eleanor; I should not have shouted. But I am angry…angry that my crown has been given to fat, greasy Uncle Softsword. I'd call John Soft-Dick too, save that he is known for pawing at anything in a kirtle…"

"Arthur!" I blushed bright red, surprised to hear such words from his mouth.

Arthur laughed. "I am sorry; I should not have spoken so crudely in a lady's presence. I forget myself sometimes. Other than our mother, I am in the company of many men each day and they tell me I must not seem over-tied to the Duchess, lest my enemies claim I am merely a snivelling brat attached to her skirts."

"No offence was taken, brother. To be truthful, I agree about John."

"He was here, you know…when Richard died at Chalus."

"Was he?" My brows rose. I had not known.

"Yes! He despised Richard and wanted me to join him in a plot against the crown. Mother did not entirely approve, because she said John was slippery and deceptive and would try to filch my birthright, but my chief advisors overruled her. They thought it was wise to join with John in amity. But..." he glowered, mouth sulky, "John betrayed me. The moment news came that Coeur de Lion was dead, he took horse under cover of darkness and rode to Chinon, where he claimed the Angevin treasury! He then fared to Fontrevaud, and wept and wailed during Richard's burial there as if he truly loved him and would not have stuck a knife into his heart had the opportunity arose. He would have, Eleanor."

I bowed my head. "I suspect you are right."

"Of course I am right!" Arthur's mood darkened again. "I will crush that John, I swear it. I am in line before him, the presumptuous boor. I almost had him in my power, you know. Mother and I took our army to Le Mans. Unfortunately, he slithered away, the loathsome snake. And now he wears England's crown."

"Life is not always just," I said in a whisper.

"Not, it's not...but I will have my crown one day, by Jesu's Toenails! As for you, sister, I will talk with mother and my counsellors about who you might marry. I promise, if it is at all possible, he will be neither too old nor too ugly. Goodnight."

Abruptly he turned away from me, mouth open in a huge yawn. Calling for his attendants, they ran in to turn down his bed and scatter fresh flowers. One brought his pet dog, a small hairy beast like a woman's lap dog gone wild, which yapped and snapped at both my brother and his servants.

I stared in surprise. Arthur grabbed up the dog and cuddled it, looking like any innocent young boy, with his golden curls dangling in his eyes and his favourite dog licking furiously at his face. But his words to me were cold and imperious, "Are you still here, Eleanor? I said 'goodnight'. You are dismissed!"

Whatever Arthur spoke of with mother the next day, I heard no more of any marriage in the months that followed. Perhaps no suitable groom could be found; perhaps it was because the arrangements for mother's nuptials took precedence. In August, when heat haze hung like a shimmering shroud over the stagnant river, my mother Constance de Penthievre, accompanied by Arthur, myself, and a party of nobles, set out from Nantes Castle to Le Mans, where we were first to make our peace with Uncle John then celebrate the union between mother and Guy of Thouars at Angiers.

My stomach lurched at the thought of seeing John and I feared I might have one of my strange, frightening headaches, but there was no helping the meeting. William des Roches, one-time supporter of Arthur, had turned his coat and negotiated a truce with my uncle. To repay him, John had confirmed William as seneschal of Anjou. With William's Breton army dispersed and William now in John's favour, Arthur was in no position to battle on against his uncle.

We had no choice but to make peace with John.

Le Mans was the birthplace of my grandfather, King Henry, and my great- grandfather, Geoffrey Plantagenet, whose bones were interred there beneath a beautiful enamelled portrait. It was a city that suited the Plantagenets well, proud and stern, shimmering in the warm September sun behind a wall built in antiquity by the Romans. The Cathedral of Saint Mary the Virgin and Saint Peter towered over all, its spire a sword blade stabbing the sky, its great west front rising atop the hill where Saint Julien had converted pagans from the worship of trees and stones.

We were to meet John at the palace of the Counts of Maine, a towered and fortified building tucked amidst the rich merchants' houses in the centre of town. I had prayed to the Virgin that he might either be delayed, change his mind, or fall ill (perhaps fatally) on his journey hither…but Our Lady did not grant my fevered request. My heart sank as I saw the Lions of England roaring from the highest parapet of the ancient palace.

King John was there.

Entering the Great Hall with heralds shouting our names and titles, we came upon the new King of England enjoying himself at table. He was greedily wolfing down peaches in cider while three wantons in scanty attire clustered around his chair, giggling and jostling for his favours.

"Ah, you've arrived!" he called out, spearing a piece of chicken on a knife and thrusting it into his mouth. Thick saffron sauce dripped into his beard. "Come celebrate our newfound friendship." He grinned, his teeth bright yellow with the saffron. "It is time we settled these foolish disputes, is it not?"

Arthur looked mutinous, but mother shot him a warning look and he kept his peace. Slowly, sheepishly, he went forward and knelt before King John. "That's better," said John, peering down at the top of his head with glee. "No more of this foolish fighting. Richard, God assoil him, named me his heir at the end. I am crowned and anointed. That is that, even though some men still whisper against me…" His eyes suddenly shrank to black, glittering slits. "Do not listen to them, nephew Arthur, for such whispers could prove dangerous…"

"Arthur will do as he is bidden," mother interrupted. "No threats are needed."

"Ah, Constance, ever the lioness ready to defend her cub. I hear you are to remarry?"

"Yes. I am sure you know it is to Guy de Thouars."

"Yes, I know of him through his brother Aimeri." He sniggered. "I am not in Aimeri's favour at the moment, due to his loss of the seneschalship of Anjou. I trust you will not plot to overthrow my recent choice, William des Roches."

"We swear to it, even though William is a traitor," said mother between tight lips. "We are not fools, John. We would not have come if we had not sought peace."

"Let us all walk together then," said the King breezily, rising from his seat and brushing down his deep red velvet gown. "As a token of our newfound family unity, let us travel to the Cathedral, Arthur and I, to visit the tomb of our ancestor, Geoffrey Plantagenet."

He craned his head, seeming to notice me for the first time. "Ah, and there is my niece Eleanor, fair as ever. How you managed to escape my wardship and get back to Brittany, I do not know. "

"It seemed your mother had lost interest in marrying me off, your Grace," I answered, somewhat impertinently. Mother glared. "It was not so hard. It seems no one in England after Uncle Richard's death knew quite what to do with me. I had no desire to wait any longer with an uncertain future."

"More like, you hoped men would acclaim your brother and depose me," John laughed. "I can see it in your face. So defiant, little Eleanor—you need not hate me, we can be friends."

He moved towards us, greasy hands with their winking crust of rings extended, the cloth of his robe pulled taut over his round belly. A short man, he was no more than an inch taller than Arthur and me. Standing next to my young brother, they looked like paintings on a chapel wall—one a devil, one an angel.

"You are very beautiful, you know." His gaze ran over me appreciatively, lingering on my breasts. It felt obscene and I shuddered. He was my uncle…but his lechery was becoming legendary; he had a stable of mistresses and bastards already. Poor Hawise of Gloucester, left back in England; he had not even had her crowned with him. It was clear to any with eyes he meant to put her aside soon.

"Now come, all of you, my dearest kin. Let us stroll in amity in this beautiful city of our ancestors!" He took my hand in what was meant to be a gesture of friendship—but it felt unnatural and unnerving. His palm was hot, damp and sticky, and nausea gripped my belly; briefly, I thought I might shame myself and spew. With a benign smile, John extended his other hand to Arthur—and for all his youth, my brother acquitted himself well in that uncomfortable moment; his boyish visage became still as a piece of carved alabaster and he clasped John's reaching paw.

Up through the streets of Le Mans we strolled, guards forming columns on either side of the road, the curious townspeople milling behind that wall of steel, eager to see the strange, portly little English King and his kinsfolk.

The Cathedral loomed ahead, spire glistening wetly in the sun; when we were in the palace, the heavens had opened and doused La Mans with a short, sharp shower. As the sun emerged again and the clouds sailed eastwards, the rain-washed tiles, the cobbles, the roofs of the town began to steam, sending ghostly tendrils up into the clearing sky.

The Cathedral door stood open, its vast porch shining and scrubbed, the interior lit by expensive tallow candles in huge sconces. Saint Peter and Saint Paul, carved in limestone, sat sternly on either side of the portal into the nave, surrounded by a plethora of smaller Biblical figures. Above the door soared a marvellous tympanum showing the Majestas Domini, Christ in Majesty upon a throne, the robed figures of the Apostles arrayed below Him like a holy army.

The Cathedral interior was dim and filled with the fragrance of old incense. Romanesque in style, it had rounded arcades and straight, single aisles filled with tombs and monuments. There had been a great fire some sixty years before, and Grandfather Henry had contributed much money to the rebuilding in honour of his dead sire. Columns from the rebuild soared around us, a forest of stone, their capitals carved with acanthus leaves, capering beasts, and grotesques that leered and capered. Beautiful stained glass allowed light and colour into the womb-like darkness—one window showed the life of Saint Julian, another the Ascension, others the life of the Virgin and the miracles of the blessed Saints. I took particular note of the one of the Jewish Boy of Bourges, where the Virgin Mary was saving a young Jew after his father cast him into a blazing oven for attending Mass. The red glass that represented the flames that surrounded the boy cast lurid bloody streaks across the Cathedral's tiled floor.

The Bishop of Le Mans, Hamelin, guided us to the tomb of our ancestor Geoffrey near the choir. The tomb itself was a simple chest, covered in the figures of saints, but above it on the wall hung the famous portrait of Duke Geoffrey made of enamel upon copper plate. He was clad in green robes and bore a sword in one hand and a shield decorated with rampant lions in the other.

John made a great show of bowing before the tomb, wailing over it as if he had known Geoffrey personally and was in deep mourning for him. Our forebear had never met his English-born grandson, having died suddenly at thirty-nine. "By the bones of our esteemed ancestor," Uncle John was saying, "by the blood that binds us, let us all be great friends. Let us eschew the fighting that took place between my brothers and me, and between my brothers and our father. Swear on our ancestor's tomb that you will support me and my rule."

Arthur suddenly bridled, an angry expression shooting over his face. "You bring me here to swear to you over a grave? I have already given you assurances of peace! I think you should swear to me, not the reverse, Uncle John...your Grace. After all, I have rebelled against no one, nor conspired against my kinsmen for a crown. Indeed, many men would claim your coronet should rest on my head, not yours."

A terrible silence fell. John's face suffused with blood; a vein stuck out, twisted, from his temple. "How dare you, I should strangle you with my own..."

I grasped Arthur's arm, yanking him away from John, placing my own body between man and boy. "Uncle John, your Highness, I beg you have mercy on my errant brother! He is just a child...a child who has spoken out of turn! He knows not what he says!"

"Yes!" Mother, who had been stunned into silence by Arthur's untimely outburst, now rushed over to protect her son. "Arthur is merely weary from too much travel. He does not understand the politics of men yet. Do not punish him!"

John's ragged breathing began to slow; he looked like a small, dark bull, huffing and puffing, deciding whether to charge. Fortunately, he appeared, in this instance, to have contained his most violent emotions. "Madam," he said coldly to mother, "take the boy from my sight. If he is not fit to take his place with great men, I bid you confine him where he belongs—the nursery!"

Arthur began to protest; mother shot him a warning glare and his advisors, sombre in their robes, looked uneasy.

Bishop Hamelin began to clear his throat and speak on the virtues of patience and mercy. John turned his beady, angry black gaze on him; I'd heard the two had no love of each other, and John had already complained to the Pope about Hamelin's lack of support for his Kingship.

The distraction gave us time to depart. In silence, our party left the confines of Le Mans Cathedral and dispersed. Overhead, the clouds had rolled in from the west again. Rain began to gush from heaven, filling the empty eyes of stone saints on the Cathedral façade and spewing from the mouths of gargoyles perched, waiting, on the roofline.

From Le Mans, our entourage hastened to Angers, where, as arranged, my mother Constance married Guy de Thouars. It was a great relief to leave King John behind, but still his malignancy clouded my daily thoughts. He was like the fabled monster in the castle moat, the creature of the deep woods waiting to pounce when one was unwary.

Guy was a lean, well-made man, the son of Geoffrey IV Thouars and Aenor de Lusignan. His neat cap of hair was the colour of dark honey, and little streaks of grey gleamed in his carefully trimmed beard. Solicitous of mother and respectful to Arthur, I hoped he would bring them nothing but good fortune. Doubts filled me, however, for his brother Aimeri had once served John. But Arthur assured me Aimeri's disenchantment with my unlikeable uncle was total; he would never bow to John again.

The wedding feast was, as I expected it would be, magnificent. Mother and Guy sat on a dais beneath a scarlet canopy flickering with gems. Guy wore a robe of damson wool while mother was resplendent in a silver bliaut embroidered with roses in white gold, the hanging sleeves heavy with threaded crystals. As she turned to her new husband, however, seeking to present him with a chalice during the serving of the many courses, her sleeve fell back and his hand inadvertently landed upon her bare arm—where the rash I'd noticed still burned against the whiteness of her flesh. He whipped back his fingers as if burnt, holding back a grimace of revulsion.

Concerned, I bit my lip. What if he should repudiate her for her unknown illness? However, I had no time to mull on such awful possibilities, for the minstrels in the gallery began to play a fast Saltarello and Arthur pulled me from my seat onto the floor while onlookers clapped and cheered. Together we danced, a well-matched and handsome couple, I in my favourite blue silk gown, Arthur with golden hair flowing and diamonds sparkling on his collar.

"You dance well, sister," he said, as we finished, breathless. "Our grandmother taught you well, though I pray she did not infect you with her unwomanly wilfulness."

"Grandmother is an elder, Arthur," I chided. "You should not speak of her thus. And remember, mother has been your strongest adviser; she has been your rock. Some would say that role was not fitting for a woman either, and that she should have cast you to the wolves and tended to her marriage with the Earl of Chester. Instead, she stood up to him…for your sake."

Arthur's cheeks flamed, but my words silenced him. He adored mother and could find no argument to give against her courage. Instead, to show his annoyance, he pushed past me, bowed before a vapid creature with long fair braids and devious cat's-eyes, and hauled her giggling to the floor. Once again, I was dismissed from his presence.

I glanced towards the high table. Guy de Thouars was drunk. His brother Aimeri, a shorter, darker man, hovered over him like a grinning crow. Mother was clearly in her cups too, and the new couple drank from each other's golden goblets and made much show, real or feigned, of adoration.

Feeling strangely out of place amidst my own kin, I made my excuses and hurried to my chamber where I lay on the bed and stared out the window into the hard-starred night. In the distance, I could hear the laughter from the feast, the squeal of bagpipes, the burr of the hurdy-gurdy, the twinkle of the lute.

Eventually, the sound of music faded away. The wedding party passed below my open window, Guy's male relatives and companions shouting out bawdy jokes as he took mother to his bedchamber.

I pressed the counterpane over my ears, not wishing to hear more. Fitfully, I slept.

A sound woke me from troubled slumber. Rolling over on my back, I stared in the direction of the window. The shutters hung open, for the night was warm, and the sky beyond was black, dotted with high, icy stars. The moon had vanished, sailing westwards—although the dark hours still prevailed, night was hurrying towards the dawn.

Out in the courtyard, a pinprick of light glimmered and my heart raced with sudden apprehension. I told myself not to be foolish; many servants would still be wandering the castle in the aftermath of the banquet, cleaning away the animal bones and remnants of food that could be doled out to the poor.

Yet still I felt uneasy, and donning a robe over my kirtle, I crept to the window. There! The light came again, flickered once, vanished—a torch hastily extinguished. Muffled footsteps sounded and a dark shape scurried across the courtyard, glanced about, then sank into the shadows embracing one of the nearby towers. Another figure followed the first and then another; peering into the gloom, I was sure I could make out men in coats of mail, black-cloaked. They wore no obvious devices and with their furtive behaviour, I knew some evil was afoot.

"Jesu, I must find Art…"

I whirled on my heel and a hand slammed over my mouth, stifling any cry. Struggled wildly, I tried to bite the hand…until I saw that it belonged to mother, haggard and trembling in the gloom.

"Eleanor, do not scream!" she hissed into my ear. "Just take my hand and come. My spies have been busy at work; they have found that John plans to capture and imprison Arthur while the wedding festivities distract the garrison! We must get away while we can."

Dragging her hand away from my face, I shook my head. "Mother, there are men hiding in the courtyard; I have seen them. John's soldiers must have arrived. Oh, it is too late…"

"Guy and Aimeri are aware of John's soldiers; they will deal with them, fear not." Mother smiled grimly. "Now come, we cannot wait longer lest we are ruined!"

"Where shall we go? Where will be safe?"

"The Court of the French King, naturally. Philip has shown favour and friendship to Arthur in the past; he has no love of the English Kings and will succour to your brother again. John will not dare attempt to harm Arthur or any of us while we are guests in Philip's court. Now, ask no more questions! There is little time. Prepare yourself for flight, Eleanor!"

Chapter Sixteen

Spring sunlight danced upon the pointed red turrets of Philip of France's castle. I walked through the herb garden with mother, whose belly was swollen with child. She looked wan and unsteady, and her hands had grown even more claw-like; she said, in confidence, that sometimes she lost feeling in them. The strange patches on her skin had multiplied too, although her ladies took great pains to hide them with gloves and concealing sleeves.

"I wish I knew what was going on, Eleanor." She gazed anxiously towards the frowning keep. Above it sailed Philip's banner, the fleur de lys; one step below was the vivid, striped banner of Brittany, and next to it fluttered the Lions of England, the most fierce and martial of the three. John was present, claiming he wished nothing more than to negotiate a Treaty with Arthur that would make both of them happy. Philip had agreed to mediate between uncle and nephew and give them both good guidance.

"I wish they would let me speak for my son!" mother said tetchily. She drifted past a huge spray of lavender, her long skirts knocking off clusters of busy bees. "They would not let me join in the negotiations. I had forgotten how limiting it is to…to…be a woman!"

"Arthur is not a little child anymore," I told her. "He must speak for himself now and show his mettle. Sooner or later, men will rally to him, when they realise his worthiness compared to John Softsword!"

"Pray Jesu you are right, but as it is, he is still too young and too hot-headed."

"He is Plantagenet. It is natural for him to be hot-headed."

"This is one time when his heritage may not serve him well…"

We both glanced up as we heard raised voices in the arcaded walkway leading to the castle gardens. The warm wind died away with a sigh and even the bees seemed to stop their buzzing

Arthur burst out into the garden in a foul temper. Wildly he struck at the flowers, tearing them out of the beds with his hands and hurling them about.

"Arthur, what has happened?" Mother rushed to him, grasping his wrist just as he reached for the stems of the primroses.

Arthur twisted free but ceased his destruction of the flowerbeds. "I have been shamed!" he snorted. "King Philip has let me down! I am angry…and saddened." Sudden tears filled his eyes; quickly he blinked them away so as not to appear unmanly. He was only thirteen.

Reaching out, he grasped mother's hand and held it as a man clings to a rope while drowning. "Philip has accepted that John is Richard's rightful heir, mama. He had to pay Philip a substantial sum and do homage for his lands in France but still…I…I…"

"Go on," said mother.

"I have been acknowledged as Duke of Brittany, as one might expect but…but—here is the worst part of all!—they say that the lord of Brittany is merely the vassal of the Duke of Normandy, and so I must do homage to that bastard John for my own duchy!"

"That is preposterous!" mother cried. I bowed my head. Why did things always goes John's way? It was as the old wives whispered, 'The Devil cares for his own.'

Mother looked suddenly uncomfortable and rubbed her belly as if she felt a pain. "Arthur, I cannot fight your corner any more," she said. "I am growing old and I am to have another child. Do you understand? I need peace."

Hearing these defeated words from mother's lips shocked me. Arthur's expression was angry, then unhappy, but finally he raised her hand to his lips and kissed it. "You have done enough for me, mama. You go and take care of yourself and the babe. I will be a man now and endeavour to take my father's place."

He walked out of the garden, leaving mother and I staring at each other in dismay. "Ah, I wish this burden did not lie so heavy upon me," mother said, pressing her hands to the small of her back.

I did not know if she meant the troubles of Arthur's inheritance or the baby that grew within her womb…or the unnamed illness that was now clearly upon her.

Arthur and I remained in Paris at the King's Court while mother and Guy returned to Brittany. A few months later, we received the happy news that mama was safely delivered of a daughter, our half-sister Alix.

We celebrated and even the King of France raised a toast to the health of little Alix of Brittany. Arthur's mood, dour for months, began to lighten. He was good friends with Philip's son, the Dauphin Louis, despite the fact that King Philip had agreed to a betrothal for Louis to Blanche of Castile, whose mother was our Aunt Eleanor, sister to John and Richard. I did not want to remind Arthur that once I had also been mooted as a bride for young Louis and was rejected; I did not want his friendship with the French prince to falter. However, the marriage served to remind me that I was already older than most women when they first wed, and for my own protection, I needed to marry well and marry soon.

But I held my tongue. Arthur has his own troubles and his own alliances to think of—with the engagement to Tancred's daughter long dissolved, King Philip dropped hints that he might wed his daughter Marie. It would be a good marriage yet it troubled me, for Marie was but an infant, a child of Philip's second wife, Agnes. More than a decade would pass before little Marie could live with Arthur as a proper wife.

Gradually, as time passed, I became more involved with court life and tried to put aside the grievances my family had with John. Arthur had not forgotten his lost birthright but to keep the peace with the French King and with John, he kept his opinions quiet. With interest, both of us listened to the gossip out of England, and how juicy it was indeed! John was swiftly making himself Europe's most unpopular ruler. He had now made enemies of the powerful Lusignan family. Whilst on a visit to Hugh le Brun, John had become enamoured of Hugh's betrothed, Isabella of Angouleme, who was living with her future husband's family prior to marriage. Isabella was strikingly beautiful—but she was barely thirteen and set to be another man's bride. Spiriting her away with the consent of her power-hungry father, the troublesome Count Adhemar, John had his marriage to Hawise hastily annulled and married Isabella instead. Shortly afterwards, they were crowned together at Westminster—the greasy, barrel-chested, thirty-four-year-old King and the slight, dainty child that was the beauteous Isabella of Angouleme.

"What madness!" I said spitefully to Arthur in the privacy of his apartments. "And poor Hawise, his first wife! He put her aside without a single protest from anyone, but I would stake my life on it that he manages to keep the Gloucester lands."

"I would too," snorted Arthur. "He has a habit of taking what isn't his." Going to the window, he leaned in the embrasure. The light flooding through lit his golden hair; he seemed much older than his age, already a young knight ready for battle. Or a young king.

"The Pope declared years ago that he should not bed with Hawise; that their blood ties were too close," I said. "That aided his quest to discard her. Bishops in Aquitaine and Normandy joined in to claim his first marriage was null and void too."

"All paid off, no doubt," grumbled Arthur.

"No doubt. Ha, this talk of John falling in love instantly with Isabella—troubadours' talk, as deceptive as a mummer's mask. He lusted for the girl, but I would wager he lusts after her lands just as much, if not more. He's not stupid. She's her father's only heir, and her husband will become Count of Angouleme. The lands are in a strategic position, so John is ensuring that none of the lords in that area can challenge him. He wants the roads to Poitou and Gascony kept free, and he'd rather be friendly with Adhemar than face an alliance between the Count and Hugh Lusignan."

Amazed, Arthur stared at me, then gave a shout of laughter. "You are not like most girls, are you, Eleanor?" he said gleefully. "Most would believe John's words of love and go mooning over this 'marvellous marriage'! Where did you learn to think like a man?"

"Mother. And our grandmother, the Dowager Queen."

"What was she like…old Eleanor? Alas, she appears to have forgotten the children of her son Geoffrey. She is all for John, despite what he did to her beloved Richard!"

"She is his mother, no matter what. As for what she is like—great in many ways, and yet, in others, not so much. Once Lionheart was dead, she lost interest in me, grandchild or no. I was cast adrift, like a leaf in the wind. Sometimes, in our years together, I came close to loving her…and then she would cool in her affections and that made me feel near hate. What she felt about me in truth, I do not know. Most likely just another pretty body to use for an alliance."

"She had no interest in me at all." Arthur's voice was hard. "At least she is out of the way now and hopefully will interfere no more. Philip is enraged with John's recent behaviour and may move against him in the near future. If John is defeated, maybe I will have a chance again. A chance at being King of England!"

"Maybe," I whispered. At that moment, a cloud moved over the sun outside the castle. The room went dim; Arthur's golden hair became the colour of ashes. I suppressed a shiver and reached for my prayer book, no longer wishing to talk about the machinations of powerful men.

Unexpectedly, Arthur and I were called back to Brittany from Paris. Mother was with child again but had fallen deathly ill. The physicians did not know if she would survive.

After a mad ride through the night, when I rode astride in order to gain speed, we arrived together at the castle of Nantes. The servants hung their heads, deep in gloom; a pall of death hung over towers and battlements. Everything was quiet and sombre.

The steward escorted us to Guy of Thouars, who gave greetings with solemn melancholy. He already wore mourning colours. "Is she…" Arthur began, sounding suddenly very young and helpless. His voice, recently deepened with adolescence, gave an unmelodic crack.

"No…no, Constance lives still," said Guy, "but I fear it is only a matter of time. It is not just the babe that makes her sicken, the physicians think she has leprosy."

"Leprosy!" I cried in horror. "No, it cannot be!" Distraught, I began to weep, thinking of the Lazar Houses set on the edge of most towns, where afflicted men and women dwelt apart from society, their fingers and toes and noses and lips slowly decaying while they yet lived. I could not bear to think of mother carried there, put away from the world to spend her last days wrapped in white rags, ringing a bell to warn others should she wander into the street. Death would be preferable…

"Hush, Lady Eleanor," said Lord Guy. "Few know and I would keep it so, for I would not have her put from me. Christ, she may yet bear my son, afflicted or not."

"Is it safe to see her?" asked Arthur. "I…I do not want to risk catching it!"

I glared at my brother. He sounded so…so cold at that moment. His words were worthy of someone cruel like John. And after all the efforts mother had made for his cause! Yet, he was young, afraid, grieving; hastily I made excuses for him.

"There are no guarantees, but my physician, who has studied medical texts from the east, says the disease spreads very slowly. I have it not, nor do you from your earlier days dwelling in Constance's household. Whether you see her or not is, of course, your choice, Lord Arthur. You must do what you deem best."

My brother took a deep breath. "I will go. It is my duty to go. I will be brave."

Smiling weakly at him, I clasped his hand in mine. If not exactly proud, I was glad he had done the honourable thing in the end. Even with the fear of contagion, I would not miss my last chance for farewell.

Together we entered mother's chamber. Doctors in their long black robes streamed in and out, their assistants carrying bowls and jars of strange, unknown potions. The windows were firmly shuttered to keep evil humours out, and the air reeked of unwashed flesh and sickness mingled with the scents of lavender and roses hung around the bed frame.

On the bed lay our mother, huge, bloated, the golden coverlet raised over the mound of her belly. Her hair hung unbound over the sides of the bed in a long, sweaty cascade. She drowsed; her breathing was ragged. Little pinpricks of sweat gleamed upon her sallow skin. I noticed the doctors had bandaged her hands, hiding the telltale sores. The dressing could not conceal the increasingly crabbed look of her fingers, however.

"Mother, we have come...Arthur and I came as soon as we heard you were unwell."

Slowly, mother's eyes opened. She tried to smile but with her cracked, dry lips, it was more of a grimace. "Do not fear for me," she slurred. "I am strong, Eleanor, you know that. I have always been strong. The doctors and herbalists will find unguents to heal my skin. It is this pregnancy that troubles me most of all; my legs are swollen like tree-trunks! The midwives tell me it is not one babe inside but two."

"Two!" I cried in shock. While there were cases when twins were born alive, it was even more perilous for both mother and babies.

"You must recover, mother," chimed in Arthur. "I need you. John has sorely angered the Lusignans and hence King Philip. He may decide to back my cause in the end."

Mother took a deep breath—to me, it seemed with some difficulty. "I...I think I grow too old and weary to fight onwards, Arthur. You must battle on your own, if you must."

Rolling on her side, she clutched the coverlet to her chin. "I would sleep, my children. Forgive me, but these babes draw my strength...all my strength."

We went from her and sat in misery within the castle waiting for more news. Sometimes I prayed for mother's safe delivery in the chapel, sometimes I went to the nursery to dandle my little half-sister, Lady Alix. She was a winsome thing with silver-fair hair and deep blue eyes; one day I was sure she would be beautiful. Guy took Arthur in hand and set off hunting and hawking so that both could keep their minds off mother's plight.

Three days on, all the male physicians were hustled from their Duchess's bedchamber and the midwives swept in; the pangs of birth had begun. Arthur and I paced the cloistered walkways near the courtyard with nervous agitation, drifting in and out of the chapel with its painted glass and arched columns. Distantly, as we passed back and forth, we heard the odd cry or scream from the direction of the birthing chamber within the tower where mother's apartments were laid out.

"What was that awful noise?" Arthur said uneasily, as one particular high-pitched, almost inhuman cry lingered in the air. "What, by Christ, are they doing to her?"

"It wasn't her," I lied. "That last sound was just one of the seagulls wheeling around the towers, looking for scraps. You know how noisy the greedy gulls can be!"

He glanced at me dubiously. "Eleanor, don't lie, I am not a babe…"

"Let us go and find a minstrel to sing to us," I interrupted. "Let us hear merry songs to lighten our hearts while we wait…"

Grasping his broidered sleeve, I made to haul him towards the Great Hall, but suddenly Lord Guy appeared. Right away, from his stance, I knew he brought bad news. He walked stiffly and his hair was ruffled as if he had run his hands through it in despair.

"My Lord Arthur, Lady Eleanor, a midwife has come to me. The children are born—twin girls. They have been named for the saints Catherine and Margaret and will be baptised this very hour for they are small and weak…"

"And mother?" I asked in a hoarse whisper.

He bowed his head. "She is with God. Such a birth was too much for her."

Arthur's lip started to tremble and I grasped his shoulder, trying to draw him close that we might comfort each other. Instead, he pulled away. "She should not have married again!" he cried. "It was her own fault for leaving our cause. I will not weep for her…"

Whirling around, he raced away into the castle's corridors without a backwards glance.

"I beg your forgiveness on my brother's behalf, Lord Guy," I said. "He has lost control of himself through grief."

"See to him, then," said Guy of Thouars. "For I cannot deal with a boy's uncontrolled moods. I must prepare for the burial of my dear wife, the Lady Constance."

Mother was buried with all ceremony in Villeneuve Abbey, which she had founded earlier in that year, almost as if she suspected her end was near."You are the truly Duke of Brittany now," I said to my brother as we walked, alone, atop the ramparts of Nantes Castle after the burial. "You, just you."

"Yes," he said, but his voice was faint and disinterested, almost as if he had not heard a word I said.

Gazing at his young face, I could almost see what was in his innermost thoughts. A golden crown instead of a ducal coronet.

The crown of England that rested on the troubled brow of our uncle, King John.

A few weeks later, messengers arrived telling us that John had brought an army into Normandy. King Philip strove to create peace between John and the Lusignans, who were still in high dudgeon over his abduction of Isabella, Hugh's former betrothed. If my uncle had a shred of honour about him, he should have listened to the grievances of the Lusignans and tried to pacify them—lands or a wealthy heiress to replace the stolen bride would not have gone amiss. But he offered no recompense at all to the injured, insulted Hugh and his family. Instead, he treated them as if all that had befallen was their fault, and that they were traitors for reacting with rage.

When the family asked for justice over their dishonour, John screamed at them that their very presence reeked of treason, and the only way they could prove otherwise would be to fight in hand-to-hand combat with John's chosen warriors.

Fearing treachery, the Lusignans refused, and I have no doubt my uncle would have done further injury to them had they agreed to the duel. King Philip, growing increasingly incensed as the war of words escalated between the two sides, at last ordered John to appear before him in Paris and explain his actions.

Surprisingly, John agreed to do so, but when the designated time arrived, he was nowhere to be found. It was a snub of monumental proportion, leaving the King of France and the Lusignan kindred waiting vainly like fools. Philip flew into a towering rage and decided to strip his unruly vassal of Poitou, Anjou and Aquitaine.

Arthur was jubilant. "Eleanor," he said to me, "God is finally smiling on our family. John has proved himself an unfit ruler time and time again, but this time, he has gone too far. Soon what was promised me will be mine!"

"Perhaps," I said, cautiously, "but I think it will take more than the loss of a few lands to shift John's arse from the throne."

Arthur roared with mirth at my profanity. "My sister, the Pearl of Brittany, is speaking as coarsely as an ale-wife again! I do love you so, sister! You...you will stand behind me in my claims?" He threw his arms around me and kissed my cheek with affection.

"I always have supported you, Arthur. From the time you were but a babe."

"You will ride with me then?"

"Ride with you? Where?"

Reaching to his belt, he brought forth a scroll. The red wax sealing it shut had already been broken but the mutilated image of Philip's royal seal was clear. Arthur held it aloft, gripping it tightly, as if in triumph. "King Philip has asked me to return to Paris, Eleanor. At last, he plans a formal betrothal to his daughter, Marie. He says he will give me men to fight the tyranny of my uncle."

"What does all this have to do with me?" I cast him a wobbly smile. I feigned enthusiasm, but the idea of such a youthful boy going into battle filled me with sick fear. "I cannot wield a sword!"

"You...I want you to take mother's place, to advise and support me. Who better? You are my nearest blood and have no marital ties to lead your loyalties astray. Mother failed me at the very end...but you won't fail me, will you, Eleanor?"

I hesitated, afraid that I could not adequately fulfil the role he desired me to take. His deep blue eyes blackened; I recognised the signs of brewing wrath. I would not have him think I had abandoned him! Grasping his hand, I kissed it fervently. "I will do as you bid me. Hail to my brother, the true King of England."

Arthur's face softened, the anger flowing from him. "My thanks, Eleanor. When all this fighting is done and over, I will see you made a Queen. I will find a royal husband for you...somewhere."

Looking proud and confident, my brother strode off towards the stables, where preparations were in progress for a swift departure to Paris. Breathing heavily, I leaned against the ashlar blocks of the chill castle wall. What madness had I agreed to?

We reached the French King's court in time for Easter. The betrothal to Marie was formalised; I watched the little princess teetering around the solar in a voluminous golden dress, hands sticky from sticks of barley sugar supplied by her doting nurses. Rather incredibly, John sent Arthur a letter asking for his 'beloved nephew' to rendezvous with him at Argentan, but Arthur merely laughed and tore the parchment into scraps, which he threw upon the brazier.

A few months later, Philip knighted my brother and granted him John's confiscated lands, for which Arthur did homage to the French monarch. Once that ceremony was complete, a council of war was called. On Arthur's insistence, I sat with him, as mother had when she was alive. The French nobles sneered and smirked behind their hands, shocked and surprised that a woman was in their presence, but they dared say nothing.

"Now," said King Philip, "I would have you depart, Duke Arthur, and attack the borders of Normandy, which I now declare as my own due to John's endless perfidy. I want him out. Two hundred of my best knights are ready to do service for you. The Lusignans too are eager to join your cause."

Hugh le Brun de Lusignan, who was at the council, stood up at the naming of his family. "We will swear to the Lord Arthur's cause!" he said. "John has shamed us…shamed me. He must not go unpunished. The Lusignan family and a Poitevin army will support his claim."

Arthur chewed his lower lip, eyes fixed on the French King. "I understand fully that the hatred for my Uncle is great and that my Lord King wants Normandy. But the province is loyal to its current master, from what my spies report. Is this move not premature and dangerous?"

Philip made a steeple of his long, ring-laden fingers. Sea blue eyes glittered, the colour of the sapphires stitched to his collar. The King was almost bald; torchlight glimmered on the dome of his head above his fleur de lys laden circlet. "Ah, my dearest son-to-be, Arthur! A great weapon lies in Normandy that we might use against John. Obtaining that weapon will be your aim."

"A weapon? Your Grace, I don't understand!" Arthur's brow furrowed. "What weapon does he have that we do not?"

"A weapon that will be potent only in our hands," chuckled the King. "At the castle of Mirabeau, King John's aged mother dwells, having recently left the nunnery of Fontevraud. Take possession of her and you have a marvellous bargaining tool. John is an unnatural man in many respects but I doubt even he would allow his own mother to be harmed. And if he is not bothered at the thought of her suffering…" Philip shrugged, "well, Eleanor of Aquitaine was always a troublesome harridan!"

"Sire, the Dowager Queen Eleanor is the grandmother of Lord Arthur!" I said sharply, turning on my bench. He also seemed to have forgotten his elder half-sisters, Marie and Alixe, were Eleanor's children through her first marriage to his father Louis.

King Philip stared at me with surprise, as if he thought I had lost the power of speech while being in the presence of such great men. "Ah, yes, forgive me, my tongue was too free.." Suddenly his face brightened as if an amazing idea had come to him. "Lady Eleanor, you were once in Eleanor of Aquitaine's court, is it not so?"

"It is, your Grace." I felt uneasy.

"You must know her well."

"I would not be so bold as to claim that; I was just a child. She did educate me, however."

"She has affection for you, *non*?"

I hesitated. "I...I presume so, but Queen Eleanor was a practical woman, my Lord King. Affection was always tempered with practicality. Her duty to me was to teach, mine was to learn and make a good marriage match. When my marriage to Leopold of Austria's son fell through upon the Duke's death, she lost interest in me and hastened to Fontevraud, hence my return to Brittany and my brother's side."

"Still, you seem to have had some closeness."

"Perhaps, but I do not know why you ask, your Grace."

"You shall ride with Arthur's army. Speak with Eleanor of Aquitaine and tell her no harm is intended to her august person...Tell her that if she surrenders Mirabeau, she will have safe passage back to the nuns at Fontevraud."

"And will she be safe? You said you considered her a 'weapon' to use against John."

"Yes, certainly...if she co-operates and implores her wayward son to hand Normandy to me, its new lord."

"You must know of her reputation from your sisters. She is not the type to co-operate under force."

"She is old now, and doubtless doddery as old women often are." King Philip waved a dismissive hand.

I dared not argue with Philip, for he was a King, but I doubted my grandmother, even at the great age of eighty, could ever be called 'doddery.' Surreptitiously, I glanced at Arthur, my eyes downcast as if in modesty, my lashes shielding my true expression. I was trying to warn him—be careful here...!

My brother did not notice my look; he seemed excited. "Yes, yes, Eleanor must ride with the army. If anyone can converse with grandmother, it will be my sister."

"So it is agreed then!" King Philip leaned back and snapped his fingers. A page brought a golden platter covered in sugared figs. "The campaign to take Mirabeau shall begin as soon as possible. My tacticians will devise a route that will, if fortune favours us, split the lands John holds in two and keep one side from aiding the other. Within days, we shall have John Plantagenet and his old mother where we want them."

Arthur sat up straight. "Within days? But…but my Lord King, my army from Brittany will not have arrived by then! Surely we should wait until they have joined me."

Heart thudding, I raised my voice to join my brother's. "Your Grace, I must concur with the Lord Arthur. Our levies cannot possibly arrive within days. It is a long march from Brittany."

"There is no need for your troops," smiled King Philip. The plate of figs had been whisked away, empty; an esquire was dabbing at the King's shiny pate with a rose-scented cloth, removing a fine spray of sweat. "Duke Arthur, have I not offered to supply you with two hundred goodly knights?"

"Yes," Arthur replied, unsure, "but I admit my heart would be filled with gladness if my own men from Brittany were to ride under my banner."

Henry pursed his mouth. "*Non*, we cannot wait. John has his spies; linger and he will detect our plans. The march on Mirabeau must begin at once."

Hugh le Brun cleared his throat. "My men are ready and waiting. I need only ride to join them and lead them into battle. With the warriors of France joined with those of Poitou, I daresay we will not need extra forces from Brittany."

"The Lord Arthur should have his own loyal men around him," I interjected. "So it has always been. The Bretons are of sturdy heart and great prowess."

Again, the lords sniggered, amused and half-appalled a woman should dare speak on martial matters.

"The Lady Eleanor is much like her lady-mother, the Lady Constance," someone said drolly. It was not meant as a compliment.

King Philip smiled sweetly in my direction as if mollifying a small child. "My men are Arthur's, my dearest lady. After all, he is to marry my beloved daughter, Marie, and join my family."

Marie is not yet six, I thought sourly, biting my tongue. *A completed union could be years in the future…or not at all.*

143

Hugh le Brun glanced down the long council table; he gave me the same kind of smile as Philip, the smile given to an infant or simpleton, but there was a kind of appreciation in his eyes too. I remembered him from Germany. He was a handsome man, broad-shouldered, with a strong jaw and weather-tanned skin; he would be seeking a new bride now that John had whisked the young and alluring Isabella of Angouleme away. I hoped his attentions would not fall upon me; at present, my sole interest was Arthur and his safety. Besides, I'd heard he had contracted a new bride to replace Isabella—Mahaut of Angouleme, a pretty replacement who was also Isabella's cousin.

"My Lady," he said, in his deep, harmonious voice, "you need not fear that his lordship the Duke of Brittany is undermanned. I swear my Uncle Geoffrey and I shall fight near his side with all our strength and that of the men of Poitou. King John has done our kin grievous harm; we will be avenged."

I dared not argue anymore, but bowed my head in acceptance of Hugh's assurances. If I persisted in my doubts, I would seem a nagging shrew, for what would a mere girl know of war? I would make my brother a laughing stock.

King Philip rose from his chair, resplendent in his furred robes. "To battle, then!" he roared. "Let us teach John Lackland a lesson!"

Under a dull, threatening sky, I trundled down the road to Mirabeau in my carriage, feeling very much a piece of the baggage, which rolled along beside me in a series of huge, wooden wains. Sitting on a pile of cushions, attended by just one maiden called Hodierna, I heard the men guarding the train laugh roughly, as common men often do, and question my identity. "Do you think she's really his sister?" asked one. "Or is he bringing his light o'love on campaign? A bit of fancy swordplay before the real swordplay?"

"Nah, he's but a boy, take a look at him, Piers. Not even the trace of beard as yet."

"Doesn't mean a thing, Rogier. When I was his age, I'd still have had a good go at a creature as comely as that…"

Pressing my hands over my ears, I shut out the ongoing lewdness. I wished I could have ridden at the front of the company with Arthur, but he told me it was too dangerous—and the other lords would never countenance it. I suspect that even though he desired my counsel, he did not want me nearby when he was dealing with his captains and advisers, who would not appreciate a woman's input into matters of war.

Uneasy, I sighed. At least he had heeded me in one thing—I had told him to send couriers to Brittany to rally our army, even though Philip insisted they were unnecessary. I would take no chances. Let them march, even if they arrived late.

I wondered what I would say if it did become possible to speak with my grandmother, the Dowager Queen of England. I sorely wished this siege was just an ordinary one, not one involving an ancient woman of eighty. A woman who was blood kin, no matter that she had not supported her grandchildren of Brittany as well as she might...

My lady-in-waiting, Hodierna, leaned over and asked me if I required anything. It was a hot, July day that threatened thunder, and she stunk of sweat. I am sure I smelt no better. "Get me some wine...and a posy to hold to my nose." I testily pushed her away. "Jesu, it feels as if I have been closeted in here for weeks."

The chariot wobbled on as the heat increased. Tension hung in the air and the promised storm broke overhead, filling the day with roars and booms. Hail hit the painted canopies above us, making Hodierna shriek in fear. "God is angry!" she cried, crossing herself.

"Don't be silly," I told her. "It is just a storm, nothing more. We have them every year when the weather grows over-hot."

But even as I spoke, I heard the driver of the chariot call to the horses and felt the wheels below cease to turn. All around were the sounds of horses slowing, men dismounting.

"Shall I see what is happening, mistress?" asked Hodierna.

I did not wait for my maid. Pushing back the heavy sarcenet drapes at the back of the chariot, I gazed out, ignoring the leers of the baggage men I had heard talking so disrespectfully earlier. By Christ's Nails, they were fortunate I did not have the foul temperament of my Uncle John or they would be sorry!

However, I had no interest in such lowly miscreants, even to chide them for their vile assumptions. Before me, in the distance, stood a great grey castle on a crag. Sullen and square, its crenellations and jagged towers bumped the black, lighting-crown abutments of the clouds. It dated back to the days of Foulque Nerra and his rival son Geoffroy, two early Dukes of Anjou, and it looked little changed—a castle for war rather than comfort.

The Poitevin forces under the Lusignans had already arrived and were clustered outside the walls; siege engines of various designs, including great trebuchets to throw massive stones, ringed the fortress. Every now and then, I heard the hiss of displaced air and a mighty *whump* as a boulder sailed through the air to strike a tower or gate. Dust clouds rose into the air to mingle with the lowering sky.

"My lady Eleanor." One of Arthur's knights approached the chariot, striding boldly through the crowds of men unloading barrels of supplies. A fresh-faced young squire leading a saddled horse followed him. "His Grace the Duke has requested that you be brought to his pavilion to confer."

I nodded and the squire assisted me onto the waiting steed, careful to touch me as little as possible lest he cause offence. "What about me, my Lady?" Hodierna hovered at my stirrup. "I beg you do not leave me with all these rough men."

"You shall come too," I said wearily. "I dare say my brother has some foresight and has a pavilion ready for us also. He would hardly expect women to sleep under the stars or on the rug on his floor."

Slowly we made our way through the forming encampment to Arthur's pavilion, a huge blue-and-white striped tent with words from scripture painted in gold around the rim and banners flying from a decorative pinnacle perched on top. I noted one of the pennants bore the Royal Arms of England—a bold statement to make publically but one that made my brother's intentions clear.

Dismounting my horse, I was escorted through the heavily guarded doorway of the pavilion. Inside, Arthur was seated before a low table, with papers and maps strewn about, pinned down by daggers. Clad in a blue bliaut, a golden belt cinched his waist and royal ermine gleamed at his cuffs. A lion dangled on a chain about his throat—another bold statement. Behind him, a hawk jigged on a perch and a trio of musicians played quietly on flutes. Arthur's collapsible couch was arrayed with silken sheets in the colours of the flag of our mother Constance. On the canvas above the bed gleamed the motto of Brittany, in Latin—*Potius mori quam fœdar*, and below it, in the Breton tongue—*Kentoc'h mervel eget bezañ saotret*.

Death before dishonour.

Despite the heat, a cold chill ran through my breast, a needle of ice reaching my heart. My temples tightened; I feared one of my famed headaches would start. Hodierna, noticing my pallor, stared in consternation and began to rub my freezing hand.

"I trust you had a pleasant ride, sister?" asked Arthur, glancing up from the map he'd been studying.

"No," I quipped, "Locked in that carriage, I felt much as a cow must feel when brought to market. I longed to breathe the air."

Arthur laughed. "You never utter false niceties, do you, Eleanor."

"Never. If I learnt one thing from our grandmother, it was plain-speaking!"

"Sit." He gestured to a quilted stool. Hodierna made to kneel next to me but Arthur frowned, vexed, and waved her away. "Squire, take this girl to the tent prepared for the Lady Eleanor. What I must speak of now is only for the ears of the chosen."

Hodierna was led miserably away by the squire, glancing at me every now and then over her shoulder. "Go," I reassured her. "I will be with you later."

Arthur gestured for his musicians to depart; picking up their instruments, they left the pavilion with bowed heads. Men began to file into the tent, captains and generals. I recognised the Lusignans, Hugh le Brun and Geoffrey. They had seemed quite urbane and courtly at Philip's royal court but now they were war-like in mail and bright surcoats marked with a lion gules, its tongue lolling and its head crowned with gold stitching. At their sides, hung swords in sheaths bearing the Lusignan family emblems of roses and mermaids.

Hugh, carrying a helmet ornamented with a lion under one arm, bowed deeply. "Glad are we to seek your company, my Lord Arthur, Lady Eleanor. All is going well; before long, no doubt will be able to cry victory. The walls of Mirabeau are old and inferior in strength; our bombardment is bringing pieces down and keeping the defenders in locked positions. The gates are another weak point—if God smiles upon us, we should break through tonight. We will not cease to harry the enemy, even though darkness will have fallen."

Arthur rushed towards Hugh; I thought he might embrace him so excited he seemed. "Bless you for this excellent news, Hugh! I will come down to the field to watch and to participate, if I may."

Hugh le Brun looked slightly uneasy at Arthur's ardour-filled words. "Perhaps it would be best to send more seasoned soldiers. With respect, your Grace, you are but fifteen and untried."

Arthur's excitement turned to fury. "I am the Duke of Brittany! I am the heir to England. I will fight for what is mine, no matter what you say, Hugh Le Brun. Cross me at your peril."

Hugh took a step back; I touched my brother's arm and instantly he calmed. "Sir Hugh, forgive me, I meant no offence. But I must learn the ways of warfare sometime; there have been great warriors who began their careers at my age, even younger. I am eager to battle for my rights against the tyrant John." He glanced at the men surrounding him, then over to me. "I know," he continued, "how perilous war can be. A man may die in hand to hand combat or be struck by an arrow from afar like my Uncle, King Richard, at Chalus. If anything should happen to me, at least I have an heir, of the rightful blood and lineage—my sister Eleanor, Pearl of Brittany."

Catching my hand, he led me forward before all the knights and captains. "If I should die, Eleanor will take the title of Duchess of Brittany…and Queen of England. Remember, in England, Salic law does not bind a woman. Remember, she is the great granddaughter of Empress Maude, who gave to us the great Henry Plantagenet, my grandfather. Far better Eleanor, Fair Maid of Brittany, pure of heart and righteous, than swart John Lackland whose vices include treachery, ineptitude and stealing other men's wives."

Hugh Le Brun's face grew thunderous as the clouds outside as he remembered his shame at losing little Isabella to the King.

"Eleanor…" Earnest, golden, Arthur faced me—the young King Arthur reborn. "I will go to attack the castle tonight. I would not risk you by having you too close, but I would have you watch the battle. There is a hill where you may observe—would you?"

In truth, the thought terrified me, but I would not let my brother down in front of these powerful men. Men he needed to stand at his back. "Whatever is your desire, your Grace, my lord Duke. I will do your bidding gladly and rejoice at your first military success."

Under guard, I was taken to a bald, summer-blasted hillock that overlooked the beleaguered fortress of Mirabeau and the smoking ruins of the village it had once sheltered. Hodierna came with me as a companion, a timid mouse scuttling at my heels. Overhead the clouds began to part, the storm hurtling eastwards, dying in its fury behind the bastions of the castle's glowering keep. A pale moon peered out, a thin ghost against the dusky blue of the early eventide sky; an aged and mottled face as cold as death. I averted my gaze from its madness-inducing glow and kept my eyes fixed instead upon the forces crawling below, small as ants as they approached the castle walls, manoeuvring the great engines into position

Near the castle, trumpets thundered a tantara, and I saw the banner of the Lusignans billow out, and beside it the banner of Brittany, held aloft by Arthur's standard-bearer. Together the two contingents converged, driving in spearhead formation toward the grim towers in the distance. Around them, fire flared in the night—arrows loosed by the Poitevin archers, their shafts dipped in pitch and set alight. The missiles bounced off the castle walls, died hissing at the bottom of the dry moat, and sailed over the battlements where they struck the intended targets of roofs and wooden walkways. Squinting, I could see defenders rushing to put out flames as the burning pitch caught on sun-dried timber.

In front of Arthur's advancing front line, the siege engines proceeded to hurl their missiles. An *onager*, named for the violent kickback of its release, which was as furious as a wild ass' bucking, rolled out to join them. A master artilleryman set about arming the onager; within a short while, its humped arm was casting forth huge clay balls that burst into flames as they smote the curtain wall of Mirabeau.

More trumpets blared; the acrid scent of the mysterious potions that soaked the incendiary bombs hurled from the *onager* filled the air. Arthur's mounted warriors and foot soldiers and the Poitevin troops of the Lusignans parted like a curtain, and down between the ranks trundled a fearsome battering Ram on a mighty wain with spikes jutting from its wheels. Most rams were simple enough, a felled oak tree with its trunk carved to a spike but this one was not—crafted to attract attention, its aim was to cause fear in those who witnessed its onslaught. Its iron head was fashioned into that of a sinister Ram, with curled horns more like those of Satan than a beast of the field; attached by rivets, the metal jaw hung open and a small blaze burned within, giving the entire war engine a particularly sinister look.

At my side, Hodierna gasped in horror and clutched the little pewter image of Our Lady that she wore on a thong. Noticing my stare, she said, "I know the Ram is a strong weapon for our side but how unholy it looks, my Lady! Like something straight from hell!"

The Ram, riding beneath a canopy made of damp animal skins to protect its wooden body from enemy fire-arrows, was hauled toward the main gate. Hidden under shields, its bearers positioned it before the ironbound wooden doors of Mirabeau. Above them, the castle's defenders hurled stones and tipped basins of boiling water and other liquids. Archers tried to shoot downwards and pick off men through gaps in the array of shields; from behind the cavalry, the Lusignans' own division of archers fired back, picking off men rushing between the jagged crenels above.

"Heave!" a captain shouted, his faint voice borne to us on the wind. "Forward!" The Ram's cruel horns slammed against the gate. A sound like thunder carried over the devastated plain. "Again!" the captain roared, raising his mailed arm to signal to his soldiers.

Creaking, the Ram swung back, then lurched forward with a violent motion, flames spitting from its jaws. The head with its coiled horns smashed against the slats of the gate once again; wood started to buckle. The fiery liquid from the gaping mouth spewed out like obscene red-hot vomit, catching on the lower part of the gate and sending flames and oily smoke twisting to the sky.

The defenders roared in rage and terror and a hail of missiles descended on the Ram, bouncing harmlessly off the iron shields and the canopy of skins.

The Ram swung back one more time and then struck the weakened centre of the door. A crunching sound filled the flame-strewn night and the metal head burst through, mouth belching hell-flame, into the interior of the fortress.

A massive roar of victory ran through the Poitevin army and Arthur's French knights. I expected them all to race in with swords drawn but they hung back…and then I saw why. They were bringing up another engine of war—a *cheval de fries*, a barricade bristling with spears and jagged blades that glittered wickedly in the wavering light of the fiery arrows darting overhead. These machines were used to stop horsemen but that was not the intent here—the cheval de fries was clearly meant to block potential escapees, mounted or otherwise, from within the castle. Anyone who might bear news to King John, who was somewhere on the other side of Normandy.

The *cheval de fries* in place, the warriors began piling around its sides and storming into the inner ward. The Ram was taken to the other gates and likewise they were shattered; more soldiers poured into all sections of the bailey, stabbing, killing, capturing.

"So Mirabeau has fallen," I breathed.

"So it would seem, Lady Eleanor." Hodierna's voice was a squeak.

I thought of Arthur, somewhere in the milling press, near his banner. I started to pray, quietly, fervently: *He that is mighty hath done great things to me, and holy is His name. His mercy is from generation unto generation to those that fear Him. He hath shown might in His arm. He hath scattered the proud in their conceit. He hath cast the mighty from their thrones…*

Another boom from the castle made me jump in alarm. A huge segment of wall had crashed outwards; flames danced with the bailey.

Swallowing, I also said one quick prayer for the safety of my grandmother, still dwelling within the beleaguered fortress. Even though she had supported her son John above Arthur, she was still my blood kin.

Cursed is our family, born of devils, and in constant war with each other!

Arthur and the Lusignans returned to the encampment leaving the unbreached keep, the castle's strongest section, ringed by armed watchers and the sinister shapes of the *onagers* and the great cheval de fries. My brother summoned me to his pavilion, despite the lateness of the hour. He was in a state of high excitement, his golden hair plastered to his scalp with sweat and his mail, which had not yet been removed, sluiced with blood.

Moving to embrace me, he halted as he realised the gory state he was in. "Today I have killed a man," he said wonderingly. "When the gates fell and we forayed into the inner bailey. He came at me with an axe, and I brained him with a mace. I am blooded, a warrior. I am now a man…"

You are fifteen, I thought, in despair. *Learn the craft of warfare but remember your limitations, my brother. Fifteen…*

Arthur made an impatient gesture to his squires; they rushed to his side and began unfastening his armour. I stared modestly at the floor as my brother was dressed in clean apparel befitting his rank and had his soiled items removed for cleaning.

When he was fully dressed and had wine brought, I lifted my head. "I saw the gates fall. Has anyone spoken to grandmother? I am guessing she has not surrendered?"

A petulant expression briefly crossed the planes of Arthur's face. "No. We were fortunate but not as fortunate as that. Along with those closest to her, she barred herself inside the keep and destroyed the wooden stair leading to the first floor. We could get a siege tower up to the doorway, but the top of the tower is bristling with archers. Geoffrey Lusignan also said the keep appears be of sturdier construction that the outer walls; sappers and miners may be of little use. He suggests we starve the defenders out."

I cringed. "Grandmother…she's eighty, Arthur."

Fire flared in his eyes. "Whose side are you on, hers or mine?"

"Yours, of course, do not mistake me! But you…you must be a just lord, Arthur. A cruel, harsh one would make you no better than John.

Besides, a long siege would give John time to arrive." As I thought of our uncle, my spine prickled; unnerved, I pulled my cloak closer about my shoulders—would the squires ever stop pouring in and out of the tent, allowing in the dangerous, cold night air?

"John is miles away at present." Arthur was confident. "But yes, you are correct, Eleanor, we cannot tarry, for I doubt he will want his mother to remain in her present plight, once he learns of it. And that is where you help me, dearest sister. We discussed such a situation at Philip's court. Tomorrow I want you to go into Mirabeau with my herald and treat with the Dowager Queen. Use your womanly powers of persuasion to make her see sense and surrender. Reassure her she will be unhurt and treated with all courtesy. Tell her I swear to see her safely back to Fontevraud."

Uneasy, I began to pace the pavilion. Deep in my heart, I knew such an effort would prove useless…

Arthur sensed my hesitation; again, his hot Plantagenet wrath rushed to the fore. "Do not betray me in this triumphant hour! This…this hesitance is treasonous!"

Shocked, I stared at my brother. "You wound me with your harsh words! I will do as you ask but I will not lie to you—I have many misgivings on this matter."

"I have no care for your misgivings." Arthur, sullen, folded his arms defensively across his chest. "Just do what I ask, that is all I want."

"My Lord…" I said coolly, as if he were a stranger and not the brother I had idolised from afar, when I was taken into wardship so long ago. My King Arthur renewed—the hope of Brittany.

I left the tent; my guards and Hodierna were waiting. The night had clouded over again, and rain began anew. The droplets falling from the sky mingled with my tears, hiding them from those about me—a small mercy.

After Mass the next day, shortly after dawn broke in a welter of flaming cloud, I strode across the churned, charred fields before Mirabeau with Arthur's herald and entered one of the ruined gates. Passing through the corridor into the bailey, I was all too aware of bodies on the flagstones and the iron reek of congealed blood. Then I was out in fresher air again, in a bailey ravaged and ransacked; dead animals and men lay about in the wreckage of wooden buildings, collapsed wall walks and fractured masonry blocks. Buzzing flies, drawn by the carnage, had begun to gather for their feast.

Up, up before me rose the great keep, the castle's strongest building, its stonework slick from the night's rain and its small windows like the eyes in a weathered skull. Archers crowded on each of its four jutting corner towers, their arrows to the bowstring. Although heralds and messengers were generally immune to deliberate violence during a parlay, this did always hold true when tempers flared…and I was well aware the men on the battlements could shoot me dead in seconds.

I reached the base of the keep. Gazed up at the livid burn marks where the wooden steps to the door had once stood. Slowly the door, slashed with black ash, creaked open and a rope ladder was hurled down. I stared at it for a moment, debating how I might climb in my long skirts with dignity, then I cast such thoughts from my mind and climbed, the herald following close on my heels.

As I neared the keep's first floor, arms reached to pull me up the rest of the way; I was drawn inwards to stand before a grim-faced crowd of men with ash-smeared faces. They looked so fierce, their gazes piercing like daggers, that I thought they might take me captive or even kill me on the spot. But once the herald was dragged inside, and in a breathless but sturdy voice delivered his message that I was here to bargain with the Queen, the captain of these stern defenders beckoned me onwards to Eleanor's quarters.

The Dowager Queen was sitting alone, her women all dismissed, when I was brought to her chambers. She had the shutters closed to bar the hideous sights in the bailey and to keep smoke from seeping in. To compensate for the lack of natural light, she had candles burning everywhere in great gold candelabras. The wavering light played on the glaze on the blue floor-tiles and made the whimsical unicorns in her expensive tapestries leap to life.

Grandmother had aged greatly in the years since I'd seen her. Once she had seemed a virtual giant, a tall, strong woman bristling with energy. Now she had dwindled from a bright flame to a dying spark, her shoulders bony beneath rich damask, the lines of her face deeply grooved. She sat with a prayer book in her hands. As I was escorted in, she shut the book with a loud snap and rose to greet me.

"Eleanor…granddaughter." Age made her voice raspy, tremulous. "You have come. I never thought I would see you under such circumstances."

"Nor I, grandmother." Sweat began to bead on the nape of my neck. All through the previous night, I had rehearsed what I would say to her, thinking up speeches noble and convincing, but now it felt as if my wits had deserted me.

The Dowager Queen grasped a carven cane from beside her seat and hobbled in my direction. "Well, out with it, girl. Why do you and Arthur torment me? Why have you killed my people and ruined my castle?"

I took a deep breath, thinking of my brother and my promise to him. "Arthur should have been King of England. He will be, with the aid of the Lusignans and the King of France."

Eleanor lifted her hand and waved it as if fanning away an evil smell. "He has become the French King's puppet. He has been set upon a foolish, ill-starred course, and you have blindly followed. Yes, Arthur was once Richard's choice as heir but on his deathbed, he changed his mind, as he was entitled to do. He named John his successor."

"People hate John, grandmother. You saw yourself how he behaved during Richard's imprisonment in Germany. He tried to steal his crown. And of late... surely you know of the scandal with Isabella of Angouleme! Christ's Teeth, she was little more than twelve."

"Well, we always knew he would probably rid himself of Hawise. She was a weak, mewling thing, though well decked with lands."

"John has a reputation and it is not a good one. How can you still support him?"

"*He. Is. My. Son.*" Eleanor's lips were tight, bloodless lines.

"So the rest of your blood is cast aside? Unless you personally benefit from us in some way?"

"You learn quickly, little Eleanor." He tone was cruel, so too her smile. "I taught you well, at least. Are you not grateful for that, if nothing more?"

"Madam, bickering will do neither of us any good. I am here to ask you to surrender. Arthur will eventually have you taken to Fontevraud. We do not want you harmed, nor do we wish ill to the inhabitants of your castle. If you will leave this stronghold, I swear not one person within your household shall suffer more. All will be free to go."

"And if I refuse?" Eleanor's sharp chin tilted up defiantly. "I note you say Arthur would send me to the abbey 'eventually.' Yes, after he had used me in an attempt to compel John. It is ridiculous. I will never cede to him."

I bristled; she was stubborn, but what did I expect? "Then Arthur and his allies will continue to besiege this castle. They will starve you out or use sappers to undermine your keep. For every wasted day,

Arthur and King Philip will hang one of the defenders once the castle falls."

Eleanor shook her head slowly. "Oh, Eleanor, you have made such a terrible mistake. A terrible mistake indeed. You know what I would advise? Go to my errant grandson Arthur, take him by the hand—foolish child that he is—and fly back to whatever strongholds you have in Brittany."

"Why would we do that, with victory so near at hand?" I said, full of scorn.

"Because, you foolish chit, John is coming. I secreted a messenger out the postern gate before your blasted trebuchets had hurled a single missile at my walls! He is coming…and his wrath will know no bounds. You, my dear, suspect what he is capable of and you are right—tell Arthur."

My head reeled. John knew! Yet even if he had deployed his forces immediately, surely he would not arrive to relieve his mother in a reasonable time? The Lusignans insisted it would not be possible…

Grandmother threw her cane aside and limped up to me, placing her hands on my shoulders. Her fingers had grown knotted and bony, tangled with lumps of blue veins. "Eleanor, for your own sake, get away." Her voice had changed, no longer angry, deepening with concern. "For all that we may be on opposing sides now, I do care for you as the daughter of my lost Geoffrey. Get away. Leave, even if Arthur forbids it. Just be gone from Mirabeau ere John arrives with his army. For it will not go well for you if he captures you… either of you."

She pulled away from me then, hobbling back towards her seat. "Go now. I have had enough. I am too old for all this fighting. It makes my head pound."

I cleared my throat. "What is the official word that I must take to Arthur?"

"You know it already." Keen eyes sparkled beneath brows flecked with silver. "No surrender."

I hastened back to Arthur's pavilion. He was waiting, all enthusiasm, with Hugh and Geoffrey and other captains at his side. Impatient, he strode towards me. "What word, Eleanor, what word from our grandmother?"

Unable to meet his brilliant, shining eyes, I bowed my head. "She will not surrender. I am sorry, Arthur."

Arthur stood in silence for a moment, then suddenly whirled around and with one blow of his hand sent the silvered cups on the table ringing to the floor. Another blow sent piled of maps and documents sailing through the air. Cowed as whipped dogs, servants darted forward to grab the parchments before they were trampled underfoot or burnt on the nearby brazier.

"The stupid woman! The evil old witch!" Arthur screamed, pummelling the air with his fists. I noticed Hugh and Geoffrey glance at each other, suppressing little smirks; inside, I cringed with shame.

"Well…" Hugh Le Brun took a deep breath, "her answer was what I expected from a lady of the Dowager Queen's reputation. We shall just continue the siege; she cannot hold out forever."

Shivers ran through me. "My lords, I bring more than Eleanor's refusal. I bring a warning. Eleanor told me something that brings great fear to my heart—she claims to have sent a messenger to her son, my uncle, King John. I fear he marches here even as we speak. Eleanor told us to beware of his wrath, for he would take great vengeance on us, kin or no."

"Of course she would say that!" spat Arthur. "She is trying to convince us to leave with lies…"

"But if it is true and John should come at greater speed than is reckoned, we could end up encircled by his forces, trapped between his army and the castle walls."

Geoffrey shook his head. "He could never get here that quickly with any amount of men. Put your mind at rest, Lady. Your grandmother's words were just a ruse."

I glowered. By the timbre of Geoffrey's voice, I suspected he was patronising me, treating me as a timid female scared of shadows, believing everything I was told.

"I know my uncle as you do not," I said icily. "If he sets his mind to a task, he will act upon it…especially if there is a rich prize at the end." My gaze travelled to Arthur, standing sullenly, arms folded in petulance. My innocent, foolish young brother would be that prize.

"I only speak of what I know of military matters," said Geoffrey, "but I do agree on one thing—John or no, we cannot waste time. We will resume attacking the keep at dawn and put as much pressure on the defenders as possible. No more parlays, no quarter. We will take this castle with as much violence as needed. You, my Lord Arthur, my Lady Eleanor, do understand what this may mean for the Dowager Queen if she continues to refuse to capitulate…."

"Yes, yes!" Arthur broke in. "It no longer matters. She has severed her ties with her grandchildren of Brittany and thrown in her lot with her tyrant son. She is an enemy now. If any harm should befall her—that will be God's will and his wrath upon her for her folly!"

He waved a hand in my direction; I sensed his disappointment in me for not convincing the Dowager Queen to act as he wished. "You may retire, Eleanor. If you are needed, I will call."

In silence, I went under escort to my tent, where Hodierna waited anxiously. She had my bed made ready, the counterpane doused in rose petals, heated stones wrapped in linen under the cover to warm my limbs. And yes, I felt cold, so very cold…and it was not all from the chill night air.

"I am so glad to see you, my Lady," Hodierna said in a timorous voice, as she took my cloak and draped it on a stool near the brazier. "I was so afraid. To go inside a castle split asunder by war…It must have been terrifying for a maid of gentle breeding."

"It was not pleasant, Hodierna." I slipped into the bed, pulling the covers up around my chin. "I hope never to see such sights again."

"I will be glad when this siege is over," the maid said, hands clasped together. "I will pray to Christ for a swift victory."

"So will I," I said, "now come, crawl in and warm me. Arthur's forces will resume the attack in all earnest at dawn. Soon…soon, pray Jesu and the Virgin, it will all be over."

Chapter Seventeen

Darkness lay over Mirabeau. I dozed, with Hodierna curled up beside me like a faithful dog. The embers of the brazier faded to nothingness.

Suddenly, a series of loud bangs made us both sit up, clutching each other in fright. A heavy object struck our pavilion. One side of the tent crumpled and was then torn into shredded tatters—on the tip of a sword blade. Horrified, we watched the cloth tear further, blowing up in streamers as the stormy wind shrieked into our tent.

"Run!" I gasped, pushing my maid out of the bed.

"But…what…what is it?"

"Just run!"

Grasping strands of the ripped cloth, we fought our way out of the collapsing pavilion. Two soldiers—the guards Arthur had set—lay dead on the ground, their throats slit, their lifeless eyes mirroring the red of the impending dawn.

All about us men tumbled, some half dressed, some half-drunk, fighting with hastily snatched dagger and sword against mailed warriors who assailed them with grim determination. A body tumbled across our path, skull shattered, brainpan showing, teeth spewing like vomit from the torn mouth—Hodierna screamed hysterically and reeled as if she might faint. Grasping her arm, I hauled her away from the hideous sight. I must find Arthur…We must find horses and flee.

Grandmother had been right. Her warning was no lie. John and his army were here to relieve her—and to take his rival captive.

Terrified, Hodierna and I staggered across the encampment, past shattered and burnt pavilions, past dead watch fires with dead men sprawled in the embers. All around the camp horns were blowing wildly and drums beating a fierce tattoo. A riderless horse galloped by, a dappled grey mare with rolling eyes; I snatched at her dangling reins but they were sticky with blood and slipped through my fingers.

A ring of steel, of enemy soldiers, was closing in on us. The numbers of attackers seemed to grow as they pushed forward with determined tread, the golden star and crescent of John's badge clear upon their surcoats. The camp was infiltrated and surrounded. There was no way out.

Arthur and the Lusignans had wanted Eleanor to surrender—they would be the ones to do so instead.

Or die.

Maybe they would die anyway. Maybe we all would.

A knight stepped out before us, holding a sword that dripped crimson. "You! Halt!" He raised his blade in a threatening manner. "I seek the King's niece on the orders of his Grace King John. Which of you is Lady Eleanor of Brittany?"

"I…I am she…" Hodierna gasped out, lying in an attempt to save me that was both brave and foolhardy.

I twisted her arm. "No, do not listen to the girl…I am she. Do not harm my maid—she is just a servant and one of good heart."

The knight approached, sinister with his bloody blade and his face obscured by the plates of the great, rectangular bucket-helm he wore. Suddenly he sheathed his sword and reaching up, removed the helmet to reveal a scarred and sweat-streaked face. A face that I recognised. William des Roches, who had once supported Arthur but then turned his coat.

"Now that I can see clearly without this encumbrance on my head, I know that it is indeed you, my Lady. You may not remember me, but I was at King Philip's court several years past."

"Yes," I said, "I do remember you—how could I not? I was there to support my brother, Duke Arthur, and my mother, Duchess Constance, God assoil her. At the time, we believed you true to our aims, but you betrayed us."

Looking uneasy, he bowed his head. "I thought your Uncle a more likely ruler than a mere stripling."

"The truth is you were angry King Philip destroyed the castle of Ballon in Maine, which you desired. My uncle offered you the position of Seneschal of Anjou instead, so in gratitude you turned traitor and supported his unrighteous cause."

A muscle jumped in the man's cheek but he did not respond. "You will be treated courteously, I can assure you, Lady Eleanor. You will not be harmed."

My brows lifted. "Is that your assurance, Sir William? Or my uncle's? You I might trust, despite your faithlessness…but John? Never."

"He has sworn…" began William.

"I do not want to hear," I interrupted. "Take us to him, and prolong this horror no longer."

Des Roches gestured to two of his henchmen lurking at his back. "Tie their hands but be gentle, I bid you or you will answer to me."

"Tie us!" I cried, as the ropes went about our wrists. Beside me, Hodierna began to weep slow, silent tears. "Are we hogs to be tied? So much for treating us courteously. Already you've proved false." Filled with sudden rage, I spat at des Roches' iron-shod feet.

Disgusted, William des Roches whirled away from me. "Bring the women! Hurry!" he barked at his men. "Let us find the others."

We were dragged to the wreckage of Arthur's pavilion. My brother was inside, in his shirt and hose and no more, but unharmed. Manacles bound his hands and feet. John's man William de Braose stood guard over him, looking like a cat that had stolen cream from a goodwife's kitchen. "Eleanor!" Arthur cried and tried to leap forward.

De Braose, a stocky brute with a florid face and wild red hair, yanked on the chain that bound Arthur's feet. He stumbled and fell to his knees with a heavy thud. "I told you not to move 'my lord,'" he mocked.

"How dare you treat my brother so!" I cried, enraged. "You maltreat your rightful King, you squab-nosed knave!"

De Braose flung back his head and bellowed with laughter. "He doesn't look much of a King grovelling on the ground like a worm."

"Where are the Lusignans?" I asked, staring that way and that. "What has become of them?"

"Captured and held by the King's loyal men, just like your precious brother. Stupid fools. Geoffrey Lusignan was caught while eating his breakfast of pigeons! He looked stunned, with the fat from the birds dribbling down his chin like drool from the mouth of an idiot!"

"What will become of us now?" I turned away from de Braose's grinning face and glanced towards my captor, William des Roches. "What are you going to do with us?"

De Braose answered, "You are to go before John later in the day, once he has bathed, supped, and spent time with the Dowager Queen. You will know your fate then. Best get on your knees and pray in the meantime, for his Grace is full wroth about the attack on his mother."

King John sat beneath a vast canopy bearing his emblem of the golden crescent and star, an insignia also once used by Richard Lionheart. He was slouched in a fancy chair rimed with carbuncles and fitted with a tasselled cushion to support his weight. He wore purple robes lined with spotted ermine and his neck blazed with ropes of rubies and emeralds. He had even affected a small ceremonial crown, to impress upon us that he was indeed King and a victorious king at that. It was a gaudy contraption with the letter 'J' spelt out in pearls and ungainly lumps of coloured gems embedded around the rim.

For a while he said nothing, just stared with a basilisk-gaze at his most prized prisoners—me, Arthur, the Lusignans and several high-ranking Frenchmen—all the while popping grapes, one by one, into his mouth.

When he finally found his tongue, he began to roar like an angry bear. "You…you dared to ride against me, against my aged mother who is half-dead with the strain of this outrage? You fools! You bloody fools!" Leaping from his seat, he kicked out at a page, sending him flying with a yelp and then overturned his own table, spilling the remnants of his grapes and a flagon of wine onto the ground. "I will have you all hung from the walls of Mirabeau, even the damn girl!"

I saw Arthur blanch. John stalked up to him, thrusting his suffused face into that of his nephew. "You swore to be my vassal. You broke your oaths. Do not pretend to be an innocent; you are not. You will suffer for your treachery."

"Have mercy!" I cried. "He is but a boy, no matter what he has done. Remember how Richard once excused you by saying you were but a child led astray by evil counsel!"

"I remember Richard's words well, Mistress Eleanor." He strode over to me, breath from his flaring nostrils blasting hot against my cheek. "They were meant to be an insult, calling me a child when I was a man grown. Well, I take no more insults from anyone—especially half-grown boys who think they are worthier than they are!"

Pivoting on his heel, he grasped Arthur by the hair and shook him as a terrier shakes a rat. "You shall be sent to Falaise, brat. I will call a council to see what my barons think I should do with such an ungrateful little bastard."

Then he turned to Geoffrey and Hugh Lusignan, standing sullenly in their shackles, a bristle of sword blades pressed to their backs. "You shall go with him, and remain in chains, upon my pleasure. And I am sure I will get plenty of pleasure from your captivity, Hugh le Brun." He smirked meaningfully. "Nearly as much as I've had from your former betrothed, my beautiful young Isabella…my Queen."

Hugh gave an angry cry and lunged at John, manacles clacking; one of the guards struck him with a mailed fist, flinging his head back sharply and causing his mouth to bleed.

John sneered and stepped away from his prisoner. "You, Eleanor, shall be taken to England and imprisoned in my castle of Corfe and others, as I see fit. Two hundred knights have been captured today, including the notables Andre De Chauvigny, Hugh Bauge, Savary de Mauleon, and Raymond Thouars. They and their fellows shall be imprisoned in diverse dungeons around Normandy and over in England. What will befall you all will depend on the actions of your overlords…and how much coin your families are willing to pour into my royal coffers to ensure your freedom."

The King clapped his hands. "Come on, my men; let's get these prisoners out and on their way. I am weary of speaking to such rabble and would fain dine with my dear, distressed lady-mother."

The guards began pushing Arthur towards a prison-cart with bars. He fought them resolutely, despite his chained hands, but he was no match for their combined strength. As he was thrown to the floor of the filthy cart, he raised his head and shouted back at me, "Eleanor, stand firm! I'll get free, I swear it. I'll come for you, see if I won't."

The cart began to creak away from the ruined camp, surrounded by a horde of mounted knights and fierce spearmen.

The afternoon light, spearing through massed clouds, struck Arthur's golden hair, making it into a bright halo. He was like King Arthur in defeat, having suffered his Mount Badon. Or a saint, wreathed in a heavenly nimbus—a saint like young, innocent Melor of Brittany, likewise captured by his power-mad uncle…

It was the last time I ever saw my brother alive.

Chapter Eighteen

Corfe Castle loomed on the horizon through the drizzle of an English morning. Set upon a conical hill rising sharply from the floor of a valley that plunged through the heart of a low ridge of lesser hills, it dominated the green landscape as it guarded the passages to Wareham and Swanage. Massive and austere, the keep was extremely tall, and even at a distance, I could see the tiny figures workers busy repairing walls and building new structures—Corfe was one of John's favourite royal castles and he was adding apartments and stronger towers.

As my prison cart and those containing a handful of the captive knights rolled on toward the castle ascent, local folk came out to jeer and mock, wives and children of the workers who had set up a settlement that now appeared to be permanent. Their jibes were not directed at me, but rather at the French lords in manacles, whom they saw as the enemy of England. I was more of a curiosity, being John's niece. One old woman cried out, "Poor child; she'll probably never see the light of day again!" and hurled a posy of wildflowers at my cart. They landed on the floor in a spray of bright petals and leaves.

Up the steep incline the carts trundled, the thick-hoofed workhorses that drew them straining in their harnesses, the wains rocking ominously from side to side. I clung to the bars, not sure where to cast my eyes—up to the louring towers overhead, my future prison, or to the unfriendly makeshift village below. Even the very soil of the hill seemed blighted and unfriendly, and I remembered, long before my Norman ancestors came to rule England, that a young Saxon King, Edward, was murdered there by the wiles of his stepmother, Elfthryth, mother of Ethelred, the other claimant to the throne. One Chronicler had written—And the greatest of betrayals is also in this world, that a man betray his lord to death, or drive him living from his rightful land, and both of these have come to pass in England: King Edward was betrayed and then killed, and after that his body was burned …

Ahead, the gate that protected the barbican was opening, the portcullis rising in a squeal of gears and chains. I passed into castle bailey, and out of my old life and freedom.

A party of sombre, older women awaited me. They were clad in dour grey wimples, almost nun-like, and there was not a smile amongst them. Their eyes were hard flints, without pity. "My Lady, if you would come this way and not linger," said one in clipped tones, as the workers high above on scaffolding stopped their labours to stare at the prison train as it entered the castle precincts.

There was no point in any argument. Pulling up my hood to cover my face, I followed the women into one of the towers. Up, up, I went on the dark, spiralling staircase, lit by torches in brackets on the wall. At length, we stopped on a floor; it must have been close to the top of the tower. A wooden door gaped open, waiting. The stern-visaged women beckoned me forward with impatience.

Inside my new quarters, tears filled my eyes. Tears of relief. In my head, I had mulled the possibility of imprisonment in a bare room with a straw pallet to sleep on and a bucket to piss in. Instead, the room was decorated in the manner a woman of rank might expect, with rugs to keep out the cold and a bed with clean linens covered by a canopy to keep bugs from dropping from the ceiling into the sheets. There were clothes chests, ewers of silver, rosewater basins, candelabras and even a handful of rich tapestries.

I cried even harder though as I thought of the knights who fought for Arthur's cause—and mine. Even the highest-born amongst them were not to have accommodation such as mine. Four and twenty of them were going into the dungeons until they were ransomed.

The foremost of the women glared at me as if I were weak or ungrateful for weeping. "I am called Ivette. His Grace the King has called upon me to serve. Anything you need, Lady Eleanor, you must ask me first and I will see what can be done. Fear not, it is not his Grace's intent to harm you. Sustenance shall be brought and books if you desire them and, naturally, you will have access to the chaplain and permission to pray in the castle chapel."

"Thank you, Ivette." I wiped my eyes on my sleeve. "For now, I would only ask that I be alone."

She curtseyed in a sharp, perfunctory way and left the room with her stony companions. I heard the clunk of a huge iron key turning in a lock, and then the clanking of armour as guards positioned themselves outside my door.

And so I spent my first night in Corfe.

It would be the first of many.

Despair could have ruled me, but it did not. I clung to the idea that soon I would be free and Arthur too. Philip of France would ransom us, since Arthur was to wed Marie, and we would rule Brittany together until his majority or until a suitable husband was found for me. In the meantime, I took it upon myself be a dutiful lady and aid the knights held captive at Corfe as much as I was able. No word on any ransoms for them had come from France, and the conditions they were held in were, in my opinion, less than adequate.

Head held high, I had Ivette take me to Stephen de Turnham, whom John had appointed my personal gaoler. Plucking up courage, I entered his chamber above the gatehouse near the Constable's own rooms. "Master Turnham, I have a request. I would visit with the knight Andre de Chauvigny."

Rising from a desk, Turnham began to cough and splutter, clearly ill at ease with my suggestion. "I fear the King would not approve…"

"Master Turnham, I beg you. Sir Andre is my kinsman. His mother Haois was great-aunt to Richard and John, and to my own sire, Geoffrey. Andre was a great crusader and a captain of many men whilst in the Holy Land. It is shameful he still languishes in prison."

Stephen de Turnham continued to look uneasy but I could tell he was thinking on my words. I knelt before him, despite my status, and spoke quietly, persuasively. "You have not been harsh with me; I think you are probably a kind man. I will not be here forever, Master Turnham. I am a royal princess. When freed, I will remember any kindness…or otherwise."

There…a slight hint of threat. Not too much…

Turnham looked surprised, then slightly worried. He licked his lips and leaned back in his chair, his gaze never leaving my face.

I rose slowly, brushing the dust from my skirts. "Master Turnham?"

"I am likely a fool, but truth be told—what harm could you do when de Chauvigny is safely behind bars?" he said gruffly. "A slip of a girl is hardly likely to foment rebellion. Look…go now but return when the Matins bell rings out at latest. If you do not return on time, I will drag you from the cells myself…and write to the King of your behaviour. Do you understand, Lady Eleanor?"

"You are too kind, Master Turnham!" I cried, with false cheer. "I will remember your kindness in my prayers."

"No need," he mumbled, blushing deep red beneath his black beard. "Now go!" He snapped his fingers and a bland-visage guard walked over. "Guyon, take the Lady Eleanor to the cell of Andre de Chauvigny. Let her speak to him but only through the grate in the wall. She is to return to the Gloriet tower by the time the Matins bell is rung."

Dour Guyon led me from de Turnham's sweltering chamber into the bowels of Corfe, sunk deep within the great pointed hill upon which the castle stood. The air changed, becoming rank with the smell of dankness, dung and unwashed bodies. I folded one of my long sleeves and pressed it to my nose to block the foul scent.

Passing the oubliette, a shaft in the floor dropping into a deep, lightless pit, I resisted an urge to peer through the floor-grate into the blackness below. Poachers and murderers were kept in the oubliette, trapped in the reeking murk, but the French knights, being men of rank, were confined in individual cells on the next level where there was, at least, a small amount of light and air.

After what seemed an eternity of walking through narrow corridors where ash rained from half-burned torches, Guyon halted and gestured to a wooden door fronted with an iron grille. I flew to the bars, peered inside. When my eyes had adjusted to the dimness, I could see a figure slumped on a bench, his hands shackled; he sat with his head bowed, not glancing up.

"My Lord Chauvigny!" I cried. "Cousin!"

He glanced up abruptly through a tangled matt of unwashed hair. "Lady Eleanor! Why have you come?"

"I come because you and your fellows have fallen on evil times because of your loyalty to the Duke of Brittany's just cause. I want to know how you fare. Has any news reached you of a ransom, a release?"

Andre got up stiffly and shuffled forward as far as the chains on his feet allowed. The metal cuffs he wore had cut his flesh; weeping sores oozed around wrists and ankles. He winced in pain. "No, nothing. King John, for all he spoke of filling his coffers with ransom money, wants something else it seems—the good behaviour and acquiescence of our fellow countrymen, and yours. We are not just prisoners, my lady, we are hostages."

"How do you know this?"

A corner of his mouth quirked upwards; his lips were dry, broken—someone had struck him with a fist. "One of our number, Savari de Mauleon, has begged John for mercy and sworn to serve him well. He is still imprisoned, but not in a foetid cell like mine, and he is not chained up or beaten by the guards. He comes on occasion to bring news and to try and convince us to support John and renounce our sworn vows."

"The disloyal blackguard!" I cried. "Another faithless traitor."

"De Mauleon warns us too," continued Andre, "of how we might be punished if the Bretons and Angevins do not cease to attack King John's territories...."

I did not want to hear. Idle threats, surely. All laws and decency forbade harming well-born prisoners of war when a ransom could be obtained instead. "I will write, if they let me...write to my grandmother, the Dowager Eleanor. Beg her for mercy and forgiveness. She will prevail upon John..."

"I fear he no longer listens to his mother, no matter her influence of old. He is as glutted with power as a crow is glutted with blood on the battlefield. He acts with rashness...some would say madness. Although he conquered us at Mirabeau, his vile behaviour afterwards has alienated even his closest friends. Daily they betray him. Did you know his enemies nearly caught his Queen at Chinon? What a bargaining tool she would have been if they had succeeded! But he has the luck of the devil. He arrived just in time with his army."

At that moment, I heard the first clang of the Matins bell. "Jesu, I must go." Footsteps thudded behind me and I saw Guyon's hulking shadow on the wall. "Is there anything...anything I can do?" I wrapped my hands desperately around the beslimed bars on the cell door.

Andre shuffled closer, stretched out his blood-caked, festering hand—just touching my fingers with his own. "One thing, if you can—send word to my wife, Denise de Deols, Countess of Devon. Let her know I think of her always and our sons, especially the eldest, Guillaume. Tell her that she must prepare him for manly duties in case I do not return home..."

"My Lady!" Behind me, Guyon's voice was a dull boom. "Master Turnham gave orders you were to leave at the ringing of the Matins bell. It rings now. Do not make me have to drag you forth in shame."

"I will do as you bid, oaf; there's no need to treat me discourteously," I spat at the guard, then, turning away from him, I nodded slightly towards Andre. "I can do little, I fear, but will see if that one request will be granted."

It took time and all the powers of persuasion I could muster but I manage to convince de Turnham it was Christian charity to send news of Sir Andre to his wife, the Countess of Devon. "When these men are freed," I told him, "they may show gratitude to a kindly gaoler, as will I. You would benefit, I swear on the Cross."

I also managed to coerce the knights' keepers to occasionally bring them out into the bailey to see the sun; it made my tears fall to see these once proud men reduced to shambling wrecks who blinked in the sunlight like blinded bats. I scolded the castle constable, William de Blunville, for their condition and insisted their portions must be increased and warm blankets given for the cold nights in their dungeon.

But then one day, messengers bearing John's badge galloped up to the castle. More knights were arriving in chains, taken from confinement in other castles across both France and England. Now the iron hatch of the great oubliette was pried opened and the newcomers unceremoniously hurled down into the reeking pit. The prisoners already resident at Corfe were wrest from their cells and thrown after them.

Walking on the walls, wrapped in furs against the January chill, I managed to escape Ivette's clutches and entered the bailey, where Constable de Blunville was giving directions to John's soldiers. "What is going on?" I cried. "Why are more men arriving at Corfe? Why are you putting them in the oubliette? They will die down there…"

De Blunville's small, cold eyes blazed as he turned on me, snarling. One of John's creatures, he always regarded me with suspicion, unlike the more placid de Turnham. He was never so discourteous or wrathful as today, however. "How did you get here? This sight is not for your eyes, Lady. You must return to your chamber immediately. Where is that hag, Ivette?"

Ignoring his anger, I flared with wrath of my own. "These men were my men, who supported me! It is my right to know!" I screamed over the cold wind buffeting the castle walls.

"I will tell you then!" he snapped. "The King has sent letters to Hugh de Neville and the constables of eighteen castles, telling them to send the French prisoners here, where they are to be incarcerated in the oubliette as befits the worst felons and traitors. Here is his letter, if you do not believe me, Madam, with his own Seal…" Hand shaking with righteous rage, he thrust a crumpled parchment in my direction.

I snatched it and read quickly…*you should do what Thomas, clerk of our chamber and Hugh de Neville tell you on our behalf concerning the prisoners that have been delivered to you…*

"And what did the clerk and de Neville tell you to do?" I hurled the parchment to the ground at de Blunville's feet. "What?"

"Get this wench out of here!" roared the Constable to the guards. "Put her back in her own cell where she belongs!"

A surge of men pressed forward to take hold of me. I screamed, beating and kicking them, trying to gouge their eyes. Ivette appeared, red-faced at having let her charge slip away, and tried to capture my wrists; I struck her with a fist and knocked her to the ground. She glared up at me open-mouth as I stood over her, victorious...then steely arms wrapped around my middle and a hand clamped over my mouth and I was carried bodily, struggling and protesting, back to my confinement in the Gloriet tower.

The door slammed. The lock clicked. An additional wooden bolt fell to hold me fast.

I threw myself at the door, pounding in ceaseless rage until my hands bled, and then I fell on the floor, gasping and hysterical.

Darkness had come. Hell was free upon earth. The truth was clear.

My Uncle John was going to murder all the captive knights.

The days that followed were the worst of my life. I was kept locked in my chamber, with bowls of pottage and a flagon of weak beer pushed in through the door by one or other of my maids—though not Ivette, who either had resigned her position or was hiding in fear of my wrath. My bed linens were not changed; the floor remained unswept. I was grateful that the tower had its own privy chute at least, so that I would not suffer the indignities of a brimming chamber pot. Small mercies.

Through the narrow window-slit on the eastern wall, I eyed the activities taking place in the castle bailey. The servants seemed subdued, running about on their tasks with heads bowed. The stonemasons working on John's new building likewise huddled together in silence, not singing, whistling or laughing in their normal way.

I prayed that my suspicions were wrong, that the oubliette was only a temporary if unpleasant measure, a warning to John's enemies. Maybe Thomas the Clerk and Hugh de Neville had informed the de Blunville of nothing more sinister than the fact they were gathering the knights together prior to release. After all, Dorset lay near the coast—on a clear day, from the highest walls of Corfe I could see the shining blue of the sea in the distance. It might be, driven by fear and distrust, I had mistaken the gravity of the situation.

But then the sounds began...

They came slowly at first. A cry here, a cry there, a shout from the direction of the prison block. But as time went by, the noises escalated. Although the walls of Corfe were thick, the sound vibrated through the stonework, a dull, vibrating mutter. The sound of men begging for mercy, screaming and shouting in fear and panic.

The bailey was empty of servants. The masons had left their wooden platforms and gone to their temporary settlement outside the castle walls. John's own soldiers patrolled the walls and courtyard and kept all but the Constable away from the dungeons.

At the end of a week, the terrible sounds—the groans, the shrieks, the begging and the heartfelt prayers—has ceased. A deathly silence fell over Corfe Castle. But not for long. The gates, which had remained barred for days, ground open and a stream of wains poured in, piled high with poorly made wooden coffins. The carts halted in the bailey and the King's soldiers finally left their appointed positions and entered the dungeons.

Horrified, I turned away as the first limp corpse was dragged out into the light, gape-mouthed and bloody-handed where he had torn at the stones of his cell in final torment. Then my stomach heaved, and retching, I ran to the privy to void my guts.

The stench of death rose from the bailey, carried on the breeze, and hungry gulls began to shriek in delight, anticipating a meal.

I pressed my hands over my ears as tears ran down my cheeks.

After the dead knights were removed, things returned to what passed as normal at Corfe. No one spoke of the murdered men again; I knew not where their bodies were deposited, whether they were thrown in paupers' graves or borne by ship to their grieving families in France. To my surprise, Ivette returned to serve me, grumbling and gloomy, the fading yellow of the black eye I'd given her adding ugliness to her face.

Once again, I was permitted to pace the castle wall walk, feeling the ice-cold wind in my hair and the faint sun on my face, with Ivette shuffling a few paces behind and my keeper Stephen de Turnham, girt with his sword, watching from a discreet distance. I ate in the Great Hall, with others of the household, but I kept my eyes fixed on my trencher, for I could not bear that my every move was scrutinised.

To my surprise, Uncle John sent me money—a sum of five marks. I thought of flinging it over the walls for the poor to gather, but instead put it aside for a time when it might prove useful. John also sent a basket of figs and almonds; Ivette, despite her bony thinness, ate most of them. I think she believed they were her payment for looking after such a disagreeable prisoner.

Despite my captivity being a soft one, I was fretful and ill at ease. The people of Brittany were still fiercely loyal to our House and the deaths of the knights were likely to goad them into action. I had no more dreams of battles for a crown; I just wanted those loyal to Brittany to negotiate my freedom and Arthur's. Yes, my brother's claim to England and the French territories had perished at Mirabeau; he would have to kneel before our uncle and plead that his evil counsellors had led him astray, but if we made peace, Brittany could still be ours to rule, although we would be sworn vassals of John. We could dwell quietly in our own lands, avoiding the squabbles of our kinsmen as best we could...when the ransom was paid But there was no indication that any ransom was ever asked for by the King.

Shortly after Easter, I timidly asked Ivette if any news had arrived from my uncle's court regarding my future or my brother's. She eyed me suspiciously. "Why do you need to know? I am not sure if I should tell you anything. I do not want to incur his Grace the King's wrath. It is all hearsay, anyway."

I continued to pester, becoming more insistent, and finally, her patience worn thin, Ivette sent me to see Stephen de Turnham in the castle solar. "I must know what John plans for me," I said, with desperation, as Turnham's servants ushered me into the room, "before I go mad. I must know what his terms are for Arthur's release."

De Turnham folded his hands as if he were about to pray and released a long sigh. "My Lady, many things have happened in Normandy of late...."

"Exactly! And so you must tell me!"

He shifted uncomfortably from one foot to the other. "My Lady, I do not know how to put this...but...your brother Duke Arthur has disappeared..."

"Disappeared!" My heart started to hammer against my ribs. "You mean he escaped?"

"No." His voice was the toll of a mournful passing bell. "While held in Falaise, the King went to visit him, expecting him to seek clemency and mercy. John spoke to him sweetly, with promise of rewards if he would only bend his stiff neck to his rightful overlord. Arthur refused; he insisted his only ally was the French King and that he was Richard's true heir and would one day claim his kingdom. The King went into a towering rage, destroying the room around him. He ordered Arthur sent to the castle of Rouen...and then he vanished. No one will say where he might be, but there are many whispers. Many..."

Sickness clawed my belly; I felt the floor tilt beneath my feet. "I don't want to hear rumours. I want only the truth. I want to speak to the King himself!"

"His Grace will not permit you to travel so far from Corfe, Lady Eleanor, but I have heard he plans to return to England before the year is out. Petition him for an audience then."

Year's end! How could I possibly wait so long to find out the fate of my brother! Helpless tears prickled my lids; the torches in the room grew blurred and shaky.

"There is more, Lady." De Turnham began to pace the flagstones uneasily. "Would you like to sit?" He gestured me in the direction of a window embrasure.

I shook my head, gulping back my tears, as a princess should. "No. Just tell me what I must know."

"Your half-sister Lady Alix, daughter of Guy of Thouars…" he hesitated and again there was a lurch of sickness; I thought he would tell me the pretty little silver-haired baby I remembered was dead. Instead, he mumbled, scarcely audible, "She had been made Duchess of Brittany."

"What? What did you say?"

"Lady Alix is now the Duchess, with her father Guy as regent for the Duchy. The people of Brittany spoke for her. They feared that if you were acclaimed Duchess, King John would rule through you."

"Neither of us should bear the title of Duchess!" I cried miserably. "What of Arthur, their rightful Duke? You do not say he is dead, only missing. Unless I get proof my brother is no more, I refuse to believe he is dead. The King is a beast but surely he would not slay his brother's only son! If he has, I swear I will wreak vengeance…"

"Lady Eleanor…" De Turnham's eyes flashed. "I beg you use discretion in your words. There are many listeners here at Corfe, ready to report to the King. The matter of Arthur is…is a sensitive one… Now, I suggest you retire to your chamber. You have had a great shock and I will call the physician to administer to you. Let me escort you…" He held out his arm.

"I can manage on my own," I snapped before fleeing the solar, pushing aside an eavesdropping Ivette and my other two maids who were lurking in a niche.

I flung myself up the stairs to my room in the Gloriet tower and behind me the door was locked and barred, the guards gathering round in their usual formation. "Such a temperamental child..." I heard Ivette's waspish voice.

Resisting the urge to shout back an insult, I grasped a crucifix that hung on the wall and clutched it to me. Bursts of zigzag lights obscured my vision and my temples throbbed. I sobbed like a babe, certain I had offended God in some terrible way, for He had allowed my world, my fragile happiness, to be destroyed like a lightning blasted Tower.

That night I tossed and turned, moaning and groaning beneath the heavy counterpane. Troubled dreams assailed my sleep. I saw my father trampled by horses in a field of mire and blood. I saw Uncle Richard struck by a crossbow bolt at Chalus. I saw my mother, bloated with her final pregnancy, her hands weak and scarred by the leprous malady that sapped her strength. Last of all, however, I saw a little boat gliding upon a great dark river. I seemed to be riding in the boat, a ghost, invisible, one with the darkness. Overhead the moon hung, an unfriendly eye, its beams making a shimmery path along the black waters. On the far side of the river, a fortress rose like a clenched fist in the shadows, its walls aglow with an eerie blue corpse-light. Suddenly the waters parted, showering phosphorescence, and a beautiful lady emerged from the depths, white-gold hair flowing in coils to her knees, a robe of white samite flaring around her form. I knew at once that she was a Fae, a water faerie, well known in the legends of Brittany. "Arthur..." she called, her voice the bubbling of the river. "*Arthur*..." At that moment, I realised I was not alone in the boat. Two figures sat in the prow, the back of the nearest towards me, blocking my view of the other. I gasped as I recognised the closer figure as being that of John—a John hideous and bloated like a toad, crouched in feral menace. "Go...go to the watery witch!" he cried, and in his hand gleamed a bloody dagger. The boat rocked on the swell; my mouth opened in a soundless scream. My brother Arthur, gold and silver in the moonlight, blood flowing like red rain from myriad wounds, slid like a gutted fish into the currents, into the waiting arms of the water-Fae, away down to the weedy river-bed, where he was lost forever....

Panting and weeping, I awoke, the crucifix slick with sweat in my hands and the rain drumming on the parapet of the Gloriet Tower.

And so I would wake, day after day, as days slipped into months and months slipped into years...and my brother slipped into blessed memory...

Chapter Nineteen

England had an heir. The bells in Corfe castle tolled in joyous celebration when word came that Queen Isabella had safely birthed her first child, a boy named Henry after my grandfather. John, the proud father, was forty, and this was his first legitimate heir. (Bastards he had many; one natural daughter Joanna was even wed to a Prince of Wales.) I felt no happiness, however; my heart could not rejoice at the birth of this infant. It should have been Arthur's son that was born to much joy, a child with Marie of France. ...or my child.

My hands drifted down to touch my flat belly. I was still young—young enough to bear children but John gave no indication that I would ever be released or ransomed, let alone married. Any child of mine would prove a threat to his throne, and I would prove a threat also, for as long as I lived.

The joy that gripped the country at the birth of Henry did not last long. Shortly before, John had argued with Pope Innocent III about the appointment of Stephen Langton as Archbishop of Canterbury. Innocent insisted on his favourite, Langton, while John strenuously put forth his own choice, John de Gray, who had served him for many years. The monks of Christ Church in Canterbury had supported John's candidate at first, but eventually they bowed to the Pope's wishes and acclaimed Langton in an act that outraged the King. He sent the knights Fulk de Cantilupe and Reginald of Cornhill to chase the monks from their monastery, driving them across the channel to seek sanctuary at Saint Bertin's Abbey in Flanders.

The Pope was furious when he heard about John's treatment of the monks. He threatened to excommunicate de Cantilupe and Cornhill and tried to reason with John through the mediation of the bishops of London, Ely and Worcester. The bishops had approached their sovereign most humbly, grovelling on bended knee before his throne, but he reacted with customary fury, threatening to send any emissaries of the Pope back to Rome with their eyes put out and nostrils slit unless he was left in peace to choose his own Archbishop.

The violent quarrel continued until January when, unexpectedly, John appeared to capitulate. He cast his henchmen from their pilfered Canterbury lands and agreed to accept Stephen Langton as Archbishop. However, his compliance would come at a cost—if the Pope insisted on installing Langton, John wanted a guarantee that in future he alone would have the right to confer bishoprics in England.

That was a step too far for the Pope. John was attempting to wrench power from the Church, to rival the power of Rome with his own decrees.

Innocent called the Interdict down upon England.

Throughout the land, in every church and every chapel, every cathedral and every oratory, every monastery and every nunnery, the Interdict was proclaimed aloud to the horror of every man, woman and child. No masses would be said. No marriages would take place at the church door. Baptism could still be performed and the last rites administered to the dying—but the latter gave little comfort to the bereaved, for the dead could not find rest in consecrated soil. The bells in churches, abbeys and priories rang out one final time, a cheerless and mournful sound—and then they were silenced.

England became a godless country, where the King's minions seized the property and wealth of the clergy and locked up the church barns, placing them under armed guard. Men of evil intent ran wild, attacking priests, monks and nuns who dared to travel the lawless roads and robbing them off wealth, horses and sometimes their lives.

Hearing of the uproar in the world beyond Corfe's gates, for the first time I was glad to dwell behind those high, stern walls, even as a prisoner. I wondered what my grandmother who had died at Fontevraud in 1204, her wits having left her at the end, would have made of such unrest. I wondered if she would have regretted the choices she had made regarding her tyrannical son.

After the initial shock of the Interdict had worn off, however, the ever-resilient people of England began to adjust to the change. They went on as they always had, saying their prayers in secret, wedding their lovers by word of intent alone, and birthing babies that were hastily baptised. Death was harder to deal with since burial was forbidden in sanctified ground, but the bones of the departed could always be reinterred in the churchyard sometime in the future.

In these early days of the Interdict, which dragged on many years longer than it should have due to John's stubbornness, a strange and unexpected visitor arrived at Corfe. I was upon the walls, Ivette my unwelcome shadow, when I spied a party approaching the castle, wending their way across the green, undulating landscape. I saw the Lions of England. I saw the golden crescent and star.

Grasping the battlements with my hands, I leaned out dangerously far, my hair, lifted by the breeze, a flaming cloud on the wind. "Is the King coming?" I cried. "Is he coming here?" Fear and hope warred within my heart; fear that my spiteful uncle would visit further evil on me—hope that he might have changed his mind about my captivity. The latter seemed unlikely, though; word had come that the Bishops of Nantes, Cournouaille and Vannes had come to court to try and negotiate my release, but John had mocked and derided them before banishing them back to Brittany.

Ivette sidled up to me and peered over the breastwork. "You need not fear, Lady. His Grace is busy elsewhere. It is the Queen who comes."

"The Queen. Alone?" I was surprised. It was not long since she had birthed John's heir at Winchester; I hardly expected her to be travelling, especially without her husband.

"Why is she coming here?" I asked.

"It is not for you, or any of us, to ask that question, Lady," said Ivette loftily, her long, thin nose prodding the air.

I watched as the entourage reached the barbican, rode under the fangs of the portcullis. The Queen was out of view; she did not ride astride but lay within a heavily canopied litter. Burly soldiers stood to attention, five deep, pikes in hand, more than mere guards, almost as if...

"Is the Queen a prisoner?" I cried.

"Shush, be silent!" admonished Ivette, waving her hands. "Let it just be said...she is in secure custody here. Now come away, no one wants to see you prancing like a moon-mazed hare on the battlements."

Ignoring my despised lady-in-waiting's rudeness, I followed her back to the Gloriet tower. So, the beauteous and scandalous Isabella of Angouleme was at Corfe, and it seemed not of her own volition. What could she have done? I was eager to speak with her.

"Do you think I will be permitted to have an audience with the Queen?" I blurted.

Ivette frowned. "I do not know why you think she would see you. She will not help your cause; she is powerless."

Defeated again, I sank down upon the edge of my bed; Ivette departed, slamming the door behind her with finality. Below, in the Great Hall, musicians began to play and the murmur of voices drifted to my ears. On normal occasions, I was permitted to eat with the household, but the arrival of Isabella was clearly not considered a normal occasion and no one came to escort me to table.

My wish to meet the young Queen soon came true, however. She had hardly been at Corfe a day when one of her servants ascended the stairs of the Gloriet, a young lady-in-waiting with thick golden braids beneath a white fur hood. "What do you want here?" Ivette said, glaring. "You do know this is a forbidden area—the dwelling place of the King's royal prisoner?"

Despite her youth, the girl glared flinty-eyed at the older woman, and Ivette flushed and backed away beneath her arrogant stare. "I know very well who dwells with you, woman," she said. "I am Lady Isoud, chief lady-in-waiting of her Grace the Queen, and I come on a mission from her to the Lady Eleanor. The Queen wishes to meet with her dearest kinswoman-by-marriage."

Ivette sputtered. I smiled sweetly, gazing at Isoud over my gaoler's shoulder. "I would be most delighted to meet with her Grace, Lady Isoud. Most delighted indeed."

The Queen of England was not as I had expected. Tales of her beauty abounded, and I imagined her to embody the feminine ideal, willowy and golden-tressed, with skin the hue of milk and roses—a more northern Helen of Troy, who was so beautiful kings and lords all desired to steal her for their own. Instead, I found myself faced with a tiny woman, less than average height, with a pert, heart-shaped face and a small, shapely mouth. Her eyes were very large and expressive, ringed by long curling lashes; a thick, glossy dark braid trailed from beneath the diaphanous veils of her headdress.

"So...you are the Lady Eleanor, my husband's cousin." Isabella sat on a chair in the royal apartments, clad in regal red with gold trim gleaming on her floor-length sleeves.

I bobbed a curtsey. "Yes, your Grace."

"I always wondered what you were like. I heard they called you 'the Pearl of Brittany' at one time. The name was well chosen; you are very fair to behold."

"Was, your Grace," I said. "I know not if I am still fair enough to bear such a flattering title."

"You are," she said, "despite the misfortunes that have befallen you. It is not just what has happened, Eleanor, although I do agree with my husband that Arthur had to be...removed."

I winced but kept my peace. I did not want to make an enemy of Isabella. I had enough enemies.

"I would intercede for you, if I could, Eleanor." The Queen spread out her hands; they were long-fingered, graceful and white, with carefully manicured nails. "But I doubt John would listen to me. Especially not now. Why do you think I am at Corfe?"

I shook my head, not daring to guess.

Isabella continued. "John and I quarrelled…bitterly. There was a scene at Marlborough Castle. Over one of his many trulls…Oh, this one was the wife of Hugh de Neville, the Constable, and she wasn't particularly willing, but what woman would dare refuse the King? She even offered two hundred chickens as a fine just so she could have one night in her own husband's bed!" Isabella let out a ringing laugh. "I was living at Marlborough too, and the situation was humiliating for me. I do not care much what John does or with whom, but not under my nose. I will not have the court mocking me! So I confronted him and when he laughed in my face…I scratched his cheek with my nails." She lifted those fine hands with their pointed tips again and smiled with satisfaction.

"You scratched the King of England!"

She laughed again. "My erring husband. But mayhap I should not laugh. He had packed me off to Corfe in close custody, and I know not how long his anger towards me will last. Perhaps he is tired of me; I have grown older and am no longer the pretty toy he liked to dandle. I have done my duty and produced an heir; perhaps he has no further use for me. Not so long ago, he took away my rights to Queen's Gold and had the sum paid directly to the Exchequer."

"I am sure he will forgive you soon enough. You are his wedded wife after all; the people would not countenance their Queen locked away."

"You may be right." Isabella laid her hand on her belly. "John also does not know it yet, but I carry another child. A man needs more than one son, especially if he is a King."

"Will you tell him?"

"Eventually. At the moment, to speak honestly, I am rather pleased to spend some time away from my husband."

Isabella stayed at Corfe until her belly began to show beneath her sumptuous gowns. Then one day she called me to the royal apartments;

servants were rushing about dismantling the bed and taking down tapestries.

"John has called for me, at last," she said. "I am not completely in favour with him as yet—I am not rejoining him, only being moved to Devizes Castle for the birth of my next child. John is not so far away, though; he frequents Marlborough often, and the hunting lodge at Odiham. When I see him, I will plead your case as much as I can. I fear it will not do much, but who knows? Maybe it will help a little. Maybe the birth of a new prince, if it is a prince, will sweeten his mood."

A few months after Isabella's departure for Devizes and the birth of her second son, Richard, I received a gift...from John. It was a beautiful saddle with gilded reins and scarlet ornamentation. Hands on hips, Ivette looked on disapprovingly, as I examined it. "So, he is going to let you ride out," she said. "Very bold and kindly of his Grace. Do not do anything foolish, Lady Eleanor. You may not enjoy imprisonment, but if you fled into the depths of Dorset, God only knows what evil would befall. Wild people dwell beyond these walls and they are even wilder without the strictures of God to keep them on the straight and narrow."

"I will stay close to my attendants," I promised. Even had I changed my mind, no possibility existed of escape. John's knights accompanied my every move on their powerful coursers. Even so, it was a pleasure to ride out amidst the dew-drenched hills, to travel to Swanage town and see the ships passing in and out of the harbour. One day, God willing, I would take one of those ships to freedom...

And when I returned to Corfe—dare I call that looming castle home?—fine dishes would await me in the hall. Queen Isabella must have mentioned a paucity of courses to the King and now I was supplied with not only bread, ale, mutton and pork but also sole, butter, beef, honey, egrets, herrings and conger eels. I had to do leagues of wall-walking to make certain my middle did not expand!

The next year brought two new visitors to Corfe. Two more prisoners, actually—the Princesses Margaret and Isobel of Scotland. Isobel was only fourteen, and in tears when she arrived; her elder sister Margaret, who went by the name Marjory, was sixteen, sullen and rebellious, pushing the guards out of her way when they stepped too near. At first, they were sequestered in the newest apartments the King had built, far from the Gloriet tower, but eventually we were permitted to meet in the castle gardens.

"How can you bear it here?" Isobel blurted out. "I heard the bad King murdered many men in this place."

"Isobel, be silent," Marjory hissed. "We must not be foolish and swift in speech."

I nodded in agreement. "Yes, it is best to keep silent, Isobel. Many listen to our words here, and will report back to John."

"Does he come here much?" asked Isobel, terrified. "I have heard he is a great ogre, huge and hulking with yellowed teeth."

I laughed, pulling both princesses into the lee of a flowering bush for privacy. "No, he's not an ogre. He's a fat little man."

Isobel giggled, putting her hand to her mouth to curb the sound.

"His belly is very big, like a woman with child…." I extended my arms out before me to show them the expanse of John's paunch.

Even Marjory smiled now, though she glanced nervously over her shoulder.

"And when he screams in rage and gnaws the rushes, his face goes as red as a bawling babe's…"

Both girls laughed together, but Isobel quickly sobered. "You didn't answer my question, Lady Eleanor. Does he come here often?"

"He comes every now and then, now that the builders have finished their work," I told the Scottish princesses, "for he enjoys the hunt in the forests of Dorset. But he never asks to see me, not even to gloat. And I am grateful for it."

"My father William the Lion said we must beware, for John is known to be lustful and has many mistresses," said Marjory. "But what hope have we, mere maidens, should his eye fall upon us?"

"We'll tell him we mean to be nuns!" exclaimed Isobel.

"Don't be such a silly goose!" Marjory rolled her eyes. "Not only would he not believe us—remember, they have the Interdict in England. We can't become nuns."

Isobel crossed herself piously. "I forgot. A godless land…"

I did not blame her for saying what many felt, but a pang of sorrow struck my heart. England was not the country of my birth but I had spent much time here, and by my blood, with Arthur dead, it should have been mine to rule. As Queen, I would not have defied the Pope and harmed my people.

"Hush!" Marjory put a finger to her lips. "That black-visaged old crow is coming…Ah, I apologise, Lady Eleanor. Your lady-in-waiting."

"You may call her whatever you like, Marjory. Ivette is no friend of mine. Or yours, I dare say."

Moments later, Ivette crashed her way between the lavender bushes and the beds of growing herbs. "It is time for you all to retire to your chambers. I also bring news—his Grace the King will be paying us a visit in the near future. He wishes to see his latest guests."

Isobel uttered a frightened little cry; Marjory nudged her with an elbow.

Cold dread gnawed my innards; I feared Isobel might be correct about his dishonourable intentions. My grandfather frequently took his wards to his bed; why would John spare hostages that shame? I tried to tell myself it was no business of mine; that my own situation was as precarious as theirs.

But, being their elder, I felt a stab of protectiveness, especially for young Isobel, who was clearly frightened of John.

My brother was now beyond my protection, but these two innocent girls were not.

John sent us a present, shortly before his grand entrance at Corfe—a sweetener, I thought, which made me even more suspicious of his motives. All three of his royal prisoners were given green robes, cloaks of lambskin, and thin, lacy slippers. My robes were of cambric and arrived with a matching cloak and a hat trimmed with miniver.

"All clad in green, we look like three sisters!" said Isobel, smoothing down her new gown with her hands. So pretty...so innocent.

"No, we look like prisoners," I said, "all identical, marking us out from the other women of his court. Marking us out, just as distinctive hats and garments mark out Jews. And look at our new slippers—so thin we would not be able to run away without our feet being cut to ribbons on stones."

The day of the King's visit rolled around. Banners were unfurled and clarions called, their brazen shouts echoing from tower to tower as the royal procession wound its way up the steep hill, surrounded by locals prodded to cheer by the King's henchmen, who circled their coursers ominously behind them.

John was riding a white stallion caparisoned in gold. He had been hunting prior and his dogs ran around the horse's legs. His falconer was trudging at his side, in conversation with the King about his newest acquisition, a handsome, fierce-eyed gyrfalcon, which sat brooding on its handler's gloved wrist. I noted the Queen was not present.

In the bailey Isobel, Marjory and I lined up near to Constable de Blunville, the chamberlain and the chief steward in order to greet the monarch. We dropped deep curtseys as John passed, and he reined in his steed, admiring us with those hot, probing eyes I knew too well. "My beloved cousins and my dear niece of Brittany," he said. "I see my gifts to you have arrived—they suit you well. You will join us in the banquet in the Great Hall."

Escorted by our ladies-in-waiting and the usual milling host of guards, we proceeded to the hall. The steward seated us surprisingly close to the King's dais, considering we were prisoners. Every now and then, John turned his dark head to look over and smile—if that quirking of his over-red lips could be called a smile.

I tried to ignore John's glances as the courses were served—the first time we had sat in close proximity since Arthur's capture and disappearance. Instead, I concentrated intently on the chilled strawberry soup and honey-mustard eggs, the salmon and bream served in tissue-thin silver foil, the venison pies shaped like crowns and topped by glazed fruits, the enormous centrepiece seal brought from the coast and baked in saffron and butter.

However, after the last course arrived, John clapped his hands and called for entertainment. First came a conjurer, dressed as a wiseman from Araby—he did tricks using sleight of hand and dazzled the room when it seemed a dove burst from his hands and soared up to the roof beams. I was sure that he'd secreted the bird in his flowing sleeves but laughed and clapped nonetheless. A series of tumblers, vaulters and nimble ropedancers, many of them female and wearing shamefully revealing garb, followed him on. John was appreciative, roaring with laughter and tossing coins and the occasional small gemstone in their direction.

Mercifully, a troupe of musicians soon replaced the last outlandish acts, and dancers from amidst the spectators filtered into the centre of the hall. I was horrified, however, when John rose from his seat and joined the dancers, beckoning young Isobel to join him.

I then lost track of what was happening for Hubert De Burgh, one of John's favourites, was bowing before my seat and asking to dance, and before I knew what was happening, I was dragged out amidst the dancers in their sweeping robes and glittering jewels.

Hubert de Burgh stood partnering me, a small man with a sad, dark countenance and bushy brows. He was not very old but his face bore signs of strain and worry. "I have always wished to meet you, my Lady," he whispered, bending near to my ear. "The opportunity was never there till now."

I said nothing, feeling suddenly sick. Had John promised me to his loyal man? But no, de Burgh was married to Beatrice de Warenne. It could not be that.

"I see you are perplexed, as well you might be. I must tell you about …Arthur."

I stumbled, missing the dance steps and elbowing a woman near me, who gasped in outrage and cast me an evil look. "You wish…you wish to…" I gasped.

"Yes." He leaned close to me again, his mouth just brushing my hair. "I just want you to know…I was his gaoler in Falaise."

My belly twisted. "And you dare to speak to me. You are as foul as my uncle. Have you come merely to torment?"

"Lady Eleanor, I pitied Arthur. I tried to help the young Duke as much as I could. John sent orders that he be blinded and castrated…"

I choked back a cry, almost crashing into yet another dancer. I hoped the others in the room would merely think I'd had too much wine and not heard the most terrible particulars of my brother's death.

"It was not done!" De Burgh hissed, stepping around me to the cadence of the music. "I refused such barbarity but pretended to the King that the job was done. The news went out, rumours spread…"

A sudden, terrible hope bubbled up inside my brain. *Could it be…*

Hubert must have seen what dwelt in my eyes, for he hastily shook his head. "John was furious when he learned the truth; he raved so much, I feared not only for my position but my very life. I was fortunate, however; the King was focussed only on Arthur. It was then he was sent on to Rouen, and there he…"

"Disappeared?" I said, voice laden with sarcasm and anger.

"Met his end." De Burgh cast down his sad, tired eyes "Although I swear I know not by what means. A rumour reached me that fishermen found his body in the river, many miles downstream from Rouen and recognising it, bore it to Bec Abbey, the resting place of your ancestress, the great Queen Maude. Remember, though, it is only a rumour."

"Why have you told me this, in this manner?" The dance required I turn my back to de Burgh; I did so gladly for, quivering with wrath and sorrow, I could not face him.

"You deserve to know the truth of the matter," said de Burgh. "Also that many disapprove of John's treatment of Arthur…and your continued incarceration."

"Yet you still support John."

"I still support John. He has given me great honours and I do think a man should rule a country, not a boy. And certainly not a woman."

"Even if the man proves a tyrant?" The vielle à roué gave one final wheezing squeal and I was scurrying away from my unwelcome dance partner, only to find my arm clutched by Marjory of Scotland. She dragged me aside, leaving de Burgh lost within the moving crowd.

"Eleanor, what can I do? The King has gone from the hall, taking Isobel with him. She is too timid and naïve to protest…and he is a King. What shall I do? I swore to my father that I would protect her!"

I had no idea what to do myself, but since I had taken on some kind of maternal role to the two hostage princesses, I was determined to assist. John would not claim another victim. "I will go find her. You stay here and wait, Marjory. Where did they go?"

Marjory pointed with a shaking hand toward a side corridor. Grasping a handful of my skirts to keep them from impeding my ankles, I raced in the direction Marjory indicated. The corridor was dark; the torches had gone out sometime during the banquet. I felt my way along in the gloom, hand falling on chill stone. I prayed I would find John and Isobel before he managed to reach his chamber. Once the door was locked from within…

Ahead, I spied the dance of a torch flame, heard the deep murmur of a man's voice followed a nervous, high-pitched giggle, a laugh that sounded more hysterical than merry.

Isobel.

I could now hear the male voice clearly, smooth yet wheedling: "I can make your confinement so much easier here at Corfe, do you understand me, little Bel? If I get what I desire, so shall you. And why not? What else have you to fill your time? Think of it as an honour. A great honour."

"Your Grace," said Isobel. "I am of royal blood, even as you are. It would not be honourable for a princess to hand out her virtue lightly, even to become paramour to a mighty King."

John's tone changed from wheedling to anger. "As I can make your life better here, I can also make it worse. Why you should be so intransigent is beyond me. Do you want to end up like my niece Eleanor, drying up with age like a plucked flower? If it is bearing a bastard you fear, I swear I would acknowledge it…"

I burst into the ring of torchlight. John had Isobel pressed into a niche in the wall, his legs spread apart, blocking her escape. "Lady Isobel," I cried, thinking quickly, "you must attend the Lady Marjory at once. She...she has fallen ill." I prayed Isobel would believe my lie and play along.

"Ill?" wailed Isobel, slumping against the wall

"Yes...it...it was the seal at table. Too rich..."

"Let the physics tend to her!" snarled John.

"She calls out for her sister Isobel. Can you not understand how frightened she is, Uncle, a hostage in a strange country?"

"I must go!" cried Isobel and as John turned to glare at me, she slipped beneath his arm and vanished into the vastness of the castle.

I was left in the gloomy passage with my uncle the King. The man who had ordered the mutilation of my brother. The man behind his disappearance. The man whose base desires I had just thwarted.

"So...you have taken it upon yourself to interfere where you're not wanted," John growled. Deep brown eyes took on the horrible reddish gleam I had noticed years ago, making him once again seem inhuman, devilish. The Pope had excommunicated him in 1209—had Satan now claimed him utterly, this scion of the Devil's Brood?

"I was wanted. Marjory wanted me to find her sister." It was no lie.

"And when you found her, instead of minding your own business, you decided to 'save' her virtue and interfere with the rights of your monarch."

"Perhaps I was saving you, John," I said. "The girls may be hostages but if you harm them while their father has kept the peace, there will be outright war between England and Scotland. Cities and towns will burn."

"I wasn't going to harm her," John scowled, crossing his arms over his barrel chest.

"I dare say her father would consider being dishonoured as harm..."

"Maybe you are jealous...and want me for yourself. Hmm, is that it, girl? Is that why you chased that little chit away? Does your long captivity, your forced chastity, make you burn for a man's touch?" Suddenly he grabbed me, pulling me in against him. Wine and spices reeked on his breath.

"Sire! You are my Uncle! This is...wrong!"

"Right and wrong can be dispensed with under the cover of night...or the sheets." He pawed at me. "I have always thought you fair, if wilful. But often wilful women are the best to make the two-backed beast."

185

"Let me go!" I shrank back as his hand clamped on my breast, squeezing roughly. "I would sooner die than swive the man who murdered my…"

"Stop, Eleanor!" His hand dropped from my bodice but his face thrust into mine, huge and grotesque. Spittle struck my cheek. "Do not say it, woman. Do not say it…or…" His fist curled, winking with rubies and emeralds. He could smash my jaw with one blow, I knew that—and the rings would rend my flesh like tiny daggers. My mouth snapped shut. My eyes filled with unshed tears of fear and rage.

John flung himself away from me. "Bah! What possessed me? Just looking at you snivelling has the effect of cold water thrown on my loins! Go back to your chamber, bitch. You will spend plenty of time there, for I tell you now, I have no plans to ever set you free. Your only freedom will be when they bear you to your grave!"

He stormed down the passageway and breathing a sigh of relief, I slumped trembling against the wall. When I had regained my equilibrium and sought out the safety of the Gloriet, to my shock I found Ivette packing my meagre possessions into a wooden chest. "What are you doing?" I asked.

"King's orders." She roughly flung my shoes and kirtles, screwed into a ball, into the bottom of the chest. "You seem to have displeased him. You are going on a little tour of the King's castles, I believe."

So I was sent from Corfe to Brough in the far north, the ancient Roman fort of Veterae, where the King's man Robert de Vieuxpont held sway. William of Scotland had burnt the castle down in my grandfather's time and although it had been rebuilt, still its grounds showed red with burning and I fancied I could scent blood upon the fierce northern wind. I had no sooner settled there than de Vieuxpont had me removed to another fortress where he governed—lonely Bowes, also once a Roman fort, its walls brooding darkly above the swift-flowing River Greta. My removal there may have been a stab at me personally—Bowes belonged to the Earl of Richmond, and Richmond was the only title I was still permitted to use. My imprisonment in that remote stone block was reasonably brief, however; without any warning, my goods were packed anew and I was taken to Gloucester, Marlborough and finally Bristol, where I tarried a while, listening to the gulls squabble on the metal parapets as I sat confined in the squat castle keep. At every stop I made along my route, the governor of the town paraded me to the locals like a fine prize horse, just to prove to them that Eleanor, Countess of Richmond, rightful heiress of Brittany, would-be claimant to England, was still alive and had not suffered the fate of her brother Arthur.

My ignominious travels from castle to castle made me bone-weary but at least, as I found out later, I had a certain little success, a tiny victory over John. My uncle had heeded my words at our last fateful meeting. Although he visited Corfe many times in my absence, the King never bothered Isobel or Marjory of Scotland again.

Chapter Twenty

The King had ordered me returned to Corfe. Something was brewing. I was told nothing of what it might be, nor were Isobel and Marjory, but we all witnessed a flurry of activity throughout the household and new supplies were sent to the guardroom. Ivette refused to say anything at first but after pressure told me that new prisoners were on their way.

"They won't enjoy the privileges you do," she said as she tussled with the lacings on my gown in her usual rough, perfunctory way. "They are headed straight for the oubliette."

Memories of the dead knights' groans and screams loomed like haggard phantoms in my mind. "Jesu, no! Not again. Who?"

"A woman…a great Lady," sniffed Ivette.

"A great Lady for the dungeon? Surely, you must be mistaken. Even if she has committed some crime, women are not treated so."

"It is indeed a woman. Do you want to know who?" Ivette taunted. She did not wait for me to answer. "It is Maude de St Valery, William de Braose's wife."

Startled, I pulled away from her. "Maude de Braose!"

"Yes, and her son William."

"But why? Last I heard William de Braose was one of the King's favourites." My mind reeled, remembering the coarse, leering man leading my brother in chains. Leading him to imprisonment and death.

"No longer. He owed his Grace much money, and the King began to suspect his motives. He was a fool in Ireland and raised a rebellion to reclaim castles the Crown had taken. He burnt half of Leominster and killed men in the royal garrison there. But Maude did a worse thing…" Ivette grinned; the barber-surgeon had recently extracted a front tooth and the hole gaped, dark and ugly. "The King asked for members of the huge de Braose brood as hostages for their parents' good behaviour. And do you know what the wicked hussy said?"

"I have no idea."

"She said she would send no members of her family to a man who murdered his own nephew."

I let out a gasp. Ivette pursed her lips disapprovingly. "Oh, Lady Eleanor, you have had years to come to terms with what happened to your brother…"

Hastily I regained control of my emotions. It would not do to let her see any weakness. "What happened then?"

"The King got word of her insolence, of course. He pursued Maude to Ireland and beyond. John's distant kinsman, Duncan of Carrick, eventually captured along with Maude's daughter Annora, her son William, and his wife and children. They were taken to Bristol Castle. You were brought back to Corfe to make room for them."

"Wasn't I the fortunate one?" I said mockingly.

Ivette ignored me and continued her tale. "At Bristol the silly trull tried to bargain with John. First, she offered 40,000 marks for her freedom, then reneged on that offer, then increased the amount when the King's looks grew black. William de Braose was forced to vouch that the money would duly reach John's treasury but before any further demands could be made, the knave slipped off to France, leaving Maude with no wealth to pay the debt. She had the temerity to tell the King he would see not see one penny of the money and so, as punishment, she is being brought here with her son. She'll cool her famous temper in the oubliette. The termagant Maude de Valery has met her match at last..."

The prison cart rattled into the bailey under armed guard. Indeed, so many soldiers were protecting it, one would think they expected Maude de St Valery to gain magical powers and burst from the cart, swinging her fists like a pugilist. Maybe they thought she might—I had heard tales of how the Welsh, who loathed her harsh rule on the Marches, called her Mad Moll and claimed she was a giantess who built Hay Castle in one night with stones she carried in her apron...

However, though tall and well-made, the woman who emerged was no giantess, merely a female of middle years clad in rumpled garments and dusty wimple. A brown-haired youngish man followed her, limping in leg-irons. The pair was hurried toward the prison tower; the doors shut firmly behind them.

At first, I endeavoured to ignore the plight of these unfortunates. Maude de St Valery, wife to a man I despised, was no concern of mine. Surely, she would come to no real harm. John, though undoubtedly cruel, would not murder a woman of rank, surely. He was trying to break her spirit, to instil fear, to get at her husband William through Maude...

I found I could not believe my own rationalisations.

I had to attempt to see Maude.

Swiftly I made my way to the chamber of the Constable, Sir William de Blunville. He eyed me suspiciously, as he always did, but at least without the hostility he had displayed in the past. "Lady Eleanor, what do you here? I am busy. Where is your lady, Ivette? Or your keeper, Stephen de Turnham?"

"I slipped away when the old besom was in the privy. As for Sir Stephen, I heard he was abed with a sore head—too much drink yestereven. Fear not, Sir William, I am not about to make a mad rush for the gates. Running in a dress and tiny slippers is rather difficult, you know."

He bit back a slight smile; when I saw that, hope leapt in me. "How may I help you, then, Lady?"

"The prisoners. I wish to see them."

He shook his head. "Difficult."

"I saw the last ones. I did not loose them all to kill the household in their beds, did I?"

"No…" Again, the tight, almost imperceptible smile. Perhaps he had learnt through the years to trust me. A little. "But I do remember you screamed and acted the wildcat at their just punishment by the King."

I flushed but refused to show him my discomfort. I dared not react in anger or I would lose my chance here. "It is Christian charity that motivates me, Sir William. Is that not a laudable thing?"

"Very. Or so the religious claim."

"So you will let me see them?"

He sighed. "I do not want another scene, and Christ knows, your life is restricted enough. I fail to see what harm you could do. Do as you did before under de Turnham's eye. A few minutes and naught more. If the prisoners need anymore Christian charity, I will send them a priest."

With a solitary guard tramping at my back, I entered the dungeon area of the castle, half a loaf of bread and a few dried figs secreted in my voluminous sleeves. I had not set foot in the prison since my knights were murdered—it seemed an eternity ago. Once again, I shivered as dank air assailed my nostrils and bleak, slimy stone rose on either side, the heavy weight of the tower's stonework bearing down oppressively overhead.

On the floor, the bars of grate covering the dreaded oubliette gleamed in the half-light. I knelt on the ground, folding my skirts beneath me. The guard William de Blunville had sent loomed over me,

190

slack-jawed, clutching his sword. He could have been the oaf Guyon's twin.

"Away!" I ordered, attempting to sound authoritative. "You do not need to stand over me wagging those great ears of yours. You have a sword as defence and the prisoners are under lock and key."

Reddening, the soldier stepped back into the concealing shadows of the nearby corridor. Leaning further over the bars crisscrossing the oubliette, I strained to see down into the darkness below. Eventually, I made out the dim shapes of a woman and a man crouched at the bottom of the foetid pit.

"Lady Maude," I called softly.

A soft rustle of cloth and strain. A faint voice. "Who goes?"

Quickly, I sprang up and pulled down one of the nearby torches, bringing it close to the grate. Illuminated by the wavering flame, I peered down again and saw a broad, handsome face smeared with dirt below a once-white wimple. Maude was standing, gazing up, her chained hands crossed before her. The man, her son William, also glanced up but did not rise, perhaps was not able to; his countenance bore bruises where the guards had beaten him.

"Who are you?" repeated Maude de St Valery. Her voice was deep, husky, commanding. I remembered another story that said she stalked around her Welsh castles wearing armour like a man.

"Eleanor of Brittany."

A moment's silence fell. Maude and her son glanced at each other. "What do you want?" Maude asked suspiciously.

What did I want? I could convince myself all I liked that I was there for pity's sake, to comfort the wretched, as a Christian maiden should, but it would be a falsehood. I wanted to know, finally, the absolute truth about Arthur's fate. Not from fey dreams, not from Hubert de Burgh's guess, but from one who truly knew. Her husband had been my brother's captor and taken him to Falaise…

I hesitated a moment, not wishing to seem crass. "Have you eaten?"

"A rind of bread," she said, "between us both."

I dropped the food from my sleeve through the bars. Maude and William snatched it up and thrust it into their mouths, slobbering, wild as beasts. "My thanks," said Maude, once she was done. She looked ashamed, wiping saliva from the edges of her mouth.

"I know why you are imprisoned. I know what you said to King John. About your children being taken as hostages. About my brother, Arthur…"

"Arthur," she hissed between clenched teeth. "Would that my husband had never laid eyes on the boy."

"What is the truth, Maude? Please tell me. I know he is dead but here only rumour and supposition, even from the likes of Hubert de Burgh. I need to know the truth. It haunts me every waking hour."

Maude's hands clenched into tight fists; nails dug into flesh. "My husband was there when Arthur was taken to Rouen…when Arthur was killed. Although he was a hard man, he did not take part; you must believe me on that. Arthur was destined for the King alone…"

"What happened?" My head grew light; I fought for control. The truth, this is what I always wanted. I would have to accept it in all its awfulness.

"It was Easter, that holy time, although John knows little of holiness, God curse him to hell. John was drunk, stinking drunk, staggering about and clutching a tankard like some varlet in a seaside tavern. His temper began to rise; it was as if the Devil himself possessed him. With the aid of his henchman Peter de Maulay, he hauled Arthur from his cell and laughed and mocked him. He then said that perhaps the night air would cool his head and he would take a boat ride on the river—surely, his loving nephew would wish to come? Arthur was fearful; he knew John's actions were not those of a sane man, but when he resisted de Maulay and others grabbed him, all laughing and drunk. They dragged him to the postern gate and roaring with mirth, John climbed into a little boat moored on the riverside. Arthur was thrown in beside him and the henchmen paddled it out into the swell of the Seine. Once they were at the deepest point of the river, John drew his sword and ran Arthur through. A great weight was tied to his body and he was cast into the river."

"So it was true…as in my dream. The river took him."

"Yes. The river took him, God rest his young soul."

"And your husband, what did he do while my brother was murdered?" My voice cracked. "You say he took no part, but why then was he there? I know his past, Lady; William de Braose had the Welsh lords murdered at Abergavenny Castle and chased down one of their sons, a child of seven, and slew him."

"I do not deny these deeds, but Arthur was different. My husband wanted money or offices for his capture; he received little. He would not join in drunken killing unless there was something of value in it for him. There was nothing. I do not say William is kindly or beyond murder but…"

"But it has to benefit him." I closed my eyes

After several moments, I regained my equilibrium and leaned forward again; the broad, pale face, a white moon in the murk, bore an expression of true sorrow. "Lady Maude, I think you have been honest with me. I thank you. Your husband's deeds are not yours to atone for anyway. I will attempt to help you—perhaps I could write to…to the Queen."

"There will be no time for that, I fear. Unless a reprieve comes in the next day or two, William and I will die here."

"John is hasty in anger but you are a woman. He would not kill you just for imprudent words and a debt."

"Would he not?" said Maude. "I fear he grows yet harsher as the years pass. He swore I would not survive without payment of a mighty sum, more than any noble could afford. My husband cannot pay this fine…and he has fled to France."

"Surely, there is something that can be done."

"Just pray for me, Lady Eleanor. Pray for my blameless son William. Pray that our deaths will come swiftly with as little pain as possible. Now go! I have told you all I know. I merely wish now to contemplate God and beg forgiveness for my sins before the end."

Picking up my skirts, I ran, the guard clanking after me, a puzzled expression on his dullard's face. Reaching my chamber, I took my Crucifix, worn smooth by my fingers over many days, many years, kissed it and prayed that Maude de St Valery and her son would receive a reprieve from the King.

It was not to be. Eleven days they lasted in the oubliette, down in the forgotten pit, foul as hell, where rats rustled through the bones of men and no sunlight ever touched.

But they could not last forever. When William de Blunville sent men into the dungeon, they found the mother and son clinging to each other, dead. Maude was seated between her son's legs, leaning against his chest, while he slumped back against the wall.

Having outlived her child, demented with the desperate pangs of starvation, in her final agonies she had eaten the flesh from the younger William de Braose's cheeks.

Chapter Twenty One

After Maude de St Valery's death, John seemed to go mad. Truly mad. It was as if my uncle railed against the entire world and wished to punish it for its perceived crimes against him. He began to persecute England's Jews, which was strange and unexpected; for he had protected them once, naming them 'his property.' When some miscreant violently robbed a Jew in the first years of his reign, he admonished the Mayor of London, saying 'If I have given my peace even to a dog, I expect that peace to be inviolable. So too the Jews."

Now he was ordering the arrest of all Jews and confiscating the ledgers that held the details of their wealth. Bringing the Jewish leaders to Bristol, he raged at them for withholding money that rightfully belonged to the Crown. Isaac of Canterbury was hanged by the neck until dead and one Jew of Bristol had his teeth painfully extracted with pincers one by one until he handed over all he owned to the King's commissioners.

The Papal legate arrived in England to attempt to make peace with John but the King refused the Pope's terms during a great council held at Northampton. In a letter, the Pope warned John that his increasingly erratic behaviour would cause his downfall, but the thinly veiled threat of deposition only made my uncle angrier and more stubborn.

Having robbed the Jews and the monastic houses of England, he decided to cross the Channel in an attempt to reclaim territories he had lost to Philip of France. His invasion never happened, however, for Wales was set ablaze by the renewed fury of its native princes—including Llywellyn, who had wed John's own bastard daughter Joanna. Castles fell along the border, their towers split by sappers like over-ripe fruit; whole garrisons were slaughtered and hewn bodies left in the burnt wreckage of once-great strongholds.

John dared not fare abroad with such trouble brewing at home. Instead, he fastened his malevolent eyes on Wales. Riding like the wind to his favourite castle of Nottingham, the tyrant dined in the Hall and then, fully refreshed and brimming with venom, brought out twenty-eight hostages that Llywellyn had granted him some months ago.

One by one, he paraded them along the castle's sheer walls. One by one, he hung them.

The last one to fall, legs kicking as the rope tightened on his throat, was a boy of only eight....

John's cruelty was beginning to rebound upon him. Whispers proliferated, even at Corfe, that his own barons were waiting to murder him. The servants, gossiping in hall and kitchens, imparted the latest rumours with a mixture of relish and fear—"*The King is going to be deposed. Simon de Montfort the Elder, terror of heretics, shall be elected King soon!*' '*The treasury has been raided by corsairs!*' '*Raiders burnt Marlborough, ravished the Queen and slew the poor baby prince Richard!*'

None of these things was true, and Constable de Blunville and his steward firmly rebuked anyone caught spreading such lies, but when one rumour was scotched, it seemed another took its place...

Like a mad dog, John now turned viciously on men who had once supported his cause. He feared they all plotted against his life. The Barons Fitzwalter and de Vescy, whose wives and daughters had been dishonoured by the King, were chief suspects in the supposed plot. The powerful Richard de Clare, Earl of Hertford, was another. There was also Earl David of Huntingdon, brother of the Scottish King, who was forced to relinquish the castle of Fotheringhay and give over his second son as a hostage.

The stripping of lands and castles from these great magnates did not solve John's problems—they only compounded them.

And then there was Peter of Wakefield.

Peter the Hermit, poor and unlettered, who was said to have the Sight, who claimed to have had a vision in which Jesus was a golden-haired child who called out, "*Peace, Peace, Peace*!" Peter, who made the fatal and treasonous mistake of predicting the King would be deposed on Ascension Day the following year, on the fourteenth anniversary of John's Coronation. "He will hand his crown to another," he had told a listening crowd, and the rumour spread all over England, even as the others had.

John heard tell of these tales, of how men believed or wanted to believe God would smite him down, and now Peter and his blameless son were in chains and heading for Corfe as prisoners.

Wretchedness engulfed me as I watched the spectacle of this poor simple man being brought into the bailey. Not even given the dignity of a cart, he struggled along between his gaolers, his hair a wild bush, his eyes rolling, his shoes in tatters and mud clumped on his legs. His son, a youth of about seventeen summers, staggered after him, looking lost and afraid.

I was foolish but I could not hold my tongue—what had I to lose? "This man is not a traitor, nor is he some kind of prophet. He is clearly mad. He should be pitied, not imprisoned."

"King's orders," grunted the burly oaf who guarded him.

"I know my uncle is seldom merciful but surely even he knows the gibbering of a moon-mad soul cannot harm him!"

"The rumours about Ascension Day have spread to France." Ivette sidled up to me like a wizened ghoul, lips in their usual sour pout. "The King is embarrassed. The miscreant gets what he deserves, in my opinion."

"My uncle plans to starve the poor wretch, like my poor knights and Maude de Valery?"

Ivette shook her head. "No, he keeps this one alive...until the day the prophecy is set to come true. Is that not kind of his Grace? For if the loon is indeed a soothsayer, then he will go free, for John will lose his crown. If he does not, of course..." She shrugged.

"Oh, get away from me, you evil harridan," I said. "You are like a blood-sucking fly."

The next few months passed with the land in turmoil. All residents in Corfe were filled with fear, save me, and perhaps the unfortunate Peter the Hermit, who sang hymns from his cell in a trembling voice and trusted his fate to God's mercy. Stephen Langton, Archbishop of Canterbury, now an exile by John's decree, had fared to Rome and complained of John's treatment to the Pope. Horrified, His Holiness wrote letters to Philip of France, condemning John and exhorting him to attack. The French king gladly rose up against his traditional foe, eager to invade England with an army and cast the King from his seat.

If he were successful—my heart beat like a captive bird. Philip had supported Arthur, even planned for him to marry his little daughter; I would be set free at long last. I, alone in the castle, longed for the sight of French ships on the horizon.

While the French army rendezvoused at Rouen, John had been preparing his own forces to attack France, with the aim of regaining the ancestral territories that he'd lost. However, once he heard that both the Pope and the French had risen against him, he called off his invasion with lightning-speed.

In a panic John, whose initial summons to his barons had gone mostly unheeded, sent out writs to the sheriffs of England. All men, even serfs, were to hasten to Dover within the week to fight the French; coin and weapons would be given out as payment. Any man who refused the summons would suffer harsh penalties. Merchants were compelled to hand over their goods to the army upon threat of fines or worse.

"The King has gone mad," said Marjory of Scotland after the latest messengers left Corfe, riding like whirlwinds towards the coast. "How can he possibly expect to rouse England in a week? A week, Eleanor! It would seem it is a mere week before the French plan to set sail. He cannot raise a mighty force in days."

"John is always lucky, though." I stared through the arch of a high window overlooking the Dorset countryside. "Always too lucky. Looked after by the devil."

A day went by and then another. Rumours reached our ears that the King's call to arms had worked—despite his unpopularity he had more men than he had expected rallying to his call. From having almost no supporters, suddenly he had many—stout yeomen with their bows, serfs with cudgels and spears, old knights dressed in the armour of bygone times. Fear had motivated them, fear of John's wrath, fear of a successful invasion by foreigners.

"I told you," I said to Isobel and Marjory, "once again Fate smiles on my uncle. Despite his evil, men come to his call."

Marjory sighed, brushing out her long brown hair. "Indeed they do. They say his navy is now larger than the French King's and that he hopes to sink the French ships before they touch shore."

"But..." said Isobel ominously, "what of the prophecy of Peter? Soon it will be Ascension Day—May 23rd."

"Peter of Wakefield is mad," I said.

Isobel glanced down, her long curling lashes hiding her eyes. "Let us hope you are wrong on that score, Eleanor. Let us hope the soothsayer is right."

Old Peter the Hermit might have been moon-mad but in the days that followed, an incredible event took place that seemed to many folk as crazy as the greybeard's prophecies. Pandulf, the Papal legate, reached England in the company of John's envoys...and the King humbly accepted Pope Innocent's terms of peace. At the Templars' Preceptory at Ewell, before a great crowd of magnates, John lifted the crown from his brow and handed it on bended knee to the legate. "I hand my crown and the kingdoms of England and Ireland to his Grace the Pope," he stated. "I do this here, of my own free will, to make good my many sins. I pray his Holiness will allow me to receive my countries back as a humble vassal. If this be done, I will pay his Holiness 1000 marks a year, and that payment shall be passed on to my heirs after me for years without end."

So it was done. John gave away the kingdom. Pleased by John's capitulation, the legate hurried back to France to tell the French not to invade, that England now was under the rule of the Pope. King Philip ranted and roared, consumed by wrath that his plans were ruined, but the legate Pandulf threatened excommunication should he pursue the invasion of England. Sullenly, Philip retreated with his forces to his stronghold in Paris.

England rejoiced. John rejoiced. The Interdict was lifted and the church bells rang out over England after many years of silence.

I did not know how to feel about the cancelled French invasion. John had won again…but…but technically, with England a papal fief, I was no longer my uncle's prisoner, but in the hands of the Pope. Surely, the Holy Father would free me from my unjust imprisonment, once he had been reminded of it….

I decided to let my cares slip away and celebrate the ending of Interdict with the other folk at Corfe. Choirs sang in the chapel and the small stone church in the valley below the castle, and priests in their vestments blessed the people waiting on the roadsides, at the castle gate, in the bailey. In churchyards everywhere, gravediggers exhumed old corpses from outside the perimeter walls and reverently placed the shrouded bones and shrivelled liches in hallowed soil. Young couples danced about, hand in hand, flowers in their hair, overjoyed that they would celebrate their nuptials at the church door, with the priest attending, as had their parents before them.

In Ewell, John himself made merry as if he had not handed his kingdom away in shame. Seated in a gaudy pavilion with a gilded lion statue on the peak, he invited men both great and lowly to visit and plied them with food and wine. Fools cavorted, bawling rude jokes and waggling their buttocks, and cooked swans, peacocks, oxen and mutton lay steaming on the table.

Ascension Day, the day of Peter of Wakefield's prophecy, came…and went.

John was still alive and well. John was still on the throne, although circumstances had changed and the Pope held the overlordship of England.

John's cruelty not changed, however, despite his vassalage to Innocent and his frivolous, seemingly carefree pastimes at Ewell. Even as he cavorted with his Fools, mummers, and harlots, he sent word to Corfe's Constable, and Peter of Wakefield and his son were hauled from their squalid cell. Roughly, soldiers tied them between two horses and dragged them from the castle all the way to Wareham, where, before a baying crowd, they were marched to the gallows and hanged.

As Isobel, Marjory and I gathered for chapel that evening, I whispered to my companions as I knelt before the Rood, "The Hermit was not altogether wrong, though, was he? By Ascension Day, my Uncle ceded England to a foreign power. Peter of Wakefield was right."

Chapter Twenty Two

If I had thought Pope Innocent might intercede from me when England became a papal fief, I was to be sorely disappointed. Master de Turnham and Constable De Blunville forbade me to send letters abroad, and when John rode back and forth from Corfe, trying to raise armies anew for his endeavours on the Continent, he sneered and told me not to get my hopes up—he was still master of England in all but name. "The Pope now considers me merely an erring son," he laughed. "Far from diminishing my rule, his support has strengthened it. He will not let hostile powers such as Philip of France come against me and soon he will lift my excommunication. To atone for my sins, I have sworn to go on Crusade and as a would-be Crusader I cannot be touched."

"And will you go on Crusade, Uncle?" I asked, barely disguising the sarcasm in my voice. "Will you attempt to emulate the heroism of your brother, the Lionheart?"

He glowered at me but reined in his temper. "Dearest little Eleanor, always defiant even in despair. I may go…I may not. The Pope will not live forever."

"Nor will any of us." I was careful to choose my words lest he invent some charge against me of ill wishing his demise. "However, Pope Innocent is quite a young man and liable to live many years yet."

John shrugged. "A few ships sent east, a few Saracens killed…I'll have done my job killing for Christ…" he sniggered—John was always sceptical of piety and even, it sometimes seemed, of God Almighty Himself. "Right now, I have concerns of greater import—the conquest of the lands in France that are rightly mine. You will play a part in that, Eleanor."

"Me?" I said, startled.

"Yes, my sweet niece, you will," he said, and without any further explanation, he stalked towards his private apartments, his ermine-lined cloak belling in the wind, the gems on his circlet flashing sullen red light.

Fears gripped me—fear of the unknown, fear of my devious uncle. What part could I play in his proposed invasion?

I was leaving Corfe, my garments and paltry goods packed and loaded onto wagons. This time it was not a punishing tour of John's castles, but a journey over the sea. A journey to the Continent with the

King's royal army. The Queen and her youngest son Richard were travelling with me, which gladdened my heart; I felt safer in female company.

"Your Grace," I said to Isabella as we rode together in her chariot, "have you any knowledge why the King desires my presence on this campaign? Fear gnaws my belly."

"Be at peace, Eleanor," said Isabella as she sipped wine from a goblet and cast a baleful eye upon the little prince Richard, who had pulled free from his drowsing nurse and was mauling a tapestry with chubby fingers sticky from sugar cane. "He is taking you to your family."

"My family!" I cried in shock. What family did I have left? Only my half-sisters, including Alix, who ruled Brittany in my stead. I had not seen any of them since they were infants.

"So he has told me. Do you not want to see them?"

"Yes…yes, I do," I said, but further uneasiness gripped me. None of the girls knew me. Alix would see me as a rival. What idea was fomenting in John's inscrutable, dark mind?

I had little time to muse upon the situation. From the moment, we disembarked from our ship near La Rochelle hostilities began. The lord of Millescu refused John passage through his territory and the King besieged his castle. It fell with little effort on the King's part. John went on to take two dozen more fortresses in short order, then stormed through Isabella's old homeland of Angouleme, trying unsuccessfully to gain footing in Gascony, where the fierce Simon de Montfort repelled his advance. Rebuffed, he surprisingly decided to march onward to Poitou and the lands of the Lusignans.

"Hugh and Geoffrey will surely never treat with him," I murmured to Isabella. We were in a safe tower in Poitou, under guard while the King fared to Geoffrey's castle of Mervent for a meeting.

The Queen was playing chess with one of her ladies-in-waiting, Souveraine, leaning intently over the large ornate chessboard on its carved, gilt legs. The chess pieces were very rich, carved from horn and bound with gold. She dropped her knight; it clattered on inlaid marble tiles. "Ah, Souveraine, you win tonight."

Swivelling around on her stool, Isabella faced me, her little mouth in a pout. "Eleanor, your fretting made me lose. I could not concentrate."

"Forgive me, my lady. I am just…fearful."

"Of what? That Geoffrey and Hugh might overcome John and come and ravish us?" She laughed, a tinkling, capricious laugh; I remembered how men whispered that she had low morals, how she had sullied her marriage-bed with lovers. They even said John caught one and hung him, dead, above the Queen's couch. I had no idea if these tales held any truth.

Isabella rose, smoothing down her damask gown. "Hugh was rather handsome in his prime. Troubadours named him 'the Emerald' in song. Ravishment at his hands might not be so bad!"

I ignored her improper levity. "I met Sir Hugh several times, the last at…" I paused, the pain of the memory gripping my heart.

Isabella did not notice my sorrowful expression. She was more concerned with talking of her ex-betrothed. "When Hugh lost me to John, he was most furious, of course. He did not pine forever, though—he married another maid of Angouleme, my kinswoman Mahaut Taillefer, daughter of Wulgrin, my sire's brother. They have a son, Hugh, and a daughter Isabella. I wonder if the boy is as handsome as the father? Did he name the girl for his lost bride?" She laughed again, and like a true sycophant, Souveraine laughed with her.

At that moment, we heard scuffling feet in the corridor outside our chamber. All merriment ceased and we fell silent. A knock sounded on the door, sharp and urgent. "Enter!" said Isabella, imperiously.

The door fell open and surrounded by guards a messenger came forward to kneel before the Queen. "News from his Grace, Highness!" he gasped.

"Well, what is it?"

"Mervant has fallen; the King took it in just one morning."

Isabella clapped her hands. "Ah, and men claimed it was impregnable. Men are such fools sometimes. What else? Surely, you have not come to tell me that alone."

"It is as you say, your Grace. Geoffrey and his sons fled to Vouvant and barricaded themselves in the fortress there. The King brought in his engines and remorselessly battered their walls and gates, but then…" he paused.

"Then what?" said Isabella sharply. She reached over and grasped the man's collar in her little, delicate hand. "Are you bringing me bad news, messenger? I do not like bad news!"

"No, no, Highness, no bad news!" The man flailed, terrified of the anger of the tiny, pert-faced woman before him. "It is…it is that Hugh de Brun came riding to the King's tent and asked for terms. His Grace offered him many rich lands for his future loyalty and le Brun convinced his uncle Geoffrey to surrender. All the Lusignans are now reconciled to John's rule and have sworn fealty on bended knee."

"Blessed Christ, a miracle," breathed Isabella, unhanding the messenger. I did not know if she was being serious or sarcastic.

The messenger licked his dusty lips. "I have one more item to tell you, great Queen. About Hugh le Brun…"

"I can't imagine you can tell me anything about Hugh I do not know," she smirked, "but speak on, man."

"As part of the agreement with Sir Hugh, his Grace has made him an offer," the messenger continued. "The offer of the Princess Joan of England in marriage for his son."

Isabella's eyes widened and for a second I thought she might spit in his face. Then she began to laugh, a little bitterly. "If Hugh could not have me, well, my daughter for his son is the nearest thing, I suppose. Perhaps he sees this as a small vengeance. Well, he will have a long time to wait for his son's bride…my Joan is barely four!" She placed her hand on her belly. "I shall miss my little daughter, but it is truly of no real consequence; another child is on the way to take her place." She laughed a little. "At least John and I do one thing well together—make healthy babes!"

She snapped her fingers and Souveraine brought over a pouch of coins. "For you messenger," she said, pressing the bag into the man's sweating hands. "Now go and leave us."

Clutching the purse to his breast, he scurried away and Isabella fell into a sombre, sulky mood that told me she was not as pleased about her daughter going to the Lusignans as she had pretended.

She looked happier when another courier arrived, bearing a letter from the King. She had it read to her in private, then returned to our quarters, smiling. "We are on the move again. The King needs more alliances. Eleanor, tomorrow we fare to Brittany."

It was strange entering the country of my birth, riding on a caparisoned white palfrey next to King John by his express command. Yes, the green hills and azure seas, the strange standing stones and the wide, cloud-streaked skies were the same…yet everything else had changed. The villages we passed through seemed smaller, somehow meaner, and the looks received from passerby were fearful and unfriendly. In my heart of hearts, I had imagined the Bretons would rush forth to greet me as their long-lost ruler. Instead, I saw scowls,

203

suspicious gazes. I realised then they did not know me, did not trust me. For all they knew, I was a fraud and the real Eleanor dead in some unmarked grave in England.

"We head for Nantes," John was telling me. "Since it stands upon the Loire, it is a strategic point to mount an invasion. If Nantes were mine, supplies and soldiers could be shipped there straight from England. I could rally against Philip from there."

I returned no answer, hating the thought of my land invaded for John's rapacious need to regain his old lands.

"Are you looking forward to seeing your sisters?" John asked, taunting. "Duchess Alix is wed now, did you know? To Peter of Dreux, cousin of the French King. I pray he will be more willing and reasonable than his kinsman."

"Yes, I heard that Alix has wed. I pray she is happy. It does not seem fitting though that she should have married before her elder sister." A jab at John.

"So you would like me to marry you to one of my barons? Choose a husband for you, as my father chose Ranulph of Chester for your mother, Constance? Perhaps someone cast in the mould of my enforcer William Brewer would do, or my doughty mercenary captain, Brandin. Does your blood grow so hot in captivity you are eager take any man?"

"I only say that it is not right to have held me for so long. After all, I am charged with no offence, Uncle. I have committed no crime. You have men swear loyalty to you daily, men who have been faithless before. Yet you let them walk free. Do you fear a mere woman so much you would not accept her sworn oath of loyalty?"

John looked slightly shaken and confused. "I trust no woman," he said, shrilly, striking his horse's flanks with his spurs and pulling ahead of me. "Least of all a fiery-headed bitch like you. Now, be silent!"

June had come, the summer's heat scorching the earth and causing steam to rise from the bed of the nearby river, when John's army approached Nantes. Shading my eyes, I looked ahead at the ancient castle walls—at once both familiar and strange. In the years of my absence, the castle's defences had been strengthened and the outer fortifications rebuilt. The standard of Alix's husband, Peter de Dreux, flapped atop the highest turret beside the flag of the Dukes of Brittany.

Suddenly there was shouting and the braying of horns. The castle drawbridge descended with a bang and Peter de Dreux charged out on a grey destrier, leading a large party of soldiers with weapons unsheathed, ready to give battle.

Taken aback by de Dreux's unexpected defensive action, John shouted for his captains to assume battle formations. Given into the care of one of his mercenaries, I was quickly hustled to the rear of the army, where the Queen and Prince waited in their chariot. I was thrust in with them, as a bristling sea of swords and spears formed a deadly iron wall around us.

Isabella grabbed my shoulders. "Your family has attacked us!"

Scarcely able to speak, I nodded. I wanted no harm to come to the Queen or the little Prince Richard, but Oh, Christ in heaven, how I had wanted to tear from my uncle's side and ride madly toward the host of Brittany, not away from them. But would they even accept me? Would they want me as their ruler after so many years? Would they deem me a pretender and impale me on their sharpened pikes?

I was soon to find out my true standing in this latter-day Brittany. John sent a message to the Queen that hostilities were over; in a brief, bitter engagement, he had captured twenty enemy knights including Robert de Dreux, Peter's brother. We were going to Nantes Castle to meet with Duchess Alix and her young husband in order to reach an agreement.

It was with some trepidation I entered the castle—my castle by strict inheritance, but Alix's by acclamation. All had changed, the tapestries, the sconces on the wall, even the coats of arms painted on shields along the ceiling. It was as if all signs of my old life had been rubbed away.

In the Great Hall I stood like a helpless fool behind John, who, careless of his appearance, stood arrogantly with hands on hips, as we awaited the entrance of Alix and Peter.

At length, my half-sister and her husband slipped from a curtained passageway and sat down upon the dais at the far end of the chamber. Alix was about fourteen, a pretty girl with silver-gilt curls tumbling under a diaphanous veil. Her skin was milk-pale, her lips small and red. We bore little resemblance to each other, and when she glanced over at me, so frosty was her gaze, I felt as if darts of ice had flown from her wide-set green eyes. Her husband Peter was a pallid, long-faced lad dressed in austere black broidered with the fleur de lys of France.

Alix spoke first, her tone as glacial as her eyes. "I do not bid you welcome, my uncle of England, but you have come nonetheless and destroyed the peace of our land. I will not spend time in wordplay with you. What is it you want?"

"Brittany on my side, of course, instead of at my throat," replied John with a grin. "I tried to communicate my good intentions to the Lord Peter in a letter not so long ago. I told him his compliance could be beneficial; the earldom of Richmond, traditionally tied with Brittany, could well fall into his hands."

I jumped, cheeks burning. Richmond! The one title I had left was Countess of Richmond, for all it was worth. So John had dangled that last small part of my inheritance before Peter of Dreux!

"It was not worth it to me," said Peter stiffly. "I would not sell out the sovereignty of Brittany for a mere title."

"You will treat with me now, though, won't you?" asked John. "Your little foray against me was ill-advised, shall we say, and now Robert, your brother, languishes under armed guard in my camp. Perhaps I should send him for a stay in Corfe…"

"You are a monster." Alix's hands gripped the arms of her high seat. "I know all about your reputation and the horrors that have taken place in your castles. Why should we treat with you? We have the French King on our side. He may be marching to our aid even as we speak!"

"You must because…Well, think of poor Robert. You may never see him alive again if you do not. Think of yourselves too, and your positions. After all, Alix of Brittany, you are not the eldest daughter of Constance of Brittany, nor are you of royal blood upon your sire's side. My dearest niece Eleanor could easily sit where you are now—the fair Pearl of Brittany. Step forth, Eleanor."

Mortified, I walked to my uncle's side. One could have heard a pin drop throughout the Great Hall. Head bowed, furious, I stood beside the smirking John—the King was attempting to pit me against my own flesh and blood in another of his cruel games.

"We won't have your puppet, English King!" cried out a Breton councillor from the high dais. Agitated, the man waved his hands in the air. "It is an outrage! This creature you parade may not even be the true Eleanor of Brittany! She could be any comely, red-headed wench you've found in the stews; the true Eleanor may well lie in an unmarked grave like her brother Arthur."

I fought back the tears that threatened. Glancing around the chamber, I sought for any known faces from the old times. There was none…no, wait…surely that old woman huddled in the corner was my former nursemaid, Aaliz? Although ancient and grizzled, still I recognised that much-loved visage from my childhood.

"Aaliz, you know me," I blurted. "You surely will speak and verify that I am Eleanor, daughter of Constance."

The huddled figure darted forward, spidery, blinking. Then the grey-haired head began to shake from side to side in an agitated motion. "Nonononono! You cannot be my Eleanor; she was taken long ago, they whisper that she's dead. They've coached you haven't they, King John and his wicked advisers? Told you my name, all our names…"

Alix cut in, raising a hand for silence. She cast a hate-filled look towards John…and towards me. "Enough of this mummery. For Robert's safety we will treat with you, John of England, as long as you promise not to try to foist the girl who is with you upon the people of Brittany."

"If the terms of a truce go well, I shall see she never sets foot on Breton soil again."

I cringed, each word a dagger blow to the heart.

"Eleanor…" Smug, he turned to face me. "Leave us; the guards will see you safely back to the Queen."

I took a tremulous step towards the arched door, then suddenly paused. As the Bretons gathered in the hall gaped and gasped, I stared straight at Alix and said, "You deny I am your sister but we share the same blood. I fought for our family's rights and now I am not only captive but also dishonoured and discredited. Well, sister, I only hope your truce with our uncle the King brings you all the happiness you deserve. Farewell, I doubt we will ever meet again. Pray for me, Alix, for the sake of our shared mother if naught else…"

Before Alix could say a single word in return, I had vanished into the hallway beyond, tears trailing salt into my mouth.

I would never come here again. Brittany was lost to me forever, a strange land that no longer welcomed, where ancient heroes were feted in song but a lost princess was buried and forgotten.

Chapter Twenty Three

After the humiliation in Nantes, John sent me back to England, back to the stern walls of Corfe, a cold homecoming indeed. Ivette was waiting, imperious and haughty, to start me back in my daily routines—mass at dawn, a meagre breakfast, walks on the walls, a brief meeting with my fellow captives Isobel and Marjory, maybe a ride in the valley with the King's guards swarming about me like bees flown from the hive.

"I heard the people of Brittany rejected you," said Ivette cruelly, as she brought a pewter tray bearing my breakfast of sops. "Your sister has thrown in her lot with the King. She is wise. Mayhap one day his Grace will show mercy and allow you to enter a convent."

I refused to respond to her cruel taunts; they were wearing now rather than infuriating. Ignoring the food she brought, I strode to the window, my back towards her. "If you have nothing more to say, Ivette…" I said, with meaning, and then, in surprise, "Messengers are arriving, many of them. They ride like the wind!"

Momentous news had reached Corfe. A battle had taken place at Bouvines between Philip of France and my cousin Otto, Emperor of Germany, along with others fighting for John's cause. Otto had three horses killed under him then decided to flee the field, while his knights died closing the way after him. The Count of Boulogne and Count of Flanders, both John's supporters, were captured in the fray. The fighting bishop of Beauvais flung himself at the English army with the cross before him, smiting the helm of William Longspee, King John's bastard brother, until it burst asunder. Miraculously, Longspee survived this assault, but he was taken prisoner.

John never reached the field, having received the disastrous news about Bouvines while on the march. Retreating with all the haste he could muster, he began the long journey back to England, and word had it that his wrath knew no bounds, for he realised that the defeat at Bouvines meant he had lost his ancestral lands forever. No welcome would await John on the shores of his English kingdom, and men shuddered to think on what evils his rage might bring upon them.

None of his barons was happy; they wanted reparations for the long, bleak years of the Interdict. Many other injustices had taken place during his reign, too. John had forced Geoffrey de Mandeville to marry John's spurned wife, Hawise, a woman too old to bear children, and charged him 20,000 marks for the privilege. When de Mandeville was unable to pay such a sum, John had levied a huge fine—de Mandeville now wanted the sum repealed. Other lords such as William de Mowbray and Roger de Montbegon held their own grudges against their sovereign. They, and many others, met John at Temple in London with a copy of an old charter from the time of my grandfather, King Henry, demanding John follow the rules and laws his own ancestors had decreed.

John refused.

The crisis deepened; enraged barons, unable to make any headway in negotiating with John, retreated to their castles and stockpiled food and arms. Across the land swords were wrought, pikes sharpened. Men prayed that civil war would not break out as in the time of King Stephen and Queen Maude, when it was said that Christ and His Saints Slept.

At Easter, an assembly was called at Northampton's royal castle. The angry Geoffrey de Mandeville was there, and Fitzwalter, whose wife and daughter the King had molested. The Earls of Winchester and Hereford, de Quincy and de Mohun, rode in with their armed entourages. De Mohun came with Giles de Braose, Bishop of Hereford, whose mother and brother had met their grisly end in the oubliette under Corfe Castle.

Despite his earlier avowals to meet the barons, John showed his cowardice and did not turn up in Northampton as promised. Instead, he hid behind the impregnable walls of the Tower of London. And when the hostile eyes of increasingly angry barons turned in that direction, he took horse and galloped west, first to Clarendon Palace and then to Corfe, perhaps giving himself time to gather loyalists, perhaps to place himself nearer the coast should he need a hasty escape overseas.

When he reached Corfe, I kept to my chambers but he caught me when I was on my customary walk upon the walls. The day was darkness and light, short sharp showers from threatening clouds, then sunlight that beamed across the valley, transforming the rounded heads of the nearby hills into beacons of fire.

The King looked strangely aged, puffing as he ascended the steps to the wall walk. I fell into a deep curtsey, as was expected of me.

"Get up, niece," he said. "Up here, out of sight of prying eyes, your obeisance is not needed."

"As you wish." I gathered my skirts, stared out over the crenellations in the direction of the sea. I did not want to gaze upon the lined, swart face with the two furrows cutting from the side of his nose into his glistening black beard. The devil's face. The murderer's face.

"I take it you have been informed of all that is happening in the world beyond?"

"I try to take an interest in the affair of England, even though I cannot participate in such actions. The Constable William de Blunville and others tell many tales."

"You know what my barons ask of me then?"

"Yes."

"God's Teeth!" A scowl twisted his features and he kicked at the nearby stonework in a fury. "Their demands are outrageous! What else will they ask for—my very kingdom?"

"They ask for justice, my lord King. That is all. Will you give it to them? Will you give it to me?"

"You are defiant as ever. You are lucky I gave you your life!"

"Lucky?" Raising an eyebrow, I laughed. Laughed at the stout little King, the murderer king, the incompetent King.

John sputtered with outraged indignation and began to hurl curses and imprecations at me. I continued to laugh; he seemed ridiculous…and I felt mad, moon-touched. I did not care if he ordered my head smitten off that very afternoon.

"You are insane, wench!" John screamed and he stormed away towards his apartments. Ivette and the other ladies hustled me to my chamber and locked the door. News came that I was banned from eating in the hall in the King's presence. As if I cared a jot! I laughed at John; I scorned his presence.

The next day the King marched out, leading a sizeable force to Wallingford in Oxfordshire. From my high perch in the Gloriet, with the seagulls whirling and screaming overhead like lost souls, I watched his departure with relief.

War had come to England, a deadly civil strife. John refused all the terms the barons had laid out. Under the leadership of Baron Fitzwalter, who named himself Marshal of the Army of God, the lords began a plan to seize John's prime castles, laying siege to Northampton almost immediately. However, the defenders held out and Fitzwalter's young standard-bearer was smitten down, his skull smashed to fragments by a crossbow bolt.

Despite their inability to take Northampton, the Army of God was not dissuaded from its cause. After leaving the town in flames, they marched to Bedford where, unlike Northampton, they took the castle with ease. Confidence rising with their victory, they then journeyed on to London. There, on a Sunday, when most of the townsfolk were in church, grappling hooks were thrown up over the city walls and a select group of warriors slipped in unnoticed. Making for the main gates, they flung them open—and, like a rain-swollen torrent, the armies of the angry barons flooded into the city. Houses and shops were put to the torch; the homes of rich Jews were ransacked before being fired. The King's faithful were captured and all their possessions divvied up amongst the rebels. London had fallen to the might of the rebelling barons.

At night, I prayed for those lords to succeed, to lay the tyrant low.

On the tenth day of June, John met his fractious barons at the watery meadows running alongside the sluggish Thames near to Staines. The place was known as Runnymede.

Confronted by thousands of armed men willing to fight for their rights, he finally ceded to their demands and placed his seal upon the document they proffered.

In the years that followed, that document would be called the *Magna Carta…*

The subject of the King's Charter was cause for great gossip back at Corfe. Many of John's most loyal were horrified that the King had submitted to the will of the barons. Isobel, Marjory and I scurried to the solar where we feverishly embroidered and pursued other maidenly pastimes whilst talking to each other in whispers about this scandalous Charter.

"Do you think John will abide by it?" Marjory's embroidery needle flashed like a tiny sword.

"I dare say he'll try and wriggle out of it," I replied. "He's a serpent. I'd wager he's writing to the Pope even as we speak."

"Do you think the Charter, if it is not repealed, might help us?" asked Isabel hopefully.

I shrugged. My embroidering had gone awry; a pretty unicorn with silvered mane now had a bent horn. "I overheard Ivette saying that the Charter states John will treat with your brother, King Alexander, for your freedom."

Isobel began to weep with joy. "Shush!" said Marjory. "We don't want unwelcome attention while we talk. Like Eleanor, I am certain John will try to nullify this Charter."

"I have heard the Charter also says that no widow shall be compelled to marry so long as she wishes to live without a husband," I said, "but I have heard nothing of its contents that might aid me. You have a brother John may treat with…but I have no brother, thanks to John's malice."

"It will come good for you in the end, Eleanor, I am sure of it!" said Isobel with forced cheerfulness. "But we all must wait."

"Waiting is all we ever do," I said dryly, and stabbed my sharpened needle through the beady black eye of my ruined unicorn embroidery.

It did not take John long to rile the barons again. Ignoring every clause within the Charter he'd just signed, he attempted to obligate the lords, in writing, to defend him and his heirs, no matter the circumstances. Angrily they refused.

War was set to begin.

The Pope, who had chastised John so strongly once, grew oddly supportive. Men whispered he truly had no idea of the gravity of the situation in England. "The lords of England are no better than ravening infidels!" he raged. "Saracens and paynims! Let all who rise against my vassal, a sworn Crusader, be excommunicated for their perfidy!"

John refused to treat with his barons, even with the Pope prepared to stand at his back. Instead, like a foul bat flitting under the cover of darkness, he took to the sea in a swift, black-sailed ship and none knew where he had gone. His return came soon enough, though—he landed in Kent with his loyal companion, Peter des Roches, and Pandulf, the Papal legate. Following in his wake was a vast host of Flemish mercenaries, ready to be released like a scourge upon the land. Land-pirates out for gold and plunder.

Learning of John's landing at Sandwich, the barons were swift to counter- strike at the approaching King. Dispatching letters to Philip of France, they begged him send his son Louis to England to wrest the crown from John. Yes, they were so angered with John's treachery and tyranny that they would even offer the sovereignty of England to a Frenchman. Young Louis willingly agreed to invade; it had been his wish to take on England for years, but first he had to raise a good-sized army and then wait for a safe time to cross the storm-ridden Channel.

The delay in Louis' departure was not good news for the King's enemies and John, bolstered by his Brabancon troops, looted Kent for days, firing villages and carrying off livestock, tuns of ale and local women. Finally, he set to besieging mighty Rochester Castle, where

William de Albini, Lord of Belvoir, held the immense keep, one of the tallest in all England, against his hated foe.

Determined to pass Rochester unhindered, John threw all his might at the great fortress guarding the sullen, sluggish Medway. Fat pigs were slaughtered and their carcases placed on a pyre that was set along. As the pigs burned, flesh sizzling and spitting, they were carried in ones and twos to a trench dug beneath a corner of the great tower and thrown in. Soon, the fat-fuelled heat of the flames that consumed the beasts broke the nearby stonework asunder and one of the keep's great bastions began to teeter and groan. As the men atop the tower fled for safety, a whole section of the tower collapsed with an unearthly roar. Still, the defenders held on, drawing back behind the cross-wall where they continued to shoot arrows at their opponents.

Starvation finished the siege of Rochester. The garrison's inadequate supplies soon ran out. A few men had tried to surrender in the days before final capitulation but John, ever cruel, had taken them prisoner and said, "You will live...but without your hands and feet,' and he ordered his leering mercenaries to cut their limbs off and before their very eyes used a trebuchet to hurl the severed parts into the keep.

Once the garrison had resorted to eating their war-horses, they knew they had no chance of holding out any longer. William de Albini surrendered, walking forth from the keep bareheaded and clad in just his shirt and hosen, holding out his empty hands. Gleefully, John clapped him in chains and sent him and his son Odenel to his favourite castle for prisoners, Corfe.

William de Albini was a broad-shouldered man in his forties who glared defiantly when he was brought into the castle bailey. His son, Odenel, looked equally outraged, perhaps to mask the fear he must have felt. Both would have known well the tales of the starved French knights and Maude de Braose.

"God help them if he casts them in the oubliette," said Marjory, twisting her crystal-encrusted rosary around her fingers...but this time, the King did not.

Perhaps restrained by the terms of his Charter, he placed both men in ordinary cells within the dungeon. Servants delivered plain, tasteless fare to them in no great abundance, but at least they were fed.

On Twelfth Night, when dull sleet and snow sluiced in freezing sheets over the castle walls, I convinced the new Constable, Peter de Maulay, to allow me to visit the prisoners, as was my wont at this time of the year. I dreaded speaking to him, as he was said to have been present at Arthur's murder, but I forced myself to show courage. I thought he might deny me, for he was even more officious than Blunville, but he seemed more interested in drink and revelling than in my activities and waved me onwards.

Carrying a basket containing scraps of bread and sweet pudding, I hurried for the cells.

De Albini's face pressed to the bars, half-overgrown by a wild, silver-streaked beard. "Who are you? Why do you come? And that..." He gestured to my basket. "You expect me that eat such fare? It could have been poisoned on John's orders. He killed Matilda Fitzwalter with a poisoned egg when she refused to become his leman."

"Be of good cheer," I told him. "I assure you the food is harmless; I have eaten of it myself. I come to you out of charity, to give you hope at this time of celebration."

"Celebration!" he groaned. "No Christmas celebration for me, I fear. Can you give me news of my son Odenel? Good news of my son is all I wish to hear."

"He is unharmed and imprisoned in the next cell. I have already given him bread and sweet things—a Yuletide dole."

"Who are you?" His hands gripped the bars. "Something about you seems familiar."

"Have I changed so much?" I smiled sadly. "My lord de Albini, you were with the contingent that fared to the court of the German Emperor to secure King Richard's release. I am Eleanor of Brittany."

"Eleanor! I thought it might be you! It is wicked what the King has done to you and yours. One day, I swear, he will be brought to justice."

I sighed. "Sometimes I fear it may not be in my lifetime."

"Lady, even if we both were to die here, in Corfe castle, victims of this unrighteous King, know this—the gates of justice have been pried open and shall never slam shut again. Men of worth will rise to combat the tyranny of rulers such as John. If we die, it shall not be in vain."

My lower lip began to tremble, there in the gloom of the dungeon. "May your words be true, Sir William. Pray to Christ and the Virgin that it may be so, if not for us, for those who come anew into this fallen world."

I fled the cells, retiring to my lonely chamber. Sleet turned to snow; the castle bailey went white, as did the village in the valley and the long line of hills marching away into the distance.

Another Christmas spent in captivity—I counted on my fingers, I was now well over thirty years of age. Hope was slipping away, slowly but surely. It was not impossible that a lord would still wed me if I was released, but I had nothing to offer now, not wealth, not titles, not lands. My looks were surely fading and at my age, a brood of healthy children seemed unlikely.

A few days later, a message came to Constable de Maulay relating to the status of the prisoners William and Odenel De Albini. At first when I heard, I shuddered, certain that an order had arrived to throw the incarcerated noblemen into the oubliette. But it was not so. John had attacked William's fortress at Belvoir and threatened young Nicholas de Albini, a clerk, that he would starve his father to death if he refused to open the gates.

The fearful Nicholas opened them, and let the King do his worst to the rebel castle.

De Albini and his son would live another day.

It was one small, positive thing in the bleak grey January of the Year of Our Lord 1216.

Menace filled the early months of the year. Pontefract had fallen to the King; York and Berwick followed. The lords of the north, in the wake of the tyrant's coming, burnt their own houses and stores so that John could not claim them for his own. When certain barons joined Alexander of Scotland, John marched brazenly over the border and ransacked the Abbey of Coldingham, his mercenaries wandering from the ruined cloister carrying armloads of church plate and sacred chalices. Pleased with the results of such pillaging, the King returned to England via Berwick and fired the town as he left, setting a torch to the castle apartments where he had stayed a few nights previous.

"At least our brother Alexander is safe," said Marjory, "and many disaffected English barons have sworn oaths to him at Melrose Abbey. Surely the Pope will not continue to protect John much longer when he realised the havoc he has caused."

"Where is Louis of France in all this?" asked Isobel, toying with the silk ribbons twined in her long braid. "He said he would come, but he has not."

"I have overheard whisperings," I said, "that he will not come before Easter."

"Easter!" Isobel groaned. "Only God knows what will happen by then! So much wickedness is afoot, I would not show surprise if the earth opened up and all the devils of Hell sprang out to attack decent men!"

"Your imagination, sister!" laughed Marjory, shaking her head. "Devils and demons. I despair!"

"There is only one devil we need fear," I said, solemn. "John."

We were not the only ones to fear the King. Even as he harried and burnt in the north, his captains and mercenaries rampaged throughout the south. Pleshey castle had fallen on Christmas Eve, even as the bells rang out to proclaim the Christ-child's birth; at the same time, horses were stolen from a nearby abbey for use by the King's forces. John himself finally appeared, capturing Norfolk's castle of Framlingham; Hedingham fell next and its owner, Robert De Vere, the Earl of Oxford, pleaded for his life grovelling at John's feet. Pleased by the submission of his enemy, the King distributed Oxford's furnishings, plate, horses, and tapestries to his Brabancons...but Oxford, at least, was spared death.

John marched on towards London, where several small French contingents had arrived to help the rebel barons. The city held firm against the King, burning his ships with fire-arrows as they attempted to creep up the Thames. He could not force entrance and retreated to Kent.

Easter came and went. Prince Louis still had not left France but it was clear to English spies on both sides of the conflict that he would soon embark upon his journey.

John was like a dog at bay. He hovered near the port of Folkestone in a ship, keeping a watching eye on the French coast in the misty distance. His intent was to stop the French fleet as they approached the shore. His ships were larger and faster than his rival's. The English fought more often at sea so had greater skill in such warfare. Without a doubt, he would win any sea battle...

My uncle did not count upon the fickle English weather...

May had come, and I was on one of my permitted rides in the countryside around Corfe. The Scottish princesses rode with me, wrapped in cloaks with deep hoods. Our ever-present guards milled around us, looking bored and sullen. The wind roared high, screaming over the hills, while white blossoms tore from the May trees and spun through the sky in a flurry like unseasonal snowflakes. Out towards Swanage clouds hung in a dark, lowering band, brooding and ominous.

Suddenly the gale stopped, almost as if a giant in the sky had paused for breath. A strange, unnatural stillness hung over the land. Clouds snaked in silent dark bands throughout the heavens and an unwholesome yellowish light streamed down over Corfe as the sun struggled to assert dominance, then was consumed by growing shadow.

"Is the storm over?" Isobel cast back her hood, blinking up at the sky. "It has suddenly grown so still!"

One of our guards, a greybeard with a scar from an old dagger wound livid on his cheek, shook his head and grabbed at my reins. "We must not linger here any longer, Lady Eleanor. We must return to the castle at once."

Isobel pouted. "But…but the wind has dropped. We have scarcely started our ride. Jesu knows we have little enough time free of the castle walls."

"My lady Isobel, I beg you do not argue," the man said desperately. "I am here not just to keep you from flight but to protect you from any kind of harm. We stand in the eye of the storm, when all grows still…for a short time. I have lived near the coast all my life and have seen this very thing happen many times. A great storm is coming!"

We fled back towards Corfe, our horses' hooves beating against the earth, our cloaks streaming out in the wind of our speed. The barbican gate loomed, a great mouth, and just as we passed under it, a boom of thunder sounded from above and the sky was alight with twisted forks of lightning. Rain began to hammer down and in the bailey stalls and stands were knocked over, and a roof half-torn from the stable. A goodwife, busy at her tasks, screamed in fear; she ran for the kitchens holding her headdress to her head, while her chickens, which had been pecking about her feet, flew through the air like feathered balls.

Leaping from our horses, we rushed for the safety of our quarters as wind-blow ostlers struggled to control our terrified mounts.

Inside the Gloriet tower, before a roaring fire, we collapsed panting and drenched, our hair straggling in our eyes.

"What a wicked night," said Marjory, as a servant towelled her wet face. "Listen to the wind! I have never seen such a storm, even in Scotland, where the weather is often fierce."

"Maybe is it a storm brought upon England by God for all of King John's wickedness!" Isobel peered out the window, her elfin features lit by flashes of lightning.

"You and your superstitions," chided Margaret, as she often did, gesturing her sister to sit beside her. "Whist now, you goose, come away from that window."

I stood in the centre of the room, water puddling around my feet from my sodden skirts. My gown was deep crimson; a defect of the dyers meant the water curling around my slippers was red. Like blood.

A strange feeling raced through me, a feeling of prescience, of foreknowledge. Like some sibyl in an ancient Greek tale, I turned to my fellow captives. "Isobel is right. Tonight this storm betokens something, although I cannot say what. I can feel it, although I cannot tell what the dawn will bring."

The sisters bowed their heads and crossed themselves.

On that night, when the wind shrieked like a crazed demon and trees were torn from their roots, the sea rose in fury and smote John's navy out in the Channel. Ships were hurled about on the swell, crashing into each other and overturning. Masts snapped, hulls were rammed; men drowned in a sea awash with tangles of silvered lightning.

England was now wide open to invasion by the French.

Louis took the opportunity God's wrath had given him. Although battered by the storm winds himself and having half his navy blown off course, he managed to land with a sizeable force at Sandwich.

John, who had massed his land forces all along the Kentish shore, suddenly changed his mind about giving battle to the invaders. Without telling his captains of his plans, he donned a dark mantle as a disguise and fled.

Prince Louis rode triumphantly into England, opposed only by small bands of royalists and the handful of mercenaries still supporting John—most of the Brabancons had vanished like mist when they realised no more pay was forthcoming with their master on the run. Canterbury capitulated when Louis' army marched into view and Rochester swiftly gave in to the Prince's demands, its castle already broken by the earlier siege. In fear of his life, not knowing where John had gone, Pandulf the Papal legate fled the country on the first ship he could find.

London greeted Prince Louis with joy, and with the Oriflamme flying overhead, he sought out Saint Paul's, where many of the barons swore on bended knee to serve him loyally. In return, he promised the return of all the lands and inheritances confiscated by John.

He was not content to take merely the capital, though, and soon marched on with his forces to Winchester, where he set to attacking its two strong castles. Within ten days of his siege engines rolling up to their gates, both fortresses had surrendered.

As he often did when all was not well, John rode with his entourage to Corfe. All the castle's inhabitants were horrified by his presence. Although a strong castle, John's recent additions had been more for comfort than strength; its height on the hill might give defenders a brief advantage, but the walls were perhaps not as stout as they might be.

Isobel was in a panic. "If the French attack, there might be a long siege. We could all starve. Or if they break in, they might kill us all…or worse…without realising who we are."

"Isobel, Isobel." I tried to calm her. "You will make yourself ill. Trust in Our Lady and Our Lord."

"Why should I trust in them?" she cried. "Have they helped any of us so far, imprisoned here for years as our lives slip away? No, they have not!"

I had no answer to that but merely held her close as she wept out her fears.

I tried to avoid my uncle during his tenure at Corfe, but, as I feared, it soon proved impossible. As I walked amidst the strong-scented lavender bushes in the evening cool, after the sun had gone but the first stars had not yet risen, he appeared suddenly from behind a thicket of herbs. I was reminded of our first unexpected meeting all those years ago at Marlborough, but the King was no longer a haughty youth seeking to heighten his position in the world, no matter what harm he might do. An air of malevolence still clung to him but now it seemed muted; the old fire had vanished from his sunken eyes. Age lay heavily on his shoulders like the huge, furred mantle of blood-red velvet that he wore despite the summer night's heat.

"Eleanor, my niece," he said, deceptively mild.

I curtseyed, mind roiling with reasons to give him for a hasty departure. "Your Grace."

"Walk with me a while, will you?" He sloped towards me; his scent overwhelmed, rich imported musk mixed with horses and sweat. Not a pleasant odour; I inhaled the nearby lavender as much as I could to get his sour aroma from my nostrils.

Silent, we strolled through the garden. Then John halted and stared hard at me. "You...you understand why I had to keep you here all these years?"

I refused to meet his eyes. "No, I do not. What risk am I to you now?"

He began to pace, his shoes kicking up little pebbles on the path. "Do you...have you ever dreamed at night of a crown upon your brow? That is what I dreamed of as a little boy. It seemed as far away as the moon back then. Once the crown came to me, I swore to fight for it to the death...and for the rights of my heirs to wear it after me."

"Unlike you, I never dreamed of any crown," I told him. "I would wear one if it was rightfully mine but I would not wrest one, with bloodshed, from another."

"Are you calling me a usurper?" At last, a frisson of the old fire kindled in his deep eyes. "Richard named me his heir at the last, have you forgotten that? The succession was never clear. As for bloodshed, your brother swore an oath to serve me, which he broke. Even the Pope said that it was not wrong to condemn him to death for his folly."

"He was just a rash boy, as you know," I said softly. "If you say you could not resist your dreams of crowns, so was it with Arthur, promised a kingdom as the son of Geoffrey Plantagenet. As for the breaking of oaths, how many times did you rise against Richard and break yours? Even when the ransom was ready to be paid, you interfered and tried to have the Emperor keep him imprisoned."

"By God, you speak too freely!" John shouted, waving his arms in sudden fury.

"Did I ever do anything but? I am cast in your mother's image, I think. If you mislike my words, send me away, or confine me more closely—after so many years, I no longer care. The world is just a fantasy out of my reach, a dream in which I no longer can take part."

For a second I thought he might pounce upon me, those calloused, dark-haired hands clamping around my throat. But he did not touch me. His shoulders slumped in a world-weary way and he sat heavily on a stone bench, his arms trailing.

"Christ, it has all gone wrong," he muttered, half to me, half to himself. "All wrong. Where will it end? All my men leave me, even those of my blood. William Longspee, my half-brother...even he has broken faith and joined my enemies."

That last fragment of news shocked me. William of Salisbury had always followed his kinsman through thick and thin. I wondered what had occurred to cause such a rift. Rumours spread that John had dishonoured William's wife Ela, but that might have been no more than scurrilous court gossip, although I would not have put such a base act past my lustful uncle. Maybe Longspee just saw at last that John's days as King were numbered and wanted to be on the winning side.

"Where are your enemies now?" I asked in a quiet voice. "Have you led them to Corfe?"

He shook his head. "God be praised, Louis decided to go take Portchester…and my castle at Odiham! Odiham, of all places, more a hunting lodge than anything else. The defenders still managed to hold out against the foe for a week, but my castle is ruined." He licked his thick lips. "Louis is now striving to bring down the gates of Dover but Hubert de Burgh is holding fast. Other bloody Frenchmen are marching to assail Windsor. God's Teeth, its gates had better hold and keep them out!"

Robes swirling, he sprang to his feet. His brow was awash with sweat; he looked cadaverous. "Fear not, I will ride from here soon. I do not want them to find me at Corfe; these walls are high but in no wise strong enough for long-term warfare. I will head toward Windsor at the break of dawn."

He stared at the sky, the pallid blue of evening fading into the blackness of night. The moon stared back, pocked as an old skull. "Where did it all go wrong?" he croaked, repeating himself. "Where?"

I wished to tell him the problem was the darkness that dwelt within his own heart but I held my tongue. Instead, I whispered the words of Gerald of Wales, the acerbic churchman who had written words as sharp as sword blades for many years. "Fortune's favour is fickle. Her Wheel is always turning."

The King marched from Corfe and all its tenants breathed a sigh of relief at his departure. However, when we heard that he had not engaged Louis's forces at Windsor, bypassing the besieged castle and marching to the east instead, we were perplexed.

"Couriers told Peter de Maulay that John burns all in his wake; the night is as light as day with the brightness of the fires."

"I know his intent." Marjory's lips were tight. "I was allowed a letter from my kin in Scotland—read, of course, by our gaoler before I received it, but I recognised that it had been written in coded letters." She held out a ragged piece of parchment.

"Coded! Marjory, you are so clever." Isobel peered over her sister's shoulder at the letter.

"What does it say?" I asked.

"My brother Alexander is on his way back from Kent where he did homage to Prince Louis. That is why John has headed east. John is trying to capture him, to take him hostage…or slay him."

Faint with fear, Isobel pressed her hand to her throat. "Oh, Jesu help us…"

"John is weary," I said, placing my hand on Isobel's shoulder. "I have seen it myself. With luck, he will never catch your brother."

But I was uneasy, for my uncle always seemed to have the luck of the devil.

It turned out, this time, though, that the devil himself came for John.

The King had been gone only a short while when Queen Isabella arrived at Corfe with her two small sons, Henry and Richard. Her entourage was heavily armed, and upon her arrival, the number of crossbowmen on the walls was doubled and the gates barred with great oak tree trunks.

Once Isabella had settled into her apartments, she sent for me. "Eleanor, it is good to see you again. I am here because John thought I should stay away from the centres of fighting and have a sea-route available if needed."

"Where would you go, your Grace, should it come to it?"

"Maybe to Normandy, maybe Ireland…I do not know. So many are hostile," she sighed. "I want this to be over, Eleanor; I want my sons to be safe and well."

"Understandable, your Grace."

"How did my husband seem when he was here?"

"I shall speak plainly—he looked like a lost soul."

"Longspee has deserted him; in fact, nearly all have abandoned his cause save de Burgh and the Marshal. Eleanor…" She glanced at me, her eyes shining in the torchlight, through tears or from excitement, I could not tell. "We must be prepared. Anything might happen now."

"I think I understand."

"Good." She snapped her fingers and summoned a page to bring her wine in an emerald-encrusted goblet. "To the future, Eleanor of Brittany, whatever it might bring."

"To the future," I murmured awkwardly.

I had no goblet and no wine.

On the night of October 18th a great storm crashed over the gaunt towers of Corfe. The very stones shook to their foundations and the wind was so fierce it tore all the royal standards from the turrets and cast them into the valleys below the steep walls.

At dawn, the storm had blown itself out and the sky was cloudless and blue as a robin's egg. Rainwater trickled down the hill to gather in the nearby stream. It was as if the world had been washed clean of a great stain.

By eventide, a rider was at the gate, mud-smeared, breathless, hair a storm-tossed thicket. His horse was near dead beneath him.

He asked to see the Queen.

Isabella drew herself up to her full height (which was not great) and sallied forth to meet him, with her ladies-in-waiting at her side and a guard around her. She held her little sons by the hands, Henry on the right, Richard on the left. "What news do you bring, courier?" she asked in a clear voice.

"Your Grace." He flung himself down on his knees. "I bear sorrowful news from Newark. A week ago his Grace, while campaigning against his eastern enemies, was smitten by illness after eating a dish of peaches and cider that curdled in his belly. He was on his way from Lynn to Swineshead priory at the time and when he tried to hasten due to his sickness, he was ill-advised and chose a dangerous route—his baggage train foundered in the Wash and all the crown jewels were lost to the tides."

A gasp ran through the assembled company. "The jewels! All of them? Even the crown?" cried Isabella. Her hand tightened on young Henry's.

"Yes, your Grace, even the crown. Nothing could be recovered."

An angry look passed over Isabella's features. "Jesu, why was my husband such a fool!"

The man swallowed, his Adam's apple bobbing up and down. "Lady, there is more news, grave news. The King was so ill by the time he reached Sleaford, he was bled by the physics, and when this availed nothing he wrote to the Pope to tell him of his grave infirmity and ask him to, once again, take England under his protection. That way the throne could be given to his heirs if the worst befell…"

"And where is the King now?"

"Lady, he…he rode for Newark in the heart of the storm…"

"So he is at the castle there."

"He...he reached the castle and collapsed. The Abbot of Croxton was in residence. He heard his Grace's confession and gave him the Last Rites. Highness...the King is dead." He glanced at the curly-headed boy at Isabella's side—a quiet, thoughtful child with a drooping eyelid. "God save the King. God save King Henry, Third of that Name!"

The crowd began to shout, "God save King Henry, God save King Henry."

I stood frozen, unbelieving, lost in the pressing crowd behind the Queen, jostled by elbows, pushed aside by those struggling to get a closer glimpse of young Henry, their new King.

John was dead. The man who had destroyed my family was gone.

Isabella of Angouleme swept around the chamber, pointing out items for her servants to pack. For a widow, she was exceptionally tearless but that did not surprise me overmuch; for after his early lust for her had waned, John moved her from castle to castle out of his way, ignoring her unless he desired to rut. He had allowed her very little freedoms, not even the luxury of managing her own estates.

"The King has been buried in Worcester Cathedral," she told me, "without a crown, alas, but at least with the coif that bound his head when he was anointed at Westminster. His servants did not dare steal that...but they took all else, his clothes, his boots, his rings! John wanted to be buried at Beaulieu, but his enemies have taken Hampshire, so it was impossible. His heart and intestines rest at Croxton, as a gift to the Abbot who ministered to him on his deathbed."

I grimaced at the thought of the customary disembowelling and Isabella glanced at me with a small smile. "Do you wonder why I do not weep, Eleanor? Well, John took me from the finest knight in the world. But at least he left me with a healthy son who will now be crowned King of England. I can rejoice in that."

Reaching to a carved jewellery box, she opened it and picked out one of her own circlets—a band of gold and silver, decorated with pearls. "It's not a kingly crown but John lost that in the Wash. This band will do to crown my son in Gloucester Abbey."

"I must make haste," she continued. "William Marshal will be waiting at the Abbey; he and Hubert De Burgh shall care for my son the King in his minority."

"And...and what about you, your Grace?"

224

"I...I shall see my son crowned and then perhaps head to my homeland of Angouleme. Did you think I would stay on as regent? Alas, I have no aptitude for such a role and none would allow it. John kept me like a child."

"And yet...your children. They are but young. The youngest, Eleanor, is but a babe in arms."

"They have nurses," she said breezily. "Royal children should grow up independent. It is far better that way."

Although shocked by her indifference, I strove not to show it. Whilst children were not to be coddled and must do their duty to the parents, it was my belief they still needed a mother's guidance in their youth. Perhaps a life with John had hardened Isabella's heart even towards her own flesh and blood. "I wish you all happiness in whatever you decide, your Grace."

She put her circlet back in its box, closed the lid with a snap. "I will see what I can do about your situation, Eleanor, now that things are...different. I will speak to the Marshal on your behalf. But, once again, I can promise you nothing. I may bear the title Dowager Queen but no one of rank in England respects my word."

So out she rode, the little king riding at her side, waving to the crowds that gathered outside the castle gates. The barons accepted the little boy, the Marshal making a strong stand for his kingship, and suddenly Louis' plans to take the English crown dissipated like sea fog. No one truly wanted a French overlord when there was a viable English heir. When William Marshall defeated Louis' forces at the battle of Lincoln, the French prince retracted his claim to the throne and returned hastily to France.

In the aftermath of John's demise, there was good news for William and Odenel d'Albini. They were released from Corfe's dungeon, although William's wife, Agatha, had to offer herself as a hostage in exchange for her husband's freedom.

Marjory and Isobel were both freed, returning to the court of their brother, the Scottish King....for a time. A few years later, they would wed into the powerful English families of the new regime—Marjory married Hubert de Burgh, of all men, and had a daughter named Megotta, while Isobel married Roger Bigod, the earl of Norfolk, a boy fourteen years her junior. It was not a particularly happy match by all accounts, but at least Isobel had her long-awaited freedom

I, alone, was left a prisoner at Corfe.

Not long after Henry's Coronation, I had received a brief message from Isabella the Dowager Queen.

I send bad news, Lady Eleanor, as much as it pains me to do so. I have spoken to William Marshal and he is adamant—In my husband's will, it states that you must never be released from captivity. Farewell and I pray God grant you ease....

Chapter Twenty Four

The new King seldom fared to Corfe but, to my surprise, he ofttimes summoned me to court at Christmas in London or Winchester. These outings were strange affairs for me now, ones where I did not fit in, was just a curiosity to be stared at in my old-fashioned gowns and circlets.

I heard highborn young women I did not know sniggering and laughing behind their hands, "Look at the old woman, still wearing her hair loose like a maiden. She looks half-mad!"

I would later gaze at myself in my brass mirror, seeing the lines, the grey hairs, the signs of age. Did I look mad? Was I mad? I assumed not, for my mind was clear, but I had lost the art of courtly discourse in my long confinement. I spoke too plainly for the courtiers to deal with.

When I was back residing at Corfe, my young kinsman the King would send me gifts in the manner of his father—little treats like cinnamon, figs, sweetmeats. I had another new saddle and the best linen money could buy.

But I did not have my freedom…or my youth.

Peter de Maulay remained the Constable of Corfe, having also in his custody the young Prince Richard. Ofttimes I was allowed to visit the Prince and even walk with him in the garden. He was a bright boy, different in character to his brother the King, and again, different from both his parents, although I saw John's restiveness in him and vestiges of the Plantagenet temper.

De Maulay unnerved me, and not just because of his involvement in Arthur's death so long ago. He swept around the castle like an evil presence, and I found his eyes were on me far more often than when he first became Constable. Once he sidled up to me, his teeth flashing against his dark beard, and whispered, "Would you like to be freed, Lady Eleanor? Would you?"

I would not answer such a one, accomplice to murder and faithful to John till the bitter end. I started making efforts to avoid the hall and dine in my chambers rather than meet him.

In May of 1221, I found out why Peter De Maulay had renewed interest in me. While asleep one eve in the Gloriet tower, I heard the terrifying sound of clashing arms in the courtyard beyond. Leaping from my bed, I screamed for my ladies-in-waiting to dress me. I was scarcely decent when a great blow shuddered the hinges of the tower-room door. My women screamed and rushed to the back of the chamber in fear.

"Open in the name of the King!" a man bawled, as another great blow shook the door.

The King's men! I was as mystified as I was fearful. Why had Henry sent soldiers?

"Peace!" I shouted back through the door. "We are but women here. I am the King's cousin, Eleanor of Brittany. I will lift the latch on the door but I beg you, treat us not with violence. I know not why you come in such anger, and demand you explain your actions to me."

Reluctantly I threw the latch. Into the room marched an armoured knight wearing the King's badge, the Plantagenet sprig of broom. Other soldiers gathered in the hall behind; the torchlight dipped and danced on their mail and helmets.

The man bowed slightly. "My forgiveness for alarming you, my Lady, but you must come with me immediately. The Constable of the Castle is under arrest and faces a charge of treason. His Grace King Henry has ordered that you be sent from here to greater safety."

"A greater safety? Where? Why? What has happened?"

"I may not speak of it. In time, you may learn if his Grace sees fit. Now come…"

"My things…" I glanced over my shoulder at my pitiful chest with its small store of clothes and wimples and keepsakes.

"It will be brought in due time. Now come, my Lady. An escort awaits."

Hand firmly on my elbow, the knight hurried me down the winding tower stairs and out into the bailey. A chariot waited, with wooden bars crossing the narrow window. As I climbed in, I saw Peter de Maulay dragged across the yard, his feet and hands bound in chains. His visage was red and he bellowed like a mad bull.

"Good sir!" I called to the knight who had taken control of my person. "Grant me one boon before we depart. Let me speak to Peter de Maulay."

The knight looked dubious, uncomfortable. "I would hardly think it appropriate, my Lady, given the circumstances. He is the King's enemy if the charges against him are true."

"He is my enemy, even if they are not," I said. "He was one of the knaves involved in the death of my brother."

The knight gazed at me with new respect, as if he had never seen a woman fired by desire for vengeance before. Perhaps he had not. He motioned de Maulay's captors to drag him over to my chariot.

I looked at the man, cursing, frothing like a mad dog, a bleeding scratch above his right eyebrow. "So now you know what it is like to be a prisoner, Peter de Maulay. How does it feel?"

Panting, he stared at me, blood running into his eye. "You have me wrong, Lady! I did what I did for you, Lady Eleanor!"

"What?"

"The French King still desires your freedom and an alliance. Your claim to England is still better than Henry's. I was to put you on a ship…"

I snarled at him, a strange rage curdling in my heart. This man saw Arthur to his death and yet he pretended to think of my freedom. He was lying. He wanted to sell me to King Philip for gold, I knew it! "What was in it for you? How much was he paying you, Peter?"

"I…I…have said too much!" he stammered, confused by my anger and suddenly aware of the confession he had made.

"You are a despicable worm, loyal to none," I said, and then I spat into his face. "I would smite you if I had a man's strength. I spit on you instead, de Maulay. That was for my brother, Arthur."

Turning, I climbed into the chariot without glancing back at the prisoner. I pulled the curtain across the window and sat in the muggy darkness with pounding heart.

I left Corfe within the hour and never returned.

After a short sojourn at Marlborough castle, I was taken to Gloucester under the protection of Walter De Audeon, and thence to Bristol, where the latest appointed keeper, Ralph de Williton greeted me. Then it was to Gloucester again, with William Talbot watching my every move. In every place I halted, my customary walk was made before the townspeople, the mayor, the local bailiffs and sheriff, as proof I was alive and unharmed. A few of the curious came to see me as I was paraded before them, but most seemed to no longer know or care who I was.

The Queen who had never been.

In fact, I was nothing now, not even the Countess of Richmond. On advice from his counsellors, Henry had stripped me of my last formal title in 1218. Alix had used the title on occasion over the years but now her husband, Peter de Dreux, was officially made Earl of Richmond. I was nothing but the 'King's dearest cousin Eleanor."

Life went on in endless dullness, broken only by the occasional visit to court. I saw Henry grow from a quiet little boy, to a rather awkward, bookish youth, to a lonely young man who was extremely pious, with a particular affinity for Edward the Confessor. His advisers still had not settled on a bride for him, despite him being beyond the age royal marriages were normally made. Henry did not whore or wench and rumour had it that Hubert de Burgh, in a drunken fit cast aspersions on the young King's manhood. After such insolence, it was hardly a surprise that Hubert fell from favour, although I felt for his blameless wife Marjory. Once de Burgh was removed from high office, other counsellors made a greater effort to find a suitable wife for Henry. Suggestions included Yolande, the daughter of my sister Alix, who now was dead, God rest her soul, having contracted an ague at only one and twenty years of age. Another possibility was the rich heiress, Joan of Ponthieu. It was a near thing with Joan but the French were furious because of the strategic position of her lands and made every effort to block the match.

Old King Philip was dead now and so too his son, Louis VIII, who reigned but three short years, so it fell upon Louis' Queen, my cousin Blanche of Castile, acting as regent for the teenage King Louis IX, to complain to the Pope of Joan and Henry's consanguinity. The Holy Father promptly denied the dispensation needed for the marriage.

Henry was desperate for a suitable wife now, and forgetting Joan sent out messengers and even his brother Richard to seek out a potential bride. He settled on Eleanor of Provence, one of the four beautiful daughters of Count Raymond Berenger and his wife Beatrice, even though her father was in straitened circumstances and she brought nothing in terms of a dowry.

Henry married Eleanor in Canterbury in January 1236, with the young bride, aged twelve or thirteen, clad in a dress of gold that held tight to her waist then flared out at the hem. At the time, I was back at Gloucester Castle in the care of William Talbot, and listened intently to the incoming tales of the celebrations at Canterbury and the little Queen's lavish Coronation at Westminster the same day.

I was happy my young cousin the King was wed at last—I had heard that he was so enamoured of his bride, he rushed up to embrace her with the excitement of a puppy leaping upon a fond mistress—but a horrid bitterness coiled within me too. Lonely Henry was married, while the opportunity for wedlock, the rightful state of man and woman outside of religious orders, was lost to me forever.

I was fifty years old, nearly fifty-one.

I took my frustrations out on William Talbot's wife, Adeline, a plump and rather empty-headed woman, who truly meant no harm but had a tongue that flapped too much. And I had grown brittle and snappish; a withered old stalk that was about to break.

"Ah, it is so joyous to have a Queen of England again!" she burbled, as she toyed with her sewing. "England needs a good Queen to bear strong sons for the good of the nation."

"She is not yet thirteen," I said curtly, "it may be some time before she breeds any heirs for Henry. And if England wanted a Queen, it could have had one—remember, many once believed my right was better than John's…or Henry's!"

"Oh!" Adeline's eyes widened in shock, for my words bordered on treasonous for all that they were true. "My Lady Eleanor…I…I did not think!"

"No, you did not!" I spat and I struck the sewing from her hands so that it fell in the dust. "Go you from me, and do not come back until you've learned to use the wits God granted you!"

Hand to her mouth, tears starting, Adeline fled. She did not return that day or in the weeks that followed, and her husband William Talbot, a quiet, sombre man, cast me reproachful looks whenever he entered my presence. Finally, I dared ask where Adeline was; Talbot told me she had fled to her family's lands in Wiltshire.

Guilt overcame me, making me morose. I wrote to the King himself, telling him of my unkindness to Adeline Talbot. *I pray you write to William Talbot, your Grace and have him tell Adeline that it is my wish she returns to Gloucester where I may make amends. In this holy season of Easter, it is unfitting to hold bitterness against our fellows. I wish to speak with Adeline and have her back as my companion if she so wishes…*

The King wrote to Talbot, Talbot wrote to Adeline and soon she returned to Gloucester…but she was always wary around me after that, always formally polite. My sharp tongue had lost me an ally.

I was not sorry when I was moved back to Bristol again, back to the mighty keep the size of Canterbury's with its odours of sea salt and seaweed drifting through the narrow window slits. The scent of a sea that could bear me back to Brittany but now never would.

It was in Bristol I fell ill of a malady that attacked the servants also and left us all bedridden for weeks. Doctors bled me several times for my health, but although they claimed I would recover, I never felt hale again.

I began to think of death.

My solitary lady-in-waiting, Agace, suggested I should beg the King for clemency so that I might be given permission to join a convent for my final years.

I refused. Indeed, I was quite looking forward to Christmas at the King's court, to which I had received an invitation. The year was 1239 and in the summer, Queen Eleanor had given the King a fine Prince, named Edward after his favourite Saint, the Confessor.

In my litter, I approached Westminster, surrounded by guards who must have thought it folly to protect such an old, seemingly unimportant woman. The high steward and chamberlain greeted me with all honours, and I was escorted into King's presence. Henry sat upon a throne, happier than I had ever seen him, arrayed in splendorous robes and wearing his crown. Eleanor of Provence sat at his side, one of the most beautiful women I had ever beheld, with a dignity that belied her tender years. She had fine eyes and skin like lilies, and dark hair flowed beneath her veil. Her neat figure was encased in red damask with silvered quatrefoils; a golden girdle clasped her small, neat waist.

I did obeisance before the regal pair; my knees, which now ached in the cold months, creaking and aching as I went down on the colourful tiles.

Eleanor raised me up with her hand. "Cousin Eleanor, my namesake," she said kindly, kissing me on both cheeks. "Be welcome."

Henry smiled benignly at me. "I trust you are well, cousin, and in need of naught at Bristol?"

Only my freedom...

"I have a gift for you, Eleanor," continued the King. "I thought it only right that you have this, as you are a Plantagenet and my dearest kinswoman." He gestured to a page, who brought forth a jewelled box from a stand behind the thrones.

The King took it from the page, held it a moment, and then pressed it into my hands. "A blessed Christmas to you, cousin."

Slowly I opened it. Inside, was a circlet of pure gold incised with scrollwork, decorated with pearls and other small jewels. A royal coronet.

A coronet that meant nothing to me now.

I lifted it from the box, held it up. The light from the torches around the room dazzled my eyes, danced on the rim of the coronet.

I placed it on my brow, saw Henry and Eleanor smile.

Then I lifted it off again, placed it in its box and handed it back to Henry.

"A fair gift, your Grace, but one I cannot accept. Let me instead bequeath it to your son, Prince Edward, for whom it is more fitting."

The King looked puzzled but Eleanor clapped in delight and the courtiers also roared their approval. For a moment, the Queen caught my eye, and I saw in her own gaze that she understood my heart in this matter, and she did not condemn me.

Even as an ageing matron, with no chance for release in this life, I remained unyielding. If I could not be Eleanor, Duchess of Brittany, royal princess, with lands and rights restored, I would not play the part of a puppet twirling in a meaningless coronet to assuage the conscience of the King…

Epilogue

And so I sit back within the walls of Bristol Castle, scratching down the tale of the Breton Saint Melor onto a sheet of parchment.

It is coming to the end now—*When Melor reached the age of fourteen, his Uncle Riwal found out he still lived, and that God had healed his mutilations. Once again, Melor was fit to rule and the common folk rallied to his cause. Riwal decided the youth must now certainly die, and paid much gold to Melor's guardian, the faithless Cerialtan, to hew off the young prince's head. When Melor's blood struck the ground, angels appeared from on high and a fountain sprang up where the blood fell. Riwal had the Prince's head brought to him to ascertain he was indeed dead, but when he laid his profane hands upon that holy relic, he was struck down and died in agony. And so it was that Almighty God meted out justice upon the tyrant...and the bones of the saint, bringing with them many miracles, were taken to Amesbury in the Island of Britain, where they now rest upon the altar of the abbey there...*

When I finish the tale of the tragic young Saint, I roll the parchment it is written on and seal it with wax, putting it aside. Then, fingers trembling, I lift the quill once more, and on a separate parchment begin to write my final will and testament, for I know in my heart of hearts that I grow old and my health fails—even my eyesight dwindles. On hearing of my malady, King Henry sends me kegs of special, curative wine, but I find it does not work: the candles still shudder in my dimming vision; my writing is a nigh-illegible scrawl on the blurry page.

In my will, I ask that after death my body be taken in a royal cortege from Bristol to the town of Amesbury in Wiltshire. The priory there is a Daughter House of Fontevraud, so loved by my grandmother, Eleanor of Aquitaine...but it is not the new little priory, founded as part of Grandfather Henry's penance for Becket, where I seek my final rest. Rather, it is in the older Abbey, sacred to the Blessed Mary and to Saint Melor, where the young boy's relics still sit in majesty upon the high altar—his naked child's skull, the long bones of his legs grown brown and yellow and smooth in the long years since his death.

I would fain lie before him, protected by the saint of my own sweet country beyond the flowing sea, my bones an eternal reminder not only of Brittany but of Arthur, my dear brother—the rightful King of England, who died in the same manner as Melor…at his uncle's hands.

When men step upon my grave, maybe they will remember us both for a brief instant or maybe longer if their thoughts run deep. Remember the King of England who never was, the Queen who ascended no throne but was imprisoned all her adult life with no trial, no charge, no guilt.

Writing these words, my last request, upon the yellow parchment page is truly my final, and greatest, act of defiance.

AUTHOR'S NOTES.

Eleanor of Brittany is a little-known figure in England's medieval history. Daughter of Geoffrey Plantagenet, Henry II's middle son, she did indeed have a valid claim on the throne by strict primogeniture. Since England did not have Salic Law impeding a woman from ruling, she was regarded as a danger by both King John and King Henry III, who kept her in 'honourable confinement' for the rest of her life, after her capture at or around the time of the Siege of Mirabeau. She had committed no offence and was never tried or charged with anything; her only crime was her claim to the throne.

Needless to say, due to the constrictions of Eleanor's life, little is known about her. I have reconstructed her story as much as possible without adding huge amounts to the tale, using the greater backdrop of the historical events that occurred in the reigns of Richard I, John and Henry III.

What we do know is that she was born between 1172-1174 (I have gone for the earlier date) and that as a young girl she was made a ward of Richard Lionheart, joining the household of her indomitable grandmother, Eleanor of Aquitaine. What an upbringing that must have been! In 1194, she enters the records as travelling to Germany with her grandmother as part of Richard's ransom; she is to marry the son of Leopold of Austria. However, she does not appear to have been sent to his household, and some months later, after orders she be delivered to him at once, along with the 'Damsel of Cyprus' (called Beatrice in the book, as per the guess of historians) , Leopold dies after an accident at a tournament.

Eleanor's whereabouts become a bit shaky at this point. Eleanor of Aquitaine retires briefly to Fontevraud and it seems at some point, our Eleanor returns to her mother's household in Brittany. At the Siege of Mirabeau where her brother Arthur is captured, John's forces take her prisoner either before or after the battle. From there she is sent to England, to a series of strong castles. Most of her imprisonment seems to have been spent between Corfe and Bristol (chroniclers differ on which), although she travelled around. I have chosen to set most of it at Corfe. Records do appear of various keepers and of supplies, including periodic gifts from John and Henry, and for some years she had the company of two other captive princesses, daughters of the Scottish king.

Only one letter of Eleanor's still exists, in which she asks King Henry to help her to make amends with the wife of her keeper at Gloucester Castle, with whom she has quarrelled!

Many sources state that Eleanor was permitted to become a nun towards the end of her life, and I used to believe this to be the case, but further research casts doubts on this idea, which probably came from the fact she was first buried in Saint James' Abbey in Bristol. There is no evidence she was allowed to take the veil.

As for Eleanor's will, she requested burial at Amesbury, which, some time after her first burial in Bristol, was done. It is uncertain whether she was buried at the new priory or in the old Abbey (by then the parish church, as it is today) dedicated to the Breton saint Melor. Geophysics have shown two graves lying in front of the high altar in the present church. One of these may be Eleanor. If she was buried in the priory, however, her grave will have been lost in the Reformation, along with that of her kinsman King Henry's wife, Eleanor of Provence.

If you have enjoyed this book, please look out for my other works on medieval queens and other little-known ladies, Richard III and the Wars of the Roses, Stonehenge, Robin Hood and more!

Follow me on Amazon for more info on my books, news of new releases, book signings etc. at https://www.amazon.co.uk/J.P.-Reedman/e/B009UTHBUE

Printed in Great Britain
by Amazon